THE GIRL BEHIND THE NUMBERS

Tatiana McArthur

Publisher/Executive Editor: Brittiany Koren
Cover Art Designer: Ed Vincent/ENC Graphics
Interior Layout Designer: Amit Dey

Category: Political Romantic Suspense
Description: A young woman stumbles upon romance while using her talent with numbers for a political cause.

Hard Cover ISBN: 978-1-951375-56-0
Paperback ISBN: 978-1-951375-57-7
Ebook ISBN: 978-1-951375-58-4
LOC Catalogue Data: Applied for.

First Edition published by Written Dreams Publishing in October, 2021.

Green Bay, WI 54311

Advance Praise for
The Girl Behind the Numbers

"With spirited characters and intriguing suspense, *The Girl Behind the Numbers* ticked all the boxes for an enjoyable read. Don't miss it."

—Karen Fenech, *USA Today* Bestselling Author

"A riveting read, *The Girl Behind the Numbers* is a pulse-pounding romantic political thriller. This exciting page-turner set in Canada—a delightful change—kept me guessing and up late into the night worrying about Charlotte and the trouble she found when she started dating her boss, a man destined to be the next prime minister."

—Dorothy St. James, Author of the White House Gardener Mysteries

"In *The Girl Behind the Numbers,* who would think a statistician crushing numbers would be involved in a love triangle, one that is surprising and unexpected? Tatiana McArthur's novel has it all: political intrigue, who dunnit, and development of an unexpected romance. If you have an interest in crime, drama, and an unexpected twist, this novel is for you."

—Susan Teti-Finnegan, Natural Health Consultant

"Charlotte Finnan is a dynamic, inspiring, strong female lead and David Reid is the down-to-earth politician with a solid moral compass I'd love to see more of in our non-literary leaders. The thrill of a fast-paced political campaign combines with the allure of new love and the intrigue of a good thriller between the pages of *The Girl Behind the Numbers*. I laughed, I cried, I was on the edge of my seat, and I ended up learning a lot about Canadian politics, which was an added bonus. It is a gripping page-turner you won't be able to put down. I couldn't put it down!"

—Lindsey Marantos, Organizational Leadership & Effectiveness Consultant

THE
GIRL
BEHIND
THE
NUMBERS

Tatiana McArthur

Green Bay, WI 54311

*To my favorite
absent-minded professor.*

Author's Note

Political parties and campaign timelines have been modified for this book.

Chapter One

For the third time in three weeks, I sat in a meeting with my boss with the phrase "I can't just quit" running in a constant monologue through my head. I'd thought about it, made a list of pros and cons, looked at other jobs, but had put off actually doing anything. Managing the predictive sales models for crude oil in my region, plus those of my teammates who were content coasting in my wake, had burned me out. Walking out in the middle of the day had been a fantasy.

I nodded along to his rambling, looking appropriately sympathetic to his nonstop complaints; some were founded, the vast majority not. I tried to break in, point out I had done good work, that I was the top data scientist for the transportation company and pinpointed more new customers and markets for us than anyone else, but got brushed off.

"You've done well, Charlotte," Victor said grudgingly, seemingly reluctant to have something he couldn't complain about, "but the numbers aren't 100%," he finished, leaning forward and making his chair groan under him.

I stopped myself from rolling my eyes. "No, but they are 99%. Given the data integrity issues we have, you've recognized that I cannot reach 100%. Asking me to do more without better resources is ridiculous. I can't keep doing this."

He scratched his chin and stared outside, ignoring me. The snow had picked up and danced around the window, too puffy to fall, so it drifted up and sideways. The other squat gray buildings in our industrial park, normally visible from the window, were lost in a sea of gray sky and snow. We lived in a snow globe.

"One hundred percent is the goal, and anything short of that you know won't count as a success," Victor said.

My internal monologue screeched to a halt. The words tickling the tip of my tongue broke free and slipped out before I could stop them. "I quit."

Some sentences in life you can take back or spin around if you changed your mind. *I quit* is not one of them.

His eyes fluttered a few times like he couldn't believe I'd had the audacity to say it. I struggled not to run out of the building giggling. What came next was inconsequential because I felt free again, floating like the snowflakes outside.

*   *   *

Within thirty minutes of the sentence popping out of my mouth, I had my parka on, my little box loaded up with my desk effects, and trudged out to my car. Finding it took longer than normal. Our office shared the massive parking lot with other suburban office buildings, and all the cars from multiple offices were nothing more than snow mounds. Snow flew sideways in the wind, peppering my face with fat wet flakes. I hated driving home at night with this much snow blurring the road markings with ice and glare. Calgary was well-prepared for snowstorms, but it still took me twice as long to get home, the whole time with brakes juddering. Every now and then, my car gave an odd lurch to the side as I hit ice.

Driving distracted me from the consequences of walking out. The thought had seriously crossed my mind before in a meaningful "I hate what I'm doing" sort of way. The time had come. The oil industry had been perfect after university, but it wasn't my work love.

I kicked off my boots and shoved my workbox into a closet. It could be dealt with later, after dinner and a hot bath. My apartment was small, but at least it came with a full-sized bathtub.

I caught a glimpse of myself in the mirror and winced; the snow had splattered across my glasses and plastered my white-blonde hair into a solid wet mass on my head. I needed to fix myself before doing anything else.

Maybe I knew my skill set—big data analytics and modeling—was in high demand, or maybe I was overly confident in myself, but I was surprisingly unworried by the lack of, well, purpose for the next day. I poured myself a glass of red wine and flopped into my squishy leather chair. I watched the snow fall, my tire tracks two-stories below, were nearly obscured already. I felt more hopeful than I had in a long time. Starting over on my own terms wasn't necessarily a bad thing. In fact, I thought, it was a wonderful thing.

* * *

"You did what?"

My cousin Eric didn't share my enthusiasm. His little guy, Henry, had just turned three, so I'd called to say happy birthday and to catch up. Eric was a big guy and with a laugh that carried through the phone without a problem from Toronto.

I grinned. I was a single child and Eric was the closest thing I had to an older brother, complete with laughing at me.

"Quit. Walked out. No idea what I'm doing next." I knew I shouldn't be so flippant about it. The wine made me a bit flippant.

"Charlotte, what—do you have anything lined up?"

I heard his wife Melissa and little Henry chattering in the background. It made my apartment feel cold and empty; the desire to move back closer to everyone became a physical ache.

I fingered the edge of my glass and shrugged. "Well, no… I mean, I'll do something, move back, be closer to everyone again. I'll find something pretty fast."

"Cocky little thing, aren't you? In such high demand you'll just get snapped up?"

I winced. I probably deserved that. "There are an awful lot of data jobs out there." I sounded defensive, and sighed. "Or who knows, maybe I'll give cello lessons or coach coding for girls. I can do something altruistic."

My cello sat neglected in the corner. I could fix that later tonight. I could join a community orchestra again wherever I ended up. I'd first heard a cello when I was eight, and the performer's fingers danced along the strings, the low notes thrumming and echoing in my chest. The performance had hooked me on playing. I wanted a job where I was happy, where I could come home from work and be satisfied enough to sit down and play again. Recently, I'd been so demoralized I only had energy for dinner, Netflix, and maybe mixing myself a martini. That wasn't a life.

Eric hollered something at Henry, prompting a squeal. I'd move back closer to family and university friends; sometimes it felt very far-flung being by myself. I'd never minded doing things or moving on my own before, but it had the unintended consequence of isolation. I saw that now.

"You realize you need money, right? Cello lessons? Altruistic doesn't pay. Hey, does that mean you're coming for Christmas? Jessica's showing up, too… Having us cousins all in one place would make the old folks happy."

"Probably. What's she up to now? Still editor in chief extraordinaire?"

He snorted in a not-so-polite way. "No, she switched jobs a few months ago. You'll hear more than you ever wanted to hear about it if you get her talking. I almost miss when she was with the newspaper."

"Worse than that? You're not selling Christmas dinner."

Eric and I were close in age, with just a handful of years separating us. Jessica was a good ten years older and made sure we knew it. After she'd graduated from university and landed a job as assistant editor in chief for one of the big newspapers in Toronto, we'd heard about how important her role was, how nothing would ever get put to print if she wasn't helping, how her boss relied on her so much, etc. The pompousness oozed. It was thoroughly obnoxious.

"She works as a campaign director now. David Reid and the Centre Party. The guy walks on water, alleluia." The phone muffled as Eric spoke to someone in the background. "I've got to go, Charlotte. Dinner. Enjoy the weeks of leisure before your money runs out."

The phone clicked off abruptly and I tossed it on the couch. It didn't take a lot of imagination to see Jessica as a campaign director; she'd be in her element amassing the troops and sending them out.

The job, or lack thereof, Christmas, and what to do next in life would wait until tomorrow. When you graduated from a university, just getting a job offer was fantastic. It didn't necessarily matter what the job was because you needed to start somewhere. Being overly fussy was nonsense at that stage. I could be fussy now and use the night to revel in my newfound freedom. Given the weather outside, that meant another glass of wine and cello time. And a delay in brushing the dust off my résumé.

*   *   *

On Christmas Day two weeks later, I was firmly ensconced in family holiday festivities. My parents' old farmhouse was huge, way more space than two people plus two dogs—and me again—needed. For the holidays, though, it was great and could easily accommodate the giant Christmas trees Mom always decorated. This year, there was a white, red, and gold themed tree, all blinking with glitter and lights.

With us three cousins, plus Eric's wife and little Henry, my grandma who liked to escape from the nursing home for the day, and my aunt and uncle, the house groaned at full capacity.

Eric's fat basset hound, Poppy, tagged along and sniffed everyone's ankles, hoping to find someone willing to toss her a treat. She'd been happy at my feet for the last half hour. Henry perched on my lap at the dining table as we tried to catch popcorn in our mouths; Poppy so far had come out the winner, getting more than either of us.

I was deep in concentration and didn't see Jessica come alongside me until her chair screeched across the wood floor, sending goose bumps across my skin—it was nearly nails on a chalkboard. I jumped, and poor Henry wobbled on my lap.

"So, I hear you're looking for a new job?" Jessica asked.

I set Henry down and sent him happily toddling off to find his new presents. I couldn't hold an adult conversation with a squirming three-year-old on my lap.

While everyone else wore jeans or yoga pants, sweatshirts, and the like, Jessica was in pressed dress trousers and a gauzy peach shirt. Her hair looked blown out, brown and highlighted, sprayed and bounced to within an inch of its life. Our green eyes were the only thing that identified us as family, hers dark, mine light.

"I am, but only for the last two weeks. Early days yet." I smiled and tried to look vaguely more professional. No matter my age, twenty-seven or not, Jessica made me feel like I was perpetually stuck at the kids' table.

She waved me off with a shrug. "You'll be fine. Actually…" She leaned towards me, smiling like we were sharing a big secret. "I'm wondering if you'd be interested in working on my team, David Reid's team, for the Centre Party."

I sat back and blinked. Getting a flat-out job proposal at Christmas dinner had not been in my plans. And in politics? "I'm not sure politics is my forte. What—"

"Charlotte." She interrupted me as if I'd missed the obvious point. "You are a brilliant data scientist. Your predictive modeling and analytics talent, especially your ability to target messages to new audiences, would be a major boost for us. You're a huge prize and can help us get undecided voters, no doubt. I'm being selfish and snagging you for myself."

I'd looked at jobs in tech fields and at a couple of schools. The realm of politics had never entered my mind, and now sat there uncomfortably.

"I'm not sure working for a political party fits what I'm looking for," I said. "I want to do something I can feel good about, and politics is dirty, no offense," I added, since she ran the campaign for a potential future prime minister and his party. I hadn't gotten the warm and fuzzies working for an oil company; I doubted politics would do it, either.

"Do you know anything about our campaign?" she asked.

My brain scrabbled through the last few weeks of news stories, Facebook feeds, Twitter, anything news related, but came up blank on specifics. I shrugged and shook my head.

Jessica gave me a look—tolerant, patient, but ready to correct. "David's one of the good ones, and I'm not just saying that because he'll be a great prime minister. You can feel good working for his campaign. Besides," she said before I could object, becoming more animated and going into full sales pitch mode, "this is something you can really impact. How many people can say they helped win a national campaign? Not in an abstract way, but *really* have an influence. You could."

She paused and narrowed her eyes at me. "It's one year, but in that year, you could have a bigger and more lasting impact on the country than most people have in a lifetime. We want you."

It was unsettling how close she'd come to reading my mind. She'd summed up the type of job I'd been trying to find.

"You're good," I said, reluctant to admit it. "Can you send me the details on the job? I'll take a closer look tomorrow."

"Absolutely." She grinned and hugged me.

We'd never been huggers, and it caught me off guard. I awkwardly patted her shoulder before pulling away, escaping the hairspray-scented cloud around her.

"Seriously, I think you'd be a great fit. The work is fast-paced and changes every day. You won't get bored and you'll feel good about what you've done. I'll send a summary to you."

It would have been easier to think about it more clearly if I hadn't just eaten my weight in mashed potatoes and drank a glass or two of wine. "Why are you offering it to me?" I asked and rubbed my head. Something felt off. "No interview? And I'm guessing there's a head of the data area for the campaign… Did they send you out to get me?"

"I already told you." Her lips pressed together in annoyance, but a second later the charming sales lady returned. "I remember my mom and dad saying how your parents were bragging about you being top in this class, top honors in that, a star student, awards at work. You would be a huge asset to us. I'm running the campaign, and if you make us a stronger team, I will pick you up and put you in. Danielle will be delighted to have you with her in data. No doubt."

Part of me said jump now and take it; the other part hesitated. "I'll look tonight. When do you need to know?"

You'd have thought I handed her a million dollars her smile was so bright. "Sooner is better. The campaign's running now."

I snorted and rolled my eyes; the stupid ads had started already. Every news story was about what party leaders were up to, how they were positioning their parties for a tough round of elections. The ungodly long election cycle ranked as one of the most obnoxious trends to have crept into Canada from the U.S. A year-long campaign was a crazy and useless amount of time.

"One more thing," I said as she stood to leave. Already she was looking at her phone, smiling to herself like I'd given her the best Christmas present of the day. "Isn't nepotism frowned on in politics?"

She stopped typing and blinked fast, startled. "Well, yes. But if my family member truly is the most qualified for the job, then it's just good business sense."

Hmph. She walked away to a quieter area, still typing away on her phone.

I reached down and scratched little Poppy's ears. She lifted her head and happily leaned her heavy body into my hand for a rub. Work wasn't supposed to interfere at Christmas. I said I'd deal with it that night and I would. However, it was most definitely the afternoon. I could hear my family laughing and talking in the living room, and Christmas cake was still available. I had my priorities.

*   *   *

Later that night, after the last scraps of wrapping paper had been removed, new presents shoved into boxes and stored off to the side and plates of cookies reduced to crumbs, I popped my laptop open to look at the info Jessica had sent me. Job searching was a little more pleasant stretched out on a couch with a mug of eggnog warming my hands and embers smoldering away in the fireplace. Poppy slept on her bed, little basset hound snores rumbling on the floor next to me.

The first link was to the generic Centre Party home page. Unsurprisingly, it detailed how fabulous they were and labeled the other parties as idiots. At least what they considered to be fabulous lined up with what I considered fabulous, for the most part. But really, it told me nothing new. It was a lot of talk and took too many clicks to find out how all these ideas would happen.

I searched a few news articles on the likelihood of any of their fanciful plans becoming reality. I found little, but what caught my eye the most was the level of criticism leveled at the party's campaign so far. Apparently, they weren't keeping up with the others. Poor data analytics were the lynchpin; their ability to pinpoint swing voters and target the campaign's message was behind the curve. Jessica really did need someone like me. The back part of my mind started to think through different models and how to code for them; the work was right up my ally.

The second link was to the party leader main page. A quick skim showed a very biased author had written it.

I typed in my own search for David Reid and pulled up his Wikipedia page. It may not have been one hundred percent true, but it was at least close, and a fairer picture. I read through his professional accomplishments (top of his law class, public prosecutor based in Montreal, Member of Parliament—or MP—from near Ottawa for the last ten years, government positions in ethics and education before being elected as current Leader of the Opposition) and personal (father had died in a fishing accident when he was five, raised by his mom and older sister, had been married to the fashion designer Marie Vandeau for ten years, divorced, classically trained violinist). I clicked through a few of the pictures. He looked too polished and smooth but didn't seem to be a slimy politician. The page was devoid of scandals.

The third link showed details of the work I'd be doing, salary, location, and schedule disclaimer. I'd be third in line for assisting with data science modeling, interpreting historical campaign data to pinpoint improvements, running and analyzing experiments to help streamline campaigning, fundraising, reaching new voters, etc.

I ran a search on Danielle McIvers, my potential boss-to-be. There wasn't a lot out there on her, and her LinkedIn profile was locked down tight. Work hours were as needed. Salary wasn't bad.

My friend Camille lived in Ottawa. It wasn't too late to call. Working for a political party wasn't one of my first choices, but what Jessica had said nagged at me, especially being part of something with a lasting impact. I wanted that. Maybe I was overly idealistic, but I liked the idea of working for something bigger than just a bottom line. And the job itself was only for a year. If I hated it, I had an out.

"Merry Christmas!" Camille's greeting blasted through the phone's speaker and I jumped. It was nice to hear her voice again.

"Merry Christmas! How's the holiday? All merry and bright?" I wrapped myself in one of the heavy wool blankets Mom kept draped on the couch and snuggled down into the cushions. I smiled, glad I had called.

I heard her walk away from whatever noise she was by and into a quieter space. Their Christmas sounded much more lively than ours. "Winding down Christmas at Tom's parents'. You?"

"Wound down at my parents', along with cousins, cousin's kid, dogs, aunt and uncle. How was the holiday?"

We chatted for a while about normal holiday happenings, how cold it was, the interviews she had lined up for the start of next year. She wrote a fashion column; openings, award galas, and fancy fundraisers all were detailed and gushed about in her spread. Her husband, Tom, was doing well and settling into his first job out of med school.

"How're things with you? Were the relatives horrible about the job?" she asked.

When I had moved back, my parents had been incredibly supportive. I felt a little guilty they were fussing over me so much. It'd probably be a different story if I'd moved back and done nothing, sitting around watching TV. Since I was actively looking for a new job, they were fine with it. Dad had pointed out when I jumped, there was usually a plan in the back of my head, maybe not fully formed, but I didn't jump without looking, never have. So no, they hadn't been horrible at all.

"Not really. My cousin offered me a job today, with the campaign she's running."

"She works with David Reid, right?"

"Yup. It might be interesting. It'd be a different experience."

She laughed. "Out of all the candidates, I'd be least mad at you for working with their party. Since when are you interested in politics?"

Hmm, I wasn't the only one with reservations. "I wouldn't be in front of the camera or sucking up to donors. I'd be telling them who to target and how. Behind the scenes, tucked out of sight." I yawned and felt my brain starting to shut down. "Would I be able to find somewhere to live in Ottawa on a normal salary? Preferably somewhere not too shabby?"

"Probably. Or you could rent our spare room. It's small, but you'd fit. We didn't kill each other as roommates in university, so we probably wouldn't now. Tom won't mind."

We had gotten along incredibly well in university as roommates, and I'd know what to expect. Coming up with reasons not to take the job kept getting harder. I got to bypass an interview and house searching—almost too good to be true. Still… "You weren't married in university. I'm occasionally awkward, but don't need to be the full-time awkward third wheel."

"Don't be stupid," Camille said, brushing me off. "Tom's working all over the place with odd on-call hours; he won't notice you're here for a few months. Think about it. It could be fun."

Second time today I'd been told that; there was a lot to think about. I yawned again, a jaw cracking, shaking yawn that signaled the end of my night. "I will. You haven't heard anything nefarious about that campaign?"

"No, not that I can think of." She paused and yawned back at me. "You'll be working long hours, but you already know that. You're young and single. Might as well do a crazy scheduled job now. Our spare room is open. It'd be nice to live together again."

We chatted a bit more before hanging up for the night. It was late, and in reality, even though I was pretty sure I'd take the job because it intrigued me and sounded like a unique experience, any decision I made tonight wouldn't matter. I doubted a long-term career in politics was in the cards for me, but it'd be interesting to see the inside of a big campaign and say I had done it.

*   *   *

Unsurprisingly, I didn't change my mind. Shortly after New Year's, I moved into Camille's house on what the weatherman had cheerfully announced as the coldest and possibly snowiest day of winter. Her house was tucked away on a quiet side street a little south of downtown. It was small but had a front porch that would be wonderful in the summer. The area felt more residential than city with no high-rises to be seen, just a tidy tree-lined road. The only downside to living away from the center of the city was the delay in the road being plowed. Thankfully, I only had a couple boxes and suitcases with me, so moving didn't take long. I seriously questioned my sanity at deciding to move someplace that was still so cold my face hurt.

"I think this is the last one," Camille said, and set down a box with snow still melting off the top. "I'm cranking the heat and making spiked hot chocolate. Want one?"

I hung up my dripping gloves and coat and nodded. "Yes, please. I might thaw out before tomorrow."

The sun had already set as we headed towards her kitchen in the back. The patio door was fogged over, the snowdrift pressed up against it just visible. More snow swirled around the top. My initial thought had been to see the neighborhood tonight, or maybe part of downtown; I hadn't been to Ottawa since a trip in high school. It was far too snowy and cold to go exploring now.

"No rush for getting everything put away; relax tonight, get through tomorrow and then figure out where your stuff goes." Camille banged two mugs and a bottle of Baileys down on the kitchen table. "You nervous for tomorrow?"

I poured Baileys in my mug and topped it off with the cocoa, the sweet warm smell of chocolate and alcoholic cream wafting up in steam.

"Apprehensive, not nervous. I'm not sure Jessica told the truth when she said I was a welcome addition to the team."

Camille sat down and tried not to laugh. "Causing problems, already? That sounds about right for you. What'd you do?"

I kicked her under the table and glared. "I did nothing. The emails I've gotten from my future boss have been rather curt. I don't think she shares Jessica's enthusiasm for my talents."

She grinned and dumped a hefty portion of Baileys in her cocoa. "Try not to be too obnoxious tomorrow. What do you actually do on your first day?"

Wasn't that a good question? "Jessica hasn't shared. I imagine they'll give the standard paperwork, HR spiel, and then tuck me away in a corner with a laptop and instructions and let me play."

"You have an odd idea of play, Charlotte."

I didn't argue, and we sipped in quiet for a while, safe and snug in the warm messy kitchen while the storm blew around outside. I was nervous about tomorrow—not about doing the job, because I knew I'd be fine with it, but with how I'd been hired. The last email I'd gotten—with the generic directions to the office building and floor and dress code—had been sent to a few other people who must be new hires as well. So, it really was a hiring kick; I'd just skirted by all the normal pre-hiring song and dance. Hopefully, no one else knew that. I didn't want it to look like I'd gotten preferential treatment.

"Do you mind if we brave going outside and get pizza for dinner? I can't be bothered with finding the counters tonight." Camille cast a forlorn glance back towards the sink and counters covered in dishes from last night. It made me smile; some things hadn't changed from university. "There's a takeout pizza place just a few blocks from here."

"As long as we don't get lost and turn into ice people, sure."

She nodded and unclipped her hair, sending black springs dancing around her face. "We can binge watch Netflix now, then get dinner. It'll keep you relaxed before tomorrow. Helping me clean the kitchen wouldn't help relax you at all."

I smiled and sipped my cocoa. "Agreed. I'll enjoy my last day of leisure before rejoining the work force and productive society."

"You're entering the realm of politics," Camille said. "I'm not sure that counts as productive."

Chapter Two

I arrived early to my new office the next morning. The storm had cleared and left blindingly bright snowbanks piled on every corner, leaving the city shining in ice. The sidewalks bustled with government and private-sector workers, some disappearing into other office buildings and others heading towards Parliament.

I tip-toed over slush puddles and paused outside the mirrored high-rise tower that was my new work home. If I looked off to the left, down the street and over the crossroad, I saw Parliament Hill, the Gothic towers and spires kissed golden from the sunrise and the maple leaf flag fluttering on top, all framed by an impossibly blue winter sky. For all my reservations about politics, I was excited to be involved in the election and here in the capital, and this morning—beautiful, crisp, and cold— felt like a good omen. I turned and went inside, getting blasted with dry heat as I entered.

I followed the large welcome sign in the lobby and went up to the fifth floor. Everything that morning shone, from the ice to the sky to the tiled black floors and brass accented elevator. When I found the conference room we'd been directed to, two people were already there—a guy about my age and a woman who looked fresh from university. The guy glanced up, gave me an obvious once over with a raised eyebrow, then looked down at his phone.

"Hi!" The woman jumped up and held out her hand.

I fumbled with my bag and coat to shake it back; she was much more awake than me.

"I'm Mia Bries."

I dumped my coat on an open chair, closer to her than I originally would have chosen, and smiled back. "Charlotte Finnan."

She sat down and jiggled her foot. "I'm the new head for volunteer outreach. Isn't it exciting to be working here and helping the campaign?"

I was not a morning person. I'd love to say I was and woke up ready to tackle the day, but that'd be lying. When I was little, my parents had to drag me out of bed, wake me up as I got dressed, and keep poking and prodding me until I ate breakfast. Things hadn't changed too much, except I was responsible for myself now. My people skills were severely lacking until about nine, after I drank coffee and ate something with a very high sugar content; the bakery across the street would be a frequent stop.

Rather than snapping out something sarcastic, I nodded. "Very exciting. I'll be in data analytics. How'd you come to be here?"

My gut instinct was right. She launched into her past, hands waving and tossing her chestnut color hair as she talked. I sipped my coffee, gradually waking up. It wasn't hard to keep her going until the caffeine hit and I could handle conversation. She was nice in a bubbly sort of way.

A couple people drifted in over the next few minutes for a grand total of five of us. I wondered how many people worked in the office on a daily basis and how it all fit together.

"Welcome, everyone!" Another fellow came in and clapped his hands to get our attention.

Mia squeezed my arm in excitement; I was curious but perhaps not quite as excited as she was. There was a good reason I wasn't the volunteer coordinator. I'd never summon the amount of giddy enthusiasm needed.

"My name is Mark and I'm here to get you settled for HR. We'll make this as quick and painless as possible so you can get going. First, here are the necessary forms for you to fill out…"

He hadn't been lying when he'd said it would be brief. There wasn't much to go over besides basic HR stuff, which boiled down to "don't do anything stupid." Here, there was the added caveat of "If you talk to the press and are not in the PR department, you'll be fired."

"We have an all-staff strategy meeting this morning in about ten minutes," Mark said at the end of his spiel. "You'll be there observing today. After that, you'll head off to your departments and get started."

We left the dark corner room and entered a much brighter, open office space. A few private rooms for those higher up the party ladder were tucked off to the side, but everywhere else was open. Light flooded in through the windows with a view towards Parliament. A sliver of river, white and icy, was visible beyond the puffs of frozen heat exhaust coming from the tops of buildings. Having a city view beat working in an industrial park.

Mark showed us into a meeting room in the middle of the building, the largest, with a long conference table down the middle and a view of the city beyond. We grabbed the seats along the back wall, out of the way. A few people started to arrive and gave us strange looks before settling down into what appeared to be their normal seats. Us newbies eyed the people trickling in, wondering who we'd be working with and who might turn into a friend—all that fun stuff. The first day of a new job was an awful lot like the first day of school.

"It's your lucky day!" Mark said, coming in and ignoring everyone else in the meeting room. "An event got postponed and David will be attending today's meeting!"

Mia gasped next to me.

In my last job, the CEO had made a surprise visit one day and walked around the office, saying hi and making polite, meaningless conversation with those of us in the cubicle farm. I'd appreciated the gesture. The lady who had worked next to me freaked out. Her voice jumped up an octave and she started blabbering when the CEO came by our area. It was embarrassing. Maybe if it had been someone I'd found to be ridiculously attractive, I would have gotten a little more flustered. The CEO had been in his sixties; David Reid was forty-four, so not old, but he wasn't my cup of tea. I didn't feel the need to gasp and go googly-eyed with anticipation.

I smiled tolerantly, using the excuse of digging something out of my bag to avoid questions of why I wasn't beside myself with joy. I wondered which of these people was Danielle, my boss, and where the other data guy was. I knew his name was Xavier, but that was it. They all could have been a Danielle or Xavier.

A hush descended when Jessica made her entrance, clearing the way for David Reid to follow. Jessica was well within her element, power suit on, heels clicking, talking in an undertone and showing David something on her phone; they both nodded seriously. I almost laughed—they looked too much like a caricature of politician and sidekick. They sat at the two open seats in the middle of the table, directly ahead of us.

"There was a bad flu outbreak at the school and it's closed today, so David will lead in person," Jessica announced. "David, take it away."

David glanced around the room and lingered over us in the back, clearly not knowing who we were or why we were there, before nodding at the first department head to start their update. The meeting launched into logistics, by-election campaign stops, and the business of making sure our MPs were elected. He certainly had the look and sound of a politician. He was photogenic: dark hair with a dusting of gray coming in so he looked old enough to know what he was doing; a sharp, tailored charcoal suit and perfectly knotted tie; the right pitch of voice, lower than expected. He was very smooth looking, no harsh edges, picture perfect and calculated to project the right image. It was obvious why he sucked people in to trust the future of the party and country to him. He oozed charisma, which seemed fishy to me. Too camera perfect came off as slimy. Or, maybe I was too cynical.

I stopped my overly critical thinking for the rest of the hour and focused on the task at hand; I didn't want to come off as a complete spacehead my first day, so I dutifully jotted down notes and questions for follow-up. Most of it wouldn't impact my work, but I hoped understanding how and what everyone worked on might help me pull together something useful to make a good impression.

The meeting ended right on time. We stood up to leave and disperse to our respective areas but were stopped before getting too far.

"Who are the new faces? The rest can go." David motioned for us to stay, and Jessica automatically did as well. The others left until the five of us stood awkwardly alone. I worried Mia might bounce through the roof with excitement.

Thankfully, we didn't have to do any sort of odd icebreaker activity. It was much more of a cursory shaking of hands, getting a name and department, and moving along. Mia did do a brief fangirl thing and asked for a selfie with David to put on the volunteer website. He readily agreed, smiling.

Jessica rolled her eyes behind his back and grinned when she saw me do the same.

"Charlotte Finnan," I said, and shook his hand. He was taller than I'd expected; I was above average height, and with heels, on par with a lot of guys. He still had me by a few inches. "Data science."

We also matched. I'd gone for the dark gray dress trousers and pale blue button-down shirt look today; so had he. It was a little weird.

He did a double take as I introduced myself, his business front slipping for just a second. "Jess's cousin?"

"Yes." Jessica jumped in as soon as he said her name. "Charlotte's a genius with modeling and predictions. She'll be able to help us a lot in those areas."

No pressure to succeed. I managed a grimace and shrugged. "We'll see."

David nodded and moved on to the guy I'd caught giving me a once over—Mike Diaz, finance.

David gave us all one last thank you and left. A handful of other people came in to take us to our new areas.

"Charlotte, I'm Xavier." A shorter, round fellow with black glasses that were an awful lot like mine came up and introduced himself. "You'll be working with me. I'll show you where Danielle and I work and help get you set up."

We headed out towards the entrance to a work area sectioned off from the door by a glass wall. The view from our space let us survey the rest of the office, the big windows giving us a view of the skyline. It was a definite step up from the dingy interior cubicle I'd had before.

A few long tables were set up with laptops. A lady who I assumed to be Danielle was at a corner desk on the phone; she glanced up as we came in, and that was it by way of greeting. She looked older than me, closer to Jessica's age, her blunt haircut and Angry Bird eyebrows making her look severe.

"Nice glasses," I said to Xavier as he showed me in.

Xavier glanced at me, noticed my glasses and laughed. "Ha! Yes. Data twins already. Take a seat," he said, and motioned to the open desks. "You can move around to wherever you want later, but for now, you're stuck here while I show you everything."

And so began my career as a political campaign data scientist. I had no worries that Xavier and I would get along. He showed me the all-important coffee station so we could stay caffeinated, and where he stashed away the good coffee.

Danielle was a different story, only giving me a brusque hello, but then again, she knew very little about me since Jessica had stepped on toes to get me here.

I tackled my first project that afternoon. I could see why Jessica'd hired me; she hadn't been kidding when she said I'd be a big help. There was a huge amount of work, with not nearly enough people. Running constant updates to models predicting which ad and message would impact a target audience, all the data pulls for finance and policy… There was a lot, and it would only increase as the election moved along.

The office was pleasantly quiet but buzzed with purpose. Everyone here wanted the same thing. I smiled and popped in my headphones. I knew what I was doing, and it was something I did well. I had an office with a sort-of view if I craned my neck. I had people who had friend potential. I'd have to thank Jessica later.

* * *

The hours, at least for the first day, weren't as bad as everyone had led me to believe. I had no doubt once the hardcore campaigning kicked off, things would be different, but as we laid the groundwork, I was out by five and had after-dinner drinks with Camille. She'd insisted a first day of work warranted cocktail hour and was already waiting at the table for me, chatting away with another group. She waved me over as I came in and greeted me with a hug.

"First day done! You haven't got fired yet?"

I glared and pulled open the drinks menu. "No, I didn't. I even did useful work today."

She shoved a plate of charcuterie at me and motioned for me to go on. "I'm all ears. Spill."

I narrowed my eyes at her and shook my head. "Rule one was, 'talk to the press and die.' All off the record now and forward, yes?"

I got a barely tolerant look in return. "Of course. This is between friends, and quite frankly, I don't care about political gossip. So, first day. Go."

"Not a lot super interesting," I said, and popped a briny olive in my mouth. "I think I'm far enough down the totem pole that all the juicy gossip will bypass me. Your political reporting crew will have the information before I do."

Camille just smiled, which led me to believe I was right. "Possibly. Tell me something. Anything exciting? Work romances that might blossom? Taking over the campaign?"

I paused for a moment to order myself a spiced bourbon drink. "Pretty much… Might as well call me prime minister."

So, a good day was capped off by a very good night. We polished off the charcuterie platter, a salad, and a bucket of mussels between us. The bar stayed at a happy full, not so empty we felt out of place and not so full we couldn't hear ourselves think, let alone talk. The brick walls took on a cozy glow from the lights, and we sat there longer than we should have.

"Did you get to meet Reid?" Camille asked. The ice melting in our drinks had been slurped up and we waited for the check.

I shrugged. "Sort of, if you count a very cursory handshake."

"I've talked to Marie, his ex-wife," she added when I gave her a blank stare. "She's been at a couple of different fashion events. She usually goes out of her way to be snippy about him, which probably says more about her than him, but I was curious if it's true. I want details."

I slid off my stool and started reapplying the layers of coat, scarf, and hat. "No idea. The staff thinks he can do no wrong and bubble deliriously about him. That's all I've got for you."

She swung her coat on and followed me out. "Something's bound to come out at some point. Office gossip usually has a way of doing that or getting out to the wrong people."

*   *   *

The daily work sucked me in from day one. In some jobs, it took a few months before you were trusted with doing anything of any true importance. With a campaign, time was not on your side, so you'd better be able to hit the ground running and take off at a sprint.

I was responsible for reviewing existing predictive models for voter outreach and creating new ones if needed. Xavier usually hunkered down in a corner to focus on putting together and maintaining the databases, and Danielle handled the information for interviews and other public appearances. Xavier was a perfect work buddy, willing to help when needed; Danielle, not so much.

In the first week, I got multiple eye rolls and huffs of breath when asking questions. If she could, I was sure she would've loved to look down her nose at me in annoyance, but I was half a foot taller. My initial goodwill started to rub thin, and I figured maybe it'd be best to keep my head down and do a good job.

Jessica and other top advisors weren't in the office often. It made it a little strange to have so little contact with the people who were our bosses, but I always liked operating and running on my own, so the strangeness suited me.

On the days everyone was in the office, we usually had an all staff, or nearly all staff, meeting for updates. I was being sucked into the campaign and drinking the Kool-Aid of how wonderful it was to work here.

*   *   *

A month after starting, Xavier, Danielle, myself, and the executive crew were gathered in a meeting room. David was very hands-on, more than I'd expected, and made time to show up when he could. Jessica had summoned us to help pinpoint some demographic information and PR data. Xavier and I had sent our information to Danielle yesterday, so our role was minimal.

I found the relationship between David and Jessica fascinating. A few days after I'd started, I had done a little more Internet stalking and knew they'd been friends since he was a grad student and she was a freshman at university; there were, then and now, rumors about the real nature of their relationship. They'd both worked for a campus branch of the party and insisted it was nothing more.

At first appearance, Jessica dominated. She projected a leader from the way she dressed and walked to the way she spit out rapid-fire directions that were instantly followed; she had the general thing down and was by all appearances driving our troops forward to victory. A lot of it, I thought, was how perceptive Jessica was, not her actually taking the lead. David had her doing exactly what he wanted, the puppet master pulling the strings behind the scenes. It was subtle, but pretty damn admirable. It'd be a lot easier to resist falling into line and step with the campaign if he wasn't so likable, but—

"Charlotte, do you have those numbers?"

I snapped to and kicked myself for letting my mind wander. I had no way to recover and no idea what numbers Jessica wanted. Damn it.

"I'm sorry, which ones are you looking for?" My face flared, flushing from neck to ears so everyone could see just how thoroughly embarrassed I was.

Xavier shuffled his feet and glanced away from me, not wanting to get whatever heat I had coming. Everyone else, from Danielle to David, looked angry or annoyed.

"This week's poll from Vancouver," Jessica said through gritted teeth. "The numbers."

I blinked and shook my head. "I didn't know I was expected to have those." I did a quick shift through emails in my head and conversations with Danielle and Xavier and knew I was right. "I'll get them now."

Danielle glared at me, thin lipped and jaw clenched. "I'm pretty sure I asked you for those a few days ago." She huffed and waved me off. "They take hours to run, so don't waste time now."

I got a few more dirty looks, including one from David, who obviously thought I was incompetent, and the meeting moved on.

I was pissed. I didn't forget things and I completed projects on time. If I'd been asked, I would have done it. I ignored Danielle and brought up the data on my laptop. What she didn't know was while I'd been working on my projects, I had updated the query and system to suit me. I crunched and analyzed data faster than anyone knew. Took hours, my ass.

I attached the file and clicked send a little hard. I was smug. During a slight pause in the meeting, I jumped in.

"I just sent the numbers for Vancouver to everyone. I added a few extra columns to take yesterday's interview into consideration."

If nothing else, I certainly knew how to silence a room. I started to get a little uncomfortable when no one said anything, and they all stared at me.

"How did you do that?" Danielle asked.

And here I thought I might have made up for something. "I updated the models you used. They're a lot faster now." I didn't add I was better at this than her, but the fact hung heavy in the room.

"You're good." David was the first one to speak, impressed. He nudged Jessica and smiled. "You were right to grab her."

And just like that, I was redeemed. Jessica looked pleased with herself, and with me. "Thank you for getting those, Charlotte. Now, we pulled even…"

I paid attention this time but searched through my emails a little more carefully. It confirmed I was right; that request had never been sent, or it had gotten sent to the wrong person. I took it as a lesson for the future to err on the side of over-preparing, especially when my boss had an obvious jealous streak.

*　　*　　*

At my desk during lunch, I scrolled through political news stories; keeping up-to-date on them made sense and it let my mind wander. The office was quiet on a Friday afternoon. After David left to go to meetings in Parliament, most of the other staff cleared out. The magnet left and all the bits scattered.

There was a fuzzy idea in my head, and I started to click around the reports and trends Danielle and Xavier had already run. My initial thought was surely they would have done it already, but nothing similar was saved.

For better or worse, politicians with strong charisma drew people to their cause. From the research I'd done, it was also generally true that a basic "boots on the ground" meet and greet approach increased polling popularity. My hunch was David would amplify this; he drew people into the campaign whether or not they wanted to be, and he was exceptionally good at in-person events. There were some models and projections to put his draw and pull into numbers, but nothing on how to use it to grab the undecided voters. Getting your party base out at events was easy, but I thought he would excel at pulling in the less enthusiastic as well.

My clicking took on more purpose, and I got sucked in. I dove into a wormhole of data and building models, slipping into flow mode. My headphones were on and blocked out the chatter of a new group of volunteers coming in with Mia in the lead, giving me a cheery wave, as well as Xavier and Danielle coming, and eventually going.

In my past job, I had been responsible for pinpointing what would bring in new customers; the ones you had were nice and important to keep but knowing how to steal customers away from competition was gold. Jessica had mentioned in a meeting that political campaigns were an industry, so the basic framework I'd used before—customer data replaced with voter demographics—slid into place over the existing models. One variable led to another. Controls were added. Ugly graphs and results populated until I fixed the bugs and my lovely data appeared, and proved I was on to something.

I blinked a couple times and looked around. My eyes were murky and bloodshot, scratchy and heavy, like they always got when I worked too long staring at a computer screen. Sunset had been several hours ago, and the already sparsely populated office was pretty much empty. I sat in a pool of light, but most of the office was dark.

I saw a crack of light sneaking through the half-open door to Jessica's office, so I figured I wasn't alone. Rather than wait until Monday, I stood up and stretched, making several loud pops and cracks which made me feel very old, and headed over. If someone had already tried this and I'd wasted an afternoon, I'd rather just my cousin knew about it than my boss or anyone else. I hoped Jessica would give me a little more leeway than Danielle. And after normal business hours, I didn't feel I was wasting her time if it was a wash.

I knocked and heard a tired voice. "Come in."

As I entered, I immediately wished I'd paid more attention during the afternoon. Rather than Jessica working late by herself, David had come back, and they were both reading and reviewing a tower of papers. Both looked startled to see me.

"Sorry," I said, and stopped in the doorway. "I didn't realize you were busy."

Jessica waved it off and leaned back with a heavy sigh. Her shoulders slumped and her eyes were half shut. "You're fine. What is it?"

I hadn't wanted to ask in front of co-workers, let alone the person I'd be talking about. "I'd been working on something and wanted to run it by you. Seriously though, it can wait until Monday—"

"Let's do it now," Jessica said through a yawn. "No need to delay."

"I'd like to see, too," David interrupted, and nudged the open chair with his foot.

Damn. He still wore his suit jacket and tie, lounging back in his chair with an ankle over his knee, looking as comfortable and awake as he had earlier in the day.

"I'm curious to see what's so important you stayed late on a Friday and want to show Jess."

I grimaced and sat down; stupid me being an overachiever. This suddenly felt more like a meeting. And seven on a Friday night was a little late for me to be leading something. I crossed my ankles to keep my feet from tapping.

"Right." I took a breath and opened my laptop. "I had an idea…"

I had to say out loud and in front of David how frozen and rigid he was on screen. Then, I had to admit he was fantastic in person and drew people in, whether they wanted to be or not. His in-person presence made audiences feel like there was no one else in the world he'd rather be talking to. It was a gift most politicians would pay dearly for, and he nailed it.

"On TV, you—you're not smooth or personable. Maybe that works for a daily role as politician, but it's not going to get votes. It's boring and forgettable." I hurried to explain, feeling my face burn. I pushed on, eager to get to the part in this where I knew what I was talking about.

"In person, it's a different story. You draw people to you and are charismatic to the point where someone like me who really didn't care about politics actually likes you…" I stopped and swallowed hard, knowing that did not come out right at all.

I clicked the model on my screen and brought up the graphs and tables I made. "I'll show you the numbers I ran," I said, not bothering to wait for a reaction. My stomach felt full of ice, and I couldn't look up at him.

Staring at my laptop, I shared my work with them. My model quantified my thought; if he campaigned at the rate and style I modeled, targeting the voters I identified, his appeal would easily spread beyond our base, Centre would have a majority in Parliament, and he'd become the next prime minister.

They were good at keeping poker faces in place, so I had no idea if they thought I was a genius or an idiot. Since neither one said anything or asked questions as I reached the end, I started going into more detail about how I got the results, my voice defensive about how and why I was right.

And still, crickets.

"So, that's it. I thought the results and hard numbers might be useful." I sat back and glanced at David. "Your in-person skills will swing a lot of votes, especially at pinpointed events and locations. The more people you meet and talk to, the better. I think it'd help win the election."

"If we were to take those numbers into strategy and model the later campaign on this," Jessica said, pointing at my laptop, "I'm thinking later campaign, right?"

Thankfully, that wasn't directed at me.

David nodded. "Halfway through and then heavier at the end. It's a lot of traveling but looks promising."

Jessica tapped her fingers on the desk and sighed. "Show me again."

So I did, one more time but slightly abbreviated. They both seemed to be paying attention, giving me a shot of hope that I was on to something.

After the second time, Jessica leaned back and stared at the ceiling. I twitched around in my seat, not sure if her reaction was good or bad.

"Does that hold true across all ridings?" David asked, this time looking at me, startling me. He had very dark brown eyes and the stare leveled at me was a bit unsettling—not unfriendly, but intense.

I had presented only one because showing the full thing was a lot. "Yes." I clicked the "enable all" button and the graph exploded out.

"Well, almost yes," I said. "There are a couple that are set in stone, but the rest show a boost in flipped voters if you're out in person." I stared back, but thankfully he didn't have other questions.

He just nodded, keeping his face bland and impassive.

"If we use this to influence our campaign strategy, are you comfortable banking the amount of money we'd have to spend and the success of the election on this?" Jessica asked.

I hoped my work would be well received. I was not expecting it to be jumped on and for me to make a decision. That decision was well above my pay grade.

"My numbers are right," I said firmly, because they were. "What's done with it, quite frankly, isn't my decision to make. But this," I said, and pointed at my work, "is correct based on the data and information I have."

I finally got a crack of a smile from both of them.

"Okay, send it to me and we'll discuss it on Monday. Are you okay presenting again?" Jessica asked.

"Yes, I am," I said.

She clicked away on her computer for a bit before pushing back. "Scheduled. Thank you, Charlotte. Good work."

I smiled at them and gathered up my laptop. I deserved a drink tonight. A drink and dessert, something with strawberries. "Not a problem. Have a good weekend." Score me.

"What are your plans for the weekend?" David asked, stopping me before I could escape. "Hard to top an exciting Friday night with us, I'm sure."

I laughed, a little surprised. His sense of humor was well-hidden, but he was more relaxed tonight than I'd seen him before.

"This weekend, not much. My roommate and I are going ice skating tomorrow. She's showing me around town. Any suggestions?" I asked.

Jessica shrugged and started tapping on her keyboard; I was wearing out my welcome. "I don't really have time for going out," she said. "The parks are pretty in the summer."

That was not helpful; it was early February.

David stood and stretched. "I'm not that much of a slave driver," he said, marginally defensive. "The museums are good," he suggested, turning to me. "Or a tour of Parliament… I can probably get you in for that, if you'd like," he said as an afterthought. "Unless you like crowded tours with tourists."

I laughed again and shook my head no. "I'll take you up on that offer sometime, thank you. I'll see you both Monday." And this time, I managed to escape and head off.

It was one of those mid-winter thaw days that almost felt warm, so I'd walked into work today. It was later than I'd planned on walking back, but still comfortable out—comfortable being a relative term since the temperature was hovering just above freezing. I was overly pleased with myself. I made a good impression today, even after the temporary slip up in the earlier meeting.

Hopefully, they saw it that way as well. I fell for the campaign, for the hustle and bustle of it, the pressure—everything. I hadn't been lying when I had said I'd been sucked in and won over. I decided to embrace it rather than fight it and get ready to rock Monday's meeting.

*　　*　　*

I woke up the next morning before Camille and Tom. They had gone out for date night last night and gotten in past midnight. She didn't know it, but we were going to tour Parliament today. I was surprised when I'd checked my emails before bed and found one from David that said he had talked to someone already and emailed me a name to call in the morning if I wanted a tour. It'd be a shame to turn it down, so I decided Camille and I would do that first, and then go ice skating.

Camille didn't mind, and after we split off from Tom at the hospital, we walked down towards the Parliament building. It was a bright sunny day and not bitterly cold, so people were already walking around doing the touristy thing of pointing at the Centennial Flame, trying to get a picture with all the other tourists crowding around it, and selfie-taking with the Peace Tower in the background. I was glad we had a separate tour.

"Is Reid giving us the tour?" Camille asked.

I made a face and winced. "No, at least I hope not. I don't want to be on work behavior during the weekend."

She shrugged. "I thought it'd be interesting. He'd probably have a lot of insider info and stories on the tour."

"Yes, but you don't work with him though."

A line of people snaked back towards the entrance to the ticketing office. We beelined towards the side, the general information desk.

I asked for Emily Gerve like the email had told me to, getting the friendly old lady at the desk to perk up and wave.

"That's me! You must be the Charlotte I was told to look out for. Just give me a minute and I'll be right there."

She was the sort of bright and active older woman I'd like to be when I got to that age. She tapped someone to sit in for her before shaking our hands and leading the way from the ticketing building across the road to Parliament.

"How did you get roped into giving us a private tour?" Camille asked as we walked through the entrance hall. Intricate carvings of various historic scenes decorated the tops of the gray stone archways. Everything about the building felt ponderous and heavy—from the historic aspect and what was done here.

Emily paused. "About twenty years ago, I was teaching history at Queen's University, and David was one of the students I was advising through their fourth-year thesis. He was one of the bright ones, and we've stayed in touch through the years. I retired and became a volunteer; he asks me every now and then for private tours if there's a friend or family in town."

She smiled and squeezed her hands together in delight. "It'll be quite something to say I was the advisor to the prime minister, if all goes well. I just won't clarify as to the when." She looked very tickled with that and launched into her tour.

Camille pressed her lips together, trying not to laugh. I thought Emily was cute, and we followed her onwards.

Emily was full of stories, and for history nerds like us, we found it fascinating. We got a full behind-the-scenes tour to see where the members of Parliament worked, the green rows of seats and dark paneled room of the House of Commons, and where the working offices were. I was pretty sure it was not part of the standard walk-in tour. Besides it being a good tour for strictly interest purposes, it was useful to see it from a professional level, too. As Leader of the Opposition, David had a nice office and a fair amount of power. We walked by a window facing the park and road to the prime minister's office building, and I paused.

A nice office here wasn't enough. His charisma sucked people in, but I thought his platform and policies were the best of the bunch. I wanted to help him win.

*   *   *

"Make sure you thank Mr. Reid on Monday for the tour setup," Camille said. We headed towards Rideau Canal and one of the skate rental pavilions. I hadn't ice skated in a long time, not since I was little visiting my grandparents' farm. My center of gravity would be off and too high, and I was sure at some point a little kid would skate in circles around me and laugh when I fell.

"Will do. Not sure he's just hanging around our office all the time, but sure. Are you any good at this?" I asked and started lacing up my skates. I wasn't an ungraceful person or clumsy. That said, ice made things more complicated.

"Nope." She stood up and wobbled. "I'm not. But I want to skate to the sausage vendor and eat maple taffy. Tom won't, so you're stuck with me. Let's go."

Camille wasn't joking when she said she wasn't good. We skated slowly through the groups of kids, who skated circles around us like I had imagined. Camille stayed linked arm-in-arm with me. I might have been a little better but still felt my legs skittering out to the sides. Camille slipped badly a couple times and managed to pull me down with her. I was going to have a seriously bruised butt.

"Your future as an ice skater is very grim," I said as I helped her up for an unknownth time.

She rubbed her hip, wincing. "Like you're any better," she grumbled, and grabbed my arm. "My taffy is dead ahead. Onwards, Rudolph. Lead us there."

I elbowed her—gently, given the ice situation—and we staggered on. "How am I Rudolph?" We stumbled to a stop as a sled cut us off. "Although, I'd rather be Rudolph than the fat Santa in tow."

Camille gave me a not so gentle shove, the ice amplifying it. We tumbled down in a pile of legs, hair, and coats. "Fat Santa?"

I laughed and staggered back up. "Fat Santa and Rudolph with a very red ass. Let's get the taffy and find something hot. My toes are numb."

She nodded and winced as we set off again. Living in the same city as my best friend had been a good idea.

*   *   *

My presentation Monday went smoothly. The heads of strategy, communications, policy, finance, Danielle, and of course, Jessica, listened, then drilled me with questions. They agreed, very grudgingly on Danielle's part, with what we'd discussed on Friday, and like everything else in the job, planning for it started immediately.

It was tentative, because a lot would change over the next three months, but we needed a rough idea of budgets and locations; David couldn't just show up at a city and expect all to fall into place.

Jessica delegated the project to Ben, the lead strategist, Mike for the financial perspective, and myself for data, and we were set. Despite not fully understanding what I was getting myself into, I was eager to get started.

*   *   *

The project group gathered together for the first time later that afternoon. I didn't know Ben well at all. He was at the staff meetings but observed more than he talked, only leaning over on occasion to say something to David when he was there. He was incredibly smart, and from what I could tell, nice, but everything else about him, from the unremarkable suits to the pale wispy hair over his nearly bald head to clear-rimmed glasses, made him fade next to Jessica and David.

I hadn't had a lot of interaction with Mike since we'd started, minus a few good mornings or forced small talk in the break room. He stared too much and stood too close. Something about him made me uncomfortable, raising a red flag in the back of my mind.

Mike was spread out in a chair and talking to David, who looked bored and grateful for an interruption when I came into the room.

"Blondie!" Mike hollered and waved me over.

"Charlotte will do just fine," I snapped.

I ignored the seat he pushed back for me and took my chances sitting next to David. I plopped my laptop down on the table and glared back at Mike; nicknames annoyed me, especially ones like Blondie. I'd always been just Charlotte—no Charlies, no Lotties. Charlotte.

Mike smiled. "Lighten up, Char."

"How was your weekend, Charlotte?" David asked before I could stand back up and stomp a stiletto through Mike's foot. David set his phone down and waited for me.

"Good," I said. I hesitated and edited a bit; mentioning a direct thank you for arranging the tour didn't feel right in front of Mike. "My friend and I had an excellent tour of Parliament and then we went ice skating. I was used to cushion her falls a number of times. But it was fun."

"On the canal?" Mike asked.

I nodded, and he launched into his prowess as a hockey player and skater. He offered tips for next time, said maybe he could help show us, and on and on and on. Luckily, Ben came in and Mike stopped.

"Let's get started," Ben said. "Charlotte, you'll show us what you've got in more detail. Mike, from a finance perspective, you'll tell us what will be reasonable. David, Jessica, or myself will be providing the strategy side, and David, you need to say how much is too much." Ben looked around. It was the longest I'd heard him talk. "Questions?"

"I think that's pretty clear," David said, and paused to see if Mike or I disagreed. When we said nothing, he motioned to me. "Charlotte, please start."

This time, I ran through the presentation and details with more confidence than I'd had the first two times. This time was mine.

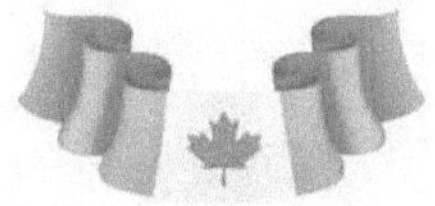

Chapter Three

My role over the next few weeks and into mid-March shifted from the entry-level work Danielle assigned me to working closely with the on the road portion of the campaign. Numbers and data drove everything: where the stops would be, who David would meet with, identifying his vulnerabilities, what message resonated with the widest audience, etc. We started tailoring the remarks he gave so we could gauge voter reactions before setting the party platform we'd carry throughout the campaign. It was incredibly calculated.

I became David's numbers guru. During meetings I wasn't involved in, he sent me instant messages through our work computers asking me to double-check something or get him a different set of fundraising figures. More often than not, it was during meetings I knew Danielle was involved in or work I knew she had an impact on. David was surprisingly snarky about her, disparaging, and made me laugh out loud with his messages. Xavier gave me a few weird looks before rolling his eyes at me. I certainly wasn't laughing when Danielle came back from those meetings with hostility radiating off her. I had a nagging feeling that on more than one occasion I had undermined what she'd said or done.

On the quieter days, I worked mainly with Xavier; he decided I was allowed to join him in the quiet downstairs area that he used, and I'd bring in pastries from the bakery for us. He'd worried I was a talker at work when I had first started. Once I proved otherwise, we worked well together.

I had no problem working with Ben, who took the primary role of running the strategy behind the project, as well as big picture strategy. David needed a platform that sold well early, was achievable, and could build long-term success for the party. After the first meeting, when Ben had picked up I wasn't familiar with the finer details of political campaign planning or any details for that matter, he'd been incredibly helpful and willing to answer my questions and mentor me, adding more strategy strength to my analysis.

Mike was a different kettle of fish all together. From the uncomfortable stares to the weekly request for drinks after work and sitting a bit too close to me, he made meetings and any unexpected encounters in the office, unpleasant.

Ben, Jessica, and David when he was there, were better at keeping their annoyance with him under wraps. Mike was loud, brash, but incredibly good at finance and getting funds to do the stops we wanted to do. So, I kept my thoughts to myself about him.

*　　*　　*

The first debate between the three main party leaders was tomorrow night in Winnipeg, and the office was buzzing. Ben had been the primary person running our sub-team show lately as David was busy doing his MP work, Leader of the Opposition role, election work, plus prep for the debate. So when I went in for our team's weekly update, I was surprised to see David sitting in the meeting room and not Jessica or Ben.

"Ben's home with a sick kid and Jess is meeting with the press," David said, and indicated for me to take a seat. "You're stuck with just me this afternoon."

I sat and glanced around. "Just us?"

He yawned and rubbed his face; for a second, he was unguarded and his exhaustion was on full display. "As far as I know, Mike's still coming. We can give him a few minutes before starting."

"Busy last few weeks?" I asked, trying to keep an awkward silence from settling in.

He laughed. "That's a nice way of putting it. This last week has been… meetings crammed into the morning, needing to be at sessions this week to question Yates," he said, gesturing vaguely towards the Parliament building and referring to the current prime minister. He shifted a bit more towards me and shrugged. "And afternoons, usually meeting with Jess or other campaign work, and this week late night debate prep. So, a little busy."

"Sleep optional, right?" I offered.

"That's for after the campaign."

"Right, when you're prime minister and running the country. Loads of free time then."

He leaned back and smiled, his shoulders relaxing and stretched out his legs. "Yes. Or maybe after I retire."

"I get crabby after a night or two of bad sleep. Better you than me."

He checked the time and glanced at the door; still no Mike. "Well, if this gets delayed much longer, no promises I'll be any better than crabby." He was starting to look less than friendly. Luckily, it wasn't directed at me.

"He and a couple other guys went out for lunch." We wouldn't have much of a meeting without hearing the money side. I could suggest all sorts of things with no budget.

"You didn't want to go with?"

I narrowed my eyes at him, caught off-guard by the teasing.

He tried to keep a smile under wraps, but it didn't work. His eyes laughed.

"No. Is it that obvious?" I'd been hoping it wasn't. It was embarrassing to get that type of attention in a work setting.

He laughed out loud now and nodded. "Yes. Obvious to anyone paying attention the answer's no."

I wrinkled my face and sighed. "Oh, shut up," I mumbled, which did not help; he just kept laughing.

"What do you do for debate prep?" I asked, shifting the attention off me and making him talk again.

Some of the humor left his face when I switched topics back to work, but he answered anyway.

"Getting my facts in order, watching the other leaders' past debates, making sure I don't look too stiff on camera," he said, and grinned. "Mock debate tonight so I can have a final run-through. That sort of thing."

"Can I watch tonight?" I asked before I could think it all the way through.

He nodded, surprised. "Of course, I don't see any reason why not. Upstairs conference room at seven."

That made me happier than it should have; I'd turned into a political groupie. Before I could say thank you, Mike breezed in and sat down.

"Sorry I'm late," he said, not looking at all sorry. "The bus was late—"

"First and last warning," David interrupted before Mike could formulate an excuse, and just like that, the guy I'd been talking to disappeared as a hardness settled on his face. "You waste my time like this again, and you'll be gone."

Mike blinked, and the cocky look slipped. "Noted."

David stood, shut the door Mike had left open, and motioned for me to start. He was intimidating when angry.

I wasted no time and shared my screen with the new projections.

*   *   *

A few minutes before seven, I went up to the conference room to watch the mock debate. An IT guy was setting up a camera to record it. A handful of other people were there already. I was pretty sure I was the only one who didn't have an official role. Jessica and David were heads-together going over something in the front, and the head of policy had his laptop open, typing madly away. It was a big room with quite a crowd of staff, closer to an auditorium than a simple conference room.

The communications head, Kaitlyn, was there as well, chatting with Ben, who had made it in for tonight. He saw me come in and gave me a brief nod hello before turning back to her. Jessica glanced up when the door slammed shut.

"What are you doing here, Charlotte?" She frowned at me, hinting I wasn't welcome.

I slid into one of the chairs towards the back. "I was going to watch," I said by way of explanation. "You won't notice me here."

Annoyance radiated off her. I realized a bit belatedly I should have cleared it with her as well as David. If I just stayed quiet in the back—

"This isn't an open invite," she said, sounding beyond irritated. "We—"

David stopped her with a look and shrugged. "I told her she could come. It's not a problem."

Jessica's mouth snapped shut. Her lips pressed into a thin red line, but she didn't argue. Jessica talked a lot and was more vocal in the office, but it was clear where the power lie. The others in the room glanced at me, but that was all the attention I got. And after that little demonstration, I certainly wasn't going to do anything to attract any more interest. I slouched down and fiddled with my phone.

I didn't need to have experience in political debate prep to know that to practice a debate you needed to have more than one person. In this case, David only practiced against a stand-in for Yates representing the National Party to the right end of the spectrum; the other party, the Workers and far to the left, wasn't a real threat this time.

As the minutes ticked on, the level of frustration and irritation ratcheted up. Jessica, the policy and PR people, and IT guy sat and waited. There was a lot of texting going on, presumably to find the missing debate person.

David paced at the front, giving the impression of a caged animal ready to explode out at the people watching. This may not have been the debate to watch.

"Matt's not coming," Jessica said, slamming her phone down.

I guessed he was the normal Yates stand-in debate partner. I wasn't sure why he wasn't coming, but it wasn't ideal for him to be MIA the night before the first debate.

David let out a string of language that in most offices would get you fired.

I shifted around in my seat and wondered if I could sneak out.

Jessica stood and frowned; her make-up had worn down throughout the day and settled into lines on her face, making her look ten years older, perpetually frowning.

I started to slide my phone back into my pocket and got ready to leave.

The movement attracted Jessica's attention and when she spotted me, her eyes lit up. "Charlotte! You can step in!"

I dropped my coat and felt sick.

"What?" Both David and I asked at the same time. I caught his eye, and while I was horrified, he looked completely confused.

She ignored both of us, her face relaxed now, as if thinking she had solved the problem for tonight.

"You were captain of your debate team at university, right?" she asked.

Being a single kid, and a single kid who had done very well at school, meant my parents bragged about me a lot. I could have strangled my parents for talking about me to my aunt and uncle. And my aunt and uncle for talking about me to Jessica. And Jessica for listening. There were a lot of people I could've strangled at that moment. I clenched my jaw and tried to reason my way out of it.

"Yes," I said reluctantly. "But there is a big difference between having prepared for a debate at university and being tossed into a debate against a very experienced politician. I'm not going to be useful here."

"I'm not sure this is a good idea, Jess," David said and glanced between us. "We need—"

They needed someone who had practiced and studied the opponent and could do a decent job acting as a stand-in. I could debate, but this was just stupid.

Jessica dismissed us both. "No. Charlotte, you'll be fine for tonight. I'll give you the talking points. We'll start in ten minutes."

For a moment, I considered walking out but figured that'd probably cost me my job. I took the sheets of paper Jessica handed me and started making notes. I had been very good at debate at university, but this really was completely different. It didn't help that for the last few months all I'd been working with were the policy and platform for our campaign. I'd be arguing against all that and working from the perspective of a party much further to the right than I'd ever vote for.

Jessica and David argued in whispers at the front; he didn't look much happier about this than I did, and that made my stomach twist.

When Jessica called time and I had to walk up in front of co-workers to try and debate the potential prime minister, I wanted to run. In school, I'd hated it when our chemistry teacher called us up randomly to write out problems on the board. Without fail, he'd pick the problem I knew I'd done wrong, and I'd have to walk up in front of everyone to show I had no idea what I was doing.

This was much worse. This was my worst nightmare of public humiliation on a professional level.

"I'm not giving an opening remark," I said as I walked behind the wobbly podium. The camera and staff were all staring at me, looking less than enthusiastic. Lights glared overhead and made my skin prickle out in sweat. The camera staring at the stage felt oddly hostile for an inanimate object.

David stood a few feet away, lips tight, notes laid in front of him; he would wipe the floor with me and I'd look like a complete idiot.

"And you know these aren't going to be Yates-like answers at all." I had no idea how to debate like Yates. I could give answers similar to his but beyond that, I was lost.

Jessica looked like she thought I was being particularly slow. "Of course you're not. David will give his. I'll ask questions, and we'll go from there. Take it away, David."

For a second, I thought he was going to push back one more time, but he clenched his jaw, gave a tight nod, and started his prepared opening statement. We were off.

David was an incredibly accomplished and competent politician, but those skills didn't always shine in debate. For the first couple of questions, his responses came out flat, sounding similar to mine, like he was reading off a sheet. Luckily, I needed the first couple of questions to find my footing. By the third question, things changed.

"You're lying," I said, interrupting him.

He stopped, clearly surprised that I said something, and that gave me a little more confidence. He'd underestimated me. "Your record on jobs is abysmal. Last year, my government saved 10,000 energy sector jobs while you did what? Your incompetence is clear as Opposition Leader. You're not fit for the job."

I knew enough of Yates to know he went personal in attacks. His campaign did not take the high ground, but I thought I might've went too far.

David stared at me. Everyone stared at me.

I swallowed down my fear that I was overstepping and kept going. If I had the upper hand, I knew I had to use it. "If Centre wins this election, jobs will be lost, the deficit will swell, and we will lose standing in the global community. An incompetent and out of touch leader is a step back."

Each time I'd said "incompetent," I could see David's jaw twitch. Just a little flex in the corner but telling all the same. A faint flush crept up from his collar, around his neck. My goading hit a nerve.

"Couldn't agree more that incompetent and out of touch is a step back, which is why I'm offering an alternative," David said. His demeanor had changed from simply going through the motions to actually participating. The first few warm up questions were in the past and he stepped up, and so did I.

I held my own fairly well against him, even with a few stumbles where I had no idea how to rebut a policy he tossed out at me. On those, I got a pass, and waved for the next question. On other topics, though, I frazzled him and got him on the defensive. That made me happier than it should have. I could poke and provoke. It'd been a while since I had debated, and I'd forgotten how much I enjoyed it.

We hit stride with each other, falling into the natural flow of the debate, and it carried us through to the end. I liked showing off I was smart; having someone keep up with me was refreshing.

"That's time," Jessica called.

I blinked and relaxed back against the wall; it had been more mental work than I'd been anticipating doing that late at night. My eyes flickered towards David and

I saw he was smiling at me. Something in the look and smile this time made me blush, and I grinned back. We were on the same page; that was fun.

"Good suggestion, Jess. And thank you, Charlotte, for stepping in; that's the most competitive practice we've had." He came over and shook my hand, still smiling.

Jessica was watching me but didn't look as happy as I expected. I had done well, and David thought so, too, so I wasn't sure what her problem was. Maybe she was tired. It was late. She got up and motioned for the papers as I walked back to get my coat.

"I suggested it for a reason. Charlotte, good job. Thank you for filling in." Despite her words, she was annoyed.

I shrugged my coat on and grabbed my bag. "Glad I could be helpful. Good luck tomorrow," I said to David and left.

*   *   *

A number of us stayed at the office to watch the debate the next night. We could all throw popcorn at the other leaders and cheer together. Mia was organizer in chief; given how good she was at encouraging enthusiasm I expected a fun night.

One of the conference rooms was rearranged for our viewing party with a big screen set up front and chairs lined up like a theater. Boxes of pizza sat on one table, with snacks and drinks on another. There was a decent crowd with thirty minutes to go before it started. I headed toward the pizza and loaded up, grabbing a few cookies while I was there.

"Looks like you have a bit of a sweet tooth."

Mike came up behind me, leaning over my shoulder to grab a piece of pizza. The smell of whatever horrible body spray he used, cloying and clinging around him in a haze, overpowered the pizza and made it hard to take a full breath without choking.

"Just getting set for the night," I said, trying to keep the conversation minimal.

He stayed too close and nodded toward his seat. "Sit with me."

Shoving toothpicks under my fingernails was just slightly worse than sitting with him for the next two hours.

"I'm good in the back."

He cut off my exit with a hand on my arm. "With me?"

The hand on my arm, holding a bit firmer and longer than was appropriate or welcome, spiked my temper. "Not a chance in hell."

It came out louder and harsher than I'd meant to say in public. A couple others in the room noticed and stared, some laughing.

Mike's joking manner dropped like a rock, melting off as his face burned red.

I took the moment and shoved past him, moving towards the back seats I had saved for Xavier and myself. Mike's friends up front laughed as he sat down next to them. At least I hadn't thrown my soda at him, but really, what did he think I was going to do? The man was an ass and couldn't take a hint. Part of me thought I should tone it down, be a little more careful since I still got a bad feel from him, but I was too annoyed to care.

Most of the people there, including me, had laptops with them. The research and social media areas were working tonight as fact checkers, and they all looked twitchy. I was happy to just enjoy my pizza and wait for Xavier; he and his girlfriend had a date, and I was in charge of saving him food and somewhere to sit. He hadn't sounded enthralled about sushi date night.

As I watched the news stations and political analysts show different graphs on the parties and leaders and polling trends, I decided to go out on a limb and send David a good luck text. I thought that'd be appropriate. After last night, it felt like I was slightly more vested in the debate than if I'd done nothing but watch.

Once I made my mind up, for better or worse, it didn't take much digging to find his phone number. Really, you'd think it'd be a little more complicated, but maybe our IT team had enough safeguards around our system that it was okay. Either way, I was glad for it. I typed the number and message in before I could second-guess myself.

It's Charlotte. Good luck!

Send.

I stared at the message for a second, not sure if I was giddy or wanted to take it back. There was nothing inappropriate about a good luck message. Finding his number felt slightly illicit, a little stalker-like, but at the same time, I thought it was okay.

I threw my phone in my bag, afraid of being caught with it in my hand as Xavier came in and sat next to me.

"Please tell me you saved me pizza." He didn't look happy.

"Sushi not to your liking?" I asked and handed him the plate I'd saved.

He shuddered and shook his head. "No. I love Addie, but she has bad taste in food. Raw fish, really?"

I checked the TV screen; just a few minutes more. "At least you have pizza tonight. Addie didn't want to join the party? Nothing says hot date like watching a political debate at work."

He glared at me, which if I hadn't known him better might have made me worried I was annoying him. "This is why you're single."

Before I could say anything back, mainly that he was probably right, Mia hollered out the debate was about to start.

There was a very distinct sporting event atmosphere in the room. When Prime Minister Alan Yates came out, we gave a magnificent round of boos. Our response was at odds with that on the TV; most of the audience was firmly in the camp of PM Yates. He was the youngest prime minster to be elected and was wildly popular among some.

I couldn't stand him. His ministers had scandal after scandal linked to them, and his way of speaking brought up all the things he had to "fix" from the previous administration instead of what he'd accomplished.

I had completely misjudged David when I'd started, and unless something came crawling out from deep within the woodwork, he absolutely was not a slimy politician. When he went on stage, there was a lot of cheering in our room. He looked relaxed and comfortable and was by far the most approachable looking out of the bunch.

The moderator went through the rules for the night and then they were off. I wasn't sure if Jessica was just good or if she'd gotten very lucky, or a combination, but the questions asked were almost identical to the ones he and I had debated last night. I didn't think that could be a bad thing, but it did leave some of his responses sounding a little rehearsed. There was an answer or two where he came off robotic and dry. On the flip side, he scored points for getting Yates flustered.

As it ended, those of us in the room felt a little let down. It had been a decent debate, but this far out it was so early I doubted it would matter six months down the road; attention spans didn't tend to last long in politics. David had to participate, but it all felt a bit pointless.

*   *   *

It was only after I'd gotten home, chucked off the parka and boots, and changed for bed, I realized my phone was blinking at me. The momentary confusion of who had sent me a text from an unknown number disappeared when I opened it.

Thanks, but luck wasn't needed. Had a good debate partner last night. Use this number in future.

I winced; sending a message to his business phone may not have been my best move. I hunkered down in bed and flipped off the light. On second thought, I turned the light back on. Texting David at night in bed with the light off felt more intimate than I wanted.

This number for future. No problem. Good job tonight.

After I'd typed the message, I wondered why I would be using it in the future. Maybe for future debates, assuming I'd be involved going forward. I hoped I would be. I had enjoyed it last night.

I tossed the phone on the bedside table, turned the light off again, and started running though my list of things to get done tomorrow. Only a couple more days and then it'd be the weekend…

The buzzing phone interrupted my planning.

Any feedback?

I wrinkled my face and tried to think of something intelligent. Wasn't this what Jessica was for, the late-night questions and planning? I didn't really mind and was glad he didn't seem annoyed with me for texting in the first place, but still.

A yawn shook my body and I snuggled deeper into my duvet, thinking— guess I was going to text him in the dark.

Impersonal at times. Stiff. Good counter points. Shouldn't you get some sleep?

I watched the little dots blink while he wrote back. Between yesterday and this, I figured I was due a bonus, or at least some brownie points, for going above and beyond.

Trying to. Good night.

I set my phone down and eyed it. It stayed silent, and I managed to fall asleep before anything else popped up.

*　　*　　*

The next few days were horrifically busy. Consensus among political commentators was a near-draw, with Yates and David at the top. I spent most days in meetings with the polling and social media areas, measuring how the debate performance had impacted what people thought, projecting it into the future.

Each afternoon, we reported on conference calls to Jessica while she and David traveled; the policies introduced in the debates were more broadly elaborated on in keynote speeches. It'd be nice when they were back.

Ben was a good strategist, but Jessica lived and breathed the campaign. I was pretty sure she would sacrifice a firstborn to win. I liked working with Ben more, but Jessica brought a spark to the rest of the office.

*　　*　　*

"You look beat," Camille said as I joined her for dinner Friday night. I'd dragged myself into the cocktail bar an hour late; her assessment was right.

I was frazzled and burned out. Thankfully, the dark and clubby atmosphere hid my tired eyes and bedraggled appearance.

I took a hefty swig of the dirty martini with extra olives she pushed towards me. "I am. I need back-to-back weekends."

She shrugged and handed me some fries. "I can only do back-to-back martinis. You'll have to make do."

I raised my glass to toast. "I'll do my best."

She hadn't been kidding when she'd said back-to-back martinis. The bar was crowded and loud enough with happy Friday night people to drown out any work thoughts. The chatter and gin blurred away the busy week, and I eased into the weekend.

Camille kept prodding me to plan my birthday party in a week.

"I don't know people," I said. Even in the din of the restaurant I could tell I sounded whiny, but I was right. "You need people for a party." Martinis made me think sharp.

Camille grabbed my phone, and for a moment I worried she'd find David listed as a contact, but no. She went to the apps and started looking for something.

"Then we find you people. You need a date."

I laughed. "Oh, really? Should I go pick someone out?" I asked and pointed to someone at the bar.

She gave me a look. "You have terrible taste and don't get to pick for yourself on this one. I added Tinder. Let's go. Date next Friday; invite them to your birthday party. Get laid. It'll help with the stress."

I flicked an ice cube at her. "That's your game plan?" Although she was right about my past luck; I was really good at finding un-dateable men.

She nodded. "Date, birthday, laid."

I took my phone back and shrugged. It wasn't a horrible plan. "I need assistance. Swipe left or right?"

* * *

By Wednesday, we had a full complement in the office. Jessica happily inserted herself in every meeting. In our data update, she fired off questions left, right, and center.

"These are the latest numbers I ran," Danielle said, and pulled up a report.

I got a jolt and recognized the report as mine, one I had sent for review that morning. I opened my mouth to say something but then closed it. It probably wasn't the right time for it.

One time I could pass off as a mistake, but it happened a second time, and then a third with my work relabeled as hers. It was my first experience with people being that level of bitchy.

"Danielle, can I talk to you for a second?" I asked. I'd stopped her on the way out of the meeting and tried to level my voice so I didn't sound quite so pissed off. She looked unfazed.

"What is it?"

"When I pass things through to you, my name is still on them, correct? Those reports you shared with Jessica—"

"I said they were *our* reports. We all work together, Charlotte. This isn't an individual effort." She looked at her watch and stopped short of rolling her eyes at me. "No need to overreact. I've got to go." Danielle smiled, a non-friendly, sarcastic smile, and that was it.

Annoyance tingled through me and made me shake. I couldn't be bothered to sit in the data room and stormed out. I'd been trying hard to play nice and send everything through for a second set of eyes, but now I wondered if the second set of eyes was taking it too far.

I marched myself and my laptop into the next meeting, the project with Mike and whoever else would be there; I had a feeling it would be a full house. It was very early, but I'd rather be there than look at Danielle's head. I wanted to throw something at her.

My solitude was interrupted ten minutes before the meeting started. The initial irritation disappeared when David came in early. In a detached way, I recognized it was a little strange the person I was most comfortable working with or being around was the one who made most people nervous. He seemed startled to see me there already.

"You're early," he said, and sat down across from me.

"I wanted to work somewhere quiet. This room was open until our meeting." I shoved my laptop back and rubbed my gritty eyes as a headache tightened its grip across the top of my skull. "You're early as well."

"Thought I'd grab a couple of minutes for myself before jumping right back into a meeting."

Well, that had backfired magnificently for both of us. He didn't look too irritated, though, finding the room not completely empty.

"Rough day?" he asked, concern creasing his forehead and making him pause with his computer.

I hadn't realized I looked that bad. "Something like that. You?" His eyes were tired, too.

He shrugged. "Just busy. It's good to be here and get updated on what's being worked on, but it makes it hectic. I'm glad to be in town all next week." He smiled, looking pleased about something. "I'm planning on trying to poach you away, partially to work with the speaking and debate side of things. That's one of my main goals next week, if you want."

The idea made me happier than it should've; breaking free from Danielle was most definitely welcome. "That's fine. I go where needed." I paused before I continued, "And I liked debating with you."

He laughed. "You might change your mind on that by the end. So as my debate partner, you didn't see any glaring mistakes?"

I thought back and shook my head. "Nothing big, but then, I might be a bit biased now."

"I'm probably biased towards my team, too, but you're the best debate partner I've had in a while. All joking aside, you really did help, and I'd be extremely fortunate to have you along for the next few."

After a rough morning where I'd felt inept, the compliment warmed me until I was glowing. "Can I ask you something?" We were having a fairly relaxed conversation, so figured I might as well.

"Of course." Some of the happy faded from his face, but he was willing to go along.

"Is Yates really as awful in-person as he seems…?"

David started laughing. It was contagious and I giggled, not quite sure what was so funny.

"Between you and me, yes. Here." He got up, grabbed a chair next to me and held his phone so I could see.

I leaned a little closer than I should have, but he didn't seem to notice. "One of my interns last summer sent me this." He glanced over and smiled. "Probably best not to share it too much or say who showed you."

"Lips sealed," I promised and grinned. We were quite close, closer than I'd normally sit with a co-worker. Close enough to see where his black-brown hair was starting to get tinged with gray, just feathered on the sides, but there. Close enough to see a thin spider's web of lines crease out from his eyes, brushing the tops of his cheeks when he grinned at me. Close enough to see a little curl of hair among the straight, just behind his ear and out of line with the rest. For a crazy moment, I thought of brushing it back. In that second, he was just an attractive man, not a coworker or high ranking official. Just a funny, kind, attractive man who brightened my afternoon. The thought startled me, coming out of nowhere, and I jerked my head back to the phone.

It was a video, a parody of one of Yates' events. He was visiting a grade school. The actor playing him did an excellent job with the squeaky voice, spewing out-of-place facts, and being baffled when a kid asked a question. It was awfully funny, and I made a complete idiot of myself, reduced to being a giggling, red-faced, eyes watering loon. I wasn't sure if David was snickering along with me or at me.

Of course, that was when the other three—Jessica, Ben, and Mike—arrived.

David closed the video and flipped back to business mode obnoxiously fast, leaving me wiping my eyes and gathering my thoughts back to work. He pulled his laptop over and slid his chair a little farther away from me; guess he had noticed we were close.

"Did the rest of us miss the party invite?" Mike asked. He glared, not happy to be left out and sat down opposite me.

"We were both early," David said, and left it at that. He looked smug, smug I had given him a minute and wouldn't do the same for Mike, and he knew it. Appropriate or not, it nearly set me off again.

I opened my computer to share the new data. I felt like I had started laughing and couldn't stop.

"Charlotte, if you've pulled yourself together, please present," Jessica snapped at me.

I took a breath and swallowed the laughs. "Ready to roll. So, after the debate…"

*   *   *

By Friday, things had quieted down. Jessica and David were off to a weekend event near Montreal. The office was quiet, and I had plenty of time to get myself nervous for the stupid date Camille had insisted was a good idea. Xavier spent a large portion of the day laughing at me as I tried to think up ways to get out of it.

But I hadn't, and I showed up at the restaurant, a very nice industrial chic place near ByWard Market. I'd checked the menu out earlier in the day and was looking forward to the food portion of the night. I arrived on time and wearing the bright blue sweater and heels I'd said I would.

James stood out front in his tight polo shirt, showing the world his arms when it was well below freezing, fake tanned to the max. His hair was overly-gelled and everything from his stance to dress screamed party boy. Camille was right that in the past he would have exemplified my normal type; boys like him were never intimidated, or cared, how smart I was. Now he did nothing for me.

"Charlotte?" he asked as I approached. "James." He offered me a handshake as we hustled in from the cold.

"Nice to meet you," I said automatically, and let the hostess lead us to a table. The restaurant was nice, with comfy oversized chairs and low lights, and wasn't horribly loud. Maybe it wouldn't be too bad. First impressions could be wrong, as I'd learned over the past few months.

We did the basic small talk, commenting it was cold out, but it'd be nice now that April was a couple weeks away. He talked a lot about going to the gym every day, that sort of thing.

"So, where do you work?" he asked as our appetizers, little tender buffalo sliders, were cleared away.

I thanked the waiter and turned towards James. "The Centre Party campaign. I'm—"

He rolled his eyes. "Politics?" He laughed, and my guard shot up. "I was way off. I was thinking you looked like a hairdresser or something."

I stared, unable to keep my mouth from dropping open. *Hairdresser?* Didn't he see the messy ponytail that was the extent of my ability? "Ah, no, I'm a data scientist—"

He nodded. "Oh yeah, I've seen all about that in campaigns now. You do all the social media numbers and the polls. Seems a waste of time when everything you see on the media has such a liberal bias. You should focus on people, not numbers."

I sipped my martini and clenched my teeth. Maybe I had judged too fast, but I didn't feel that logical arguments would work with him. I took the path of least resistance; he wasn't going to be worth my energy. "Something to keep in mind."

"Personally, I can't stand Reid, but whatever. I think Yates has done a great job. Your office is downtown, right?"

I swigged back the rest of my martini and ordered another glass; it was most definitely a "two martinis before dinner" date. "Yes, it's—"

"I'm downtown, too. Bank right across the canal," he said helpfully, and pointed. He then was kind enough to add in how much he made, what type of car he had, and how much he was projected to make next year. I was grateful when my trout and his steak arrived; maybe his mouth would be occupied with food rather than nonstop talk. As a positive, because I really was trying to find a positive spin to the date, the trout was excellent.

"My ex-girlfriend was a real bitch," he said through a mouth of mashed potatoes.

My face had shock written all over it; I hadn't thought people really did this on first dates, but he just continued blithely on.

"She hated eating out. I'm glad you—"

I thanked my lucky stars the moment my phone rang. If nothing else, it gave me an excuse to stop his monologue and escape from the table for a moment. When I saw who it was, I frowned and really did need to leave.

"Sorry, we can get back to your ex in a moment, but I have to take this." I stepped away before he could object and went out front to the entryway to talk.

"Hey," I answered. I hoped I didn't have to go back to work; I wasn't sure why else David would call on a Friday night.

"Hi." Another group of people came in the restaurant, laughing and talking loudly, so I relocated again.

"Sorry, did I catch you at a bad time?" he asked, and did sound genuinely sorry.

"No, I…" Ha! This was my exit strategy. "Actually, can I call you back in ten minutes?"

"Yes, but—"

"Five minutes. I'll call back."

I resisted doing a happy dance in the restaurant foyer and ordered an Uber before heading back to the table. It was hard to look appropriately bummed out about being called into work on a Friday night.

"That was my boss," I said, and fished some cash from my purse. James had already made it clear he didn't like to pay for his date's dinner; the ex had always expected that. "I'm afraid I've got to run back in. I'm really sorry."

"Jackass!" he said loud enough for other tables to look at us. "Blow him off."

I grabbed my coat, pulling it on fast, nearly tripping myself in my rush to get out. "Really can't. I've got to go."

I was rude and made a break before he could say or do anything else. Usually, I sucked it up on a bad first date, but this was a golden opportunity to escape.

Icy little droplets of rain pelted down outside, stinging my face and trickling down the back of my coat, melting cold against my neck. I tucked myself against the building and zipped up to my chin. My phone was blinking with text messages and a voicemail I ignored. I called.

"You didn't need to call back," he said before I could say anything. "If I interrupted something…"

I rolled my eyes and wished my Uber would hurry up and get here. "I told you it's not a problem. You saved me from an awful date. What's up? Do I need to go to the office?"

I heard him start and stop a few times. My car pulled up and I gratefully jumped in. "No office," he said immediately, and I relayed my address change to the driver.

"So…everything okay?" I was struggling to come up with a reason he'd called me. I wasn't important enough to be called in for a crisis.

"I was actually just looking to talk," he said.

"Oh. What about? Did something happen?"

"No." He sighed loudly into the phone. "I need a few minutes to relax and not think about work."

My eyebrows shot up somewhere near my hairline. "And you want to talk to me?"

"Well, I did call you," he said. Phrased like that, it had been a dumb question. "You're free to hang up on me if I overstepped. No explanation needed."

"No, you're fine," I said quickly. "It's just…not what I was expecting. Do you want to hear about the really bad date you just saved me from?" I had no idea what to talk about, but it wasn't a big deal to chat for the few minutes it took to get from downtown to the house.

"Bad date is fine."

I paused before starting. "As a work colleague or more friend-to-friend?"

"Friends. And again, you're more than welcome to hang up or tell me to fuck off if you don't want to."

I laughed. "No, it's fine. Just needed to know if I should edit the story or not." Although, the answer did change things a little. Friends were good.

Fully realizing the absurdity of relaying my abysmal date to him, I spent the next few minutes going over my first and last Tinder date. Rehashing it out loud made it more ridiculous. I sounded like an immature flake. He didn't interrupt, so he could have thought the same thing and regretted calling me. I should have thought of something else to talk about, but random surprise small talk wasn't my forte.

"So, my grand birthday party will involve five people, with me as the awkward fifth wheel between two couples, and probably will be a great disappointment to my housemate."

"Is your birthday tomorrow?"

"Not until Tuesday. Camille, my housemate, insisted mid-week parties are no fun, so the weekend it is."

"Is it a big birthday you're having a party for, or just because?"

I shrugged. "Not unless you count twenty-eight as a huge deal. Camille likes birthday parties. And I like dinner, so really, it's not bad, just not something I'd go out of my way to plan."

"Twenty-eight? You're only twenty-seven?"

I didn't point out that was how birthdays and age usually worked. He sounded shocked, not necessarily in a good way, and I didn't want him to all of a sudden go weird on me.

"Yes, for another few days."

He had thought I was older; I could hear that in the silence on the phone. There wasn't anything I could do about my age, so I prattled on, trying to fill the awkward space. I was happy talking and didn't want it to end on something silly like that. I didn't want him to feel awkward, either. "I don't feel the need for a big party for twenty-eight, but as long as strawberry cheesecake is involved it should be fun."

There was another pause before he continued. "Good cake choice. How do you know Camille?" he asked.

This was more stable conversation, so I launched into our time at university and the general mischief Camille and I had gotten into. As the Uber pulled up to the house, we were well into recounting various university escapades. Turned out we'd both spent a summer backpacking through Europe, had hiked some of the same places and frequented some of the same bars and pubs; every now and then, you got a smack of just how small the world really was.

I waved at Camille as I went upstairs. She looked at me curiously and gave me a thumbs up. She thought I was talking to my date. That certainly hadn't been a thumbs up.

After the initial oddness of him calling wore off, it was easy to talk. Politics weren't mentioned. Mostly it was fun, and it really did turn into talking with a friend. He sounded less stressed, too. I counted that a success.

"I'm afraid I've got to get back to work," he said eventually, sounding sorry to stop the conversation.

It startled me; we'd talked through the last hour. Even more startling was the thought that we could have kept going for another hour. Easily.

"Montreal Tech breakfast and lunch tomorrow?" I asked. I thought I'd seen that on his schedule.

"Yes, and then a Canadiens game in the evening—but with business on the side, so not really to watch—and then home."

"Do you like hockey?"

"Yes." His smile carried through the phone with no problem. "And I like the people I'm meeting with, so it's not bad at all."

"Do you have plans on your day off?" I asked. It didn't seem like he had days off. "Or does Jessica have something scheduled?" A little part of me was vaguely aware I was delaying hanging up.

He laughed. "I'm sure she'd love to have me scheduled for something, but my plan is sitting in my study and catching up on emails most of the day."

"Rebel," I joked. "Enjoy your day off."

"I'll try to."

I rubbed at the velvet edging on my chair and waited for him to say something. I was curious to see how this ended.

"Hope your party goes well. Good night, Charlotte."

"Good night, David." I clicked End and tossed the phone on the bed. I stared at it for a moment, letting the last hour settle into place, very aware I had a smile on my face while doing so.

Camille stopped me from thinking too much, knocking on the door almost immediately after I had hung up; she'd always had a bad habit of eavesdropping when it suited her.

I shoved my phone under my pillow and sat on it before she got a chance to see or grab it. I felt like a kid hiding something from Mom, like sitting on it was going to help. I almost laughed at myself.

"Date night went well?" she asked, sitting next to me on the bed. Her eyes were big and bright, matched by a slightly crazy grin. "Was he gorgeous? Is he coming on Tuesday?"

No, possibly, and no…but I didn't answer the questions out loud that way. "You are never, ever setting me up with anyone on Tinder, online, or a blind date again. You have lousy taste in men."

She tipped over laughing at me. "Tom might disprove your argument."

I conceded that point; Tom was a winner. "You used up all your ability on him. Picking for me, you are clueless."

She frowned at me, head tilted, and eyes narrowed. "Says she who came in all giggly and talked on the phone for the last hour. Do you have secret friends I don't know about?"

I didn't think she should be privy to that information quite yet. "Possibly," I said. The blush that crept across my face made the *possibly* show as a *definitely*.

It had been odd and a surprising twist to my failed date night, but really, not a bad twist. However, it made me a little nervous; on the surface, it felt like the start of a scandal.

*   *   *

After ten years, I should have expected Camille to be right. The weekend party had been a brilliant idea. Camille, Tom, Xavier and Addie all got along well. We stayed out late at a brewery eating burgers and fries before end of night drinks at a bar. I ended up with one too many birthday shots, making me grateful for Camille's foresight to leave Sunday as a sleep-in day.

I roused myself in the afternoon to buy food for the week, but that was the extent of my activity. Later Sunday night, I fiddled with my phone and sent one quick text to David because, well, I honestly didn't have a good reason besides wanting to.

How were the emails?

When Camille and I had met in college, I'd been annoying. I'd probably been annoying before college, too, but Camille was the friend who pointed it out to me.

We'd hit it off right away on move-in day after I'd bumped into her, wandering around looking for the dining hall. I latched on, became her shadow for the next few weeks while we settled in as freshman. She'd told me later I'd been marginally suffocating the first few weeks we knew each other. While it hadn't led to the demise of our friendship, I still second-guessed every time I called or texted or asked new friends to do something. I wasn't aiming to hang out with David, but I hoped the text wasn't too pushy.

Fifteen minutes passed and all I got were crickets. It was late, though. I was tired and did have to work tomorrow, so I abandoned phone watch and proceeded to get things laid out for the morning—clothes picked and set on my chair, bag organized and next to the clothes, everything ordered for running out the door in the morning. My room was small—cozy—and keeping things organized helped.

The little message light was blinking when I got back.

Thrilling beyond belief. How was your party?

I turned the lights out and crawled into bed, biting my lip to keep from smiling.

Fun. Everyone got along. Good food.

I didn't know where I was going with the texts. I didn't really have any reason to text him, which made it more awkward. There had been no point to the first one, except I had been curious.

Strawberry cheesecake?

I grinned, impressed he'd paid enough attention on Friday to pick up on me saying that.

Alas, no. Chocolate lava cake not a bad substitute. Hockey game good?

Texting might be the way forward for this. Camille couldn't get overly nosy.

Bad game, productive meetings. Jess doesn't do hockey well.

I laughed. I couldn't see her doing hockey well at all. It was easy to see her forcing interest but looking like she'd rather be anywhere else; sports had never been Jessica's thing.

No. Might be out of her depth on that one.

Out of curiosity, I Googled the game and pulled up pictures of them in the box with other business folks. David looked much more relaxed and at-ease at a hockey game than she did.

Yes, thankfully she's rarely out of depth. See you tomorrow.

I hesitated but decided to just ask. *You don't mind I texted you?*

The response blinked back awfully fast.

No.

Ha, not too pushy after all!

Excellent. Good night.

Good night.

I set my phone on the bedside table and didn't feel nearly as silly as I'd thought I might. Although, I thought, keeping my new texting partner under wraps for the time being was probably best.

Chapter Four

I woke up on Tuesday and was twenty-eight. The morning would be rushed. Grandma, a quirky little ninety-five-year-old who swore by a shot of whisky and piece of chocolate a day, had insisted on being the first to wish me happy birthday for as long as I could remember. Obviously when I'd lived at home, my parents had that honor, but she'd call bright and early before breakfast to make sure we had a chat. It was a little harder now for her to be the first one, but she had managed quite well the last few years. I fully anticipated her calling in the morning and needed time to talk. When I checked to make sure she hadn't called yet—one year she'd called at 4 AM—I saw a message; she wasn't going to be the first one.

Happy birthday Charlotte. Hope you have a wonderful day.

I tried and failed miserably at not smiling, being overly pleased. David had left it at 4:30. He didn't have much on Grandma. And no sooner did I think that than she called.

"Happy birthday, my little Charlotte!" she croaked out. It made my heart happy to hear her sounding so strong. "Did I get to be first today?"

"Well, you're the first I'm talking to," I said.

"Oh," she said, and sounded mock disappointed. "Someone already said happy birthday? That's very early."

I flipped on the light and squinted in my mirror; no new wrinkles or gray hairs yet. "It is," I agreed. "He just left a message—"

"Oh! A boy?"

I mentally kicked myself. Early mornings were not my sharpest hours of the day. "Just a friend," I said, clarifying before she started to ask about a wedding or future children.

"A friend who wishes you happy birthday before 6 AM," she said with a cackle. "Well, is he a nice-looking boy?"

I rubbed my face and sighed. "Yes, Grandma, he is very nice looking. As a friend," I repeated. "I got the card you sent," I said, not-so-tactfully changing topics.

We chatted for over twenty minutes and nearly made me late for work. She had to tell me all about the nursing home charades tournament she was helping to organize. I made her promise to send pictures.

Xavier was the only other person who knew it was my birthday. I'd told him last week to absolutely not blab it around because I didn't want balloons or to wear some silly hat all day or stand awkwardly while people sang happy birthday to me. So when I got in, there was only a sticky note on my chair saying happy birthday, along with a Nanaimo bar from the bakery he knew I liked, and that was quite all right.

"Pastries in the main meeting room," Xavier said as I started to get settled. He was eating one and had a cup of coffee in his other hand. "And good coffee."

"Say no more. You had me at pastry." I wasn't one to say no to sweet treats in the morning, especially on my birthday. Between the pastries and bar, I'd be sugared up for the day.

Any thought of the sweet treats on my birthday being a coincidence evaporated when I walked in the room. Giant boxes full of strawberry cheesecake Danishes sat on the tables. I grinned for multiple reasons and helped myself to the biggest one I could find—the one with the most strawberry chunks and icing—and a cup of coffee.

When I sat down at my desk, I saw the first email in my inbox. I settled myself down with napkins and headphones before opening. It was from a sender I didn't recognize, and because I was in a good mood, I assumed it was something fun, maybe something for my birthday.

Bitch.

I blinked and glanced around, thinking it couldn't have been meant for me or was a very strange joke.

Bitch? It had to be spam email that had somehow gotten through. Maybe another party or hacker had meant it for Jessica, since she had far more influence and was more likely to be targeted with weird emails.

Absentmindedly, I picked at my Danish, sending little flakes of buttery pastry and cream cheese icing everywhere. It was delicious. I'd have to ask where it was from.

Bitch? I looked at the sender's name again and was surprised it'd come from within our office. I typed the name into our staff directory, but it pulled up a blank.

Hmm. I couldn't take it seriously because I couldn't see myself being disliked or annoying enough to warrant it. Maybe it had been a missent prank. It was obnoxious and childish if someone really was sending me emails like that, but was most likely just a screwed-up joke. I pushed it out of my head and focused on my to-do list.

*　　*　　*

The staffing change announcement came later that day during our data science meeting with Jessica, Ben, and David.

"How do you eat so many pastries and not look like an elephant?" Xavier asked as we sat down.

I was on my third Danish for the day and was thin, so it was a legit question. David covered a laugh with a cough as I shrugged.

"Happy chance of genetics."

Xavier scowled at me as Danielle pulled up the previous week's summary and started presenting. It took a while; with it being the week following the first debate, there were quite a few changes to previous numbers. We'd been busy and had a lot of work to show for it.

"Thank you, Danielle." Jessica shut her computer at the end and glanced briefly between Ben and David. "Before you head back to work, we made a workload change for your department."

Xavier perked up, as did Danielle. I felt a little spark and tried not to look too eager.

"We're moving Charlotte to focus on the debate and speech side of data," Jessica said, her voice short and clipped. "All other requests will flow through you, Danielle and Xavier, but the numbers and models for the campaign tour, the speeches and debates will be through Charlotte."

Xavier looked happy with that setup; he liked working behind the scenes and hated doing the debate prep.

Danielle's face went stormy. "I thought the point of bringing on new hires was to balance out the workload," she said bitterly. "And while I'm sure you three discussed this, as the department head, I think I should have been included in those discussions."

Xavier and I shared a glance and kept our heads down. Guess I hadn't been a welcome addition to start with. Danielle probably should have been consulted, but surely, she had known the power structure before she'd started the job. I'd been fielding more and more IMs, not only from David, but from Ben as well. Danielle was great with doing the fundraising numbers, but she manipulated other data to show what she wanted, not the numbers' true story. She was good, but not always accurate.

Jessica gave David and Ben a very pointed look. It was clear Jessica and Danielle were on the same page about this.

"Instead of having only two people focusing on data requests, including speech and debate, there will be three," Ben said and shrugged. "Charlotte is stronger in that area; you two are stronger in the rest."

Danielle shook her head. "I should have been consulted on the strengths of my team—"

"Your team's strengths are well represented in the work you each do," David interrupted, smiling, though it didn't reach his eyes. "I'm well aware of the talent levels, and the move represents that." It was slight, but there was a bit of a barb. "The change is effective immediately. Charlotte, you'll be added to our meetings going forward." He stood, signaling the meeting and any discussion was done.

Xavier and I stood in a rush and headed for the door while Danielle stayed behind and grabbed Jessica. I didn't want to know what they were saying.

*   *   *

I sent David a text when I got home that night saying thank you for the Danishes. I'd felt a little strange all day eating them and not saying anything. The house was quiet. I hated to admit it, but I was glad Camille had made me have a party on Saturday. With both her and Tom out and Xavier busy, a birthday completely alone would be depressing. As it was, I was happy having the house to myself, opening the present from my parents that had been tempting me for the last week (a giant box of strawberry candies and the new headphones I wanted), and looking at places to go on vacation once the election was done.

As I set my alarm for the next morning, after I was in bed, glasses off, ready for sleep, my phone chimed with a new text.

Glad you liked them. Good birthday?

I hadn't expected him to write back.

Good birthday. The weird email resurfaced in my mind and I quickly blocked it out. I'd have to look into it tomorrow. *Quiet night so glad I had dinner out on Saturday.*

I settled myself down into bed and curled up on my side. He'd typed back already. Guess he was done for the night if he could respond right away.

No big birthday night meal?

Deli lasagna I picked up on the way home. Wasn't very hungry after pastries. When's your birthday?

I was curious. I knew I could just Google it, but that felt like cheating.

April 27. No pastries needed.

I smiled.

Balloons? Confetti shower? Mariachi band singing happy birthday?

Ha. No. I'm more of the quiet birthday night variety as well.

That seemed odd to me. Not that I expected him to go for the mariachi band or confetti shower, but as a politician of his caliber where he was so personable and public, smiling and laughing through mobs of people, I thought he'd like a party.

Sure you're in the right career?

We'll find out in October. I like having downtime, like now, or just a birthday dinner. Can't do events and meetings nonstop.

Guess that was a fair point.

Get back to downtime then. Just wanted to say thanks.

Is that a hint to go?

Not a hint. Didn't want to interrupt your downtime.

Best birthday present you've gotten?

He seemed happy to continue to talk to me; that was fine by me. The question was an easy one.

Got a puppy for my 7th birthday. Spaniel named Peanut. You?

Hard to top that. I got a fishing trip when I was 14.

We texted back and forth a while longer about fishing trips and Peanut. I managed to find a picture of me with Peanut when I had been a gangly, braced-teeth, big-glasses fourteen-year-old with Peanut the Cocker Spaniel next to me licking my face.

David sent me one from his fishing trip, holding a walleye grinning from ear to ear. We'd both been dorky-looking teenagers.

After we stopped texting for the night, I went back to the pictures he'd sent. He looked completely carefree and delighted. The way he had talked about it, fishing was clearly his happy place. I tossed my phone on the other side of the bed and smiled. It had been a happy birthday.

*   *   *

David was busy the rest of the week in Parliament. Jessica worked with the other MPs. Ben and Kaitlyn used the week to get me up and running on the strategy side and what supporter and voter data I should focus on. I'd be their point person and needed to know what each one of them expected. Rather than having the information dripped down to me from assistants or second-in-commands, they'd prefer to cut out the middle person and do it themselves.

On Friday, Kaitlyn congratulated me on having a big head that absorbed a lot of information and taking it all in stride.

"Happy hour?" Kaitlyn asked at the end of the day. She was still perky, her short brown pixie hair looking as perfect now as it had at 8 a.m., blue eyes bright and ready to go. Both Ben and I looked closer to tipping over.

"I've got time for a drink," Ben said. "It's been a long week."

I nodded. It'd be nice to get to know both of them a little better since moving forward, we'd be working close together. "Sure, sounds good. Lead the way."

We ended up at a beer and pizza place. It was a little hole in the wall I would have walked by if it'd just been me. I recognized a couple of the other tables, not from our office, but from TV. It seemed to be a political hang out. I wasn't sure if that made me feel politically elite or like a complete imposter.

"It's a little stuffy," Kaitlyn said as we grabbed a high table. "But it's got the best pizza and breadsticks you're going to find."

It was an old-fashioned bar—emerald green booths and chairs cracked with age, dark wood everywhere with brass railings along the bar. It smelled like yeast, a brewery and bakery rolled into one. In addition to the standard TVs showing sport events, there were some running news stories and financial updates—not the typical bar viewing.

A few of the people recognized Kaitlyn and Ben; they stopped over to say hi, chatting about work and families. In a strange way, it made me envious. I didn't want to be the imposter or outsider. I wanted to be in the loop and part of the circle.

"Okay with beer?" Ben asked after the last person, an MP from Vancouver, had left.

I nodded. "That's fine. Quite the spot for political junkies?"

Kaitlyn gave me a smile and shoved the basket of nuts toward me, a fancy mix in toasted garlic and crispy herbs. "You're one of us now."

I made a face and mock grimaced. "You make that sound like a threat."

"It can get nasty later in campaigns, but it's not too much of a threat."

"So, how did Jessica get you?" Ben asked. He'd lost the tie and suit coat, sleeves rolled up, and with the stress from the office gone, he looked much younger, closer to forty than the sixty I'd originally thought. "You didn't seem as enthusiastic as most who join us."

I explained how Jessica had highjacked my low-key Christmas, selling the job and turning into a full-blown saleswoman.

The beer arrived, dark, malty, and a definite step up from the average pitcher; no wonder this was a popular spot.

"You're sucked in now," Kaitlyn said, looking pleased. "I figured as much when you voluntarily showed up to watch a debate practice."

I had no defense to that and happily sipped my beer. "How about you two?"

Kaitlyn had followed the most straightforward path: an internship in college, entry-level job after graduation, working her way up to communications head now. Ben and David had been friends growing up as kids through school, and then university.

"David called to ask if I'd help out with his first campaign," Ben said. "I was bored working as a project manager, so I said yes. I'm still hanging around ten years later, happy to do whatever's needed." He was being modest. Ben was a razor-sharp strategist and very little escaped him. His advice carried more weight with David than nearly anyone else's.

We paused as the pizza and breadsticks arrived. The bowl of nuts I'd polished off by myself was removed to clear space. The pizza smelled of spices and garlic with just enough crust to be chewy and crisp, with big chunks of pepperoni and golden gooey cheese. This pizza had never seen the inside of a freezer. Ben and Kaitlyn were easy to sit with. Neither resented training me, even if they were several levels above me.

"I think it benefits everyone if you know what you're doing," Ben said, helping himself to a slice of pizza. "You're a fast learner—"

My phone cut him off. I'd left it on the table earlier and it sat quietly next to Ben and Kaitlyn's until now. I checked it quickly, saw David's name, and flushed. "Sorry, do you mind if I take this?" I asked.

Both shook their heads no. Kaitlyn looked at me a little suspiciously as I swiveled my chair around to give some semblance of privacy.

"Hi there. Is it okay if I call you back in about an hour or so?" I asked.

"Not another bad date?" David asked.

I laughed. "No. Just out for pizza with Kaitlyn and Ben, from the office." I rolled my eyes at myself; he knew who Ben and Kaitlyn were.

"The Ambassador Pub?" he guessed.

"Yes." He must frequent here as well.

"Eat the nuts at the table; they're good. Call back when you want. No rush."

"I already ate all the nuts. I'll call you later," I said over his laughing.

I hung up and turned back to the table. I shoved my phone deep into my purse to keep it from distracting me. "Sorry about that," I said.

"When we talked families, you didn't mention a boyfriend," Kaitlyn said, looking at me from over her beer, eyebrows raised in perfect peaks.

Ben's eyes narrowed.

"No," I said fast and firm. "Not a boyfriend." The idea jarred me. A phone call or two did not make him a boyfriend at all. The label "boyfriend" didn't fit with him anyway; he seemed far too serious and mature for that.

"Hmm." Kaitlyn's eyes bored into my face. "We'll see. Your face goes bright red when you're being questioned. Did you know that?"

On cue, I felt it heat up again, burning from my neck to forehead. "Yes. I did. Weekend plans?" I asked, blatantly moving the conversation away from me.

*   *   *

I called David back on my way home, once I'd settled into my bus seat.

He answered almost immediately. "Hello, Charlotte."

I heard other voices in the background. "Hi. I'm sorry. Are you busy?" Maybe he hadn't called to just talk this time.

He muttered a good-bye to someone, and I heard a door opening and shutting. He wasn't always working; he probably had friends or a girlfriend or someone.

"No, not at all," he said, almost immediately. I could tell he was smiling. His voice did that, carried his smile with it when he was happy. Why had I noticed that? "I just finished dinner with my sister's family—my nieces and brother-in-law. That's all."

I didn't know how to respond. His private family life was none of my business and seeing him as an uncle was strange. "Oh. Are you sure? You can stay—"

He laughed. "Charlotte, stop. I'm leaving. The night was terrible…that's why I called earlier. It was an escape attempt."

Despite myself, I smiled. "Why was it terrible?" I heard a car door close on his side. The others on my bus faded. "Or, you don't need to say either. I didn't mean—"

"You can ask whatever you like," he said quickly, firmly. "Open book here. My sister views me as her little brother, probably ten-years-old and likely still to get in dust ups. My nieces are much more attached to Marie—my ex—than me. Can't blame them; designer who gets them into fashion shows or a politician uncle. Not really a contest."

I pulled a loose thread on my coat and nodded. "Your nieces sound silly. Seems like you'd be a good uncle." My experience was very limited, but if I thought about him and Henry, if Jessica got him to come along to something, I could see David playing with him. The image came to me with no problem, easy, like it was already a memory.

"You're too kind," he said. Again, that smile was there. "You worked with Kaitlyn and Ben most of the week?"

"I did…most of the week. They've kept me busy."

"You're getting everything you need?"

I couldn't tell if he heard it or meant for it to show, but there was a drop of concern, just enough to negate the chance of it being a formal question.

"Yes," I answered honestly. "They've been great. Very patient."

"From what I've heard, you're taking it on faster than either of them expected. I know it's not really the area of work you were hired for."

I blinked a couple of times and bit back a smile. "It's fine. You get scouting reports on me?" I asked.

"I may have checked in a couple times this week. I have a tendency to be overly meddlesome. Just wanted to make sure I hadn't overloaded your plate."

"What'd they say?" I asked. Curiosity got the better of me and I wanted to know. He shouldn't have brought it up otherwise. Somewhere in the back of my mind, I registered this was an incredibly casual conversation for me to have with him. There was also the part of me that liked having him as a friend, regardless of who he was.

"That you catch on fast, you're sharp, good to work with… Glowing reviews."

Warmth spread up my neck and across my face. I thought he was exaggerating. "That's very generous of them. They're good teachers."

"And not bad for after work dinner," he said. "Good time?"

I was still full and happy from a night out with new friends. I smiled. "Yes. Nice way to end the week."

"It's a good place to go. I used to go there quite a bit."

"You'll have to be in the office next time we decide to go," I said without thinking. Part of me liked the idea a lot. Adding David into a future repeat was easy.

He half laughed, but a sigh answered the offer before he spoke. "Once upon a time, probably, yes," he said. "But not now. It's harder for me to go out for simple things like dinner. A few places I can, but one with that number of people and cameras who watch that place… Not anymore."

It sounded lonely. He'd in no way said it like he was trying to get pity. His role came with a lot of power and a lot of privilege; it also came with restrictions.

"Where do you suggest to go then?"

"Torino," he said almost immediately, catching himself and laughing. "Torino…it's a little Italian place next to my house. Excellent martinis and tiramisu. The owners are friends of mine, so no pretense. I'd—" He stopped himself short. "That's where I'd go."

Thankfully, I had enough sense to not say we'd go there next time. "I always take martini and tiramisu recommendations. What kind of martini?"

"Really?"

I shifted around in my seat and wished I was home. I wanted my room, to be in my chair or perched on the bed, comfortable. Not sitting in a jerky, smelly bus with a curious old lady eyeing me, not so subtly eavesdropping. "Really. Martinis are my favorite."

"In that case, I'll text you a list of places later. They're my favorite, too, and I've had time to find the good spots around Ottawa. They do an excellent dirty double martini at Torino."

I nodded and bit my lip instead, trying unsuccessfully to keep the grin away. "Sure. I'd take that."

I wanted to ask about his week, about what he did outside the office, but instead I heard a half-mumbled curse.

"I'd rather talk to you about martinis and restaurants tonight, really I would, but your cousin has called twice and will show up at my house if I don't answer. And I don't feel like dealing with that tonight."

"She'd just show up?" I asked, unable to keep the surprise from my voice.

"Yes. And…I'm usually done dealing with people after dinner with Sophie—my sister—and I can't deal with Jess tonight."

I pressed my lips tight for a second and wondered where that put me.

He seemed to get there as soon as he said it. "That came out wrong. This is different because…we're not working. Just talking."

"Yes—"

"This is fine. But Jess…" He trailed off with a sigh. "Next week, instead of heresay from Ben or Kaitlyn, we can text or call? Make sure you're settling in?"

The lie was clear as day in the question. But it gave some form of legitimacy to this. Both of us realized calling and texting wasn't standard procedure. If we didn't acknowledge it though…

"Sure, that should be fine. If you want a more detailed update, just give me a call. Any night's fine. Okay?"

"Okay," he agreed, and we were set.

Before I fell asleep that night, I pulled up news clips from the Parliament debates over the last couple of days. I felt a bit stalker-like watching him, embarrassed to be staring at him even on video. The awkwardness he had in televised debates disappeared when he argued with and questioned ministers and Yates in Parliament. He was brilliant.

*   *   *

Over the weekend and the next week, a text message or call when I was free and David wasn't busy became our new daily norm. It was one of those unexpected friendships you didn't see coming but ended up fitting. It felt easy and helped me ignore the emails—two of them now, one calling me a bitch and one telling me to quit, if I knew what was good for me.

By mid-April, I was crazy busy scrambling to get everything in order before David went to Beijing for trade talks and meeting leaders, just in case he won.

The office buzzed, everyone grabbing a meeting or update or word before he left. Next week would be comatose by comparison. My plan of arriving early to the final all-department meeting on the chance of maybe catching him alone before he left failed in spectacular fashion. Nearly everyone was already there and seated, minus Jessica, who would be coming from an interview.

"Blondie! Saved you a seat."

Mike smiled broadly at me and indicated the seat next to him. It was the only seat open, minus the far end with the new interns, and it was also next to David, who I had no problem sitting next to.

But Mike... The interns still looked like deer caught in the headlights staring around. I couldn't sit there. I liked to be closer to the action.

"All right if I sit here?" I asked David. He sat at the head of the table. I knew the seat to his right was for Jessica, but I didn't want to presume Mike knew what he was talking about with the one on the left.

"Of course." David gave me a little smile and went back to work.

I sat on the edge of the chair, as far from Mike as I could get, and set about getting my laptop pulled up to the agenda.

"I got you something," Mike said loudly, attracting attention from a few other people. He slid an envelope at me and tapped it. "Open it." He winked.

The wink nearly had me getting up and joining the interns. Other people watched curiously. I hated being put on the spot like this.

Figuring the best way out was just getting it over with, I opened it. "Hockey tickets?" I asked, dumbfounded. Two tickets for the Ottawa versus Pittsburgh playoff game tomorrow night.

"Buddy of mine plays for the Senators," he said, the brag coming through loud and clear. "Got me these two club seats, plus VIP passes."

I was not a big sports person but had gone to hockey games in the past with friends, mainly for the social aspect, not because I'd explicitly wanted to watch. Absolutely no part of me wanted to be social with Mike.

I slid the envelope back towards him, very aware there was a larger audience watching now, including a few who looked jealous of the tickets.

"I'll have to pass. It's not really my thing." I wasn't sure if he'd thought I'd agree because other people were watching, but that wasn't happening.

"Oh come on, it'll be great." Under the table, he rubbed the side of my knee with his hand to emphasize. All that did was make me lurch away from him, nearly spilling the bottle of water David had next to him.

"You can't say no to these," Mike said, completely oblivious. "What else are you doing on a Thursday night?"

My Thursday night plan was to talk with David before he left, rather than just text—not that anyone was going to hear that. I tamped down my anger at being forced to do this in front of everyone.

"No. And no to dinner or drinks or anything else," I said to cover my bases.

My answer slowly sank in.

A vein started to pulse visibly in Mike's neck and the cocky look he had on his face slipped into frustration. "Really? Nothing at all? I don't even get a chance?"

"The symphony," I said, knowing he wouldn't go for it. "I love the symphony."

He laughed, and while I was glad I had been right, his reaction still annoyed me. "Like classical music? The stuff old people go to?"

"Yes," I said, failing to keep my voice down. "I used to play in one and am rather fond of it."

"What do you play?"

The question came from my right, not left, and startled me. I hadn't known David was paying attention. I happily turned away from Mike. I took a breath to calm down, ignoring Mike's fuming on my other side. "I play cello."

David tried to smother a smile and nodded. "How long have you played?"

I thought back. "Twenty years," I admitted, and wrinkled my face. "That makes me sound very old."

He rolled his eyes. "No, it doesn't. Are you any good?"

I bit back a smile; he was teasing me. This sounded more like when we talked at night, not work. "Yes, I am. I was in the Toronto Youth Symphony and did the summer tour with the National Youth Symphony in college," I said, proud of the achievement. "You play, don't you?" I remembered reading he had.

He nodded. "Violin. I did the summer tour as well, a while ago. What are the odds?"

Of course he had. Of course we both played strings. Because we didn't have enough in common as it was, might as well toss that in as well.

"Do you still play?" I asked. It was none of my business, but now I wanted to hear him play. Maybe I could find something on YouTube.

"Yes. I'm good, too. Have you been to the orchestra here since you moved?" David asked.

I shook my head. This was much firmer footing for me than hockey. "No, haven't had a chance yet."

"It's good; you should try to get there sometime. If not this season, then maybe next." He paused. "Did Mrs. K. still bring in the little spiced cookies for some of the orchestra practices when you were there?"

I knew exactly what he meant. The conductor's wife had made giant batches and brought them in as a snack at the end of rehearsals. I grinned.

"She did. I got the recipe from her before I left. She noticed I had a sweet tooth and shared."

He laughed as Jessica came barreling in.

"Sorry I'm late," she apologized, getting the room to drop quiet in an instant. "Let's go ahead and get started."

*   *   *

"Didn't change your mind and end up at the hockey game?" David asked when I answered the phone later that night.

It was only 7:30 PM, so he must have had an easy evening. I switched off the TV and resettled more comfortably onto the couch. Camille had a work event and Tom was on call, so I had the living room to myself for the night.

"No. I thought that was pretty clear," I said over him laughing. Jerk. "Thanks by the way, for stepping in before I hit him."

"Happy to keep fistfights to a minimum in the office."

"Any suggestions on how to repel him? You must be used to getting all sorts of obnoxious people hitting on you."

He gave a little snort of a laugh. "Are you saying I'm good at repelling people?"

I rolled my eyes and stretched out on the couch. "I'm saying I bet you can if you want to."

"Hmm."

The silence felt louder than anything else, and I winced. "Sorry, work topic. Anything exciting tonight?" I asked.

"You don't have anything to apologize for," he said. "Your no should be enough. He was being an ass."

His answer made me smile. It was nice to know I had backup. "I know. It's just annoying he's doing it at work. So, have you?" I asked. "Have you had to repel? Tell me the worst case."

He groaned. "You really want to know?"

I grinned. "You're seeing mine in action. Your turn. Play fair. Or," I added in case he had no desire to go into this with me, "you can tell me to knock it off and hang up. That's fine, too."

"No, I'm not hanging up. Let me think."

I stayed quiet, pulling at the hem of my T-shirt while I waited. At least I'd offered him an out.

"A few weeks after my divorce went through, I was at a town hall event. Someone thought since I was single, I needed…attention. She threw a bra at me and tried to kiss me. I guess the police were more the repellent than me, but that's what I've got."

The image made me laugh. I hoped that's what he was going for.

"Actually," he continued, the humor dropping from his voice, "my ex-wife, Marie, was probably the hardest."

Marriage made me feel very young and sheltered. Only a handful of my friends were married, a couple with kids; the rest were still single. No one was divorced. "I was just kidding. You don't need—"

"It's fine, Charlotte," he said. "She didn't want to end anything because my publicity helped her business. That's all. She wasn't staying because of a personal attachment."

"Guess that's a little harder to get out of," I muttered, feeling silly.

"Yes, but also easier to avoid. She was my choice. You just got stuck with an asshole co-worker who harasses you at work and the creepy old politician who calls you at night."

I half-laughed, baffled he thought of himself that way. "Not creepy and not old. So really, I'm just left with the co-worker."

"Good. Otherwise, I couldn't tell you I was close to knocking him out today, too…not overly professional behavior."

"Maybe, but it's good friend behavior." I squeezed my eyes shut and gave myself a mental shake. Shouldn't go further than that. Being friends was more than I could have asked for or expected.

"I am curious, though, about this violin playing… Is there a video of you anywhere? I want to see if you're really good or if you were just bragging."

Not subtle, but I needed to switch topics before my thoughts started going somewhere they shouldn't.

He let out a puff of air. "I have no idea. Anything out there probably wouldn't do me any favors. Hold on."

The phone went muffled and scratchy. For a minute or so, there was nothing. I checked and we were still connected, so I waited. Maybe someone'd come to the door or an email had popped up. It wouldn't have been the first time.

After a while, my phone chirped with an incoming FaceTime request. I jumped up and double checked in the mirror to make sure I didn't have salad plastered on my teeth before I accepted; my teeth were clear, and while I wasn't in work attire, a T-shirt and ponytail weren't inappropriate.

The screen flicked open and showed what looked to be an office or a study. The phone rested on a desk or chair arm and focused on a music stand; tall windows stood behind the stand, heavy gray curtains drawn for the night. A bookshelf, full to the point of almost crammed, was on the left.

David sat in front of the music stand, maybe six feet or so from the camera, violin in lap. He wore a sweater and jeans. Seeing him like this at home was different, more intimate than just a phone call. He was more relaxed than anytime I'd seen him. I felt incredibly shy.

"I didn't mean you had to give a live demonstration," I said, although it was a bit late to say so now. I tried to keep my hands from fiddling with my hair or picking at something, eventually giving up and just sitting on them, leaving my phone balanced on my knees.

He shrugged and looked oddly happy. "Not a big deal. You asked if I was as good as I said. And you said it's better than a hockey game." He smiled before turning to the music stand, lifting the violin and starting to play.

When he'd said he was good, he hadn't been lying. He played a Bach sonata and made the strings sing through the phone speaker, rich and clear as crystal. I listened, meaning to stop him after a moment, but I let him play all seven minutes of it. Partway through, I lost the awkwardness from earlier and enjoyed watching his fingers fly over the fingerboard. I got lost in the music, hearing it swell and soar between us.

After the last note finished, I clapped. He did a little bow for me. "Maybe not the full symphony tonight, but not bad?"

The smile on my face answered for me, but I nodded anyways. "Not bad at all."

I watched him nestle the violin in its case and latch it up. I wanted to see beyond just the office, suddenly curious about where he lived, but really, it was none of my business.

"So, should I ask the same? Any videos of you?" he asked.

I stifled a giggle. That sounded dodgy, but I knew what he meant. "No. Well, not that I'm aware of."

He settled into a wingback armchair in the same room. It looked settled and well-worn, a small table set up next to it with a haphazard stack of books on it and an empty crystal tumbler. I wondered if he normally called from there at night.

He raised his eyebrows at me, hinting.

I hid my face on my knees and groaned.

"Really?" Maybe I should have seen it coming.

"You don't have to, absolutely don't need to," he said.

I looked up and sighed; hiding didn't work with a camera watching you. He looked like he hadn't meant to put me on the spot. "I'll play." I had practiced earlier tonight, so I wasn't particularly rusty. "Just ignore the trip upstairs and my slightly messy room." I hoped I hadn't left anything embarrassing lying around.

"Happy to ride along," he said while I walked up the stairs.

I glanced around my room before heading in; my work clothes lay on the bed, getting more wrinkled by the minute. My dresser was a little more cluttered than I'd like it, but overall, it wasn't bad. I propped the phone up on my nightstand along the wall from my cello corner. He'd have a clear view of me sitting and playing. I wished I'd put on something a little nicer. And had left my make-up on.

"Is this okay?" I asked and stuck my head back in front of the phone.

He smiled, his eyes crinkling. "It's fine, Charlotte."

I settled back nervously. "Yell at me to stop any time," I said.

The last time I'd played simply because someone wanted to hear me play was when Grandpa had still been around, nearly five years ago. Since then, it'd been concerts or practice. David hadn't minded me watching, so I could do this, too. And, I really wasn't bad. I grabbed a piece I'd done more times than I could count, matching him Bach for Bach, and played.

It wasn't the smoothest I'd ever been, but also nowhere near the worst. The first couple minutes, I was all too aware of him out of the corner of my eye. When I glanced up, I could see him on my phone watching me. But then, I got used to the camera, blocked it out, and relaxed into the music.

I smiled as I hit the last note, the tone vibrating through me and leaving me tingling and warm. Not bad. I peeked up and saw him watching rather intensely, head resting on his hand with a finger tapping on his lip. I gave him the same little bow he had done, and his intense look dropped.

"You weren't lying when you said you were good." He stood up and clapped. "Absolutely beautiful."

I shrugged but was secretly pleased. "Told you so," I said, and snatched my phone off the table. Rather than heading back downstairs, I dragged my chair over and used the bed as a footrest. "Did you want to turn the camera off?"

He shook his head. "It's fine."

The problem with having the camera on was that he could see my face light up when he'd said to keep it on. "Okay."

"Who's the little boy in the picture on your dresser?" he asked, pointing back to where I'd been playing.

"That's Henry." I got up and held the picture closer. "It's from a year ago at his second birthday. He's Jessica's nephew," I added. Henry sat on my lap with blue frosting smeared across his face and hair, offering me a sticky fistful of cupcake. "Her brother's kid."

"Cute. I think I remember her saying something when he was born. Do you see them much?"

I settled down in my chair and continued on with the evening chat. The shyness from earlier wore off and was replaced with a ridiculous flutter of butterflies every time he smiled. The camera made me forget we worked together and why we couldn't meet for dinner or a drink.

"Are you all packed for next week?" I asked after a while. It was late, and I imagined he'd have to go soon. I needed to hang up before Camille got back, anyway.

He grimaced and shook his head. "Not yet."

I laughed. "You're gone for what, ten days, and not packed?"

"Nine days," he said. "I pack suits, ties, and shirts. There's not a lot of thought that goes into it."

"I suppose. Not quite a vacation, is it? Anyway, should I let you go start?"

He yawned. "I probably should." His eyes looked tired, but everything on his face was relaxed and happy. "Calls and texts next week probably won't work so well…"

"I know." I'd expected that. Silly as it was, I didn't like it. "Twelve hour time difference?" And a twenty-hour flight to Beijing.

"Hmmhm," he said. "You didn't check or anything, right?" He smiled now, mouth turned up and teasing because he knew I had.

A blush heated up my neck and I scowled. "Just curious," I said, sounding grumbly and defensive. "It's fine. You might be a little busy."

"A little. I can call once I land back here, though, if you want?"

The offer caught me off-guard. "You don't have to do that," I said automatically.

He half-shrugged and shifted around in his chair, making it groan. "I know I don't have to. But, would you want me to?"

Part of me wished the camera was off. I wasn't sure I wanted him to see how much I liked the idea. At the same time, I was glad it was on because I could see him, and saw while he sounded casual about it, he looked the same way I felt.

"For what it's worth," he added before I could respond, "I'd like to."

There wasn't anything on the surface that said this offer was different than our usual daily calls, but there was something special about being the person someone called right after they got back from a long business trip. He felt more than just a friend at that point.

I nodded. "Yes."

He didn't show much emotion, I guessed just due to politician practice, but his eyes said everything. He liked that answer, too. "So go pack then, and call me when you get back in the country." I failed at looking nonchalant; my little video picture beamed.

He didn't do any better. "I'll call after I touch down," he said. "Can I ask you one more thing, more as a work colleague?"

My guard jumped up. "Sure," I said, a bit hesitantly.

He opened his mouth and closed it, looking lost for words.

"Just spit it out. You're making me nervous the longer you take."

"Do I need to do something about Mike?" he asked. "From a workplace harassment perspective—"

"No," I said firmly. That wasn't where I'd thought that was going. "For right now, no."

He didn't look convinced but gave me a curt nod. "Tell me if that changes."

"Isn't that something that would go through Danielle rather than you?"

He rolled his eyes. "Danielle can barely find her way to the office in the mornings. Come to me."

I laughed, even though it wasn't funny. "If something changes, I will. Seriously, go get packed."

He rubbed his head and stretched, looking far too long for the chair he was in. "I know, I know. Have a good week."

I felt myself going shy again. Saying good-bye for a longer time was more awkward than a good-bye until just the next day. "Okay. You have a good trip. And flights, and whatever else." I wondered if FaceTime would happen again when he got back.

"I'm sure I will have a good trip, flights and whatever else. I'll call you once I land back here." The look he gave me, the little smile making his eyes crinkle just a bit, made my breath catch for a second.

"Bye, David."

"Good night, Charlotte." And the screen blinked off.

We didn't say more than normal friends would say. I never wanted to be the pathetic party staffer falling for the celebrity candidate; he certainly didn't want to be the dirty politician going after a younger woman. All of that was the stuff political scandals were made of. There was a lot to lose if one of us gambled wrong. Still, I thought the line was starting to blur.

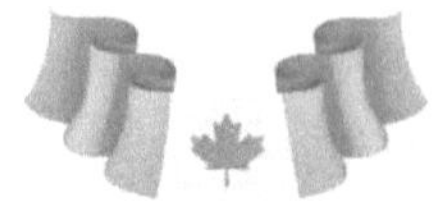

Chapter Five

L *eave the campaign.*

After carrying the FaceTime high with me through the weekend, the first email I saw on Monday morning brought me crashing down to Earth. I'd put the "Bitch" email out of my mind, along with the "Quit" one. This email was harder to pass off as a prank. It seemed incredibly juvenile that someone was doing this, like I wasn't welcome to the club so they were trying to scare me off. It was also unsettling that someone clearly didn't want me here and went through the effort of using a fake email account.

I went over to the desk of the friendly IT guy I trusted. I'd sent him the email address last week to check out and hadn't heard anything back. He glanced up at me as I came over and winced.

"Sorry, Charlotte. Completely forgot to reply." Ryan scrambled around on his desk, papers shuffled and piled haphazardly, before he handed me a sheet.

It wasn't much, and my face showed the disappointment.

"There wasn't far for us to look," he explained. "It was sent from this office, but we don't have an employee named 'Charlie Garth' and he's not listed in our past records, either. I did wipe that email address out though, so that should take care of it."

I managed a smile. "No problem. Thanks for looking into it, Ryan."

"Report it to HR maybe? Should be taken care of now."

He looked so confident in himself I didn't bother voicing my doubt. I said thank you again and went back to my desk, feeling no better than I had before.

The email certainly didn't signal the start to a wonderful week, but it wasn't a harbinger of doom, either. The meetings we had were prep work for when David got back. There was a group monitoring his trip, just in case he said something wrong and we needed to cover, but overall, it was a quiet week planned.

I jumped in and helped with some of the electoral modeling for Xavier, collecting and wrangling our voter data so strategy and policy folks could tweak campaigns.

Danielle, Mike, and Jessica holed up most of the week planning fundraisers. I was overly sensitive. Every data meeting I wasn't involved in made me think I'd been left out on purpose. When I saw the three of them together, discussing whatever event and fundraiser they were working on, my guard went up and I wondered if that was all they discussed. The workload during the week wasn't hard, but the level of second-guessing wore on me.

The call from David on Friday night when he landed was nothing more than a courtesy call. It was eleven at night and both of us sounded like we'd rather be asleep than talking to each other.

When I called him on Sunday, we talked for much longer on FaceTime. He asked about my week, not in a business sense, but just me. I asked about Beijing, not the policy side since I'd read all the reports, but what he did and what Beijing was like. We set times for calling later that week; he'd be in Parliament most days, with late meetings and business dinners. I had plans with Camille one night and Xavier another. Calls were planned around schedules, and that was that.

Even without coming into the office, David managed to keep us plenty busy. The heated debates in Parliament spilled into public interviews, making us all work non-stop. He was pushing hard to get a trade deal through, working with other parties to get the votes. Both sides were snide, manipulating whoever they could to get their way.

Our models fluctuated more than normal with the additional media attention. On top of it, I was left scrambling the first part of the week after Danielle had used my databases for her fundraising work, trying to rewrite the coding. It had broken, so I worked Wednesday night until late fixing it.

I almost ignored David's call when I saw it flash up on my screen, but my head hurt and a break wasn't unwelcome. When I saw myself on camera, hair slipping from a sloppy bun and plummy dark circles under my eyes, I wished he hadn't called on FaceTime.

"You're still working?" he asked, seeing the empty office behind me and forgoing any other greeting. The smile left his face and instead worry crinkled his forehead.

I nodded. "I had to redo part of a report before tomorrow. Late night tonight."

"Whatever it is can probably wait until morning—"

I shook my head, cutting him off. I explained the report was the one he, and everyone else, used for midweek updates. He referenced the numbers in speeches and press releases. My report had to be right.

"Did you at least get dinner?" he asked with a sigh. "I can drop something off if you need it."

"We had pizza left in the office fridge from a few days ago. I'm fed," I assured him. The worry was misplaced, but also endearing.

The way his lips tightened said everything he thought about cold pizza for dinner. "I'll let you finish up then. And thank you for doing this."

"It's really nothing…I mean, it is my job, right?"

His lips twitched in a half smile. "Yes, but I'm still thankful it's you doing it. We'll talk tomorrow."

He hung up and I stared back at my computer screen. I'd rather have spent the evening chatting.

By the end, nearly eleven at night, I was ready to strangle Danielle. The coding was fixed to how I had everything originally set up. I locked down the file so she couldn't modify it. I had no intention of sharing the password with her and sent a rather harsh email letting her know I had undone her changes. If I hadn't caught the changes she'd made, I'd have sent numbers that weren't even close to correct, making everybody look like an idiot, and making me look incompetent.

But I realized, as I got off the bus and shuffled up to my room, careful to avoid the squeaky stair, I'd added pressure to myself as well. I didn't want to lose my friendship with David; that wasn't an option. If I hadn't caught that mistake, I didn't know where the line between friend and work would blur. He would have made a public spectacle of himself, spouting off wrong information, and it would have been partially my fault.

Unsurprisingly, things deteriorated between Danielle and myself the next morning. She pulled me aside before my butt hit the seat.

"That email you sent last night is not acceptable." Her face went an odd shade of white. Sharp as stone, her eyebrows set in angry arches. "Those files need to be shared."

Lack of sleep blurred my brain-to-mouth filter. "No. I spent hours last night fixing what you broke. You want to use it, go ahead and save your own copy. But those data tables as they currently exist will be maintained by me."

She spent the better portion of the next ten minutes telling me I was wrong, how selfish I was, not a team player, and on and on.

If I had any doubt I was wrong, I'd be more worried. But I knew I was right, and even if she'd love to fire me, I was certain multiple people higher than her wouldn't let that happen.

"I'm not unlocking it," I said again when she let me get a word in. "You can take this higher up if you want, but unless Ben, Jessica, or David tell me to give universal access to those files, I'm not."

I stood and walked out before she could respond. After last night, I didn't really care if she liked me or not.

Sitting in the same area as her was awkward. Normally I joined Xavier downstairs when Danielle annoyed me, but today I wanted to make sure she didn't schedule something without me. I grabbed my headphones, a cup of coffee and cream, and got down to work, sending the report I'd stayed up all night to fix. Danielle stayed clear of me.

In the afternoon, Jessica called me into her office. I wasn't sure if Danielle wanted me there, or if Jessica and Ben had decided it was common sense. Danielle sat rigid in one chair, arms and legs crossed, one foot tapping away.

I sat down opposite her.

Jessica and Ben looked thoroughly annoyed. My heart stumbled a moment, thinking maybe I had overplayed my card this morning.

"You know why you're here," Jessica said, glaring at me. "Explain."

So I did. Before Danielle could jump in to say that the report data could be interpreted differently, I reasoned why it couldn't and showed the discrepancies. I explained what I'd had to do to fix it last night.

"I'm not staying until eleven every night to fix what isn't broke. What I have set up works; you both know that. I'm not letting anyone touch those files and risk the integrity of the data I send you."

Danielle broke in, complaining I wasn't working as a team and saying many of the same points she'd made earlier.

Jessica interrupted her and looked disgusted. "This is ridiculous," she snapped. "Act like adults, both of you. Charlotte, knock it down a peg. Danielle, don't touch the numbers we send out to the media or the files that run them. Both of you, out."

I managed to not roll my eyes when I left. It was late in the afternoon and I was done for the day. I packed up and headed out, taking a detour to walk down by the river trail around Parliament Hill.

The weather wasn't bad for April. Everything smelled like spring, with a hint of damp earth and little green buds starting to poke out, promising buttery yellow daffodils in the next few days. The air felt soft and warm. It was a good pick-me-up. It'd be nice to be here over spring and summer. I liked living in Ottawa. While it was a little ways into the future, I thought I'd stay once the election was done. I'd find my own place to live and a new job. It may not have been as exciting as Toronto or Montreal, but the pace and quiet suited me just fine. It was something enjoyable to think about and got my mind off the day.

Later that night, David laughed at the kerfuffle I'd caused. He said both Jessica and Ben had called to tell him. Laughing was a better reaction than being angry.

"I think you're the only one who's laughing about it," I grumped.

"I'm laughing because there isn't a chance in hell they'll fire you, and that you were cocky enough to dare her to try."

"I don't think Jessica and Ben, or Danielle, thought it was quite as funny as you do. They looked pissed."

He shrugged it off. "You were right. I'd rather you be cocky and arrogant and give me the right information than polite and send me wrong data."

Being called both cocky and arrogant didn't give me the warm fuzzies about doing a good job.

"Is that supposed to be a compliment?" I asked.

He rolled his eyes. "Yes. It'd be better if you and Danielle got along, but you have every right to push when you're right, and you ought to."

"I can tone it down with Danielle," I said, cringing a bit. Although I wasn't sure how to improve that relationship. "I didn't—"

He shook his head and interrupted before I could say anything more. "No. That's not what I meant. That wasn't a work critique. I meant it would be nice, like it'd be nice if Alan Yates and I got along better. Doesn't mean it'll happen, or that I want it to."

It was hard taking him at his word. It wasn't the first time I'd been called arrogant, but it was the first time in a positive sense.

"Did she really ask to have me fired?" I had thought she'd just complain.

"Sounds like it." He didn't sugarcoat it, but he also sounded completely non-bothered by it. Easy for him. "She—" He sighed and rubbed his face before leaning back in his chair. "Between us, she's not fit for the job. Jess brought her on at the start because she was a close friend. She is exceptional at the fundraising side, but other than that she hasn't delivered, and I can't get Jess to see that. That's why I was less than pleased when she mentioned hiring you," he said but grinned. "Her track record of data scientist picks was lousy."

I stuck my tongue out at him. "Sorry you're not rid of me yet."

"You have multiple people who will fight tooth and nail to keep you."

Except the person sending the emails. The thought chilled me, like someone walking over my grave. I wanted to stay.

"Hey." Something must have shown on my face, because the joking left David's voice and his expression turned serious. "It never got to that point. Jess and Ben are on the same page as me."

I waved him off and smiled, shoving the emails out of my head. "I know. How did question time with Yates go this morning?" I asked. I didn't want to think about my day or the emails anymore, so I relaxed back, listening to him.

*   *   *

We had an all-staff meeting on Friday. David was in the office for the first time in a couple of weeks and wouldn't be back in for another week. Everyone was keyed-up, and he was in a good mood since the trade deal had passed. I found my seat along the back wall, saving Xavier a spot. Danielle would present for our area. I'd programmed my name on the bottom of my slide to stop her from taking credit for it.

The room filled slowly. I busied myself with my laptop, balanced rather precariously on my lap. I didn't trust Danielle and wanted the ability to research or update on the fly. Also, it had the benefit of keeping me occupied so I didn't do anything terribly obvious, like smile or stare when David came in.

He sat next to Ben, directly across from me, wearing a slim suit and the dark purple tie I'd told him I liked. I was being silly, but it made me happier than it should have to see him in person and to see his eyes flicker towards me as he sat.

Brains are funny things. Perceptions can swing from complete apathy towards someone to behaving irrationally and biting back smiles for no reason, making me glance across the table more than I should. It didn't help I could feel David doing the same. It also didn't help that the few times we both looked up at the same time and there was in-person eye contact, he looked happier than he should have.

After the third time, his face split into a grin and he looked away sharply, rubbing his face in an attempt to clear his head.

I didn't catch him again after that. It was one thing to pretend on the phone each night we were just talking to relax; here it was different. I wasn't sure how long the charade would last before I accidentally stepped over the now very blurry line. Or maybe he would. Or maybe we both already had.

Xavier came in and my runaway thoughts got roped into place. He and Addie were off on vacation this weekend to her family's cottage, and we talked travel plans until the meeting started.

I paid more attention during Danielle's presentation than I normally would, ready to jump in if necessary, but it was unneeded. It skimmed over most of my work, but since the important people were already well aware of what I worked on, that was okay.

"Go over the third slide again, please, the one on pipeline infrastructure. How did you get that information?" David asked as Danielle sat down.

I paused from shutting my laptop. He knew that was the slide I had worked on for Danielle. I had taken it because she hadn't been able to finish it. I'd told David about it last week, not complaining, just as commentary. She wouldn't be able to come up with the explanation, and he knew that.

"Isn't that the slide you did?" Xavier whispered.

I nodded.

"Does she know what he's asking?"

I shook my head no.

I looked back at David while Danielle ran through a repeat of what she'd already said.

David looked smug. He had that little smile that looked polite, but his eyes were hard and he knew exactly what he was doing. Danielle was flustered.

"But how did you disseminate the data into that result? I can see what it's showing, but why did you set it up that way? Tell me how you got it," David asked again.

Danielle's eyes flickered towards me; if looks could kill, I'd be dead. "Charlotte, I believe this was one you assisted with. Could you take it?"

I stayed seated because I had no desire to be more visible than I needed to be. David liked to poke hornet's nests. I got he was trying to make a point, but I'd rather not be under the hornet's nest while it was poked. I gave him one semi-glare as I answered.

He just smiled and thanked me before calling on Mia for the volunteer update.

Partway through the communications piece, my phone vibrated. I glanced and saw exclamation points from Camille. That was odd. I frowned and opened the text with a picture.

A friend from a local paper sent this to me. Heads up and get brownie points! It hits the internet in 10 minutes.

I scrolled to the picture.

"Fuck."

I flipped my phone upside-down hard and froze.

Xavier heard me and looked rather taken aback. "You okay?"

I nodded, thinking. It was a picture of a young David, maybe college-aged. Two ladies in very tight, barely-there outfits sat on each side of him. He had an arm around each one, hands on bare waists, a joint in one hand. They all gazed drunkenly at the camera; the image was a complete 180 from the person sitting in front of me or the one I talked to at night. Ten minutes, and that hit a lot more than just the internet. *Shitty shitty, fuck fuck.*

I looked up and picked my course of action. I couldn't do anything with this myself. I pulled up the picture again and stood. David's eyes followed me, but I couldn't look at him. He and Jessica sat next to each other, which only made this more awkward.

"Jessica." I tried to keep my voice down as I knelt next to her chair. The pretty slim slip of a pink dress I had worn today became a hazard as it trapped my legs together. My heels plus the tight skirt made me wobble and bang into David, causing his frown to deepen as he steadied me. Jessica startled.

"What, Charlotte?" This close to her, the hairspray and perfume was nauseating.

"This," I said. "It's being published at eleven."

I kept my phone down so she craned over a little to see it. When she did, her face went white and rigid. For a moment, she froze.

"What is it, Charlotte?" asked David, touching my shoulder.

I turned towards him. I didn't want to show him. I didn't want to be the person who burst his dream, but I didn't have a choice. I tilted the phone towards him so he could see.

His jaw clenched and the hand on my shoulder jerked away like he'd been electrocuted. He and Jessica shared a look; I wasn't sure which of them would erupt first. I didn't want to be in the middle and I scampered back.

"This meeting is done." David stood and pointed at research, PR, and communications. "You three stay. Everyone else out, now."

The hand not stabbing angrily at those staying was white-knuckled at his side. Jessica's face went from white to red to splotchy.

I grabbed my laptop and followed the herd out. The shouting started before the door had closed. Jessica let David handle it. Research, who was supposed to find all pictures like this before the election and remove any evidence of them, was screwed.

"What did you show them?" Xavier hissed at me. We both hunkered down in our office, eying the conference room warily. David's shouting was muffled here, but still audible. Jessica started to chime in. Chime might be too nice of a word.

It was going to hit in a few minutes, so there was no reason not to show him. I showed Xavier my phone and his jaw dropped.

"Oh…how did you get that?" he asked.

"Friend of a friend of a friend. Just gave me a heads-up."

The conference room door opened and one of the research underlings walked out, clearly upset, and made a beeline for his desk. A few minutes later, he left with coat, bag, and a few other things. Evidently, this had been a firing offense.

"I'm thinking we should get our heads down and work," Xavier said, wincing as the office door slammed shut.

I nodded and we cracked on.

Xavier and I, and even Danielle, stayed in hiding the rest of the day, along with most of the office.

PR and communications folks did their thing for damage control, scheduling spokespeople and Jessica to make statements, a last-minute press conference for David to recover his public image, replace the debauched picture with a more prime ministerial one. The article published along with the photo was lightweight stuff in terms of dirt, and by itself, would be forgotten in a day.

By mid-afternoon, someone had tracked down the women in the picture. Both confirmed that while the image looked bad, they had absolutely nothing but nice things to say about David. It'd been one very drunken night, nothing more.

It was a start, but the picture wouldn't just go away.

*   *   *

Camille and Tom were out on a date night, so I treated myself to Chinese takeout, my favorite wine, and binged on Netflix. My desire to look at the news was near zero. The only thing likely to be covered was the lack of covering on those two ladies pressed against college David's side. There was no need to see all the talking news heads and other party leaders going to town on it. The blatantly political move to publish it made me angry and my head ached for David; it wasn't fair this could crash everything.

I felt twitchy and ornery, so rather than feeling like a twitchy, ornery, fat TV toad, I hauled my cello downstairs and started to play. There was something calming about being wrapped up in music. My mind stopped thinking and running in circles, and it all poured into each note. Muscle memory came back. When I relaxed and stopped over-analyzing everything, I sank into the music.

My phone ringing jerked me out of the song. The bow skipped up the strings, causing an awful scratching noise. I winced and grabbed the phone. I hadn't expected David to call. I hadn't wanted to call myself in case he wanted nothing to do with anyone.

"Hi," I said.

"I'm sorry."

I got up and settled the cello back down into its case. "Why are you sorry? Or, why are you saying sorry to me?"

He laughed, but it was obvious he didn't find it amusing. "Really? You need to ask?"

The rude sarcasm didn't help, and I started to get annoyed. "Well…yes. Try, 'Charlotte, I'm sorry for…' Help me out."

"Because I look like an ass." The tension in his voice spit out loud and clear. "When you're trying to look good—I don't want you to think… That's not me—"

Huh. He was worried what I thought? "David, we all did something stupid at university. You have the rotten luck of picture evidence of it, and it's public. It's not a big deal—to me, at least," I clarified, since he'd started to laugh when I said it wasn't a big deal.

"It is a pretty big deal. Everything I've been working towards for the last decade could go up in smoke because of a photo that was taken—"

"I got it." I shook my head and squeezed my eyes shut. All the nice work the cello playing had done for my stress seeped out. "I know what it means."

He sighed. "Sorry. I know you do. The timing, with polls close…it's shitty."

I didn't bother commenting back. It was.

"I'm being awful," he said suddenly. "Can you FaceTime tonight? I'll stop being a grouch."

In spite of him being a grouch, I started the camera instead of answering.

His face appeared, looking haggard.

My initial irritation faded, and I felt bad for being snappy. "Well, I'll hammer you in a few weeks with debate practice, polls will change, and you'll be fine. I'm guessing you don't hang out in public with half-clothed friends anymore, at least not with photo evidence?"

That got a real laugh. "No. I'm pretty boring and old now."

"I'd argue both those points," I said before thinking it through.

He was quiet for a minute. His room was darker, casting his face in shadows and angles, making it hard to read him.

I wondered if I'd overstepped. "I mean," I explained, looking pretty much anywhere except at the camera. I felt myself starting to babble. "It might actually help with young voters… You have a sexy badass vibe in the picture." That didn't help at all. That wasn't helpful in the slightest; damn wine I drank too fast.

Luckily, he laughed, and it was contagious.

"Sexy badass?" he asked, failing at keeping a smile off his face. He didn't look too upset. "You're a lousy advisor. How much have you had to drink tonight?"

I glanced at the bottle. "A couple glasses of wine," I admitted. "You?"

He held up a crystal tumbler with a good slosh of amber liquid in it. "Whisky."

We both fell silent, but now it was closer to normal, not the tense atmosphere from the start. I had the stupid wish we were doing this in person, not just phone and video. I wanted to make him laugh and smile so some of the stress lifted.

"So, if everyone has done something like that at university, what's yours?" he asked, taking a sip of his whisky.

I wrinkled my face up and sighed. "Probably at a Halloween party—"

The house door opened, and Camille and Tom barreled in from dinner. Tom waved and Camille started to say something before she noticed the phone.

I waved her off and jammed my headphones in before she could hear. She couldn't see the screen unless she came over and was very nosy.

"Sorry, housemates just got in," I explained. "So, Halloween. We were very drunk and dressed up like '80s workout models—bad hair, leotards that weren't appropriate to wear in public. There would have been ample opportunity for a picture that rivals yours." Thankfully the one taken was embarrassing, but not horrible. I winced in memory of the very woozy night.

Camille stopped on her way through and did a double-take at me.

I threw a pillow at her to get her out of the room.

David laughed—at either the picture description or me throwing something. "No pictures at all?" he asked, looking hopeful. "It'd make me feel better about myself."

He was joking and I smiled. "Not readily available. You'll have to use your imagination."

"My brain is shot, so I guess I'm out of luck. Tell me about your weekend plans."

And so, the pictures were dropped and we slipped back into the comfortable routine of our evening chats. This time, I was a little more aware of Camille popping into the kitchen to get something, pausing by the living room in an obvious attempt to eavesdrop.

"I've got to head off," he said after half an hour. "I've got interviews early tomorrow." That, and he looked drop-dead tired.

"That's fine. You really didn't need to call or say sorry, you know. I saw your press conference this afternoon with the apology, unless you're making personal calls to all the staff." I was rambling and strangely nervous. But I wanted to ask. I'd had another glass of wine and he'd had another whisky, so if I said something wrong, I could apologize later. Write it off as a wine-induced mistake.

He shook his head. "I'm not calling everyone," he said dismissively. "Just you." He paused and looked off to the side before he came back to me. "I did need to call. That was one night at a party, not something… That's not me now."

We were dancing around each other, both waiting for the other to say or ask it. The question formed in my head and slipped out before I caught it.

"So this isn't," I started, waving my hand between the camera and me. "You don't—" I trailed off and wasn't sure how to phrase it. I squeezed my eyes shut; everything would tilt after it came out.

"Is this normal?" I finally asked, locking eyes with my little phone camera and wishing this were in person. "Do you normally have someone you call on a campaign or is it…? Are we…? This is something beyond friends, right?"

He didn't answer right away, keeping his reaction muted and flat so I couldn't tell if I'd screwed up—

"It's…something else," he said, looking uncomfortable. "You—this every night has nothing to do with the campaign. You mean much more to me than just a work colleague or friend. And you're okay with that?" he asked, sounding unsure. "You're welcome to tell me to get lost and call me a dirty—"

"Yes," I interrupted, and cut him off.

His face went horrified, probably thinking I said yes to him getting lost.

"I mean, no." I couldn't get the words out right when my head was a ringing jumble. I paused and took a breath. "Yes, I'm okay with it, and no to getting lost. I don't want you to go or for it to stop." A silence hung in the air, highlighting what I'd said. "Of course I want more, if that's okay."

"Yes, absolutely," he answered in a rush, and sounded relieved as well. It was getting tiring pretending there wasn't something there. Guess he felt the same.

I grinned. "Okay."

He grinned back at me, this time holding back nothing. "Okay."

I couldn't sit on the couch like an idiot with happy bubbles ricocheting through me. I couldn't just sit and stare at him.

"I'll let you go," I said. I wished he were in the office next week.

"Call tomorrow night? After nine should be good."

I nodded. "Okay. Good night."

He tried for a moment to keep it under wraps but gave in to a smile that etched across every inch of his face, from cheeks to eyes. "Good night, Charlotte."

I hung up before I did or said anything stupid. There were an awful lot of reasons this could be an incredibly bad idea. Generally, workplace relationships were frowned upon. And this was a workplace relationship with potential to go very, very public. I'd given zero thought to what it might look like, with him in the running for prime minister.

At the same time, talking to him made me happy. Being around him made me happy. I wanted more than just a phone call at night or "just friends" relationship.

"Who was that?"

I jerked out of my runaway thoughts, which were somewhere around state dinners and how on Earth we'd see each other with any amount of privacy, and saw Camille standing in the doorway. She didn't wait for an answer and sat down on a side chair. Her eyes were suspicious.

"Friend from work," I said as casually as possible. "It was a rough day—"

"Same friend you were talking to before your birthday? And who I've seen you texting every night?"

"Yes. Thank you—"

"What picture were you talking about before?" she prodded.

"Eavesdropping much?"

She gave me a look and ignored me. "Is it him?"

I didn't need to answer because I could feel my face heating up. With my pale skin, a red face was a dead giveaway.

"It's nothing," I said, and she rolled her eyes in exasperation. "We talk sometimes and that's it." True, up to tonight.

"I don't need to tell you what could happen if this gets out."

"You wouldn't." I glared at her and resisted the urge to shake her.

"Of course not," she replied, like it'd been particularly stupid for me to ask.

I relaxed.

"I'm your friend first and foremost," Camille said. "I won't say anything. But you do know, right?"

It felt a lot later than ten. "I do."

She looked skeptical but nodded. "You all got dropped in it today." And just like that, we moved on…for now.

*   *   *

For something that felt like such a big deal, amazingly little changed, at least over the next week or so. David, along with most of the other department heads, was at the party convention all week, strengthening the platform he'd built for the past year and lambasting Yates' government. He pivoted from presenting himself as the opposition to a real alternative.

When there was time, we talked at night, not long, but enough to erase any doubt about this being more than just friends. It was easy to let things build quickly once we realized we were on the same page; with the brakes removed, it was effortless to fall into the relationship.

It was comfortable to be with someone who wasn't an "opposites attract" sort. We clicked into place with each other. I felt like champagne—golden, bubbly, and fizzing over with butterflies. I was almost glad he was out of the office because I was being stupid enough on my own.

Xavier noticed and poked until I admitted there was someone. The whole office noticed on Thursday, David's birthday, when a red tulip bouquet was delivered to me. My face matched the flowers as I dug the card out.

Thank you for the lack of mariachi bands and confetti shower for my birthday. See you soon.

I forgot I'd threatened him with those and laughed out loud, shoving the card in my bag.

"The first few weeks' thing fades," Xavier informed me. "You'll start nagging him to do the dishes, or he'll start whining about your long hours."

I doubted that.

"You love Addie. Don't burst my bubble."

He looked smug and plugged in his headphones. "Tomorrow at dinner, don't mention you got flowers. It'll make me look bad."

I grinned and turned to my laptop. Staring up at me was a new email from the mystery stalker. My grin faded fast.

After the first few, I'd thought about automatically sending them all to my delete folder, but that seemed like sticking my head in the sand. I thought it was better to know. There might be a hint of who it was or how serious they were.

I know where you live. I'm watching you.

The threat was implicit. I flung it into my folder with the others and promised myself I'd look at it later. That was more than just a nasty name or a warning to quit.

I rubbed the silky red tulip petals with my fingertips and stared out the window, spring sun bright and streaming into the office. I didn't know what to do about the emails.

*   *   *

I came to the conclusion that a long-distance relationship wasn't only defined by the actual distance between two people, but also their ability to be around each other. Besides getting a bad case of butterflies when I saw David, there wasn't a big change.

I didn't know what I expected the first day I walked into one of our meetings, arriving early on purpose. We hadn't arranged anything and never mentioned the idea to each other, but there was little I could do to stop the silly grin from spreading across my face when I saw he was there early as well. I felt slightly better when he looked up from his computer and his face matched mine.

"Early again," he said.

I lost my ability to formulate intelligent thoughts, so I sat down across from him. Talking the last few weeks at night had been so easy. In person, I went tongue-tied.

"You, too…some coincidence."

It was worse than an awkward first date. A bubble of nervous laughter tickled up my throat and spilled over. I was grateful this meeting was in a conference room with no windows and the door was partially shut. I didn't want others to walk by and see me laughing like this.

"You okay?" he asked.

Thankfully, he looked amused and not horrified that he'd gotten himself into something terrible. On FaceTime, every now and then he'd look absolutely delighted and his face would light up. He had that look now, eyes bright and creased with a smile that covered his entire face.

"I'm good," I managed to get out.

"Didn't change your mind now you have to see me in person?" he asked, clearly teasing.

I spared one look back at the entry way to make sure no one was coming and reached for his hand. When he squeezed my fingers back, warm and solid and tight, it made everything more real.

"How do we do this?" I asked. On the phone, the secrecy thing seemed an annoyance. Now in person, the enormity of that secret loomed.

His eyes flickered towards the door before lifting my hand and kissing it. He smiled the whole time and let his lips linger before letting go. "We'll figure it out. We'll find time."

Inexplicably, I believed him, 100%. He sounded absolutely confident that we would figure it out.

When we heard footsteps coming towards the room, we dropped hands, pulling back to nothing more than two people sitting in a room together. Our relationship started on stolen moments.

We couldn't go on a normal date. We couldn't go out in public together. We couldn't let anyone in the office know there was anything between us. It was obvious the candidate having a romantic relationship with a party staffer would not reflect well on election results. The surface optics looked bad, and while I certainly didn't give two hoots about the seventeen-year age difference, voters could easily disagree.

So, we were long distance, even though we saw each other most days or sat in meetings a couple feet from each other. It was maddening.

*   *   *

My parents were coming up over the weekend for a visit, and we were going out to a fancy dinner Saturday night. It'd be great.

I'd gotten to see David nearly every day during the week after the convention. That should have made me happy. But I started getting the emails every day. In a week, I'd been told they knew where I lived, that I was an arrogant bitch, and that I was worthless. They ranged from name-calling to threats to demands for my departure with no apparent pattern in between. The onslaught of messages twisted into my head until I was sick opening my inbox every morning. The person sending them knew what they were doing, making sure their tracks were covered. It was sophisticated and put me on edge.

Danielle didn't like me. There was no way to sugarcoat or work around it. I heard her talking to others in the office about me, complaining I was an entitled brat who expected responsibility to be handed over to me. I wanted to think of her as an idiot but couldn't. She wasn't good at the data analytics I worked on, but she was very good at her role with money and fundraising. She'd be able to figure out how to go around our spam filters and set up a ghost email account.

Mike went from being an obnoxious loudmouth to making me feel increasingly uncomfortable around him. Or maybe it was the emails, plus him. Since the delivery of the tulips, he'd gotten worse. He asked me how the boyfriend and I were getting along, what we did on our dates, and gave me suggestions on what I should wear—outfits that accented my legs or showed off my chest.

"Guys like it when you play hard to get," he said one morning as I tried to escape from the coffee station. "Hot tease."

I ignored him and walked away, sloshing hot coffee and burning my fingers.

"It's a turn on," he called as I left the room.

I couldn't bring myself to file the workplace harassment complaint. It was nothing. All of it would pass.

*　　*　　*

It felt like we'd only just finished wrapping up from the first debate before it was time to start prepping for number two. I was grateful for it. It had me spending more time with Jessica, Ben, and Kaitlyn than anyone else.

Ben helped me frame my arguments to follow Yates' style of debate better and Kaitlyn worked on my body language.

David was there occasionally to start with, and more often as we got going. One of my roles was to get him to snap, to poke and prod until he got angry; he found it amusing how easily I could find the right buttons to push. He got it out of his system in practice, so he was cool as a cucumber in the real one.

*   *   *

Two weeks before the debate, things changed. After a couple days of not seeing each other due to schedules, I thought the text I received would be from David. I thought it would be an update on the late meeting he'd had with an ethics committee, or maybe just something funny. Maybe a text saying the meeting was running long and he was looking for a break. When I opened it, I was ready for bed, my thoughts soft and eager for the sheets.

Ungrateful cunt

I blinked, the words not sinking in. Mysterious text messages at night happened in movies, not real life. Not to me.

Who is this? I typed back.

Rather than wait for the response, I got up and locked my door for the night. On second thought, I slid a chair under the doorknob as well. It seemed sensible. I left the light on as I checked the blinking reply.

Self-centered slut

A second later. *Cock tease*

Leave before it's too late

I slammed my phone down on my bedside table. Any warm and fuzzy pre-bedtime feelings were replaced with horrified disbelief. Obviously, it was from the same person who'd sent the emails.

But finding my phone number, sending from an unknown number so I couldn't block it, and sending messages at night when I was home was more claustrophobic and chilling than at work. I could write off the emails, or had been trying to write them off, as a workplace jealousy issue. Sitting in my bedroom at night, the threats became more personal.

It squashed any hope of sleep as my mind ran around and around in tired circles. I didn't know what to do. I didn't know if I should tell anyone. I didn't know if they were just angry words or if someone would go from emails to texts to something more physical. It made my locked doors and locked windows, checked and double-checked, inconsequential. The blanket I pulled around my shoulders did nothing to stop the shivers that started up my spine and shook my body. The person didn't need to break into anything physical to get to me. Technology was enough.

Chapter Six

The texts continued.

Each night there was a new round with different names and threats or repeats if the person wasn't feeling creative. I guessed stalkers got tired. Even in the mornings when I arrived at work and saw Xavier had booked a three-hour meeting—which was an excuse for both of us to have quiet work time—or I received a surprise anonymous coffee delivery from David, or had lunch plans with Kaitlyn or Mia, I was uneasy. I wasn't sleeping, and while my work was still accurate, I was tired and rude.

The extra hours for the debate prep were both a blessing and a curse. As a plus, they kept me very busy at night and I didn't have the luxury of being distracted. I also got extra time with David and the occasional sneaked touch, or what he'd try to make a casual side hug after a debate run-through.

Sometimes, I caught myself leaning on him more than I should have, wishing I could rest into him, head on shoulder. When I was tired and scared and a side hug was all I could get, it was hard not to.

As negatives went, the practices left me drained, and without fail, there was some nasty message waiting for me when I checked my phone after a session. It wore me down.

*　*　*

On the final practice day before the debate, winter decided to make one last visit in May. Wind rattled the windows with the occasional peppering of ice, and I wanted to kick myself for walking to work. The text this afternoon—

telling me I was a piece of shit, telling me bad things happened to ungrateful, pretty girls like me—didn't help. I didn't want to walk home by myself, and I didn't want to get an Uber or wait for the bus. I didn't want to be anywhere by myself.

"Okay?"

I glanced up, alarmed. I hadn't heard David or Jessica come in.

David watched me as he headed over to the podium. I wanted to tell him everything, because it was getting harder and harder to deal with it on my own. But I couldn't. He shouldn't be worrying about me.

I smiled and nodded. "Let me know when you two are ready." I looked around and realized it was only the three of us. "Anyone else coming tonight?"

Jessica shook her head and started setting up the camera. "No. The weather… We'll just do a run-through tonight. I think we've covered everything the last few nights."

They sat down and started reviewing the final change points from last night. I had my notes in front of me, all the reasons why David was a character of ill-repute: that he was washed up and out of touch; didn't have a firm hand on policies; was untrustworthy and not able to keep Canada safe… It all made me angry.

"Let's go." Jessica headed back to the camera to start recording and we took our spots.

It was supposed to be a mild-mannered walk-through. We were supposed to hit the main points, make sure David's comebacks were sharp, and that was it.

I started to let some of my emotions get the better of me. Rather than floating the criticism in a softball, I got rather pointed, which made me more angry at myself since I wasn't at all upset at David.

"The moral character of the Centre leader is summed up in one picture: drunk, high, and sexually amoral—a complete absence of judgment. That is *not* the leader for Canada—"

"Enough, Charlotte." Jessica stood and stopped the camera. She looked angry, and to be honest, so did David. "We're not going for the kill here.

Take a break. You need to get a grip." She walked out, slamming the door on me.

I wanted to bang my head on the wall. Tonight was not something I could mess up. I sat down on the table edge, clattering my glasses on the side and rubbed my face. *Focus.*

"What's going on?"

My hands were gently pulled from my face, and I looked up. He did look annoyed with me, but also concerned. This was the first time we'd had a moment truly alone. I stood and let him pull me into a hug—not just the side ones we'd had, but a real one that was tight and solid. For a moment, I forgot the texts, the emails, the panic. I enjoyed the feel of his cotton dress shirt under my chin, the warmth of him against me, knowing where my arms fit around his back and his on mine, feeling his head resting on mine, and my lips on his neck. It was nice to feel not so alone. The relationship became real and not just a dream.

"Hey." He pulled back a little to look me in the eyes. "You're not you tonight. What's going on?" he repeated.

Jessica wore high heels that clicked loudly, so I'd hear her coming back. Instead of answering, I leaned up and kissed him for the first time. He startled at first, but then returned the kiss, smiling against my lips. It was easier to think about the kiss and be happy in the now rather than worrying.

He stopped it too soon. "You don't need to tell me now." He smiled and kissed me again. "But I need to stop kissing you so you can get that grin off your face before Jess gets back."

He was right. "You need to not look so pleased with yourself, too," I said.

The clomping of heels announced Jessica's return and we both took extra steps away from each other, David busying himself with notes, me poking at my phone, trying hard to not smile. David was a very good kisser.

"Let's try this again. Charlotte, try not to be a bitch." Jessica smiled and sat down.

My happy kissing mood popped; I could have punched her.

"You could try that, too." The undercurrent in David's voice made Jessica snap her mouth shut. "We'll pick up with my rebuttal."

I did marginally better at keeping myself under control the rest of the practice. David did well, and I managed to keep my replies civil. We sparred back and forth, enough to feel confident about the debate.

When we started packing up and heading out for the night, my earlier thoughts came storming back. Someone wanted me gone. It was dark out, Camille was interviewing someone at our house so I couldn't call her, and Xavier lived thirty minutes from here.

"Hey Jessica, is there any chance you could give me a lift home?" I asked as we locked up the room. She wasn't my first choice, but still.

She looked at me oddly. "Why?"

"Because I walked in today and it's doing *that* outside," I said, and pointed at a window coated in some form of slushy mix.

"I don't have time to drop you off tonight." She shrugged. "I'm sorry."

"I can give you a ride," David offered. "You don't live too far out?"

I blinked, surprised. "No, about fifteen minutes from here."

Jessica stared at him like he'd sprouted two heads. "Do you really think that's a good idea the night before…?"

She stopped when he started shaking his head. "Twenty minutes isn't going to make any difference tomorrow. We're well prepared." He smiled and clapped her on the shoulder. "We've done well."

She didn't look convinced but got on the elevator without another word. I filed in with them and kept my mouth shut. Out of all the ways to get home, riding with David was probably the safest, and not bad company.

The elevator stopped on the ground floor. Jessica gave us a nod good night and headed towards the front. David touched my lower back and indicated the back entrance. We picked up a bodyguard as well, who followed us out. The hard ball of tension that had been building between my shoulders the last couple of weeks relaxed a smidge.

"Thanks for the ride," I said as we stepped outside.

Sleet blasted us in the face. David jumped ahead of me and opened the back passenger door. I gratefully slid in, getting a slightly startled look from the driver.

"Yes, such a hassle to finally spend any amount of time alone with you." He shut the door and relaxed back with a smile. "Peter, we need to make a detour to…"

I filled in and gave my address. Peter the driver nodded and off we went.

I shivered, from both cold and stress, and closed my eyes. The seat heater was on and the warmth seeping through my coat felt wonderful.

"Are you that cold?" David asked.

"Just chilled. I'm fine."

He undid his seatbelt and relocated to the middle seat, tucking an arm around me. "Better?"

I nodded and leaned into him. "Much better."

"You're still not going to tell me what you're wound up about?"

I smiled and shook my head. I wished I lived farther away. My head fit on his shoulder. "Not right now."

He sighed. "Later?"

I probably would later, when it turned out to be a nasty prank and I could laugh about how paranoid I'd started to get. "Later."

I closed my eyes and found his hand. He gripped it back and landed a kiss on my head, leaving his lips there for a second or two. For our first time being able to talk in person without the threat of interruption, we were both very quiet. It was a novelty to have any sort of physical contact. Maybe that was just something I'd always taken for granted, but having him sit next to me, knowing how I fit against his shoulder, or how the scratchy wool of his coat felt under my cheek, or where his breath hit my head when he rested his against mine… I just wanted the moment.

Far sooner than I liked, we pulled up in front of the house. "This it?" David asked and squeezed my shoulder slightly.

I nodded. I could see Camille sitting in the living room with someone. It made me feel better that there were multiple people in the house. Getting myself to leave the car wasn't easy.

"It is."

His arm moved, leaving my shoulders cold again.

"I'll see you tomorrow night, before the debate?" he asked.

"I'll bring the popcorn."

He hesitated for a second and then kissed me. It was strange at first, since I was all too conscious of Peter in the front, but David quickly took my attention back.

He stopped again, sooner than I would have liked, and clearly sooner than he would have, too. "You…" He just smiled and kissed me briefly one more time, leaving his hand on my cheek. "I think this might last a very long time."

And just like that, I was full of happy bubbles; the chemistry part had been the wildcard. No doubt now. "I know. Might be stuck together a while," I said and tried to keep my grin under control. I took a deep breath and tried to bring myself back down.

"Call me if you need anything, okay?"

"Okay," I nodded, giving his hand one last squeeze and dashed out into the rain.

I made it inside and shut the door without someone trying to kidnap or attack me. Camille was still in interview mode, so I dumped my wet, squeaky boots at the door and tiptoed upstairs.

I heard the front door shut a few minutes later and Camille came upstairs.

"Sorry about that," she said, and sat down on my bed. "I thought you'd walk home and would be in later. Did Jessica give you a ride back?" She'd said it like it was the obvious answer, flipping through a magazine I left on the bed.

"David did." *And he'd kissed me.*

That got her head to snap up fast. "Still interested in entering the world of politics full-time?"

I threw a pillow at her. "Yes. Very much so."

She tossed the pillow back at me and sighed. "Enough to give up your career if he wins?"

"You have a career; I have a job. There's a difference. I don't have anything lined up after the election, and I really don't see myself starting a career jumping from one campaign to the next."

My explanation didn't fly; she looked disappointed. "You're really content to be reduced down to pretty arm candy for him?"

The only other thing in throwing reach for me was a book; throwing that at her head would have been a little harsh. "No, Camille. And that's a long way off. This is a good thing. Just leave it there."

*   *   *

The debate went smoothly. I was backstage before the start, saw the prep and the media madness, then watched the debate from off-stage, the lights bright on stage. Kaitlyn muttered to herself through most of it, nodding as David responded. Ben stared stonily. Jessica made me smother giggles when she made disparaging remarks about Yates and MacCallum from the Workers Party.

When I wasn't snickering at Jessica, I fidgeted with anything I could get my hands on and watched the other candidates. It confirmed my thought from several weeks ago. Yates really was a ratty human, pointy faced and squeaky voiced, playing in garbage level politics. Overall, though, David was unequivocally the winner of the night. He stayed calm and level-headed. His policies came through as reasonable and common sense. He'd nailed it.

*   *   *

Like after the first debate, the following week was a whirlwind. Xavier and I worked together again on updates, I got pulled into help with the debate analysis, and I was thankfully well clear of Danielle and Mike.

David suggested one night after an afternoon of breaking down every single flaw he had in the debate that we—Jessica, Kaitlyn, Ben, and myself—head out for dinner, giving in and agreeing to go back to The Ambassador for pizza.

It was a perfect night where it was okay for us to joke around and for all of us to relax for a bit. It was fun to be around David after work for once and to see the other three away from the office. It helped blot out the emails and text messages I was still receiving most days.

*   *   *

What didn't go well was my outing to the police station the following week, emails printed and in hand, to see if they could track down the person sending them. I was tired of being jumpy and paranoid and exhausted. Thankfully, the police station was only a block away, close enough for me to dash over to.

My expectation that the police would jump on it, reassure me they'd have no problem tracking the culprit down, and it would all be done in a few days fell woefully short of reality.

"Ma'am, this really isn't a lot to go on," said the police officer, who looked barely old enough to be allowed out of school. He handed the papers back to me. "Are you sure you don't have any idea who it might be?"

I fought down a rising sense of hysteria. I was running around and around in circles and the person just kept sending these emails.

"I told you no," I said through clenched teeth. "There are people at work who don't like me, but I..." I thought back again and shook my head. Danielle and Mike were my first choices. I ran through everyone else: Ben, Kaitlyn, Jessica, Xavier… I couldn't think of a reason any of them would do it; the rest of the office seemed even more unreasonable. That left me with Danielle or Mike, but I wasn't confident enough to throw this at them without proof. No one made perfect sense and I knew that. I hated I couldn't be more certain. "No. I don't know."

The officer tried to put on a sympathetic face and shrugged. "We'll be happy to help once there's something to go on. You let us know if anything new happens. If you already checked the server and IT, without a lead, we can't do anything."

"That is obvious," I snapped, shoving the emails in my bag. I would not cry, even though I was angry enough to scream.

I had to sit outside the office on a bench for a moment and let some of the frustration fizzle out before I went inside to work. It was a beautiful day, where the sun finally felt warm and I started to believe I could soon emerge from layers of coats without getting frostbite. I hated being this anxious. I'd picked this bench because I knew there was a security camera above it and a constant stream of people walking on the sidewalk. Who did that?

The chair wedged under my door handle and the kettle bell I kept by my bed wouldn't stop anyone getting in the room, but I figured they were better than nothing. I stayed awake most nights listening for I didn't know what, but what else was I supposed to do?

None of it addressed me getting safely to and from work. It didn't stop something from ending up in a drink and me waking up in the back of a van. It didn't stop someone from kidnapping me. I could leave like they wanted, but the thought jarred so hard against everything in me, I couldn't. I pulled out my phone and did something stupid instead.

Where do I need to go for this to stop?

Engaging with the person was probably a bad idea. But maybe this way they'd lay off for a bit while I figured out my next step.

My phone blinked back fast.

Alberta or British Columbia.

The response baffled me and made my head hurt. Across the country? Again? I'd been thinking Toronto. Leaving David out of the picture, who was a big part of the picture, I liked living in Ottawa. I liked my job. I liked being this close to Camille again. I liked having my family a few hours away. I didn't want to leave. The big tour we'd been working on started in a couple of weeks. Leaving wasn't an option.

Fuck you

It was a bad idea to send it, but I still jabbed the send icon with more force than necessary. I'd take precautions. I would be smart. I wasn't going to run and give up everything. I'd figure it out.

Back in the office, I heard the arguing before I saw it. I glanced warily over at Jessica's office. They weren't screaming, but voices were most definitely heated.

"What'd I miss?" I asked Xavier as I filled up my coffee cup for the afternoon.

He shrugged. "No idea. Ben, David, and Jessica have been holed up in there. It just got to that level in the last few minutes."

"Charlotte!" Our guessing was cut short by Danielle barking at me. "You didn't send those reports before lunch. I need them now."

I kicked myself and knew she was right. I had forgotten. "On it."

Xavier gave me a sympathetic look and let me crack on.

I got them sent with no problem in a manner of minutes, giving me time to forward the text messages, minus the last one, to my inbox to store away. On second thought, I printed them out, too. If this person could create mystery email addresses, they could probably figure out how to get into my personal folders. Privacy wasn't a given anymore. Paper was better.

Maybe it was someone from another campaign? Or was that way too cocky for me to think I was so valuable to the team?

"Charlotte, can you come in here for a second?"

I glanced up to see Ben, looking irritated and worn. That alarmed me. He was normally unflappable.

"Sure. Do I need anything?" I asked and followed him out.

He shook his head. "No, I don't think so."

We stepped into his office with Jessica and David glaring daggers at each other. The tension was palpable; I was walking into the middle of something I didn't want to be involved in.

Ben slumped into his chair and motioned for me to pull up a seat as well. "We'd like you to be the data representative on the road campaign," he said, the tiredness coming through loud and clear. When he said *we*, his eyes glanced toward David. So, Jessica wasn't on board with it.

"Really? Not Danielle?" I asked.

Part of me was ecstatic. It'd be wonderful doing this from a business and job standpoint. I'd be in close proximity to security personnel and I'd be around David a lot. But it would piss off Danielle. It'd be awkward if I were the only non-department head going. Also, the idea of traveling with Mike caused my stomach to flip. At least, I assumed he'd be the pick for finance.

"Danielle can't debate, she can't get models put together as fast or accurately as you can and she wasn't involved in any of the planning," David said tightly, addressing that more towards Jessica than me. I had a feeling the points had already been made. "You're more valuable on the road," he added, turning back to me.

"And is far less experienced, less familiar with this campaign—" Jessica said through clenched teeth.

"And we already made the decision," Ben said before the conversation spiraled into an argument. "David and I agree you're the best person to have on the road. You know the schedule already and the travel logistics. You know the job. Think it through, but you're the first pick for data."

I smothered a smile, pleased with the compliment. "No time needed. I'm in."

"Good to hear," David said. He needed to wipe the smug smile off his face before Jessica clawed it off. "We'll have the road team assembled by the end of the week and meet before heading off. I think that's all we needed from you at the moment."

"Does Danielle already know, or do I need to tell her?"

It wasn't something I wanted to do. There was nothing about the conversation that would go well.

"We will have that discussion with department heads," Ben said, suppressing a smile. Evidently my enthusiasm for telling Danielle myself was apparent. "Thank you, Charlotte."

I took the hint and got up. "Thank you." I smiled at David and Ben; it made me happy Ben had my back, too.

"Jessica, you hired me because I'm good. I've got this." I got a very tight smile in return and wasn't sure if it helped or made things worse.

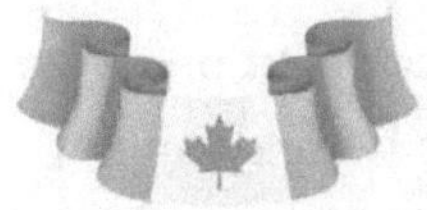

Chapter Seven

"How did Danielle take it?" I asked David that night as I flopped onto my bed. "Is she likely to kill me?"

"It was fine," he said casually. "Not happy. Questioned it, but in the end agreed. I think she's glad you're leaving. Actually..." His look darkened a bit and he winced. "Mike was the only one who wrote back asking why you were getting preferential treatment when he worked on the project as well. Jessica and I put him in his place fast. There was no chance he was coming."

I was relieved to hear Mike wasn't going, but knowing he was disgruntled made my stomach twist. I glanced over at my door, with chair jam in place and kettle bell sitting on the desk. I felt paranoid but wasn't sure where the line between paranoia and taking appropriate precautions was drawn.

"This is based on my work only, right?" I asked. I knew it had nothing to do with the cousin factor, but that didn't eliminate favorites being played.

"You think you got this because I pushed for it?" he asked, sounding baffled.

"It crossed my mind."

"That's insulting to both of us," he said bluntly. "First, you know damn well you've earned it; you don't need me to tell you that. Second, I want to win this very badly. Except for maybe the thirty minutes a day I talk to you, I eat, sleep, and breathe this campaign and would do just about anything to get those votes in October. If that means taking Danielle over you, I will. In a heartbeat."

I knew I had earned it, but the reinforcement was welcome. "Good thing I'm better than her."

He laughed. "I agree. It works out pretty well."

We chatted a little longer before hanging up. He was genuinely happy about traveling the next few months and mentioned multiple times how we'd be together more, and all the things we'd be doing, even though I knew since I'd helped plan them.

It would be good. I was overreacting and everything would be fine.

*   *   *

The rest of the week was supposed to be wet and horrible, but this morning was picture-perfect late May, complete with chirping birds and the residual smell of mowed grass from last night. We hit the road in five days. I hadn't had a text or an email in over a week, since finding out I was the data person for the tour. I started to hope the idea of me out of the office was enough. Maybe I didn't have to move.

I was in a good mood and paying more attention to the pretty tulips, bright orange and pink in someone's yard, enjoying the quiet of the morning. If I had been a little more aware, maybe I would have noticed.

Someone slammed into me hard from behind. I'd assumed the footsteps behind me were one of the many joggers in the area. I lost my balance and skidded down on the pavement.

My first thought was some idiot hadn't looked where they were going. But when I tried to get up, a hand held me down, hard and painful.

"Consider yourself warned," he hissed.

It was close enough to my face I felt his breath—hot, wet, and carrying memories of last night's beer—on my cheek. He shoved me one more time before he jumped up and sprinted away. Nausea roiled in my stomach, making me swallow repeatedly so I didn't embarrass myself on my neighbor's sidewalk.

The next footsteps I heard were a neighbor's, running up behind me.

"You all right?" he asked, and helped me up.

I was shaky, so the extra help getting up was appreciated. I nodded and tried to look convincing. "Jerk just ran into me," I lied. "A little scratched up, but no major damage." My hands were scuffed, dirty, and starting to bleed. Same went for my knee. My glasses, thankfully, made it through with just a little scratch.

"Would have tried to get him myself, but he took off pretty fast," my neighbor said. "Sure you're okay?"

I nodded. I just wanted to get moving and to my desk. If I paused right now, I would panic.

"Fine," I repeated. "Let's get the bus before we miss it."

I chattered completely mindlessly the rest of the way. If I kept talking, I couldn't think about what just had happened or what it meant. The friendly neighbor went with it and waved me off when my bus came.

Usually in the morning I stood on the bus; I sat most of the day, so whatever vertical time I could get, I took. Today, I collapsed into the first available seat. The heels of my hands were pretty gnarly. I absentmindedly picked some of the dirtier looking bits from the cuts and tried to take deep breaths to slow my heartbeat.

So, we'd moved from emails and texts to physical threats. Given the physical and sexual nature of some of the texts, I should be glad a shove was all I'd gotten. I'd go to the police station again at lunch to make a formal complaint. Maybe once that little worm of an officer saw physical proof, he'd do something. But how would I get home tonight? How long was the warning? Three strikes and you're out? We hit the road in a week, but that was work, and this person clearly wanted me out of my job. But there'd be security and other people almost always nearby, but then, I'd thought that this morning…

The bus pulled up at my stop and I got out. I couldn't go into the office like this, so I made a detour to the bathroom and locked myself in. I looked a mess, my face leached of color so my normally pale eyebrows showed as soft brown smudges against my white forehead. The bad florescent lighting threw shadows on my face, making me look gaunt and tight, something from a horror film. I needed to get to next week. I leaned my head against the cool door and took a few more breaths until I stopped shaking. I needed to clean myself up.

Five minutes and a lot of cursing later, I looked a little better, the cuts stinging but washed off and much smaller than I'd originally thought. I had worn a dark gray skirt today, so no worries about ripped knees or stained whites. With my dress shirtsleeves rolled down, the cuffs were just long enough to cover most of the hand scuffs—pink cuffs on pink hands. It looked like I'd tripped a bit, nothing serious and nothing to raise alarm over.

"You're safe here," I told myself in the mirror. The girl staring back didn't look convinced.

I headed out to the elevator. I was sticking with the story that I'd tripped on a curb this morning. Hopefully, I wouldn't get too many questions and no one looked too closely.

The elevator dinged open, and I stepped out. When I saw David getting out of the one next to me, I wasn't sure if I was happy or not. My self-control was pretty minimal.

"Good morning, Charlotte." The happy smile and voice dropped abruptly when he caught a better look. "What happened?"

It took a moment to get myself under control before I answered. I couldn't go for a hug here and I couldn't start to cry. I couldn't. "Just took a tumble this morning, tripped on a curb." Trying to sound offhanded about it failed.

His jaw clenched and he stood rigid. "Really?" he asked.

I couldn't answer this time but shook my head no. "Later," I whispered. I forced a wobbly smile and let him open the door.

*   *   *

I was quite the office joke. It was so funny Charlotte was clumsy and had tipped over. So funny on the outside, but inside, I was winding tighter and tighter. I jotted down what I remembered of the guy, but it wasn't much; he'd been medium-height, White, wearing black track bottoms, a black hoodie, and had had a hat pulled on. That wasn't a lot to go on. It could have been anyone. He could have been hired by anyone. I had new models to run.

What the hell happened?

My phone blinked with the text message from David.

I chose to ignore it for a moment and took care of the emails crowding my inbox. Danielle had scheduled a meeting to go over assignments while I was out; our sub-planning team was meeting for two hours today. Lobbying groups had started their attack ads, for and against us. I needed to focus on work. I deleted a happy hour invitation from Mike.

I wrote back to David twenty minutes later. *Can't explain in a text. Tonight?*

He clearly wasn't paying attention to whatever he was supposed to be focusing on, as he wrote back almost immediately.

Lunch. Come to my office in Parliament. I'll have Emily get you in.

I took a breath. I could do that and stop at the police station on the way back.

Okay.

*   *   *

Emily was expecting me and met me at the visitor entrance. There were a couple groups of school tours, but otherwise it wasn't busy. It was easy to spot her.

"Hello again!" She waved at me. "I've got your visitor pass. A couple signatures and we'll be off."

I thanked her and signed the forms. She tutted over my hands and clipped the visitor badge on for me. I felt somewhat pathetic having an older lady help me with a clip, but it was very much appreciated. Both wrists were jammed and bruised, and they hurt.

"Did you take a tumble?" she asked nicely as we made our way through the front public rooms and into the actual workspaces.

People were funny when they were trying to be polite. That I took a tumble was fairly obvious. Better, though, than asking flat-out, "How did you fall on your face?"

"I did. Sidewalk jumped out at me this morning."

We reached the waiting area, which was an outer office area for David. I was used to seeing him at the party office, not in his Parliament role. This was his real office. In spite of my situation at the moment, I was curious to see him here.

The secretary smiled when she saw Emily.

"Hi, Em. He's on a call, but said you two can go in."

I got a smile in turn and followed Emily through. The whole thing felt like I was in trouble and being led into a principal's office. It was completely off-base, but David wanted answers.

He was talking on the phone, but waved me in.

"It was good to see you again," Emily whispered as she left and shut the door behind her.

An oversized chair sat in the corner, so I lowered myself gingerly there, my knees as stiff as my wrists. David's office was large, but not as big as I thought it'd be. It was funny how a room could feel like a person. He had shelves of history books, atlases, and some others I couldn't make out. There were a lot of pictures from different campaign events or just MP outings, visits at schools, and meetings with the performing arts center.

He hung up after thanking someone for their support and came over.

"What's going on?" he asked again and sat on the arm of the chair. He picked up one of my hands and kissed the back, keeping it wrapped in his.

I reached into my bag and pulled out the email and text printouts. "This," I said flatly and handed them over.

I leaned against his side while he flipped through them. Having him read it all was easier than me explaining. They spoke for themselves.

He was very quiet, his mouth pressing tighter as he read. "Is this it?" he demanded.

I glared. "Is that it? Yes, that is it. Some psycho is—"

"I meant, are these all of them?" he said more gently.

I relaxed back and tugged his arm around me. He obliged readily. "Well, I sent one text back last week telling them to fuck off, but other than that, yes."

He looked somewhere between annoyed and amused, but just squeezed my shoulder. "And this morning?"

I told him everything I remembered. Retelling this part was awful, but having my head resting on his side so I could feel the warmth under my cheek and hear the steady thud of his heart was oddly calming.

He skimmed through the papers again after I finished, frowning. "Who is Charlie Garth?"

I shook my head. "Not a real person. I checked with IT, and they said the account was set up for a new employee. It's a ghost account."

"I'm guessing you already went to the police?"

"Sort of." I explained the less-than-enthusiastic response I'd gotten earlier. "That's my next stop on my way back to work."

He got up and rubbed his forehead. "This is why you've been distracted and irritated?"

I wrinkled my nose and shrugged. "I've not been that bad," I muttered and got him to crack a smile.

"Not horrible, but I could tell something was going on. You can't—we can't...you've got to tell me when something like this is happening."

I wandered over to the window, taking in the sweeping view across the front of Parliament and the color explosion of the tulip festival on the lawn. It was such a pretty day for something so ugly to have happened.

"You have plenty to worry about," I explained. "I hadn't thought this was anything serious." The thought the glass might not be bulletproof crossed my mind. I turned away and leaned against the desk.

"This," he said, and tenderly picked up my hands again; plum bruises had started to seep across my palms. His voice tremored with anger, rough and tight. "Isn't okay. Any ideas who—?"

I shook my head again. "Not really." I felt stupid voicing it. "I thought— Danielle doesn't like me. Mike wants in my pants and doesn't like being told no. Maybe one of them? But I didn't recognize the voice as either of theirs this morning, so I don't know. Maybe they paid someone?" It all sounded ridiculous.

He blinked a few times, clearly never having thought of either of them in that light. "Either way they were able to follow you this morning..." He stopped and looked at me sharply. "How are you getting to and from work?"

Wasn't that a good question? The thought of walking again made me lightheaded. At the same time, I felt completely pathetic being so scared.

"Taxi, Uber? I don't know. Maybe I'll see if I can convince Xavier to give me a ride some nights." I had an irrational fear of getting in a stranger's car and being kidnapped. I'd be shoved into a trunk, taken out to the woods, chopped up and buried in little pieces so I was never found. I wasn't going to share that thought with David. "I'm looking forward to next week when your security people are going to be around all the time," I admitted.

He looked slightly miffed. "And me."

"And you."

He brushed a flyaway piece of hair off my forehead and smiled. "You could stay with me."

That startled me. "I thought we were all about keeping this under wraps? I think showing up at work together might cause some problems."

He shrugged. "Work from home the next two days."

"I could just as easily do that from my house," I argued. "And how would I pack for the trip?"

He waved off my objections. "Whoever this is knows where you live. They'll know if you're home. We can arrange for you to stop by on Sunday to get what you need…and we'll get to see each other every night after work. You'll be safe and we can be together. Win-win."

"What if that puts you at risk?" The thought made me somewhat nauseous. "I can't do that."

He handed the papers back to me and shook his head. "I have security."

I tucked the emails back in my bag. He seemed remarkably unconcerned about his own safety. "You don't think I should do what they're asking, right? You don't think I should leave?" I hoped I knew the answer.

The carefully put-together face he'd had on since I'd showed up cracked. "No," he said without hesitation. "I want you to stay."

He came up behind me and squeezed my shoulders. "Maybe next week… You'll be out of the office a lot now. Mike and Danielle aren't going. Maybe it'll stop. And like you said, my security will be everywhere. The police will have to address this now. We'll be covered."

He was right. "Good. I'm not ready to be rid of you just yet."

"Good," he repeated. "And the rest of the week?"

I picked up my bag; if I wanted to make another police station stop before my afternoon meetings I needed to get going. "This makes me feel like a wimp," I said. "I don't like the idea of having to run to my boyfriend when something scary happens."

"Your boyfriend would very much like to keep you safe and to personally beat the shit out of whoever is doing this," he said just as directly. "And then prosecute them and throw their ass in jail."

His words got me to smile, and he softened. "You've carried this for two months by yourself. Let me help. That's not being a wimp; it's being smart."

I still had a suspicion I was being a wimp, but he made some sense. "You win." I gave in, and he beamed. "How do I get to your house?"

He waved me off. "I'll text you. Be careful. Let me know if anything else happens this afternoon."

"Okay." I wanted to leave right away and blow off the afternoon, but instead he opened the door, business front back on and gave me a blank smile.

"My secretary can show you the way out. Thank you, Ms. Finnan."

*   *   *

My trip to the police station was only slightly more useful than last week. This time they agreed to take a statement and a description of the runner. I still wasn't convinced anything would happen. The officers were disinterested and going through the motions. I wondered if it was too late to push for police reform as a policy.

The afternoon meetings went smoothly, minus a few nitpicks from Danielle and Mike. Both made me twitch and start over-analyzing. Danielle was only following up to make sure I had done my work, just teasing when she asked and laughed about what happened to my knees. Mike was being awful and annoying when he half-cornered me in the coffee area, telling me I looked good, saying I must like it rough on my knees. It wasn't fine, but it was fine.

David said he'd leave at six and I could meet the car in the same place as when he had given me a ride home. We'd make a stop by Parliament to pick him up, and then on to his house.

I was still hesitant. I wanted to stay with him from a strictly personal standpoint, but at the same time it felt a little forced.

Camille didn't answer her phone when I called to let her know the story, so I left a voicemail saying I'd be out. But what would I do about clothes? I had no clothes. I had no toothbrush. But I'd be safe.

The car was waiting like David had said, and Peter the driver opened the door for me.

"Hello, Ms. Finnan."

I smiled shyly and settled in the back. "Hi."

Luckily, I didn't have long to sit and wonder if I should be making polite small talk with Peter. The drive was short, and as soon as we cleared security and pulled into the private parking area, David came out, talking on his phone.

Peter got the door and let him slide in. I wondered what had David told him, or was it not really a big deal he was taking party staff home with him?

"Sorry about that," David said and shoved his phone in his pocket. "All set?" He looked happy about this, at least about me staying with him.

"I don't have any clothes."

He looked bemused and opened his mouth a few times before responding. "You look fairly well-clothed at the moment."

I smacked his shoulder with the back of my hand. "I mean for tomorrow. Or Friday, or the weekend. And no toothbrush."

"I have a spare toothbrush. And there's a ladies' clothing store near my house. You can pick up whatever you need while I start dinner. It'll be fine."

The idea of him doing something domestic like cooking dinner made me smile. "You cook?"

"Yes, I do feed myself," he said, sounding affronted. "I'm not a bad cook."

"I'm sure you're not," I said. "I just thought you would have a cook or something."

"I take care of myself just fine, thank you," he said drily. "Like I said, you'll be okay walking to the store, and I'll handle dinner."

He made it sound so easy. "Are we going on the assumption my stalker won't be able to find me?"

"Peter, is anyone following us?" David asked.

"No, sir," he said immediately. "We are clear. You'll be safe, Ms. Finnan."

My face flamed red. This made me feel like an overreacting idiot. Then I looked at my hands and remembered the hot breath on my cheek from this morning and I shivered. "Okay," I said.

David's house, or condo really, was about ten minutes east of the office. He'd explained earlier he'd argued hard, and won, to stay in his own home rather than the large residence reserved for the Leader of the Opposition. Thirty-four rooms for one person was extravagant and a waste of money to maintain just for him. So, he still had his condo and a huge house for any official entertaining. I was happy to have a normal place to stay for the next few days. Traveling in a car with blacked-out windows and staying in a building with extra security was all welcome. I didn't want anyone seeing me or who I was with or where we were going. Anonymity was my friend.

We pulled into an underground parking lot with a handful of cars and some elevators. David thanked Peter, and up we went to the sixth floor.

"It's a little messy," he apologized as he opened the door.

In my mind, I'd pictured a massive apartment-style mansion—huge rooms, ridiculously expensive furnishings, artwork and decorations done by a professional. Instead, it was a nice condo, no mistake, but it was also incredibly accessible. The kitchen sat off to the left with breakfast items still by the sink. The living room was a decent size and had furniture that looked comfortable but didn't necessarily match. A book was tossed on the couch, read recently. The ceilings weren't double height, and while it did have a nice view looking towards downtown, it wasn't the highest or the best view in the city. It was all incredibly normal looking. It felt like a home, not a magazine page.

"It's perfect," I said.

He looked somewhat skeptical but shut the door behind me.

"I think you're being kind. If you were expecting housekeepers and cooks, I'm afraid you're going to be disappointed."

I sat my bag down on the little table by the door. "I wasn't expecting that at all. Or, if I was, it was just because of bad stereotypes, not because I was hoping for it."

He gave me a quick tour of the bedrooms, bathrooms, and study. All of it looked well lived in, with items displayed for a reason and not just for show. His violin rested in the study, a music stand set up in a corner with music sitting on it.

"Make yourself at home. I'm going to change." He smiled briefly and disappeared into his bedroom.

I meandered back to the living room and looked out the window; the street wasn't crowded. There were people on it, but it wasn't as busy as downtown. I didn't see anyone who matched the description of the guy from this morning. They all looked respectable. The store David had mentioned was just a block away. I could make that.

"All right?"

I turned and saw a very different David than I had so far, even at night on the phone. He had changed into sweatpants and an old campaign T-shirt from ten years ago.

"You didn't say you have glasses."

He shrugged. "It never came up. Are you okay with pasta for dinner?"

The simplicity of the question made me momentarily forget the horribleness of this morning. We were here, like a normal couple, and that made me incredibly happy. He hadn't come near me since this morning. Maybe he thought I was twitchy about being touched now or he wasn't sure what hurt.

I crossed the room and wrapped myself around him, smiling when his arms came up tight around me. This was what I wanted.

"You don't have any idea how worried you had me when I saw you this morning," he mumbled into my hair.

"I wasn't that rough looking. I could have easily fallen off a bike."

His head shook against mine; his face was bristly on my forehead, just a soft scratch. "The way you looked… You looked like you were about to launch yourself at me in the office. That's what scared me. I figured it had to be bad for you to…" He trailed off. "You're safe here."

"It is a little bit of an awkward first date." I reluctantly loosened my grip on him and stepped back. I needed to go before the stores closed.

"How is this a first date?" he asked. The glasses softened some of the angles on his face; it was a good look for home.

"Well, first dinner, first time over, first time we're not at work. It's a first. We might hate each other outside of work."

He laughed. "You're going to have to try pretty hard to get me to hate you. Did you find the store?"

I picked up my purse and nodded. "Yes. Key?"

He fiddled around with his keys and handed me a key fob. "Down the elevator to the ground floor and first door on the left. I can watch you most of the way."

Oddly, the offer made me feel better. I wasn't sure what he'd do from up here if something were to happen, but it was reassuring.

"Don't eat everything before I'm back." I grabbed one quick kiss and ducked out the door.

The ladies' boutique was fancy and beautiful, a bit pricier than I would normally frequent. The pjs were soft silks and cool cottons, delicate and cute. There were some other items—sweaters, T-shirts, and yoga pants—on sale, so I grabbed those as well. On second thought, I splurged on a couple of items closer to sexy than cute, figuring I'd cover my bases for the weekend. It was an expensive shopping trip. Overall, though, it eased a minor worry of having no clothes.

The walk back was devoid of any excitement whatsoever, even with an extra stop at a pharmacy nearby to pick up a few extra things for my stay. That made me happy.

It also made me happy to open the door to the scents of garlic and basil cooking on the stove and the sound of happily bubbling pots.

"Success?" David asked. He had set the table already and had wine poured. It looked like a fancy midweek meal to me.

"Success," I declared. "I am set to be housebound here for the next few days. Anywhere in particular I should put these?" I asked, wiggling my bags at him.

He glanced up with a slight lift of his shoulders. "The bedroom's fine. Make yourself comfortable."

I smiled and headed down the hall. Maybe it was a bit presumptuous, but I went for the main bedroom.

His bed was unmade from this morning. I pulled out the pair of lounge pants and a pale peach top and changed. The shirt caught on my hands a bit as I pulled it on and stung my scrapes. One pant leg needed to be rolled up; the rubbing hurt the cuts on my knee. But overall, it was a good buy.

David was leaning with elbows on the counter when I came back, reading over a stack of papers, pen in hand, phone at his side.

"Still working?"

"Yes, but without a tie and with a glass of wine." He grinned. It made my heart stutter. "Do you mind if I work over dinner? Jess usually calls later in the evening—"

"I don't mind," I said. "Do whatever you need." I walked over and stole a sip of his wine. He had good taste.

"Thank you," he said, and sounded quite relieved. He poured a glass for me and slid it over. "My ex-wife…she hated it when I worked over dinner. I didn't want to start this off on the wrong foot."

Stupid lady. Stupid lady on a lot of fronts. "It's fine. As long as I'm fed, it's all good."

*   *   *

David's boast earlier, that he was a good cook, was modest. The dinner was excellent, with fresh pasta smothered with spicy tomatoes and briny olives, but quiet. He had a stack of documents and policy notes for review. I was perfectly content to sit and enjoy dinner. I wouldn't need to jam my door or window shut tonight. I might fall asleep without listening to every single crack or creak of the house, wondering if it was an intruder or just Camille and Tom.

I got to relax with David, in person. Every now and then, he glanced up at me and smiled, a little nudge under the table where our legs rested against each other.

Camille rang back when we were finished eating. I excused myself and took my phone into the first room I found, which was the office. I settled myself into David's chair, the one I saw him sit in most nights, and told her everything; she was the closest thing to a sister I had. And of course the stalker knew where I lived, so it impacted her and Tom.

I expected to get an earful about staying here the next few days, all the attention that might get. Instead, she thought it a sensible idea and agreed to pack a bag for me so I didn't need to make an appearance on Sunday.

"Just be careful, okay?" Camille asked. It rattled me that my normally cool as a cucumber friend was worried. "I'll keep an eye out here for any weirdos, and when you're back in town you can come home."

"I will. Thank you, Camille."

I came back out quietly, hearing David talking on his phone. He had his business voice on, so I guessed it was the call from Jessica he'd mentioned before. I meant to get a glass of water and sit out of the way, but he flagged me over. There was a momentary debate between the chair on the side or the couch, but my mind was made up for me when David gave me a slightly exasperated look and motioned me over to him.

It was hard to argue with that, so I plopped down nearly on top of him, using his side as a backrest. He gave me the speech and a pen.

"Assist," he mouthed to me, looking pleased to have a hand.

Rather than a relaxing evening reading, I ended up turning pages and jotting notes for him. I wasn't sure I was that useful. The extra commentary I scribbled on scrap paper got David to muffle laughs.

Towards the end, Jessica tried to extend the call, asking what he'd had for dinner, evening plans, etc. He shut it down quick.

"She is a fantastic manager and a wonderful friend but does not know how to take a break." He stretched and rubbed the back of his head before resting back, looping an arm around my waist.

"Eric, her brother, would time her when we were younger to see how long he could keep her talking about how well she was doing at the university. I think the record was nearly half an hour. I guess that's when you knew her," I added. In a weird way, it bugged me she'd known him longer than me.

He laughed and tossed his phone across to a chair. "That sounds about right. She's a good person, but there's a reason—a lot of reasons—I prefer to talk to you this time of night."

"I can go sit in another room and call you if you want," I offered, getting the arm around my waist to tighten.

"No, you're perfect here." He picked up my hands and turned them over to the scuffed-up sides. Compared to what I'd thought they might have been this morning when everything had been raw and oozy, they weren't so bad now. My knees had started to scab already.

"Makes me look pretty tough," I said, trying to make light of it.

He shook his head. "You are. Although I prefer you let me in on how tough you're being in the future." He still sounded annoyed.

"Well, lesson learned. It seemed a little much to land the 'oh, I'm being harassed and threatened' line right after we started talking; most guys would run off. I didn't want you to run off."

He kissed the inside of each wrist and rested his head on mine, his lips tickling my hair as he talked. "I'm not most guys. Even if it would have been right after we started dating."

"Have we been dating?" I wondered out loud. It was a very unconventional type of dating.

"Yes. You are the person I want to talk to last in the day and the person I most look forward to seeing in the mornings." He laughed. "It'll be strange tomorrow… When I get into the office, I normally glance over to where you sit. I'll miss that."

"You'll still see me in the morning."

"I know," he said. "All sleep crusted and disheveled."

I elbowed him gently. "Not disheveled. Radiant and glowing in the morning."

"Bet we can do disheveled and glowing." He planted a kiss on the side on my neck and another along my jaw. My head turned a fraction, enough to find his lips and pulled him to a kiss. He kissed in a way that made my nerves fly alive from toes to stomach to head. I'd known that a little bit from the previous ones, but this time there was no chance of interruption.

And just like that, any intelligent thought went flying from my head for the rest of the evening, and I let him lead me to the bedroom.

*　　　*　　　*

A little piece of me had worried the physical chemistry would be terrible. As it turned out, that wasn't a problem. All things considered, I thought he was right; we might be stuck together for a long time. As I laid there with him still laying partially on me, I was okay with it.

"What happens if you win?" I asked.

"I become prime minister," he answered, knowing full well that wasn't what I'd meant.

I nudged him with my leg before hooking mine back on top.

"With us, you mean?"

I nodded. He couldn't see me, but he could feel it.

"I'll take you out for dinner," he said, his smile coming through. "I've wanted to do that for months." He paused and sighed. "You'll have to deal with media, and I'd get you security detail, because there's no way after today you wouldn't have your own. It's not going to be a normal relationship, which you probably already knew."

"I know. Would I still be able to work?" I asked, even though I had no plans after the election. In the dark, it was easy to spin out the future. Outside factors faded in the gray shadows and the only thing that could possibly influence the future lay hip-to-hip, skin-to-skin next to me.

"Of course. Why wouldn't you?" he asked, rolling over to face me.

I shrugged. "Don't know. This isn't exactly something I have a lot of experience in."

"You could do whatever you like," he said. "Things would change if we were to…"

"Stick together a while?" I offered.

He brushed a strand of hair off my face before he kissed me. "Something like that. Get some sleep. Some of us have to go into work."

I rolled over and curled up against him. "I have to work."

"I know. Someone has to make sure I know what I'm talking about."

*   *   *

All too soon, his alarm bleeped shrilly, bright and early at 4:30 AM. He groaned and turned it off.

I peeked my eyes open and stared sleepily at him. "You wake up very early," I said.

He grinned at me. "What color do you say your eyes are?"

His own, so dark with sleep the brown was nearly indistinguishable from the black, were only inches from mine, brilliant black holes pulling me in close.

"Sea glass green is what my grandma calls it."

"Hmm." He nodded. "I like waking up next to sea glass green eyes." He stretched, pulling the sheets off my shoulders. "You can stay in bed. I need to start work." He gave me a quick kiss on the cheek and slid out.

David was out the door at seven sharp. I, on the other hand, dressed in my new shorts and one of his T-shirts, taking the casual dress idea seriously. He'd showed me where everything was before leaving, how to work the fancy coffee machine after making me a cup with plenty of cream and sugar, showed me where food was—all the important things.

Figuring I might as well start work, I logged in with my work laptop and sent my working from home note to all.

*   *   *

Our plan went smoothly. Working from his office was easy and caused no hiccups. We quickly agreed after I incinerated fish for dinner, nearly stinking out his house, that David was in charge of cooking. I was better at loading a dishwasher.

Saturday he was out until late afternoon, attending meetings in his home district a couple of hours south. And then, we had a full day and a half to be together.

Camille was wonderful and had packed me a suitcase that was delivered Sunday morning, along with my cello. David played violin a couple of times and I wanted to play with him. So we did, filling his home with the rich velvet tone of strings, able to anticipate each other with ease.

Aside from one text message on Thursday reminding me I couldn't hide forever, the four days were perfect. Hiding everything again would be hard.

*   *   *

Sunday night was mellow. We both packed and laid out clothes for tomorrow. David shut down in the afternoon and set aside work for the rest of the day. In addition to his cooking skills, he mixed mean dirty martinis with the perfect amount of tang, and we both drank a couple. It was very domestic.

Later at night, I didn't think he was watching the show I'd turned on, something about preserving the polar and arctic regions. He seemed pleased to be sitting next to me, acting as my backrest. The reason I was here sucked but being here for the last few days had made me happy.

The sigh he gave when his phone rang nearly ten at night had me leaning forward to grab the remote by my skinned-up knees. I got a quick thank you kiss on my head as I muted the TV. It was Jessica. I could hear her bubbly chatter. At least she was excited; it couldn't be bad news, then.

David took the remote, laughing as he switched to CTV. I'd never know if the elephant seal pup I'd been watching got his dinner.

"What am I looking—?"

The lead story made it clear what he was supposed to be watching. It was why Jessica was talking a mile a minute.

While we'd enjoyed dinner, phones muted for everyone but the favorites, we had missed a lot. A story had broken over the Workers Party Leader and an affair with a junior level assistant in his office.

I numbly grabbed the remote back and unmuted the sound. I heard Jessica giving David his own rundown. Judging by the stony look, it wasn't all good.

"…Breaking earlier tonight, reports emerged alleging Workers Party Leader Marcus MacCallum and junior staff member Evelyn Paine were involved in a relationship. Mr. MacCallum denied all accusations in a press conference shortly after the story broke, stating all claims were fabricated. Hours later, Ms. Paine released a counter-statement through an attorney containing text messages of an explicit sexual nature. The two sides…."

The news story continued on with a firing, a conversation overheard, anonymous sources, and MacCallum stepping down after being caught, literally, with his pants down.

"Jesus, they're killing each other."

I wasn't sure if David had meant that for Jessica or me, but he was right. They kept talking, David agreeing it was good for us even if the Workers had never posed a threat for the election, saying he'd discuss talking points with Kaitlyn tomorrow, tweaking policy to draw in more of MacCallum's voters, reaching out to our candidates in those ridings. He spoke calmly, his business voice smooth and in control, chuckling at Jessica when she laughed.

The arm draped across my shoulder tightened. He seemed reluctant to let go when I pulled away, giving me a glance before staring ahead. It didn't take more than half a second before he was back to being delighted by the turn of events.

I felt sick and foolish. For me, it didn't take much imagination to put David and me on the screen. To imagine someone finding out, leaking it, viewing it as some lack of decorum or moral failing, and calls for David to step down. The story would be spun as him taking advantage of the younger party staff, abusing his power. It'd ruin him. There'd be backlash for me, too, but that paled in comparison to what David would get.

I tucked my knees up under my chin and thought about it. Maybe I should leave. The calls would stop, the texts, the threats, and it'd leave David free. After the election, after everything played out, we could try again. I'd only been around for three months; his dream had been around a lot longer. We could wait.

While he finished talking, I tried to busy my mind with how I'd update our stops and data. I tried to detach and think about it objectively; he was able to, so I should be able to as well. It didn't stop me, though, from looking at the crying young lady on TV just a few years younger than me, angry and defiant that MacCallum had painted her as delusional.

David and Jessica smelled blood and had no problem going in for the kill. My numbers ran in useless circles in my head as David ended the call.

It took a moment for the silence to trigger.

"I can leave," I said. It wasn't more than a whisper, but when I said it aloud it sounded right. "That can't happen." I motioned at the TV.

The two of them probably had at one point felt something for each other… It horrified me it could end with a juvenile spat played out on national TV.

David's jaw clenched as a flicker of annoyance played on his face before speaking. "I'd never do that."

For being so smart, he could be incredibly stupid. All the tension that had seeped out of me the last few days crawled back, and I sighed. I was exhausted.

"I meant me. You can't be linked to me." It seemed clear and obvious. The smile I was trying for didn't quite work. "I can't…you can't lose everything you've been working for because of me, because of a relationship with a staffer on the campaign. We could wait until the election's done, put this on hold…"

I trailed off as I met his eyes. He looked like I was speaking a completely foreign language, forehead drawn, head tilted.

Rather than answer right away, David leaned over and kissed me, smiling as our lips met.

"When I called you that Friday night in the middle of your bad date, I knew I was taking a risk." For a second, he stared over my shoulder before blinking and shaking his head. "I was risking you leaving the team and losing your skill set. I was risking losing you as a friend. I was risking you running to Jess or Danielle or the media and reporting me for harassment. And," he added before I could say anything, "if I didn't call, I'd risk regretting it for the rest of my life. And that made the rest pale in comparison."

He grabbed my hand and didn't let go. He was good at making an earnest argument. "Even if this does come out tomorrow, or in a few weeks, or whenever, I will stand up in front of whatever press conference they tell me to and I will happily admit to it all and continue campaigning with you by my side."

Really, there wasn't a lot else I could throw at that. It tossed my anxiety clear out the window, thankfully, and made me wonder how I'd gotten so lucky. Some of the fight and panic faded, and I rested my head on his shoulder again.

"Then I'll stay. I knew it could get public when we started, and here I am." Here I was, still shocked it was okay for me to be leaning against him. It didn't mean others would be okay with it, though. "Do you want me to delete my texts from you?"

It was the wrong thing to ask. He rubbed his face and sighed, looking more stressed than he had earlier tonight. "No. I know you wouldn't release anything. That story isn't us."

Before I had a chance to respond, he stood up, shutting the TV off and stretching. "It's our last night at home; let's get some sleep in our own bed before it's separate hotel rooms the next couple weeks."

I followed him, the words "home" and "our bed" settling into my brain. It should be easy to figure out; home was where you lived, where you went at the end of a day. My room at Camille's should have been home in Ottawa, but I still felt like an interloping houseguest. My apartment in Calgary was supposed to have been my home the last four years, but it'd always felt empty.

Now that David had said in a completely off-handed, natural way that this was home, I wondered if he was right. There wasn't a lot of me here. I had a few things in the bathroom—toothbrush, basic things, a rose-scented lip balm I liked. I had a drawer, a nightstand. It wasn't necessarily the location, but all the little things that had fallen into place seamlessly over the last few days, snug and right, everything clicking together like puzzle pieces. *Home.*

While I waited for David to finish brushing his teeth, I decided to do a quick double-check of my text messages, just in case. There shouldn't be anything that would cause a problem, but I felt better checking.

A few scrolls showed messages back and forth about meetings, dinners, after-work events, a couple good lucks, random texts about something funny one of us had seen… You'd have to stretch a lot to get anything twisted into a scandal.

Somewhat against my better judgment, because it felt a little creeper-like, I clicked the link to the text messages from the news story. If I found anything similar to ours, I'd know what to delete.

After the first couple of pages of mundane texts, my eyes bugged out and my mouth dropped open. We had nothing resembling these. They were *Fifty Shades of Gray*, but not the soft version.

I kept scrolling despite myself. He'd messaged her about where he wanted her in his office, how far over she'd bend on his desk, how deep he'd—

"What are you looking at?"

I hadn't heard David come in. He flicked the main lights off and slid in next to me, trying not to look too curious. I felt caught doing something illicit and blushed. He moved closer and nudged me.

"I uh… I thought I'd double-check our texts, just in case," I mumbled, but couldn't keep an embarrassed giggle from escaping. "They seemed pretty standard to me, so I thought I'd see what was in the released messages that had caused the fuss. Did Jessica tell you what was in those?" My face went deep red. Jessica better not have read these out to him. The thought made me hot and prickly.

He shook his head.

I wouldn't be able to read a single text with a straight face, so I shoved my phone at him. "Read."

His eyes flickered at me once before starting to scroll. He muttered something under his breath, looking completely dumbfounded. He got further down in them than I had. His face went blank like it did when he tried not to give anything away. In the last few weeks, I'd gotten good at reading him.

"So," he said slowly, his face momentarily flickering in amusement before going back to the serious look. "Going forward, do you want me to start detailing exactly where I'm about to—" His voice broke into a laugh and I lost it.

"No!" I laughed. The stress from earlier tonight erupted up and out in a release. I tipped against him and tried to stop snickering, unsuccessfully. "No. If anyone gets ahold of our texts, the only scandal is going to be that we're too boring. Clearly have zero sex life."

"We wouldn't last half a news cycle in comparison." He leaned over me and switched my bedside lamp off before lying down. It was funny how fast this had become normal; I could fall asleep within minutes after we'd laid down, curled up along his side.

The earlier merriment faded as we settled in.

"You won't get in trouble or censured by an ethics committee or anything, right?" I asked. It was one thing to survive a media cycle politically, but the consequences could go on beyond just an election.

With one sigh, I could tell the question annoyed him. Maybe I should have kept my mouth shut tonight, because really, at 10:30 PM as I was half lying on his chest, it probably wasn't the best time to ask.

"No chance of it."

"You sure?" I asked before I could help it. He had answered awfully fast. Almost too fast.

"Well, yes," he bristled, clearly irritated. "I wrote the law, so I know what's in it. I know what lines I can push and make sure neither of us is out of bounds."

There was no reason that should have made me smile, but it did. I tilted my head and kissed the underside of his jaw.

"This is probably me being odd," I said, and kissed him a little further along his neck, "but it's damn sexy when you talk like that."

"When I talk like what?" he asked, sounding lost—happy lost, though.

"Casually tossing out that you wrote the law. Powerful and sexy."

He chuckled and rolled over to face me. "Should I recite a list? There are others." The room was nearly black, but I could still see him smiling in the dark.

I shook my head. "Save it for later. I trust you have it under control. It's just easier for me to worry about something else for a change. I'm getting good at worrying about other things."

It startled him, which wasn't what I'd been going for. His hand pulled back from my waist and he sat up.

"You haven't had any other emails or texts since Thursday, have you?" he asked.

"No." I tugged him back down and slid over closer to him. "Nothing."

But tomorrow they'd see me again, and there wasn't much I could do to stop from tensing up. Boring things like ethics were a better worry to focus on.

"Don't waste your energy worrying about backlash against us whenever we do become a public couple." His arm wrapped up around my back and tugged me in. "Leave that to me."

I took his advice. For the rest of the night I forgot the stalker, forgot the news story, forgot any other complications that might come. When David leaned forward and kissed me, and kept kissing me so my mouth was fully occupied and not asking obnoxious questions, I happily left it to him.

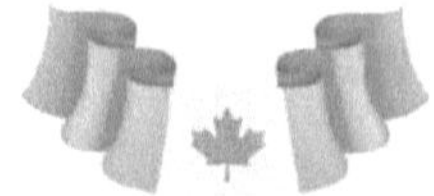

Chapter Eight

Monday morning was a hot mess. It started off on a good note, mainly because David wanted a repeat of Sunday morning, making our coffees, the newspaper, and us being lazy for thirty minutes. When we finally started the morning routine, the happy glow faded.

"I kinda liked being under house arrest here." I sat on the bed, ready to go as soon as my taxi arrived, watching David do his tie. After only four days, he'd been right about this being home. I didn't want to give it up yet.

"You make it sound like I was keeping you under lock and key," David replied. "I don't think that was the case." He straightened his tie—cobalt blue to go with the crisp white shirt and dark gray suit—and pulled on his suit coat. "But I am going to miss this, having you here."

My phone buzzed, announcing my ride was here. I had to arrive at the departure point ahead of him; it would look marginally obvious if we arrived together.

"That's me," I said.

It seemed silly to feel down this morning. I should have been, and was, excited to look forward to the next few months. It would be busy and exhausting and hectic, but there was nothing else I'd rather be doing. Jessica had been right when she'd sold me on this. The job hit all my interests and I loved it. Plus, I'd get to see David on a daily basis.

But I wouldn't have the little things, like him making me coffee or kissing my cheek as he woke up. I'd miss our nights when he was just a guy out of the sharp suits. The last few days had been a teaser to what could be, and I didn't like that it was ending. I wanted it all.

He sighed and glanced out the window. "Peter is talking to your driver now. I'll be just a few minutes behind you."

I tugged on my jacket over my dress and slipped plum-colored heels on. Camille had packed a wonderful wardrobe; that's what happened when a fashion editor gathered your suitcase for you. "I know. Text me when you can tonight."

He rolled his eyes and kissed me. "You know it. Get going."

I gave him one last hug, reluctant to let go. It might be the last one for a few weeks. I charged out before I flung myself back at him.

Peter smiled and hoisted my luggage into the back of the taxi. "All set, Ms. Finnan. Mr. Abas has directions and will get you there in no time."

His words made my eyes start watering. I didn't want to leave Peter, either, and I barely knew the guy. *Get a grip, Charlotte.* "Thanks, Peter."

He waved me off and we drove away.

The leaving point was off a side street near our main office. As we pulled up, it appeared most everyone was outside, including extras from the office who came to watch. I was happy to see Xavier had come out, too.

"Is here okay?" Mr. Abas asked, pulling to a stop.

"Yes, it's fine. Thank you." I started to get cash out, but he stopped me.

"It's already been taken care of, Miss. And if you need a ride again, just give me a call. Happy to take you wherever you need." He smiled and handed me a business card with his number on it.

I really needed to get a grip. "Thank you," I repeated and got out.

"You're not dead," Xavier said as he came over and handed me a sickly-sweet-looking pastry with globs of caramel-covered nuts. The sweet burnt sugar smell made my mouth water.

"I'm not dead," I confirmed, and ate a sticky mass of nuts nearly gluing my fingers together.

"This is quite a send-off." On closer inspection, it looked like the entire office had turned out.

He nodded, looking grumpy; it made me smile. "Mia thought it'd be a great idea to have a big to-do. Good for morale. Give Reid a confidence boost."

"That's a very Mia-like idea. Have you seen Jessica anywhere? I think I need to check in with her."

Xavier laughed and led me to where he'd last seen her. "It's like a giant school trip. Jessica as the chaperone, head-counts… Make sure you hold hands as you cross the road."

I kicked at him, but he managed to avoid me. "I'm going to head back in and enjoy the quiet office. Just wanted to make sure you hadn't died of influenza and had adequate sugar for the morning."

As far as work husbands went, Xavier was pretty good. "Thanks. Very much appreciated. Keep me up-to-date on any exciting office gossip."

He rolled his eyes. "That's me. Office gossip headquarters. See you in a couple of weeks." He waved and went back in.

Jessica hadn't moved very far and was in full command mode, barking out orders directing people on where to put their luggage.

"Good morning, Jessica. Ready and reporting for duty."

She glanced up from her tablet. "Morning, Charlotte. You'll be on the bus behind me. We leave in ten minutes." She looked at me again with an expression I couldn't quite read. Curious? "I like your perfume this morning. It's nice."

I blinked and sniffed my arm. It smelled of citrus and pepper and cedar, spicy and full of sun and sea. I smiled before I could stop myself. I smelled of David. I'd run into the bathroom to grab my toothbrush while he'd been spraying his cologne. It wasn't strong in the slightest and I wouldn't have noticed if Jessica hadn't complimented me, but now it was all I could think of and my smile stayed in place.

"Thanks," I said. "Mom got it for my birthday."

"She has good taste," she said blandly, and dismissed me.

I was on the main campaign bus; the other bus a little ways down was for the press corps following us and the PR interns. At the moment, the press and media attention swarmed around us. I started pulling my luggage towards the drop-off point, pausing to switch from my normal glasses to sunglasses. The sun was starting to glint between the buildings, burning off the damp morning chill. It would be a lovely day.

"Let me get that for you."

Before I had a chance to protest, Mike came up behind me and grabbed my bag.

"I had it just fine," I said, having no choice but to stalk after him. He thudded it down at the luggage drop.

"Wouldn't hurt you to say thank you." He was arrogant and staring; it made me uncomfortable. "You look good today."

"I'm not a big one for lip service. I say thank you when warranted. I'll send you the updated itinerary options as soon as I get them over the next week."

He smirked. "I'll take lip service from you."

I debated for a moment whether it was worth punching him or not; there were a lot of police and cameras and I'd probably be the one in trouble. Why did he have to be so good at his job? It'd be a lot easier if he was horrible and Jessica would fire him.

"Try not to be an ass. I'll email updates as needed." I stomped off, which was far more difficult when I had to weave through reporters. I should have punched him.

My violent thoughts were diverted when David's car pulled up. Unsurprisingly, Mia had nailed the idea of a surprise send-off. He looked startled to see the crowd of office staff, but it quickly turned to genuine delight. He smiled and waved.

The crowd dispersed after a few minutes, with most heading back into the office and the rest of us making our way towards the buses. My phone started buzzing and I pulled it out eagerly, still wrapped in the happy glow from this morning.

When I saw who the sender was, my smile froze and melted away, leaving me standing cold in the sun. The trickle of panicky anxiety settled back into my stomach and the spot between my shoulder blades re-knotted almost instantly.

Two more warnings before you're dead.

I squeezed my eyes shut and wanted to go back to this morning. No, I wanted to go back to yesterday, when David and I had had a normal day together. I hadn't been paranoid yesterday. I hadn't been thinking about how my parents would handle organizing their only child's funeral, how they would be left standing at a gravesite as I was lowered down. I wanted this person gone, but I didn't know *who* I wanted gone. With one text message, the terror was back and driving me mad.

I opened my eyes and found nothing else had changed. My busmates had moved on. My luggage had been loaded. The press, for the most part, had vanished as David stood talking with Jessica and the head of PR. He was talking to them but staring at me. He'd seen it all play out on my face.

I turned away and went on the bus. The inside was closer to an RV than anything else. There were a handful of seats, a couple tables for working, a teeny kitchenette. There was a full bathroom in the far back; it didn't look much bigger than an airplane bathroom, but I could see a toilet and sink. A small bedroom was blocked off, I guessed, for David.

Without paying much attention, I dove into the first seat I found. Initially, I put myself against the window; it was more comfortable to lean against and I liked watching the scenery roll by outside. But the text told me I was going to die, so I moved to the aisle seat. You could target someone more easily through a window.

We loaded up a few minutes later, with David and the rest of the staff heading towards the back to review today's speech and agenda.

When my phone buzzed after the bus lurched south towards Toronto, I nearly didn't look at it. I really wanted to throw it out the window at the moment, but it was my work phone as well as my private phone. This time it was David.

What?

That was it. What a horrible way to start the summer. The tour through Canada was my thing, what I helped plan, and what would help give the campaign a huge boost. I was supposed to help David. Now, I was an added distraction.

I rested my head against the seat and thought back to this morning. We'd been good then. He cared and wanted to know.

This

I forwarded him the text.

It was surreal to me, even with my hands and knees still healing. The idea someone disliked me enough to want me dead didn't sit at all with how I saw myself. I wasn't overly obnoxious, I hadn't done anything at work to get anyone in trouble, and while I contributed to the campaign, I really didn't think my skills were worth someone from outside targeting me; I'd say Jessica or Ben would be a more likely target. But someone was after me. It didn't make sense.

I had imagined myself dying when I was old and wrinkly—preferably in my sleep, or from laughing too much, or as one of those sweet old couples who died hours apart. Being murdered in a hit had never crossed my mind. David must have threats, too, or maybe the security detail intercepted them all. Still, I didn't think he had problems like this.

When we were ten minutes out from the first stop—a high school outside of Toronto to lay out our education platform—David came over and motioned me to make room for him.

"Pretend we're reviewing this," he said, and handed over a stack of handwritten notes. I took it but shook my head. He shouldn't be sitting next to me.

"Go run over your speech," I said. "You don't need to be here."

"That's what we're doing now," he said, his voice tighter than when I'd left this morning, the tension back in his jaw. "I'm going to discuss this with campaign security." He was better at acting—he always was—and made it look like we were reviewing something, pointing at random bits on the pages, flipping between them. "It needs to be addressed. Are you okay with them talking to you?"

I rubbed my head, squeezing my eyes shut. "Yes, that's fine. Just have someone tell me when and where."

David didn't say anything else for a while, just sat silent next to me.

I skimmed through the pages, not reading a single thing before I handed it back.

"We're going to figure this out," he said finally, standing up. "You're not going to…"

Better not to say it.

"I'll be smart." I sounded more confident than I felt. I obviously wasn't going to do anything stupid but didn't know what the smart course of action was either. "Go back to work. It's okay."

He laughed, but without a trace of humor, as he turned to go. "There is absolutely nothing okay about this."

*   *   *

All of us extras got to attend events on the stops. The first day, we lined the very back nosebleed seats in the auditorium at the high school. The audience packed into the stuffy room, amplifying the underlying scent of locker rooms and stale sweat.

I found a spot against the back wall, wedged between Kaitlyn and some security detail to my right. Unless I got shot at point blank, I'd be good.

David strode onto the stage with the local MP candidate, Lara Wright, to copious amounts of cheering and screaming. The media lights snapped and flashed. He waved and smiled one way while Lara worked the other side; David stole the show without trying.

He approached the podium to more yelling and cheers. The crowd settled down and he started off thanking the school for inviting him, for the incredible welcome we received, for the opportunity… It was a lot of butt-kissing.

"I'm supposed to be speaking to you today about schools and the policies we're going to put in place to make sure every child has the opportunity to get the best education they can. Well, I have to apologize to my campaign staff in the back, who are probably panicking about me going rogue, because that is not what I will be addressing today. Instead, I want to discuss the problem of cyberbullying and what we're planning on doing…"

The twitch of panic jolted down the line of us in the back.

"What the hell is he doing?" Kaitlyn muttered under her breath.

I shook my head. As far as I knew, it was a speech on education and schools. David pulled out a couple sheets of notes, which I'd never seen him use, and he launched into a fiery speech on cyberbullying. He had facts and figures on the number of suicides and deaths caused by cowards who hid behind their keyboards and used phones to terrorize and threaten students and co-workers. He must have written it in the last couple of hours. He went on about how the lack of response on the topic was causing schools and civil society to erode.

Even if it wasn't a personal topic for me, it was a powerful speech. It was obvious he was feeling it and emotionally involved. It was raw and powerful. Given the silence in the auditorium, and the eruption of applause when he finished, it was clear the change in topic was well-received.

"Where's that been the last few months?" Kaitlyn asked, almost to herself, and then laughed. "He keeps this up, we've got it in the bag." She grinned, directing me backstage.

The rest of the team was just as delighted with the new speech as Kaitlyn. I hung out in the back, not feeling safe or comfortable getting near David. I was too likely to hug him or cry or something else pathetic. We caught eyes once on the way back to the bus, but that was it. We were off to downtown.

*   *   *

My plans for a quiet afternoon were disrupted before I could even get close to settled in the hotel room. Kaitlyn had left with Jessica to attend an afternoon publicity event for women in the Centre Party. David and Ben were going to a radio interview. Everyone was supposed to be out, and I was going to be locked away in the hotel room, replaying the threats over in my head until I froze in place with panic. Instead, I got a text from Ben telling me I was now attending the interview and to come down immediately; they were in the car already.

I'd taken out my contacts, stretched my feet out of my heels, and pulled my hair up and off my neck, a welcome respite in the humidity. There was no way I'd be involved in the actual interview, so I grabbed my bag, glasses, and put on my flats.

The SUV was waiting for me out front. Peter, who was part of David's permanent security detail, gave me a friendly smile. I grabbed the middle row of seats for myself, glancing back expectantly for an explanation. Kaitlyn did all the prep for the interviews. Ben was here for policy and strategy tweaks. This wasn't my forte.

"I need you to review this and make sure it won't sound like shit in my voice. I'd normally have Jess do it, but I'm afraid you're up," David said, and handed forward a few sheets of paper I recognized as Kaitlyn's talking points.

"Glad to be sloppy seconds." I sighed and took the sheets, sounding far crankier than I'd meant. Judging by David's face, and that Ben had looked up, too, I had caught everyone off-guard. I mustered a smile and waved them off. "Sorry, long day. Of course, I can."

They both gave me one more look, David clearly knowing why, and left me to it.

There were only a couple of places when I read through the answer in David's voice that it came off sounding arrogant or scripted. I scribbled notes. Kaitlyn was good. It would have been fine without me looking at it, and David probably knew full-well where the notes would be. I wasn't sure if I was grateful for the excuse to not be by myself, or if I was annoyed David had been manipulative to get me here. Or if I was annoyed and irritated with everyone.

Once there, a station employee whisked David away. Ben and I were herded into a sitting room with a view into the soundproof studio and hard plastic chairs; we were the managers and he the star. A smiling lady handed David a bottle of water. She touched his arm and shoulder way too much before finally leaving him.

"So, we just sit and watch now?" I asked.

Ben, and David through the glass window in the sound room, were busily typing on their phones. There wasn't much of my work I could do on a phone.

Ben nodded. "We do. Today is a little different with the change in topics since last night."

It took a moment for me to remember what he was talking about. Last night and MacCallum and his staffer. Had that only been last night?

My phone buzzed, making me jump, and Ben gave me an odd look. If I was going to be like this all summer and autumn, I'd have no nerves left by election night. Thankfully, it was a text from David.

I glanced up through the glass, curious; he was trying not to smile and staring pointedly not at me.

C-102 D: An Act to Reform Party Finance Transparency. C-87: An Act for Legislative Ethics. Just a co-author on those, so I get to list two at once.

Some of the tension eased up and out in a giggle before I could do anything to stop it. People said laughing eased stress for a reason; it was a release, and David had hit the spot. That really shouldn't surprise me, I guess. When I looked up, he was typing something back, failing at keeping the smile from his face.

Wanted to see you smile this afternoon. Success. We can talk tonight about the two laws listed above.

Deal, I typed back as the two radio DJs entered the little sound studio. I set my phone back in my purse and rubbed my face. I shouldn't have told him I thought that was powerful and sexy. He'd have too much fun with it, although I really didn't think that was a bad thing.

"How long?"

My runaway thoughts lost somewhere in last night pulled back to the room. Ben looked at me expectantly, resigned.

"Sorry, how long what?" I asked.

He sighed and gave me the look he had when he was about to blast an idea out of the water. Patient, but thinking the other person was rather dense.

"How long have you two been happening?" he asked, this time looking towards the interview in full swing.

For a moment, then two, then three, the only sound in our waiting room was the DJ announcing the guest for the afternoon, Centre Party leader David Reid. David thanked them for having him.

I opened my mouth and shut it. Lying wouldn't help.

"How did you know?" I asked, sidestepping his question.

Ben didn't look surprised in the slightest I hadn't denied it. His lips pressed thin for a moment, clearly not happy, before answering. "I've known David since we were ten, through teenage crushes, one-night stands in college, marriage, divorce, and everything in-between. I know how he acts when he's involved with someone new. So how long?"

Hearing the list knocked a bit of my high down. David wasn't my only one, either, but I didn't need it laid out so plainly.

"Just over a month." When I said it out loud, I had to mentally count back. Only a month?

"Really? Nothing before that?" he asked, leaning back and crossing his arms. He eyed me over his glasses, daring me to deny it again.

Ben did this in policy and strategy meetings. He knew the answer to something, or thought he did, and asked questions until others gave it to him. It proved him right without needing to say anything. It was amusing when directed at someone else; now, it was patronizing and annoying.

"We talked for a while," I admitted. "Maybe since March?"

That seemed to be closer to the answer he'd expected. While we had our conversation, the interview in the radio sound room played overhead on speakers, David talking about the news from last night while I discussed our relationship with Ben. It was bizarre and disjointed.

"Since he seems to be going along with it in the middle of an election he's been working towards for over a decade, I'm going to say it's pretty serious for him," Ben said, his face tightened before he turned to me straight-on. "You're not the first party staffer or volunteer who's gone after him, but you are the first to have succeeded. Is it serious for you as well, or is he just a distraction and a story for the future?"

My mouth literally dropped open. I snapped it shut before I looked too dumbfounded. Being accused of using David just for fun took my headache to a steady throb. Last night I'd said I knew what people would probably think. Being hit over the head with it by a friend was a harsher dose of reality.

"You look like you're about to rip my throat out for suggesting it's not serious, so I'll wager it is for you as well."

I unclenched my jaw and glared at him. Some of the accusatory look dropped, replaced with resignation. "Serious," I said. "Does anyone else know?" The idea we'd been far worse at keeping this quiet than we'd thought made me queasy.

"No." He shook his head and smiled. "Kaitlyn would let you know if she did. Jessica…would let both of you know loudly. Just me."

He was right. Kaitlyn would ask if she had an inkling; Jessica would ream into both David and me if she did. We weren't around anyone else enough for them to notice.

"How long have you known?" I asked.

The deep lines on his forehead eased some, making him look less like he was ripping a proposal to shreds and more like a friend again.

"I got suspicious a week or so after the first debate and was fairly certain once we started prep for the second. What just happened here," he said, motioning at my phone and David. "That's obvious, too."

I winced. We'd been sloppy. At the same time, I didn't think we could have done much differently. We always would have ended up together, even if he hadn't called and if I hadn't texted him back. At some point, something would have given and we'd still be here.

"It didn't have anything to do with me coming on the road trip," I said, feeling defensive. The idea Ben might think I was being toted along because of a relationship rankled me and sat almost worse than the suggestion that I was using David.

Ben laughed loudly. "No, it didn't. I pushed just as hard as David did to get you over Danielle. I probably pushed more than him."

My startled look made him laugh harder. "Really?"

"Really. You're stronger, and quite frankly, more enjoyable to work with than she is. Easy choice."

Hmph.

We settled back and listened to the rest of the interview. David did absolutely fine. It was a strong end to the first day, but my thoughts were still in a jumble.

"Does he know you know?" I asked as we walked to the front of the building. It sounded like the start of a bad comedy.

"No."

We got no further in the discussion before David joined us. Conversation shifted to business as we reached the car. This time, I slid in the back after David, figuring if Ben knew, and Peter was driving, there was zero point in me not doing so.

David tripped over his words as I sat on the seat directly next to him, looking alarmed as I leaned my head on his shoulder, grabbing his hand and arm in the process.

"Is everything okay?" he asked me.

There was no move to pull away or look of surprise that a staffer had grabbed his hand and leaned against him, or any attempt to make it look like anything other than what it was. He was startled, but gripped my hand back, interrupting his conversation with Ben.

"He knows," I answered, shrugging. "He's known for a while. And it's been a rough day."

He sighed, giving Ben a look that clearly said they'd talk later, and tightened the hold on my hand. "Yes, it has. This morning was a long time ago." He touched the side of my cheek briefly, a brush, and turned back to his conversation.

*　　*　　*

After the second day, and then the third, and fourth, I felt more settled. Every day was a travel day, but they started to pick up a rhythm: packing in the morning or night, settling into the hotel room, sharing a room with Kaitlyn, getting the remote work flowing with Xavier and the passel of new data interns. From the very first meeting we'd had on this project, Ben flat out said one of David's roles was to determine how much was too much. The assumption was, if he was still running, we'd all run, too.

There was a reason elections were framed in racing terminology. A candidate ran. There were races. An election neared the finish line. David, and Jessica for that matter, were elite runners. I was the couch potato who'd never run and was now asked to keep up for the full marathon. It wasn't pretty.

I was part of the core team, starting with preliminary work for the third debate in a month's time and working daily with communications and PR numbers, but I related more to the interns with us who had started out bright-eyed and eager to change the world and now looked like sleepwalking zombies.

David teased me for having low stamina. The whole thing energized him a ridiculous amount. He wooed and charmed friendly crowds, even the mixed-bag ones. He sold his message, getting even the crankiest audience member to concede he might have a valid point or at least to respect his point. He gained a head of steam and pulled the rest of us along.

We hit the Atlantic coast first. We made our way from city to town, town hall to factory, hospital to university. My favorites were the coastal cities flooded with seaside light. Finding a spot to work in those cities was fun, taking my laptop and finding a not too breezy spot by the sea to sit for a few hours, close enough to taste salt in the air. When all the stops were in the morning or afternoon, we grabbed dinner; David and I commandeered Ben as a chaperone a couple of times. Kaitlyn and I had working cocktail hours together. By the second week, the group of us started to gel tightly and we functioned like a well-oiled machine.

David had been right about two things. For the two glorious weeks we were on the road, the emails and texts stopped. After I'd talked to campaign security the first day, there'd been absolutely nothing. The first few days of threat-free silence seemed ominous. But then a third day, and a fourth, then the full business week had passed, and still nothing. The full two weeks we were away from Ottawa, there wasn't a whisper of a threat or the stalker.

Secondly, David had said we'd still see each other every day, and it really wouldn't be as bad as I'd initially thought. He had been right. And now that Ben knew, it made it a little easier. It was one less person to hide our relationship from.

The first two weeks flew by. Early—and at this stage it was very early—polls suggested a positive trend toward Centre Party candidates among likely voters. It was premature to read too much into it, but it was a good first step.

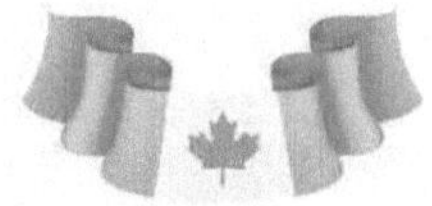

Chapter Nine

Camille and Tom were gone the weekend we were due back in Ottawa for a two-day break; her sister had had a baby and understandably, he was a bigger draw than me. While seeing Camille would be wonderful because part of me wanted a break from campaign talk, staying with David for the weekend was pretty nice, too.

On Thursday night, we arrived back at the same side street we'd left only two and a half weeks earlier. We unloaded quickly, luggage tossed out, and everyone disappeared into cars of spouses or taxis. There wasn't a mass of people to greet us, aside from our normal traveling press, making it easy to disperse. A few reporters waylaid David. He'd given me a spare key so he could take as long as he needed, and I could go home. Mr. Abas stood at the end of the block in a line of cars. He gave me a wave and grabbed my bag for me.

"All right there, Ms. Finnan?" he asked, and hefted it into the trunk.

I nodded sleepily and slid in with a sigh. "Yes. Glad for a day or two off."

He merely smiled and pulled into traffic.

I was looking forward to having our bed, not just a hotel bed. I was looking forward to not wearing dress clothes for two days; I'd wear shorts and a tank top all day. I was looking forward to sleeping in, or at least lying in bed as long as I wanted. And even if he'd be working tomorrow, and I probably would be, too, I was looking forward to having David all to myself for the next couple of days.

"Ms. Finnan, we're going to have a change of plans."

Something about the tenor in his voice made me snap to attention. He was still friendly, but there was an undercurrent of tension now.

"What's wrong?" I asked. It amazed me how fast my heart could go into overdrive. Mine felt like it would leap out of my chest. My legs and arms got a jolt from the first hit of adrenaline.

"We're being followed. Don't look back," he said sharply.

I froze where I was, staring ahead, feeling my neck tingle and itch.

"We have a backup plan, so just do as I say," Mr. Abas said.

I remembered David said Mr. Abas had worked for years as a private security guard. He knew what he was doing.

"I'm going to take you back to your house, okay? We don't want them to know where you're staying. I'll wait in the car to make sure you get in and all is clear inside. I'll be right outside," he added again, as my face went horrified at the thought that all might *not* be clear. "Right outside. You have a back door at your house, yes?"

I nodded stiffly. None of it seemed real.

"Good. You'll wave me off and I will drive around the block and wait for you. Walk around the house so they see you there, and then come out through the back door and straight to my car. Your housemate's out?"

I unstuck my throat and nodded again. "Yes, both she and her husband are gone this weekend."

"Good. Repeat back to me what I outlined."

I heard myself answering, realizing I must have heard him and must know what was going on, but at the same time, I found it baffling it was happening. Someone had waited for me to get back, followed me home, and then what? There were too many terrible scenarios I could imagine, every detail crystal clear and horribly vivid. All of this, the fear, had been gone for two weeks and in a second, it was back in my face suffocating me.

"You're sure someone is really following—?"

"Yes." The answer was quick and definitive.

I wanted to look. The entire back of my neck crawled. I'd love to say I was tough, but I didn't have any idea how to fight someone off; I wasn't strong or particularly speedy. Getting hurt terrified me.

"Call Mr. Reid," Mr. Abas said. "Let him know you'll be just a few minutes late."

He was right. I fumbled for my phone and dialed. We were about five minutes out from Camille's house. Five minutes to think about the fact that someone disliked me enough to hire someone to follow me. I thought that must mean it was someone in Ottawa.

David answered immediately. "Did you have trouble getting in? I'm only a few minutes—"

"Someone's following my car," I blurted out. My voice went hoarse and croaky. The tremor in it was obvious. "We're making a stop at Camille's house before looping back. So they don't know where I'm staying this weekend."

"Are you sure?" He sounded as disbelieving as I felt. "We just got back. There haven't been any texts or emails."

A flurry of panic raced up and down my back. "I know, but Mr. Abas has a plan, and I'll get out and back on my way to yours as soon as I can."

"Charlotte. Shouldn't you call the police? Why are you going to Camille's?"

He had a point.

"Should we call the police?" I asked Mr. Abas.

He shook his head. "Afterwards, yes. I don't want you in there alone longer than you have to be. We're not going to spook him into acting fast."

I agreed with that. The idea of me just sitting in my room with the door locked while I knew someone was outside waiting to come in made me nauseous. The idea of someone rushing in after me was surreal.

"Did you hear that?" I asked David. We were hitting green lights; we were getting close.

"I did. Shit…What's your plan?"

I rehashed it again, this time a little more consciously. I'd go in. Make sure no one was lurking inside. If someone was, Mr. Abas would be right outside. I'd wave him off. I'd make it look like I was home for the weekend. I'd head out the back door, cut across my neighbor's lawn, and back to Mr. Abas' car. He'd drive us to David's. Sounded simple, minus the stalker who would be in a car or van outside the house watching me.

"And if someone's in the house? Or someone comes in the house after the car's gone—"

"Stop it," I snapped and drew a shaky breath. "All of that's gone through my head. I just wanted to let you know I'll be late." *That's all. Just a little late.* "I'm nearly there now."

"Call me as soon as you're in the car again." His voice was strained.

I should have lied about why I was going to be late. Too late to think of that now.

We turned in front of the house. A second jolt of adrenaline made me shaky. "I will. I've got to go. Talk to you in a couple minutes." I hung up before he said anything else as we parked.

Mr. Abas jumped out and got my door for me. I stumbled out, all legs and not a bit of grace. How would I run without falling on my face?

He pulled my little suitcase out and handed it to me.

"Just wave from the front window when you've checked everything, okay?" He gave me a firm handshake and smile, but his eyes were all business and darting behind me. "Wave, wait a minute or two, and come straight out the back."

He let go and left me on my own, standing on the road.

Okay, move. The faster I did it and the smoother I did it, the quicker it'd be over. I grabbed my bag and bumped it up and over the curb to the front door; the wheels clattering over the sidewalk sounded obscenely loud. The door was still locked. Hopefully, that was a good sign. I fumbled with my keys before getting to the right one. *Just go in.*

I stepped in and shut the door behind me, not locking it yet in case Mr. Abas needed to get in. *Be quick. Be thorough.*

I left my bag by the door and made my way through the house. The living room on the left looked clear. Guest bathroom downstairs and hall closet were clear. Who would have thought a bogeyman in the closet could still be real at this age? I wondered if I needed to scream if it would be like a dream where you couldn't actually get it out. Or if I had to run, would it feel like I was wading through sand?

The kitchen in the back, with the door leading to the little backyard, was also clear. I checked the knife block and all were accounted for. That was something. I grabbed one of Camille's heavy cast iron skillets. I'd read somewhere you were more likely to get a knife turned on you than being effective with it. The skillet felt good. It was heavy and reminded me of my kettle bell.

I had to go upstairs next. With downstairs okay, I had a little more confidence. Only two bedrooms and two bathrooms. My bedroom door was partially open, as expected. I kicked it open, banging it hard against the wall. Nothing. My bathroom got the same treatment. A loud bang, but empty. I felt strange going into Camille and Tom's room but slammed my way in regardless. Empty, along with their bathroom.

I let out a shaky breath and headed back downstairs. Stage one done.

Mr. Abas was sitting in the car out front. I waved from the front window. He gave me a nod, pulled a U-turn, and drove off. *Okay.*

I grabbed my bag and dragged it to the back door. I needed to stay here a few minutes. They had to think I was in for the weekend. I locked the front door, flipping the deadbolt into place. My exit had to be fast.

Stilettos wouldn't work in the soft backyard. I kicked them off and took the stairs by two. In my bedroom, I shoved on my old sneakers. On second thought, I lost the pencil skirt and changed into workout shorts. I could haul ass across the lawn easier.

I was about to burst, all jitters and shaking with a barely suppressed scream tickling my throat. I couldn't sit in the house. Besides, I'd been upstairs and downstairs. It looked like I was home. I just had to sneak out.

Before I went back down, I stole a look out my bedroom window. My heart jumped to my throat and I stumbled back, tripping on my bed. There was a van outside. A van that hadn't been there before. It was the kind a college friend had referred to as a rape van, the utility kind with only one side door and no windows. The man sitting in the driver's seat thankfully wasn't looking at my room, but at the downstairs space. It was real. A man downstairs in a van was watching my house, watching for me. I wouldn't survive a kidnapping. I couldn't be kidnapped.

I rushed back downstairs, slung my purse over my shoulder, and grabbed my suitcase. Our backyard wasn't big; our neighbor's wasn't, either. If I headed straight out, he shouldn't see me from the front. I could make it.

I stepped out on the cement patio, locking the door behind me. I hoisted my suitcase up and carried it in front of me, ignoring the handle. *Move fast but not too fast.* If I slipped or fell, it'd be slower.

Escaping ended up being easier than I thought, and far less eventful than I'd imagined. My neighbors peered at me through their back window, probably curious about the odd lady in a silk dress shirt and athletic shorts running with a suitcase.

I saw Mr. Abas' car waiting on the next street and beelined for him. It felt like it took an hour to get across the lawn, but really, it was only a matter of seconds.

Mr. Abas jumped out, opened the trunk, tossed my bag in, and was back in the driver's seat before I could do much. I scampered in and we were off.

"It was a van, wasn't it?" I asked, my voice faint and lightheaded. I couldn't breathe. The clock in the car showed the whole thing had only taken ten minutes. "A dark blue van?"

He gave me a curt nod. His eyes were checking mirrors, clearly focused on making sure the van stayed in front of the house and didn't follow us. His driving was different, too: faster, more aggressive through the rush hour traffic. I sent David a quick text saying I was okay and on the way.

Thankfully, the ride back home was completely uneventful. I peeked over my shoulder every minute or so, but there was nothing. What if I had just gotten a taxi? I never would have noticed being followed, never would have thought to check out the windows, never would have been ready for someone to break into the house. Everything could have ended differently. It terrified me.

Mr. Abas handed back a card. It had the van and driver description, and a license plate number. I called the police.

They promised to look into it right away and ring me back, and also agreed staying with a friend tonight was a much better idea than staying by myself.

We pulled up in front of David's building as I ended the call.

"All clear?" I asked as I stepped out. I felt invisible eyes I knew weren't there pressing into me, right between my shoulder blades at the base of my neck. I glanced around; people were going about their business. Nothing was out of the ordinary.

"All clear," he confirmed, and handed me my suitcase. "Now you go inside and take care. Call me if you need a ride or anything." He gave my hand a pat and went to leave.

"Thank you. I—" I'd be dead or in a rape van without him. "Thank you," I repeated.

He waved me off. "You're welcome. Have a good weekend."

He waited until I was in the building and past security before pulling away. It was all incredibly normal, like nothing had happened. The only change was when I reached David's door, there was an additional security person who wanted to check my name and ID. I barely opened my purse before the door swung open.

"She's fine," David said brusquely and picked up my bag. "Come in."

When the door clicked shut, I collapsed against the wall, slumping to the floor. My legs went to jelly. This was apparently the point when the adrenaline left me a pile of limbs and nothing more.

David dropped my bag with a clatter.

"You're okay," he said and sat down next to me, up against the door, wrapping his arms tight around my shoulders. "It's safe here. You're okay."

"I know." My voice was still shaky. "I know. My legs are all wobbly." I smiled, also a little wobbly. "I probably need to call Camille."

He nodded. "You probably do." He turned my head towards him and held his hand there, cupping my cheek. His eyes were scared. "Call her and…"

I leaned against his hand and sighed. "Camille, and then dinner?"

He swallowed and gave a single nod. "Okay. And welcome back."

I leaned forward and kissed him. It was okay. I was where I wanted to be tonight. I wasn't dead. And the police had something to search for. It'd been too long since we had been alone.

"Can I call from out here?" I asked. I really didn't want to be in a room by myself at the moment.

"Of course; I'll keep banging pots to a minimum. Come on." He stood and pulled me up. "They might be able to find him right away, and that will be the end of it."

It was a nice thought, but I suspected that wouldn't be the case.

*   *   *

Camille was horrified when I called her. For all of her hesitancy around anything to do with David and me, she pushed hard for me to stay glued to him and his security. As I sat on the couch with my knees tucked under my chin after dinner, David next to me with a firm grip around my shoulders, I had to agree this was much better. He'd barely left my side.

"I'm afraid to meet Eric for dinner tomorrow," I chattered out loud. I couldn't stop shaking. Cousin Eric and his family were in town, and while I loved to see them, the image of the van sitting outside my window made me want to lock the door and not go outside ever again.

"Ahh." David sounded like that solved a puzzle for him and squeezed my shoulder. "Jess asked me to join her for a meal tomorrow night, saying family was in town. I didn't peg it as the same thing until you just said it."

I craned my neck around to glare at him. "You didn't say you had date night with Jessica planned."

I got a barely tolerant look. "No. I said no, but…I could say yes. You get dinner, plus security, and I get dinner plus you."

It was a neat and tidy solution to the problem. "You'd want to go out for dinner?" I asked, a bit skeptical. "Not that I don't want you to come along, but I thought you were looking forward to getting away from Jessica for a bit?"

"Well, yes. But she's also very different and more relaxed outside of work. And you'll be there, and you said Eric is friendly. So, yes?" he asked, and started kissing the back of my neck. "Please?"

His five o'clock shadow tickled and scratched along the side of my neck. I squirmed away and started laughing. "Okay. Yes."

He stopped and tugged me back over. "Sounds like a date."

I rolled my eyes. "Date night with two cousins, cousin's wife, and my little three-year-old cousin."

"Date night," he repeated, sounding very happy about it.

*   *   *

I had the place to myself the next day. David stayed in bed so long he was nearly late for his meetings in the morning. I did nothing to encourage him to get going, which was a fail on both of our parts. I spent part of the day being useful and doing laundry, and then the rest hiding in the study. There was still extra security stationed outside the door and building security had been alerted as well. It wasn't enough to me. A police officer had called back and said while they were able to find the van, reported stolen earlier in the week, any signs of the driver had been wiped clean.

David and I agreed I would get to the restaurant first. He'd come straight from work so I'd meet him and Jessica there. When I arrived, I'd text him so he'd know I had made it. Mr. Abas agreed to wait outside until David arrived as well. We were covered.

I wanted to wear a sundress, but in the past when I'd seen Henry I'd turned into his personal jungle gym. A flimsy sundress would not hold up well against a climbing three-year-old, so I opted for a more practical fitted T-shirt and shorter skirt. I made an effort with my hair and make-up, figuring if David really thought of this as a date night, I could treat it like one as well. I ditched my glasses for contacts; glasses were just trouble with a toddler.

Getting to the restaurant was completely routine. Mr. Abas picked me up and dropped me off, and no one followed. No one tried to grab me as I walked the few steps from the car to the entrance. The ordinariness of it all made me shiver. There was nothing ordinary about someone waiting outside my house to kidnap me. The normalcy was a façade.

The hostess directed me towards a back private room. There was one door in and a single high row of windows letting in the evening sun. Only one door for the security folks to watch and easy to keep curious people away. The main dining room hummed with people, so any conversation we had would be muffled and hidden.

"Auntie Shawo-lit!" Henry spotted me, slithered out of his mom's grasp, and toddled full steam at my knees.

"Hey there, shorty." I leaned over and scooped him up before he tried climbing a leg. He was a solid little kid and could have taken me out if he'd hit my knees right. "And hi to you two," I said to his parents. I smiled over Henry's blond mop and took the seat next to Eric's wife, Melissa. Henry squirmed and grabbed at his toy train sitting on the edge of the table, shoving it at my face. Clearly, that was the main draw of the evening.

Eric came by and gave me a half hug over my shoulders, tickling Henry in the process. "Glad you could make it. Jessica said she and her mystery guest will be here soon."

I frowned uneasily. "She didn't tell you who?" Springing a high-level politician on a relaxed family meal didn't seem wise.

He shook his head.

Before I got a chance to give them a heads up, Jessica and David breezed in. Jessica gave me a double take; clearly Eric hadn't mentioned I would be here. Sibling communication was not their strong suit. Eric and Melissa gawked.

"Can you go say hi to Aunt Jessica?" I asked Henry as I pointed her out, getting him to pause in yabbering about trains. Jessica hadn't gone for a Henry-proof outfit and was dressed up in a strappy sundress that made the most of her curves with heels, turning from business to night out. She was quite pretty when she wasn't running us ragged.

David had made an attempt at casual, at least for him, losing the suit coat and tie, shirtsleeves rolled up. He'd even unbuttoned his shirt a little.

Henry shook his head at my question and latched onto my arm. "No."

My natural instinct was to jump in and introduce David; it should be me since he was my significant other and was meeting my family. But I couldn't.

For appearances, David was Jessica's guest. It would have been strange for me to barge in and take over.

Jessica recovered from the initial surprise of me being there and played hostess beautifully, smiling and nudging David forward, introducing Eric and his family. I kept Henry occupied. Everyone else was standing, trying to make polite, awkward conversation. Henry stayed firmly on my lap and tried to converse with me, patting my head and destroying my earlier attempt at making my hair look nice. I smiled at Jessica and David.

"Wasn't expecting to see you tonight," I said to David.

They moved to sit down, David motioning Jessica to sit next to Eric and taking the seat next to me. Henry eyed him suspiciously.

"Jess invited me. A night out with family and friends sounded appealing."

Conversation halted when the waitress came to get drink orders. It felt like an awkward dinner party. A lot of the tension was between Eric and Jessica; I knew she should have said something about David coming. Eric should have said something about me, too.

"How was your dad's birthday last weekend?" I asked Eric, trying to get the conversation going.

It thankfully worked, although it left David at a bit of a loss. I crept my leg under the table and nudged him partway through Eric and Melissa's retelling of the event, getting a smile. Henry squirmed with excitement when he heard the word "presents" and mention of his name, and I needed to hand him back. Besides, trying to balance a wiggling toddler on my lap, plus a martini glass wasn't going to work.

"Too bad it didn't line up with your off weekend," Eric ended, looking at Jessica.

She rolled her eyes with a huff. "Dad understood," she said dismissively. "And I did call. We've been so busy with the campaign it just didn't work. We had back-to-back—"

"Jess," David interrupted, smiling. "Let's not talk campaign tonight. We can have a night off."

I expected her to look annoyed; talking campaign made Jessica giddy. Instead, she nodded back. She was apparently in a good mood tonight.

"You two met in college, right?" Melissa asked, looking between David and Jessica.

Jessica stopped making faces at Henry and beamed. "What was it, nearly twenty years ago now?" she asked David.

"About right. We were both involved in campus campaign activities," he said, sipping his beer, lost somewhere in the past. "Quite a long time ago now."

"That makes us sound very old…you would have been what, twelve years old, Eric? And you would have been eight, Charlotte. Guess we're the two dinosaurs at dinner." Jessica laughed.

I paused in sipping my martini. It hadn't been deliberate, but I didn't appreciate her pointing that out. I didn't need to look over to my left to know David wasn't pleased, either. Our ages worried him more than me.

"We would have been a little young to be involved in politics." I smiled tightly and took a heftier sip from my glass than I planned. It didn't matter now.

Eric laughed. "We had more important things to do. Remember that sled jump we made at Grandma and Grandpa's?" And he was off, retelling how we'd built a large jump on a sledding hill. I'd flown through the air because I was too small and landed squarely on my head. We'd tried to hide the noticeable lump on my head and likely concussion so we could continue on the next day. Jessica had been away at college and never took part in our winter escapades.

David asked if we'd spent a lot of time together growing up, which led to Eric launching into the many misfortunes he'd gotten me into when we were growing up, from throwing worms at me on fishing trips to wandering through brambles berry picking.

Once Eric and Melissa were used to David as David, not the candidate, they relaxed and things started to go better. Conversation flowed and we had a good time. The only downside was remembering David and I were not there together. I caught myself a couple of times about to reach over and try a sip of his beer or getting too casual with him.

A couple times, he moved to rest an arm across the back of my seat, turning it into a stretch. At work, we were overly cautious about being familiar around each other; here, when we were both relaxed, we were slipping.

"So, what do you high-powered political folks do on your days off?" Eric asked.

Jessica laughed. "No days off. I was going to see if we could meet tomorrow?" she asked David.

"No." David answered the question fast and firm. "Working as well, but at home. Sorry," he added, looking at the slightly taken-aback Jessica. "I'll be holed up in my study. What about you, Charlotte? Any plans?"

I grinned at him, probably more directly than I should have. "Nothing firm, but—"

Any other thoughts of Saturday plans were blown out of my head by a sharp, echoing metallic bang.

I jumped, dropping my fork and nearly falling out of my chair. It sounded like a gunshot. In half a second, I imagined someone barging into the room, pointing a gun at me, and shooting. I didn't know if I'd duck and cover or run.

"Someone dropped a chair," David said, sounding startled as well. His hand had landed on my shoulder as I jumped, whether to calm me down or shove me under the table, I couldn't tell. His face was pale. He gave my shoulder a little squeeze before letting go. "It's okay."

Henry laughed at me, along with the rest of the table.

I gave a shaky grin and shrugged. "Guess I do need a break. Just a bit wound up." I laughed along, but a little of my good mood had evaporated. I was more paranoid than I'd realized.

My knee got nudged under the table, followed by a hand. I slid mine under and grabbed David's, not caring if anyone saw. Jessica, Eric, and Melissa were talking about some mutual friend they'd all had growing up. No one noticed.

"Okay?" David asked again, this time a little quieter.

I nodded and squeezed his hand before letting go. "Okay," I lied.

*   *   *

The weekend passed too fast. David worked most of Saturday; I spent the day in the study with him, not wanting to be in a room by myself if I didn't have to. Our suitcases were repacked and refreshed.

I never said it to David, but I was scared of heading out again. Being home made me feel safe. Having David around all the time, being six stories up, having the one entrance for security to watch made me less stressed; choices and freedom were good, but sometimes being confined to one area—a safe space—was better.

Monday, for our Canada Day stop, we'd be at a fair. It was supposed to be fun, but it'd be so wide open. There was no way the entire crowd could be monitored. Grabbing me would be easy. Any scream would be swallowed in the noise of happy fair-goers.

*   *   *

Over the next few weeks, there was nothing, no sign or hint of me being in danger. We left Ottawa without a hitch. There were no unpleasant encounters with Mike. Danielle didn't make a scene before I left. It was all business as usual.

We had half a day off in Saskatoon for Canada Day; David went to a pancake breakfast in the morning, then did a whole lot of hand-shaking and baby-kissing at the event. Kaitlyn and I spent the afternoon weaving through the music stages set up for concerts, finding a table and enjoying a drink or two while listening to music.

Sitting with my legs stretched out, feeling the sun on my face, the air hot and heavy with humidity, funnel cakes, and dust, it was almost a perfect afternoon, but I scanned the crowd nonstop, petrified to let Kaitlyn out of my sight. I wasn't alone the entire day. I was careful to the point of exhaustion.

Ben and Jessica joined us in the afternoon. Towards evening, when newscasts and press conferences finished and we'd moved back toward our firework viewing area, David joined us, settling into the seat next to me. The cloudless day turned his skin bronze. With one of Kaitlyn's margaritas in hand, wearing shorts and a polo shirt, he was picture perfect summer relaxed. The sunset bloomed across the prairie sky, a peach and raspberry explosion. Fireworks lit up the night after dark, the booms shaking the air in red and white glitter.

The margaritas made David and I reckless. That night was the only one during the campaign I snuck into his hotel room. Thankfully, we weren't caught.

There was nothing to be afraid of.

*   *   *

It started a trend.

David killed his events. They were every bit as successful as I'd thought they'd be all those months ago. Our voter base turned out in predictable droves, but the undecideds, the curious voters, came out, too. The more places we visited and the more data I fed into my model, the larger our crowds grew. The initial positive trend in support gained steam and our numbers started pulling away in every poll. Public opinion at our stops leaned toward Centre Party candidates with regularity and showed David as the preferred prime minister.

My job role shifted for the next three weeks. The final debate David would participate in was coming up. In addition to the normal prep, I also needed to practice it in French, as the debate was in Quebec City. One of the social media interns was from Montreal, so I spent a considerable amount of time sitting with him in whatever spare classroom or office or park bench we found, brushing up on the language. It'd been a while since I used it; I wasn't sure how well I'd be able to debate. The prepared retorts, at least, wouldn't be a problem.

Five days before the debate group flew back east to Quebec, David stormed into the classroom where my French buddy and I were working. Both Marc and I looked up, startled; I was proud I hadn't overreacted too much.

David's jaw was clenched, his face red. "Charlotte, a word." He didn't bother saying anything else before walking out.

Marc gave me a sympathetic look and shrugged. "We can finish later."

I nodded and gathered up my laptop and bag.

David waited outside the door; everything, from the rigid way he stood to the sharp glint of his eyes, was hard. "What—?"

He shook his head and strode off down the high school corridor towards an empty room; later that evening he'd give a speech on STEM education. Now though, his mind was clearly elsewhere.

It couldn't be personal; if something were wrong with us, he wouldn't pull me from a meeting. Professionally, there hadn't been any mistakes. I hadn't missed a deadline. All the analysis I provided was accurate…unless Danielle had gotten a hold of something without me noticing. Or maybe something deep, dark, and horrible had crawled out from David's past and I was about to be hit with it.

When we turned into the empty room and shut the door, I looked at him closer. He was worried, not angry.

"Have you gotten any more texts or emails recently?" he asked.

The question wasn't at all what I expected. It took a moment for me to shift my thinking.

"No, nothing since the van…" There was no need for me to add in "that was going to kidnap me." We both knew that. The way he was acting made me nervous. "You know I would have told you if something— David, what happened?"

Tension eased from his face. "The meeting I just had with Mike." He ran his hand over his head, a flare of anger still there.

He shook his head, seemingly to himself, before grabbing my arm and pulling me close. His arms came up hard around me, not so much a hug as a confirmation that I was solid and here and okay. It did nothing to make me feel better, though.

"He stepped far beyond the line of appropriate comments," he explained, letting go and taking a step back. "He left a lot unsaid, but it wasn't hard to read between the lines and know what he was suggesting. I snapped."

Maybe it was because David had never had to deal with catcalls or unwanted innuendo, but I was oddly calm once I knew what he was worked up about. I didn't need to know exactly what had been said, but it wasn't hard to guess. Mike wanted one thing; I wasn't a co-worker, I was a trophy for him to win. He'd probably made some crack to David about traveling with me.

"I've heard it before. It's not—"

"Do not say it's not a big deal," he said, spitting the words out. "I've gotten where I am partially because I'm good at reading people. I wanted to make sure you hadn't received anything else."

I shook my head. "No. How confident are you? Enough that I should take this to the police?" I didn't like Mike. He was a misogynistic pig. But I wasn't about to report him to the police and start that circus unless I was 100% sure. There were pieces that didn't point toward him.

"I don't have proof," he said, and looked torn. "Just… We were lazy before when we were away from home and you almost got… Let's be more careful. What he said, plus me threatening to have him fired, it makes me uneasy."

I paused, curious about what Mike had said, but not enough to ask. David was right. When we were away from Ottawa, the texts and threats stopped. Being on constant edge was hard, though. I didn't sleep. I didn't work well. But I didn't like the alternative. I wouldn't always see the van before it was too late.

"I'll shadow you the next few days, like you really have a choice," I added, smiling a bit. With three days of debate prep to go, he'd be hard pressed to get rid of me. "And then we'll work it out?"

"We will." He came forward and kissed me. "Sorry if I scared you. I love you, and I am worried."

His words hung there for a moment, evaporating some of the earlier gloom. It seemed strange it was the first time either of us had said the words out loud.

"I love you, too." I squeezed his hand as we headed towards the door. "You were right to tell me. We'll be careful," I repeated, wishing rather than believing it'd be enough.

Chapter Ten

Over the next few days, I made a more concerted effort at being careful. If I needed to go out anywhere, I made sure someone went with me. In my emails to everyone, figuring I could be wrong suspecting Danielle or Mike, I was overly polite and not as blunt as normal; I overlooked a few things I knew weren't neat or as concise as they could have been in the spirit of not ruffling feathers. I stayed closer to David than I probably should have.

There'd been nothing to indicate I needed to be on edge, but I lost sleep again listening to every bump and twitch in the hotels we stayed. Those around me started taking the brunt of my stress. It made me feel awful.

A small group of us, plus the traveling press, flew to Montreal for a few days before arriving in Quebec City for the debate. Our bus was back to ferry us between the cities. We all worked closely, so David was nearby all the time. He showed up in meetings where he wasn't needed. Most times, it was fine. He had a tendency, though, to get involved in discussions, sidetracking the conversation and wanting to know all the details about everything.

By the last day in Montreal, the day before the debate, Jessica barely batted an eye when David tagged along with us on a touch base meeting. I wondered how long it'd be before people noticed he only jumped in on my meetings.

"Where would you like to discuss the model updates?" Jessica asked, glancing back at David, annoyed he had interrupted again. "We could go for a walk outside?"

I looked outside at the campus and the beautiful summer day, the sun starting to creep up; really, it was a no-brainer.

"Let's go outside," I said, smiling. The sun was shining and the final debate practice had gone well, so really, I couldn't think of why I'd want to stay cooped up inside.

Jessica nodded and led the way.

Our walk took us across the campus and around half the edge of a park. The security detail kept most curious bystanders away. Granted, it was summer, so the number of students was minimal. There weren't many people wandering around this early on a weekend.

The purpose of the meeting was to go over campaign stop suggestions based on the last few weeks of data. What it ended up being was Jessica and David walking ahead of me, deep in conversation; for being cranky at the start about the extra company, Jessica switched gears rapidly.

The sidewalk wasn't wide enough for me to join them without shoving one of us onto the grass or blocking the whole path. I could hear them talking, but the topic veered from what I'd wanted to discuss to fundraising activities, which was not my area of expertise.

I shouldn't have been thinking about the next time we'd be in Ottawa and what I wanted to discuss with Xavier or how nice it'd be to meet up with Camille, or about dinner with my parents when they visited. The weather and the good feeling about the final debate lured me into a state of complacency.

The runner had no problem stepping around Jessica and David. They both hugged the curb just fine.

I stepped off to the side, as I should, and thought nothing more of it.

The runner didn't run straight. He ran at me.

Before I could mentally curse myself, yell, or do anything, I was shoved down and knocked into the road. There was traffic this time, and I was all too aware of a truck barreling down the road at me.

It's remarkable how fast the human mind can work. Time slowed in that second. I heard the truck coming behind me. I had to roll left. No matter what I hit or what I bruised or hurt, I had to roll left. If I stayed right, the truck would hit me.

My tailbone hit the pavement first, then my head. Hot diesel fumes brushed my face, a horn blared too close to my head before two hands grabbed my arms, yanking me back onto the sidewalk.

It seemed silly how earlier in the day I'd thought it was warm. Now I couldn't stop shivering. My butt throbbed, and so did my leg and my arm.

I squinted down at my leg, but someone blocked my view—a lot of someones. I tried to move so I could see my leg, but someone gripped my shoulder tightly, so I stopped moving. My attention focused on the person holding me still and I frowned. Why did David look so pale?

"Charlotte, are you okay?"

It sounded like he'd asked me already, and I wondered if he had. I tried to nod, but something was pressing on my head.

David barked out orders at the security detail hovering over us.

Security guy shook his head; he couldn't go after the person who had hit me. He had to stay with David.

"Have some water." Jessica knelt down and handed me a bottle. She was shaky, too. Seeing your cousin go flying might be a bit of a jolt.

I took a sip and tried to pull myself together. It was harder than I expected. My thoughts landed coherently for a moment and then scattered like butterflies. Concussed. That was the word.

"I'm fine," I heard myself say, and forced a smile. David needed to back away. He was too concerned. "I should probably go back to the bus." That seemed sensible.

I was held down firmly by David, who didn't let me budge. "You hit your head hard and you are bleeding. Paramedics are on the way."

He shifted slightly, and I saw my right leg was scraped up along the side. It was red and angry but not bleeding. Road rash. There were other people milling around. Maybe one was a truck driver? David held something on my head.

I didn't remember getting to the grass. "My head hurts."

"You're bleeding all over the place," Jessica said, sounding stunned.

I reached up to where David's hand was. My hand came back red and sticky, blood seeping into the whorls of my fingerprints. "I've got it," I said, and replaced his hand with mine. He had to back away. "How'd I get here?"

Thankfully, David got up, borrowing a bit of my water to rinse his hands off; the water ran off red and made me queasy. The worry stayed on his face. I needed to look and sound less pathetic, but I wasn't sure how.

"You didn't get out of the way for a runner," Jessica said. "They couldn't get around and bumped into you."

I frowned but stayed quiet; I was pretty sure I had been well out of their way and it had been deliberate to run into me. That I remembered. Warning number two. If shoving me into the path of an oncoming truck was just a warning…

"Marcus," David continued the story, indicating the security man, "saw you fall and pulled you back. The truck driver, Dane, had swerved and probably would have missed you."

I smiled at both Marcus and Dane, but it wasn't convincing. *Probably would have missed me.* If Marcus hadn't been there to pull me away, I'd be in much rougher condition. And if this really looked like an accident, Marcus wouldn't be as twitchy as he was. He thought it had been deliberate.

David knelt back down and checked the back of my head again, carefully peeling the wad of cloth away. What used to be his fancy pocket square for his suit was destroyed and soaked in blood.

My butt hurt. My head hurt. Everything hurt.

"I can hear the paramedics coming," Jessica said. "I assume you won't be joining us for the rest of the meeting, Charlotte?"

I couldn't tell if she was joking or not. "I'd say that's a safe bet. I don't think the police and medics were necessary."

At least it wasn't a full ambulance. I touched the back of my head again gingerly; it tingled and stung. The amount of fuss being made over me was silly. "You two can get going. I'll head back to the bus."

In retrospect, driving to Quebec City after the event tonight rather than doing it tomorrow morning would be awful; there was nowhere for me to lie down for the afternoon. My butt and lower back and head weren't going to like that. How would I sleep?

"The paramedics will help get you all set up," Jessica said, and handed me back the water bottle. "You should be patched up in no time. Call me if you need anything, okay?" She gave me a smile and squeezed my hand.

"Shall we?" She turned to David and motioned back towards the walk. "I think we should—"

David stopped short. He was livid. "Jesus Christ, Jess… Your cousin's bleeding on the sidewalk and you want us to just leave? Cancel the meetings we had. I'll talk to the police. Charlotte, take as long as you need and we'll go back with you." He shot Jessica one more disbelieving glare before handing me over to the paramedics.

"You really don't need to wait for me—" I started, but got glared at, too. I shrugged apologetically at Jessica.

Jessica looked taken aback by David's response but nodded. "Sorry. Clearly, I wasn't thinking. My brain's shot." She gave me an equally apologetic look and started the schedule adjustments.

The paramedics took their time assessing my head and gently probing my lower back and tailbone, which was very awkward in public. The disinfectant squirted on my head made me yelp and my eyes water but was better than having road grit embedded in my head. Apparently, a number of small scrapes had caused all the blood, nothing major. They diagnosed me with a mild concussion, advised me to rest a lot and take it easy the next few days, with a generic painkiller as needed. It was much ado about not much. They probably could have continued on with the meeting without me.

David talked to the police. I was grateful he'd handled that part, even though I knew perfectly well it wasn't normal for the candidate to do this much for a party staff member. I didn't remember anything of any use, and I wasn't sure I could handle a coherent conversation in French right now. English thoughts were challenging enough at the moment.

I noticed a line of cameras across the road. There was a crowd of gawkers nearby. The scene would be all over the news.

The police talked with me briefly, but there wasn't much for me to tell them. No, I hadn't seen him. No, I didn't remember what he'd looked like. It was a lot of no's. The officers were nice and offered us a ride back to the bus. All I wanted to do was sleep.

"Actually, could you drop me off at a hotel?" I asked. If I had to pay for one day extra myself, so be it. I couldn't sit on the bus. I needed to stretch out on my stomach on a bed.

"Why are you going to a hotel?" David asked, opening the door for Jessica. It'd be a cozy ride with the police driver and Marcus up front, and the three of us sandwiched in the back.

"I need to lay flat." I winced as I lowered down to the seat.

David volunteered to take the middle in a very gallant gesture; Jessica had a skirt on and my butt wasn't okay riding on the middle lump seat.

"I'll pay good money for a bed right now," I said.

David shook his head. "Just the bus," he directed, and we took off. "You can use my bed. We'll be out all afternoon. There's no reason for you to pay for a hotel."

He didn't give me a chance to protest, just turned to Jessica and resumed fundraising discussions.

I was okay with that option. Once the shock started to wear off, the full enormity of it hit me. I didn't want to stay in a hotel by myself. I didn't want to be anywhere by myself. A panic bubble rose in my chest, choking off my lungs. I liked knowing what would happen next, confident A led to B or that C caused D. I had no idea what to expect from this person because I was running in the dark. The next time— and I had no doubt there'd be a next time—I would be kidnapped or killed. Unless I left.

I managed a shallow breath and let it out slowly. I was shaking again, this time from anxiety. It was enough to get David to glance at me.

He shifted, moving so his leg pressed against mine and his arm was more firmly against me. I couldn't have him worrying about me. He needed to be focusing on the campaign and stops and policy and nothing else.

Panic started to rise in me again. I closed my eyes and matched my breathing to his. Slow and even.

When the car stopped, we thanked the policeman for driving us back. The bus was nearly empty, like David had said it would be; most of the group was meeting with local volunteers this morning.

The only person in at the moment was Ben, who looked shocked when he saw me. "What happened?"

David nodded at Jessica to give him the rundown while he escorted me to the teeny bedroom. David opened the door to a cramped space, a twin bed and a table. I wasn't sure if it was the leftover adrenaline finally wearing away, if I'd finally realized this person really wanted me dead, or that the room smelled like home and David, but I started to cry, little tears leaking from my eyes.

David stepped in, out of sight of Jessica, and pulled me hard against him.

I rested my face against his neck, taking a couple of deep breaths to try and calm myself down. Neither one of us said anything.

"Sleep here," he whispered, and let go. "Sleep, and I'll make sure someone checks in on you for the concussion."

I wiped my eyes with the back of my hand and nodded. "I don't think… I think I have to leave." My voice shook.

He gave me one very brief kiss. "No decisions yet. We'll talk it through later." And with that, he stepped out and shut the door.

I slept awkwardly on my stomach for most of the day, getting woken up by different people at different times, all making sure I wasn't dead and my pupils weren't doing anything weird.

Kaitlyn helped me change from the dress clothes I'd been sleeping in to yoga pants and a T-shirt. Ben brought me soup, saying it was the only thing his kid could keep down when he'd had a concussion from hockey. Jessica stopped in to apologize again for sounding like an insensitive moron earlier and hovered in a mother hen-like way, offering to call my parents for me if I wasn't up to it. It was kind of sweet and made my decision that much more painful. Everyone was willing to help me, and I'd do the same for them. Except someone had ruined it.

Later in the evening, David came in to see me. "There will be two security guards here while we're out," he said. "One outside and one inside."

I rolled myself into a sitting position, squinting against the pain radiating from the base of my skull and butt. There was no way to sugarcoat it. "I'm going to leave," I blurted out before I changed my mind. "It's probably for the best, for me and you."

He looked so handsome in his suit, solid black with a white shirt, but just like that, the confident dinner-event face dropped, replaced with surprise. "Leaving the campaign or us?"

"Campaign," I clarified. "My job." It never occurred to me in my fuzzy concussed state he might not have been interested in a long-distance relationship. If he didn't think we were ready for one, I might have ruined it. "We can do long-distance for a little while, right? Just a few months?"

"Yes," he started and stopped saying something before nodding. "Stuck together, remember?"

My smile wavered. "Go do your thing. Chase me out of here when needed."

He didn't look okay. Heading into dinner tonight and the final debate tomorrow, he needed to be at his charismatic best. I reached over and grabbed his hand. I tried to think of something witty or encouraging to say, but I had nothing.

He squeezed mine and stepped away.

I lay back down on my stomach and grabbed my phone. Saying I'd leave was one thing; typing in the response was another. The idea of moving across the country with no guarantee any of it would stop filled my chest with so much fear it was hard to breathe. Both options had the possible outcome of me dead. But the fight instinct I had since this had all started was gone, scattered into smithereens when I had landed on the road. Moving and running away scraped against every one of my normal instincts, but normal was long gone and the flight instinct grew. I just wanted it to stop.

I batted the idea around for over an hour. Pros and cons organized themselves into lists. The cons list was long. But I thought I was right. I'd end up dead if I stayed here. The added security strain, plus worrying about where I was, would end up distracting David. Being by myself terrified me but staying low and covering my tracks might work for a few months. I needed to give the election time to finish before I slipped back. I responded to the last text message.

How do I know this will stop if I leave?

Asking felt pointless. I knew there were no guarantees. Three months seemed like an eternity to hide by myself. My phone lit up right away; clearly, they had nothing else to do tonight.

You won't hear from me again if you leave. Erase yourself.

A shiver rippled down my spine; I knew what they meant, but it sounded far more ominous than I liked. Erase myself. Moving across the country where no one knew me or my address. Gone.

Okay.

A piece of me died when I sent it. It felt like an idiot move on my part. There was safety in numbers and being part of a herd; I was making myself the sickly antelope who dropped back and became easy prey for the lion. Unless the lion didn't see where I went.

Give notice tomorrow. Relocate to Alberta and this will stop.

Being immobile and somewhat stuck on my stomach made it hard to get appropriately angry. I didn't like having my hand forced, but if the police couldn't do anything, and as the lump on the back of my head demonstrated, this person was serious about removing me. I didn't know what other choice I had.

Alberta it is.

I threw my phone down. It was only for a few months. I'd quit tomorrow and after the election, I would move back. The campaign would be done, and they'd have no reason to care where I was.

* * *

I was asleep when the door opened. A scream started up in my throat before I remembered where I was, why the door might be opening, and who'd likely open the door.

"It's just me," David whispered.

I heard other people on the bus.

"What time is it?" I mumbled and tried to sit up. Rather than making me feel more awake, the position shift caused bile to rush up. I lay back down and focused on not moving. I couldn't shake the taste or smell of blood yet... There'd been so much on my head.

David didn't turn on the light, but I saw his silhouette taking off the suit coat and tie. They were done for the night.

"Eleven," he answered. "We've got a few hours to the hotel." He hesitated for a second before turning back to me. "How are you?"

I rolled over on my side, wincing, but it kept the nausea at bay.

"Painfully honest or overly polite answer?" I asked, trying to smile. The bus gave a grumble and lurch as we started towards Quebec City.

"Painfully blunt, please."

A few flimsy walls partitioned a bus full of people from us. Starting tomorrow, I'd start searching for a new job and somewhere to live because I was moving in two weeks. It made me want to scream.

"I want to stay with you tonight." It slipped out. Out of everything, that was how I was. "I want you next to me tonight because I'm scared and hurt, and I want a few hours of feeling like I'm home. But," I added before he interrupted or I made either one of us feel any worse, then reached for his hand and got a death grip back. "I know I can't. I want to stay with this job and everyone and finish it off to election night, but apparently, that's not an option anymore. I don't want to move to Alberta and leave my family and friends and be by myself again. What if I step across some imaginary line and it starts up again? What if this happens again and I'm hours away and by myself? I can't..."

The panic bubble rose in my chest again. I hated the suspicious, paranoid person I'd become. "I'm terrified this won't stop and I'll have made myself an easy target because I'm alone. What if—?" The words choked and froze in my throat.

"Charlotte." David cut in and knelt down next to me, checking the door again quickly. "Breathe, sweetheart." He rubbed my back, realizing I was about to have a panic attack. His head rested against mine for a moment, letting me take a few breaths with him until we fell in sync.

"Whether you stay here or move, I love you and you're absolutely not in this alone. And you know you only need to say it and I will stay with you tonight. I will lay down with you right now and hold you all night if you want, the rest of the bus be damned, if you ask."

And even though that was exactly what I wanted, I couldn't bring myself to form the words. I kissed him, but shook my head no.

"I'll be better in the morning." I wasn't sure how, but I would be. "You're not risking this whole campaign because I need a hug." As I said it, some of my common sense came back. "Three months of laying low and then I'll be back—after the election."

He kissed my forehead, sighing before he pulled away. I knew he wanted us to go public, and despite trying to play it calm, wanted to stay with me tonight. We couldn't yet, though.

"You are stubborn and I love you." He rested his head against my forehead for a second before getting up. "We'll get you to a bed soon." And he walked out.

*   *   *

The next day was terrible. From arriving at the hotel in the middle of the night and David waking me up, insisting on helping get me into the room himself, to giving Jessica my two weeks' notice bright and early the next morning, to last-minute job searching to see what was available—it made my head spin. The last thing I wanted to do was move away, but I was terrified the stalker would take that as me backing out of the deal. And of course I couldn't live with Camille again or move back to my parents'. The thought of me bringing the threat to them made me sick. The headache from the concussion and the lack of sleep didn't help.

The afternoon spiraled down as I sat in on the last pre-debate meeting. Whether or not I was able to contribute, the headache and still-blurry thoughts made it difficult. It wasn't much of a meeting, just a final check nothing had changed. I commented having the seats behind stage would be welcome tonight, as I wasn't sure standing for nearly two hours was a good idea.

"You're not going to the debate tonight." David barely glanced up from typing on his laptop as he said it.

The others in the room looked between us warily.

I was just as confused, even more so than I'd been most of the day.

"Did my pass get revoked already?" I asked Jessica since she'd know that more than David. That'd be faster than I'd expected.

She shrugged. "No, it's valid."

Clearly, I wasn't the only one confused.

"It'll be crowded, noisy, and hot, as you well know," said David. He hit a key with more force than necessary and looked up. "After yesterday…you're not going tonight. That's not what you need."

I wished I could think sharper and faster. He was going all bossy protective boyfriend on me in a setting where it was unacceptable. I'd be annoyed if he said this in private, let alone at work.

"I think I've got a good grip on what I need," I said carefully. This wasn't a conversation I wanted to have with everyone watching. "I'm fine."

Any hope he'd leave it alone was dashed in short order. "Charlotte, you're being ridiculous and childish. You're not—"

"What are you going to do, fire me if I go?" I snapped back, getting several heads to turn. "You don't get a say in how I take care of myself." Not in this capacity.

"David, there's really no reason she can't," Jessica suggested hesitantly.

"Especially on the last debate," Ben said. "We'll all be there watching." He glanced at me.

I swallowed down the retort. They'd all be babysitting me.

David's jaw clamped shut and his body stiffened. The effort of not yelling at me was taking serious control.

I took it as my cue to leave. "I'll be in my room the rest of the afternoon." I gathered up my bag and paused to let the headache pulse away after standing. "Let me know if you need anything between now and then," I said, looking at everyone besides David. He was steaming mad at me. Good for him.

"I'll see you tonight." I smiled in a "there's nothing you can do about it" way and left.

When I got to the room, I admitted begrudgingly to myself that I shouldn't have challenged him to fire me or been as snarky as I was. We'd been acting like a squabbling couple, not coworkers. I dropped my bag with a thud and sat on the bed, wincing. Today sucked.

I napped for a couple of hours, figuring it'd help later tonight. David had been right that the debate atmosphere wasn't the best idea, but I was still going.

Kaitlyn came in after a while, waking me briefly to make sure I was all right. The unasked question hung in the air about what the hell had happened between David and me earlier.

She gave me a moment to fill in the silence before leaving again, not pressing any harder. We were close enough friends now that she knew not to push.

My conscience started to gnaw at me as I got ready to go. I didn't want David going out there being that angry or worried about me. There was time for me to stop by his room and apologize quickly.

I sped up, pulling on the softest dress I could find; it was bright grassy green and felt like a T-shirt but gave the impression of being a formal shirtdress. I loosely French-braided my hair so it didn't tug at the cuts on my scalp; the raw red scrapes were still visible under my white-blonde braid. My bottle of aspirin, a water bottle, and some snacks got tossed in my bag, and I headed out. It was the first event I wore flats and glasses to and I felt underdressed; when I was in heels and contacts, I looked older. I could pass as a college intern tonight.

Peter was on duty at David's door and smiled when he saw me. "Doing okay today?"

"Usually if I've got a headache this bad I did something fun the night before. Been better," I said. "Is he free?" I nodded towards the door, then winced at the movement.

"Just Jessica. Here, before you go in…" He stepped aside and gave me a card. "My number, just in case you need something at any point. He wanted you to have it before you leave."

I dropped it in my purse. "Thank you." It was all I had at that point. "Thank you for being willing to do that."

"No problem. Go on in."

He stepped aside and let me knock. The voices stopped; I heard footsteps coming towards the door. There was a pause, and then it opened.

David was still mid-getting ready, shirt untucked and not fully buttoned up, suit bottoms on, just socks and no shoes. I saw Jessica sitting in the room behind him looking out to see who it was. If I hadn't known any better, the situation appeared suspicious. I raised my eyebrows at David and got him to roll his eyes. It was encouraging.

"Come in." He held the door open wider so I could go through.

I wasn't having this conversation with Jessica there. "Jessica, do you mind if I have a minute?" I asked, surprising her.

She looked nice, a bit more elegant and glamor than she normally went for, with a sleek black dress, heels, and a deep red lipstick, her hair straight rather than bouncing everywhere.

For a moment, it looked like she would argue. "Please," I said again. "I'll be out of the way in no time."

"Jess, a moment."

That was all it took for her to move, when David asked.

She nodded and walked out, smiling at me as she left. The door shut with a thud and click before I started.

"I'm sorry."

We spoke at the same time, the same guilty and sheepish looks on our faces.

I shrugged and plowed on, since I was the one who had come down and disrupted his getting ready time. "It wasn't appropriate for me to say a lot of that in front of anyone."

His lips tugged up in a barely there smile. "Me neither. I'm frustrated I can't protect you or be with you right now. That wasn't a good place for it to boil over."

"Anyway, that was all," I said.

We didn't have much time, so there wasn't any point in prolonging this. He needed to get ready. Jessica was waiting outside. I had to catch the team bus over.

"Are you feeling any better?" he asked. "Your head?"

I turned around and motioned for him to look himself.

He moved the hair around my braid a bit, carefully, before kissing it. "You have too much hair; I can't see. Do you need anything before tonight?"

"The hair hides a lot," I said, and turned into him. For a second, I just stayed there, with my head on his shoulder and felt momentarily better. It was towards the end of an awful day, so maybe all I needed was the hug and knowing I wasn't alone. That went a long way. "I really will be absolutely fine tonight. I won't do anything stupid."

"I know." He gave me one last squeeze and let go. "One second before you go."

He beelined for the closet, punching in numbers for the safe. "I was going to give this to you when we got home, but now seems better."

I tried to look over his shoulder. "You didn't need to get me anything," I said. Especially anything that needed to be kept in a safe.

"No, but I thought it was pretty and wanted to get it for you. Think of it as a late birthday present." He turned and handed me what was clearly a jewelry box. "Open it later. I'll see you there."

I took the box—the kind that held multiple pieces—and numbly dropped it in my bag. "My birthday was in March." It was late July now.

He rolled his eyes and walked me towards the door. "Very late present, then."

"Well, thank you in advance." I wondered if I could just hide here tonight. His room was dark, a shirt tossed on the bed, shoes shoved under the desk. I could borrow a T-shirt for a nightshirt and sleep here, pretend I was home, burrow under the covers and wait for him to come back after the debate, then curl in bed next to his back. Even if we were angry at each other, I'd rather be here. Realistically, I knew it wasn't an option.

"And *bonne chance* tonight," I smiled.

"My brilliant debate partner has made sure I'm well prepared." He cupped my face and kissed me. "Now out with you, beautiful girl, before Jess gets irritated."

Before Jessica came back in, I finished doing up the last couple buttons of his shirt, getting a grin in response. "She doesn't need to see your chest," I said.

"I will try to be more modest. I'll see you afterwards?"

I nodded and swung the door open, finding a mulish-looking Jessica leaning on the wall across the hall.

"He's all yours. And you look very nice tonight, by the way," I said as she walked by.

The miffed look lifted for a moment and a smile came through. "Thank you. Still coming?"

"Still coming," I confirmed, and made my way towards the bus.

*   *   *

Once I was situated in my seat, I reached into my bag and pulled out the sage green box, curiosity getting the best of me. I glanced around. I was the only one on the bus except the driver.

I opened the snap. Nestled in the black velvet were a pair of earrings and a matching necklace. The earrings were simple little flowers, light pink petals of some quartz-looking stone and a diamond center; the necklace was a thin string of little gold flowers that matched the earrings. They were exquisite and delicate, each little petal slightly offset, the color fading perfectly towards the middle into the white of the diamond. It was all too pretty to not put on. It was extravagant, but the gift made me grin from ear to ear—or pretty flower earring to pretty flower earring. I settled back into my seat, staring at the necklace with the little flowers on it and waited for the others.

It was a short but scenic ride to the conference center for the debate. Our route took us past the Chateau Frontenac lit up for the night and imposing on the hill before winding down along the river, dark and vast looking at high tide. The lights of Laval twinkled on the opposite shore and the twilight was beautiful. A perfect way to start the night.

The debate went off without a hitch, and without me passing out or causing a disruption.

David spared me only a passing glance with a ghost of a grin when he saw the necklace and earrings before he took the stage.

He owned the debate, getting Yates on the defensive from the opening welcome. He was prickly, more than he should have been in a debate, but overall, he nailed it. It was a solid way to close out the debates and that chapter of my job. At least I could end this piece on a high note.

*   *   *

The remaining weeks blurred into one giant day. When I got a job offer for a three-month contract setting up fuel models for a transport company in Edmonton and found a short-term apartment to lease an easy bus ride to work, I wasn't happy or relieved. It all felt wrong. I got angry with myself for not putting more of an effort into finding out who was behind the threats. I started doubting that moving would fix anything. I still did my job well, but something went out of it, or out of me. I was empty.

I fielded questions from Ben, an extremely unhappy Xavier, and from Camille when I broke the news I was moving. Jessica had grilled me when I gave my notice, wanting to know if there was anything she could do to keep me around. Kaitlyn was upset and spent the better part of a day trying to get me to stay; she meant well, but it made me crumble inside.

My explanation of burnout fell like a rock. They all knew I loved my job; Ben knew I loved more than just the job. They knew I was lying and it made it all worse. Camille was the only one who knew an inkling of the truth.

*   *   *

We were back in Ottawa on a Thursday night, the plan to be in town for a couple of days before taking off for the next leg to the north. My last day was Friday. My last night with David was Thursday; he had a dinner Friday night and I needed to pack for my flight. I still hadn't fully accepted I was leaving. Delaying packing for a three-month move across the country until the night before probably hadn't been smart.

We followed David's plan for Thursday night. He mixed pre-dinner martinis for us, our drink of choice, and cooked dinner. He poured us glasses from a bottle of red wine, ensuring that on top of being depressed tomorrow I'd feel hungover as well. We spent quality time wrapped around each other. It was all we'd get for three months. We wouldn't have another weekend to just be David and Charlotte, or to kiss, or laugh without worrying if we let our guard slip. Our phones were muted, the TV stayed off, and for a few hours on Thursday, nothing outside the house mattered. If I didn't think about it or acknowledge it, maybe tomorrow wouldn't really happen.

*   *   *

In addition to the hangover, morning dawned with a heavy fug of gloom. We moved through getting ready and heading towards breakfast in silence, exchanging only a touch here and there. I didn't know how to leave.

While David showered, I raided his closet for a dress shirt. It was cool out for late July; wearing a long-sleeved shirt and my jeans would be just fine for casual Friday. I numbly started pulling out the clothes I had here, the couple shirts and bottoms to pack away. It seemed incredibly final, which was why I'd saved doing it until now.

"What are you doing?" he asked.

I glanced up to find David standing partway between the bathroom and closet, boxers and glasses on but nothing more.

I shrugged and let my arms drop. "Your shirt seemed comfortable today."

He smiled, shaking his head. "I don't care about that; I kind of like it. I mean that," he said and pointed at the drawer I'd emptied.

"Packing?" I said, not sure why he looked so upset. We both knew this was it.

He strode over, took the top I was holding, and shoved it back in the drawer. The others I'd laid on the bed were scooped up and dropped in the drawer as well, unfolded and messy, before he shut it with a thud.

"What—?"

"You're not moving out." His voice was clipped and his hand held the drawer shut.

"David." I half-laughed and half didn't know what to say. "I'm moving tomorrow."

"But there is no point in moving out from here," he clarified. For a second, his stony face flickered with emotion. "Leave what's here here. If I win, then it'll move with me and be waiting for you in a few months. If not, it will still be here and waiting for you. There's no point in moving it only to move back. You're coming back."

There were a couple of tops, a PJ set, some bottoms, and a dress. I had planned on taking them because they were all comfy, but it wasn't worth arguing over.

I nodded. "I am coming back. I'll leave what I've got here."

He looped an arm around my waist and kissed me. "Thank you."

"Get dressed," I mumbled and smiled against his neck, still a little damp. "I'll be in the kitchen."

By the time he came out, I'd nearly finished my cereal and was ready for coffee. David made my coffee at home since he'd figured out my sugar to cream ratio better than I could. Any trace of last night or earlier this morning was gone when he came in; the tie wasn't on but the suit was, the business look was, and the brisk, steely politician had arrived.

"Coffee?" he asked. His tone startled me. It was remote and not my David; it wasn't even my work David. He was detached and it felt like we'd gone apart.

"You don't get to do that already. And yes to coffee, please," I added.

"Do what?" He barely glanced back. He put out the cream and coffee cup I'd claimed, a swirled green and white pottery mug, the biggest one I could find in his house.

"The remote thing. I get you yet this morning, so you don't get to check out until we're at the office."

The coffee making paused for a second, the cup clattering on the counter before he nodded. "I'm not in a good mood this morning."

I snorted and shook my head. "Me, neither."

He finished and took both cups. "C'mon, then. No remote thing." He nodded toward the couch, sitting down and indicating the spot next to him.

"Sorry," he apologized as he opened up his morning brief.

"Nothing to apologize for." I leaned over and kissed the corner of his jaw, finally getting him to smile. "Read your stuff."

He squeezed my hand, kicked his feet up on the coffee table.

I'd take quiet; that was as good as I'd get this morning.

"Are you working today or just doing exit interviews?" David asked eventually, setting his phone down. We needed to leave soon.

I shrugged. I hated how that sounded. *Exit interviews.* It was all so final. "Helping Xavier with final questions and tying up loose ends, but that's all. Why?"

"Would you double-check some of the data Danielle—"

"Of course," I said. He knew that. "And you know you can always ask me going forward, too. I'm not disappearing completely."

He shifted, moving his arm from around me. "No chance. The whole reason you're moving is to get away from the campaign. I'm not jeopardizing that." He checked his watch and winced. "We need to get moving."

Now wasn't the time to argue. Instead, I nodded and stood. All I could do was follow him into the bathroom, brush my teeth, set my toothbrush back in the holder, and clench my jaw to keep myself from shaking. Everything felt wrong.

I waited for him to finish, tying up his tie, applying his two dabs of cologne. We'd both gone quiet. Maybe it would have been easier if we weren't so similar, if one of us cracked jokes in sad situations. As it was, we were the same and both quiet. He straightened his jacket and sighed.

"I like that suit," I said as we headed towards the front. It was the soft charcoal gray one paired with a pale blue tie that made his skin glow. His hand was crushing mine.

A little smile flickered across his face. "I know you do."

The plan was the same as the first time I'd left here. Mr. Abas would pick me up and drive me to work. He'd have my suitcase as well this time and would drop it off at Camille's for later tonight. I'd go to work like normal, and Mr. Abas would pick me up at the end of the day. I was still too scared to take the bus or a normal taxi.

We reached the door, and that was it. We'd see each other throughout the day and probably say good-bye at the end of the day, but this was our real good-bye.

"I will see you in a few months," David said.

It was silly. I was moving so I could be safe but leaving terrified me. I wrapped my arms around his neck and latched on. I wasn't brave or tough or any of those things.

"I kinda love you, so no forgetting about me," I mumbled into his neck. Now that we were here, unreasonable thoughts bubbled to the surface. Fuzzy pictures of him with other women started flitting through my head, completely unwarranted, but there.

He laughed and kissed the top of my head. "No chance of that happening. You have become indescribably dear to me. You're who I want to see when I wake up." He tilted my head up and kissed me. "Who I want to see when I walk into the office in the morning." Another kiss. "Who I find to talk things over with." Kiss. "Who I want to have dinner with." Kiss. "Who I want to fall asleep with." Kiss. "No chance of me forgetting you."

I smiled and pulled his head back down for one more. "Good. I'll miss you."

"I love you and will miss you, too." He sighed and gripped me tight. "It will go fast and then you'll be right back here with me."

I had promised myself I wouldn't cry until tonight when I was in my room by myself and packing. David gave me a run for my money. My eyes squeezed tight, pressed into his neck, and I nodded. "I hope you're right."

*   *   *

My last day was not one of my better days. Xavier had been down since I'd told him I was leaving. The pastry on my desk when I walked in for the last time made me duck back into a bathroom before anyone saw me getting weepy. I had a new job. I had a short-term lease. I had erased myself from Ottawa as requested. But leaving where I wanted to be crushed me.

Exit meetings and activities filled the morning. Danielle got one last crash course on the models I'd built and coded. I showed her how to pull the data and what to look for so she could hopefully continue some of what I'd done. She was excited about joining the tour and wouldn't stop yapping about how wonderful it was. She also couldn't stop talking about how she'd been right that I wasn't cut out for the job. I wanted to scream at her but held my tongue.

The final meeting with my project team, plus Danielle now, was one of the most unpleasant meetings I'd been in. This was my project and it worked. It was my baby, and I knew the people I was handing it off to wouldn't do as good of a job as I had. I was snappish and recalcitrant, making everyone ask more questions than needed. I got angry with myself because really, the person I was hurting the most was David.

The others didn't help. Danielle jumped in with improvements she'd make to my models; Mike agreed, wanting to move towards the areas heavier in fundraising instead of those I'd targeted. What I had carefully constructed the last several months was torn apart and discarded in front of me. Ben and Jessica were both annoyed we kept getting sidetracked.

"This is a waste of time," David interrupted.

Up until now, he'd been quiet and seemingly more interested in the tabletop or staring out the window. Everything about him looked tight.

"You four," he glared at the others, "get it together before tomorrow. This is unacceptable." He stood abruptly, slamming his laptop shut. "This meeting's done," he said, and stormed out.

There was a moment's silence before Jessica said anything. "Charlotte, you can go. You three, stay." She was quieter than normal and the worry lines on her forehead stood out prominently. I took the dismissal and walked out.

By the time five rolled around, I was ready to go. There was nothing I could come up with to legitimately delay leaving. Convincing myself to go was like trudging through mud; my movements were slow and clunky, my brain screaming not to go.

"I think I'm off," I announced to Xavier and Danielle. "Stay in touch?" Although for Danielle, I'd rather tell her to go to hell.

Xavier got up and scowled. "You can't lose me that easily. Breakfast next time you're in town?"

I nodded; I could not cry yet. "Absolutely."

He gave me a quick hug. Some of the IT and research people I'd worked with at the start came over. Mia as well; her natural good nature still intact, complete with promises of lunches soon. Danielle made herself scarce once people started coming in to say good-bye.

When Mike showed up, I was disgusted but not surprised; it would have been more shocking if he didn't take the chance to force hug me. He grabbed me before I could duck out. Maybe if I wasn't leaving or if I thought I'd see him again I'd put up more of a fight, but I was out of fight.

"See you around, Blondie."

The hug was too tight, his hands too low on my back, and the small but unmistakable pelvic thrust at the end of the hug, small enough that no one else would notice, made me want to cry. Instead, I just backed away, wishing it were over.

The hard ones came next. Kaitlyn and Ben had noticed I was about to leave. Kaitlyn hugged me randomly already, so she wasn't a surprise. Ben was a surprise hugger.

"I'm going to miss you; you were my other buffer between these two," he said, indicating Jessica and David, who'd both come over now.

Jessica shook her head. "David and I are wonderful to be around." She gave me a perky smile and brief but firm hug. "I'll see you around. We'll keep tabs on each other. Maybe cousin dinner again next time you're here?"

"That'd be nice. I'm sure Eric will let me know."

Then, I fixed a happy, neutral look on my face; it probably looked crazy more than anything, but it was all I had as I turned to face David. He was better at this than me and looked at ease. It was only around his eyes I could tell there was tension.

"It's been a pleasure working with you, Charlotte." He came over and wrapped me up tighter than the others had.

I bit my cheek until it stung to keep from crying. I took a deep breath, wishing I could kiss him, or he could rest his cheek on my head, or anything more than the one squeeze I gave him before we both let go. Our real good-bye had been this morning and this scraped open the wound.

"Likewise," was the only thing I managed to choke out. "Thanks again, everyone." I picked up my box, gave one more wave, and dashed out before the tears started.

*   *   *

I'd purposefully saved all my packing at Camille's for tonight. Having something to keep me busy was the goal. Camille offered to help, but after catching my mood agreed to let me be. I jammed on my headphones, grabbed the half bottle of wine left in the fridge, and started. Bubble wrap flew, trash bags filled, and clothes were either folded or crammed, based on the likelihood of wrinkling, into suitcases. The wine dwindled down to the bitter dregs. I labeled some boxes to stay in Ottawa, ready to be moved from here into David's. A couple suitcases and a few smaller boxes would fly cross-country with me tomorrow.

The packing kept me distracted fairly well. With the music cranked up loud enough to leave my ears ringing, there was only so much capacity to think about other things. But when my stupid playlist switched from Drake to Adele lamenting about someone like you, my focus slipped. It wasn't hard, especially after a half bottle of wine, to picture myself watching the news in the future, seeing David and a beautiful wife and a couple of cute kids who all had his dark eyes. He'd win and she'd be there, and I'd be stuck halfway across the country wondering if he ever thought of me.

I flung the little toiletry bag I'd been holding with more force than necessary into a box. I'd turn up like some pathetic old groupie at an event and watch him like a sad—

I jerked out of my depressing thoughts when my ringtone blared shrilly in my ears. I let out a string of language I didn't normally say. I was loud enough Camille shouted at me.

"All good!" I hollered back and answered my phone before my eardrums burst.

"Hey." I answered in a rush without looking at it; I had a moment of panic it was the stalker again and I hadn't left Ottawa soon enough, but it was just David's normal nightly call.

"Hey."

"Aren't you supposed to be at a dinner?" I punched the volume down so I wasn't being yelled at.

"I'm hiding in a bathroom."

Despite my earlier mood, I broke out laughing. "Why are you hiding in a bathroom?"

He chuckled back and sighed. "Because it was the only way I could get a chance to talk to you tonight. How are you?"

And just like that, I was back to the Adele mood. "Shitty. You?"

"Same. You could guess that, though. How's the packing?"

I shoved a box out of the way and looked around my nearly empty room, empty enough my voice sounded echoey and it looked far bigger than it had a few hours ago. "Just about done. I've been throwing things violently into boxes for about a half bottle of wine."

"It's only a few months," he said, sounding a bit patronizing. "You can survive that long without seeing me."

He'd been joking, but it annoyed me.

"This isn't just about you," I snapped harsher than I'd meant. "If we can't make it long distance for a little while, then we probably don't love each other enough to make it work…" I knew I wasn't coming off right, but I couldn't help it.

He didn't say anything, so I switched gears. "It's you, but it's more than that. This isn't my choice. I don't like it when my choices are taken away; I don't want to run and I'm angry that I have to." I huffed and flopped backwards on my bed. "Sorry, rant over. How's dinner?"

"Charlotte…" He sighed. "You… You're keeping yourself alive right now. That's smart, not running. And for the record, I'm furious with myself for not being able to keep you safe here."

It made me smile a little. "You should probably head back to dinner."

"Text me when you land tomorrow. I'm going to miss having you around every day."

My face flooded hot; I didn't want to cry again. "Same. I'll talk to you later. Call me whenever you're alone and get a chance."

He laughed. "I like the sound of that. Do I need to wear or not wear anything in particular?"

I blushed and giggled like a dork. "Not what I meant. Go back to dinner."

"I will. I love you." He hung up before I got a chance to say anything back.

Maybe this wouldn't end up like the Adele song.

Chapter Eleven

There were pluses and minuses to being in Edmonton, the capital city of Alberta. As a plus, the threatening texts and emails completely stopped. For the first time in months, I started to feel secure. My rental had a friendly cat outside, who I named Herring. He frequented the front stoop and liked it when I scratched his ears. I wasn't a cat person in normal circumstances, but he was huge and gray with tufty soft ears and purred as he circled around my ankles.

As a minus, work was dull compared to what I was used to. I missed Camille, and Xavier, and Kaitlyn, and Ben, and Jessica. I missed David. There were always people around him, so I wasn't sure how much we'd be able to talk.

It felt like I was an exchange student for a semester. An awkward pause, an ugly patch in life that didn't match with the rest. I'd be here for my three-month contract, but not long enough to really settle in. My apartment on the outskirts of Edmonton looked like a college dorm room; it was little more than an extended studio with a teeny, little stovetop and miniature fridge and freezer. It had cold cinderblock walls no amount of creamy beige paint could warm and a tiny bathroom. It was all very clean—a little worn, but clean. The landlord seemed friendly. All things considered, for just me for a couple of months, it'd do.

David and I agreed on my move back date of two weeks post-election. He wanted sooner, the day of the election or a day before; I wanted time for things to settle before I was added back into the mix. Win or lose, he'd be busy.

On Monday, I got the basic HR spiel, handed a company-issued laptop, and was herded out to my desk. It was in a large cubicle farm with low ceilings and fluorescent lights. The only space available for me was in the middle of the customer service call center area. It was very loud. If I stretched on my tiptoes, I could see a window several rows over, a view over the parking lot. But, I had nearly complete control over the project, and I could wear jeans and sweatshirts to work again. Noise-cancelling headphones made up for a lot, so again, it'd do.

On the first day, a large flower delivery came at lunch, a bouquet full of sunflowers, the little card saying nothing more than *I love you.* It brightened my day.

*   *   *

If nine months ago you had told me one of the first things I'd do when I moved to a new city was reach out to the local Centre Party branch and fling my services at them, I would have laughed.

I did exactly that Monday night. I'd been cranky and restless all day; I wanted to help. As I emailed the headquarters in Edmonton, I felt a little tingle of unease. The point of this stupid move was so I was away from the campaign. Running straight back to it might be counterproductive.

But, I reasoned as I clicked *send,* I wouldn't be stepping on Danielle's or Mike's toes. It wasn't the same campaign. I'd be a volunteer in a riding and for a member of Parliament candidate that probably wouldn't flip towards Centre. But I'd feel useful. I wanted to feel like me again, not the scared shell I'd become. This was my first step.

Perhaps it was something I'd picked up over the last few months on the road, but I threw myself into my work a little too hard, going non-stop, working ten to twelve-hour days. The first week flew by, and on Saturday, I walked into a dumpy little building that had obviously been a bank in a former life. A few college-aged kids and a handful of retirees for Centre Party volunteer orientation wandered in as well. The rain last night had washed out the air and left it smelling of wet leaves ready for autumn. A watery sun bleached the blue from the sky, making me feel like I was walking in an old Polaroid.

The room we met in was littered with campaign signs and stickers stacked on desks; Rita LaGarde's face beamed out from all corners, encouraging voters to elect her as a member of Parliament. When I saw the matronly coordinator waiting by the door, handing out forms with a yawn, I longed for Mia's over-the-top exuberance. I was pretty sure the matronly Kerry here wasn't demonstrating the level of enthusiasm Mia required.

On a positive note, a muted TV set up on the side ran a live stream of David's morning event; it was a community breakfast with a town hall to be held after his talk. So far, the stage was still empty.

I grabbed a seat in the back and started filling out my form. The standard volunteer interest boxes didn't really fit. While Kerry welcomed us and told us to help ourselves to the coffee and bagels in the back, I frowned. Working in a phone bank held zero appeal. Mailing I could do, but really, it wouldn't swing much of anything. Canvassing was a possibility.

I checked the "Other" box and listed what I was good at—data or debate help. I wasn't sure those were open to volunteers.

"New to the area?" Kerry asked.

She smiled as I dropped off the form. Evidently, I looked more out of place than I realized. I wore my purple campaign shirt today, thinking I'd blend in; I was the only one aside from Kerry wearing a Centre Party-branded anything.

"Yes. Just moved here last weekend." Had it really only been a week ago?

She skimmed over the form and placed it off to the side by itself. "We'll find something for you. Where'd you move from?"

Part of me wondered how much I should say; paranoia stuck with me, even if I had wimped out and run across the country. I knew the regional volunteer leads met weekly with Mia. Maybe I should have used a fake name, but then it would never stop.

"Ottawa," I answered. "Moved here for a job."

Kerry's eyes perked up. "Did you volunteer there as well? A bit closer to the action, eh? Is that where you got your T-shirt? I see the volunteers on TV with those."

"I did some data work." My eyes flickered back to the TV, to the event I'd helped orchestrate. Just a bit of data work.

"Wonderful. Help yourself to coffee and we'll get started soon." She dismissed me with a curt smile, greeting the person behind me with a mechanical hello.

I dawdled at the breakfast area, grabbing a coffee that smelled like cardboard even after I dumped a hefty amount of sugar and cream in it, and a tasty bagel. Everyone else was still mulling over the forms.

I perched on the side of the table and un-muted the TV to low. David's speech was done, but it still showed him waving and shaking hands with the crowd. Jessica or Kaitlyn had convinced him to lose the tie and suit coat; the simple rolled-up dress shirt fit the event much better. I knew he'd feel awkward not in his full suit, but I liked the casual look. The crowd there seemed to, as well.

We started the meeting with a rundown of the different opportunities, which probably should have been done before we'd signed up for everything, policies for volunteering, and the "talk to the media and die" line. I had brushed up a bit on Rita LaGarde last night so I knew what I was walking into today. She was young, a couple years younger than me, ambitious and eager for a seat in Parliament. The seat had swung left to right in the past, so it wasn't inconceivable for it to swing our way this time. Rita was very green, and I knew the amount of funding support from the party wasn't fantastic here. David had opted not to campaign here because it'd be a single stop without a chance to flip anything nearby.

At the end, we were sent on our way, assured the appropriate contact would reach out to us soon to get us rolling. It wasn't what I'd been hoping for; I wanted to get sucked into something for the afternoon or the rest of the weekend. Monday felt a lifetime away.

*　　*　　*

I got my assignment and schedule later in the week. There was an opportunity to help with the voter database. It sounded like a glorified data entry position, but it kept me busy.

David kicked the campaign schedule up a notch, adding in more visits, more talks, more of everything so every day was nonstop for him.

I kept working, he kept working, and we texted every day.

I unpacked my boxes over the first couple of weeks. David saw them sitting in the background one of the rare nights our times lined up for FaceTime. He wasn't impressed and let me know. Both of us were snappish as the long distance rubbed. It was easier to assure him I would unpack and look like I lived in a house rather than out of boxes.

Unpacking took a couple of nights. When I sent David a picture a few days later with everything organized and put away, I got another bouquet, a colorful and scented riot of lilies, with a note apologizing for being grumpy.

We'd been working ourselves ragged to the point of not making time to talk and agreed to make more of an effort to at least try and call for a minute or two every day. Text messages were backups only.

My days flowed into a routine, and I started to make headway at work and at my volunteer job. Both places trusted me and gave me freedom to work. My three-month contract was ample time, and I was confident I'd be done a few weeks early. I wasn't sure what I'd fill my days with then. Moving back early wasn't an option, despite how much David wanted me to, because it'd be right before the election. The last thing he needed was me showing up, my silent but at-large stalker reappearing, and the voters not taking kindly to a twenty-something girlfriend for their potential PM.

It'd also been nearly a month since I'd heard from my stalker; the headaches from the concussion had finally faded. I should have been happy. They'd kept their promise, that if I moved away, I wouldn't hear from them. The absence of death threats was nice, obviously, but felt false. I didn't know what might set them off again, if they'd start when I moved back to Ottawa, if Rita LaGarde started making ground and it became clear I was still involved, or if they would never start up again because I was no longer working with the campaign. I was free, but I didn't know on what terms. They had found me once. Who said they couldn't do it again?

*   *   *

When I walked into the volunteer area a month or so after starting, expecting to go to the computer terminal I normally used, I found volunteer organizer Kerry, Rita herself, and one of her advisors sitting in the room on a Tuesday night, engrossed in reading a magazine. The door chimes tinkled, drawing attention to my entrance, and they all looked up at me, stunned. Obviously, they were waiting for me.

My mind spun over the last few times I'd been here; I hadn't messed around where I didn't belong in databases.

"What did you do in Ottawa?" Rita asked me directly.

My bag dropped to the chair with a thud. I was terrified of telling them. I was terrified they would say something and the emails or texts would start again, and this time, I was by myself. They clearly knew something I didn't, though, so lying was stupid.

"I worked as a data analyst."

Rita's eyes narrowed and everything on her face went pointy.

"This came out today." She stomped over and pushed the magazine in my hands.

I wondered what on Earth I could have possibly done that had landed in a magazine and took a look.

First thing I saw was a full-page picture of David. I struggled to keep a neutral face. The photo was a close-up and in sharp black and white. He was sitting, leaning forward with elbows on knees, a direct stare into the camera. It was an excellent photo. I made a note of the magazine and would get my own copy when I left.

After I stopped gawking, I looked at the article, which was what they all seemed to be waiting for. It couldn't have been anything about us; he would have told me, or Kaitlyn would have called yelling. It wasn't.

It was a piece focused on David—part policy, part personal. The article outlined the background between him and Jessica. When I saw the picture of Jessica, I got a hint of what was going on. She was directing a meeting, one in Montreal from last month; now I saw the pictures, I did remember a camera crew and interviewer there. In the aftermath, I'd forgotten.

While the camera focused on Jessica, giving her a very good photo, you could see the rest of us, Ben and Kaitlyn and me, around the table. It was small, though. I flipped to the next page and winced. There was another full-page spread, this time of David and me working on the debate. Again, it was in Montreal, one day before I'd gotten shoved into the road and everything had gone to shit. Jessica stood in the foreground, but the camera focus was on the two of us at the front of the room, shoulder-to-shoulder, looking at a page of notes. I was smiling, apparently agreeing with whatever he pointed out to me. We were good at hiding facial expressions; he had been hitting on me very hard, very quietly in that picture. So they had seen that photo, which meant I was about to get grilled.

"Data analyst for the party," I clarified, unsticking my throat. "And I got roped into debate prep."

Rita snatched the magazine back and blinked rapidly at me; she did that a lot in interviews. If I could have, I'd tell her to knock it off; she looked shifty blinking so much. "Why did you leave? This looks bad. Why didn't you say anything? Were you fired? Are you trying to sabotage us—?"

I couldn't stop the eye roll and sighed. *Sabotage? Really?* "No. Of course not. I left for personal reasons and on good terms. If you need a reference, I can call Jessica Hage or David Reid right now and get it for you. Do you want me to?" I sounded prickly even to my own ears and pulled out my phone to start dialing. "I can tell them you need a reference—"

She looked startled and shook her head. Kerry and the policy guy had their mouths open, staring at me.

"No, there's no need to waste their time. We were just surprised." Some of the pointiness left Rita's face.

I put my phone away, shaking a little but relieved; I really didn't want to call Jessica or try to straight-face a conversation with David in front of them.

Rita continued, "Reid called out the improvements in data and debate prep as being one of the drivers for the poll surges. Did you help with that?"

David needed to keep his mouth shut, but it still made me happy. I nodded.

Rita went quiet for a moment before she stared back. "Can you do it here?"

"Maybe," I said. "That's why I volunteered. You have your own analytics team, though. I can make suggestions, but I can't get more involved." Already, I felt myself pulling back. Anonymity was safer.

"Okay, we'll see if we can move you around."

"Can I read the article?" I asked before Rita went back to whatever she had planned for the night.

She shrugged and handed it back, giving me one last odd look before leaving with the policy guy.

Kerry stayed in the room with me, eyeing me curiously. A headache started throbbing behind my eyes; rather than deal with Kerry asking more questions, as friendly and good-natured as they'd be, I pushed my headphones on and logged into the recording of David's speech from earlier. I didn't care what he talked about; I just wanted to hear his voice.

Later that night, after I'd slipped out before anyone asked more questions, I stopped by a store and bought my own copy of the magazine, just because, and sent David a picture of it with a question mark. A heads-up would be nice next time.

It wasn't until late, which meant he was up really late when he wrote back with an apology. He hadn't seen it yet, either.

It really wasn't a big deal, I assured him, and let him get to bed. I needed more to do. I needed to stay so busy I could ignore the distance and make the months speed towards the election.

*　　*　　*

Weeks flew by as I kept myself busy to the point of exhaustion each night. Rita's data people reached out and asked if I'd help them. For better or worse, I heard myself say yes, but only if my role was small and not public.

They were happy for the offer and fully understood I was just assisting with whatever was needed and not stepping on toes.

My suggestions were well-received, and Rita's policy and communications team knew what they were doing. Her numbers started ticking up a percentage point here and there, still behind, but not as much. I doubted it had much to do with anything I had done.

But Rita's movement in the polls was enough it triggered back with the campaign team. Ben sent me a text from one of their daily meetings, complete with a picture.

We played guess where Charlotte moved.

The picture showed all the polls; Rita had gone from solid, out-of-reach deep red to toss-up yellow. They were happy. Rita's team was happy. I was nervous they had all pegged me as being behind the numbers; I hoped it stayed between Ben, Jessica, Kaitlyn, and David. To me, it looked like I'd placed a giant target on myself.

I wrote back telling him I had nothing to do with it, but doubted he believed me.

Volunteering took up three nights a week.

My work hours were from eight to five, but I usually started at six. I was ahead of schedule, and at this pace, I'd finish the contracted work about the same time as the election. The people were nice, but remote and not overly engaging. At the end of the day, everyone drove straight home; kids needed to be picked up, husbands or wives to see again. There weren't office happy hours. I answered a few questions about who I got flowers from each Monday, but that was the extent of our interaction.

The company was big enough for the onsite gym to offer fitness classes throughout the day. In the past, I'd avoided the gym; I preferred hiking or doing something outside rather than Zumba-ing my calories away. However, the spin class and the circuit training class after work lined up on the nights I wasn't volunteering. I started exercising.

Camille expressed concern at my sudden fitness mania; I wasn't sure if she was just being silly because it was out of character, or if she really was concerned. Sore muscles and being physically tired helped me sleep.

Fitness classes took up two nights a week.

That left me with two nights, Saturday and Sunday. Saturdays I devoted to cleaning. I'd never been a clean freak, tidy but not spotless. My apartment became spotless on Saturdays. I found a farmers' market, complete with picnic tables, fire pits, and food trucks to visit in the mornings. I'd pick up a treat for Herring the cat; he was fond of the slivers of smoked salmon I gave him. The afternoons were for cleaning.

In the evenings I cooked, finding new things to make, things that took a long time and had many steps; there had been only one spectacular fail at the start where I'd needed pizza delivered instead. When I moved back, my cooking might be edible, and David could load a dishwasher instead of cook.

Sundays were loose ends, so I took Sundays to explore. I found museums, parks, and on occasion tagged along to some of Rita's events.

And so, I had my schedule.

Chapter Twelve

"You're busy next Thursday," Camille said as soon as I answered the phone.

I scratched Herring's head, pulling a burr out of his fluff, then shooed him off my doorstep. "I am?" I fumbled with my keys and shoved the door open. "What am I doing Thursday?"

"Going to Vancouver with me." Her voice was brimming and ready to burst with whatever she was hiding. It wasn't hard to picture her bouncing from foot to foot.

I tamped down the little flutter of excitement, clattering my bags on the counter. "Vancouver? Spit it out, Camille."

She laughed. "There's a new art and fashion museum opening. I believe a certain party leader will be in attendance and talking about the importance of the arts. I thought you might want the extra ticket I snagged."

"How did you—?"

"I'm good, my friend. I got you a ticket. You can hotel with me, or not. Get a plane ticket and a fancy dress and I'll see you there."

* * *

So, I found myself unexpectedly in Vancouver in the middle of September. The hotel was beautiful. It was airy, with light streaming in through the double-height windows; the fountains outside caught the mid-morning sun and glittered and splashed rainbows across the turquoise and yellow armchairs in the lobby, making the room a kaleidoscope. The check-in was empty, so as soon as I staggered in with my large dress bag and carry-on in tow, one of the doormen rushed over to get it.

He bustled me over to the check-in counter, where I was quickly taken care of. After my stuffy little apartment, this was definitely welcome.

We were on the fourth floor. David usually stayed on one of the upper ones. "Ms. Finnan?"

I looked up from texting Camille, letting her know I'd arrived and saw Peter standing by the side entrance. I grinned and waved. It felt like I was on vacation and stepping back into my old campaign life again, at least as an observer.

"Hello, Peter. How are you?" I detoured from my path to the elevator to join him. Now that I had a moment to look around, it was obvious David and the entourage were here. Besides Peter, there were a few other security folks hanging around. "Keeping busy?"

"Pretty much, being run ragged," he agreed, but shrugged in a good-natured way. "David didn't mention you'd be here." He said it as more of a question than statement.

The teeny niggle of unease I had about doing this as a surprise resurfaced. In theory, it had seemed like a good idea; now that I was here, I hoped it wouldn't be too much.

"He doesn't know, actually." The uncertainty in my voice came through loud and clear. "One of my friends got me an extra pass, so I was going to show up as a surprise."

Peter laughed loud enough it echoed in the lobby. I wasn't sure if that was good.

"He's not expecting anyone else tonight, is he?" I asked, mainly joking, but a little paranoid.

He waved me off. "No. He's been wound up tighter than a spring the last few weeks. You staying with him tonight?" he asked, lowering his voice.

It was strange for me to be discussing this with someone other than David or Camille, but at the same time, being with David meant my private life wasn't private.

"I'm not sure. We'll see how it goes."

Peter smiled again. "We'll see you tonight and get you in with no problem. Everything else okay?" He looked concerned, and I knew what he meant.

I nodded. "So far so good. All quiet on the western front." Even as I said it, I got the crawly feeling someone was standing behind me. The thought had crossed my mind that showing up like this was pressing my luck. One night shouldn't matter; I'd be in and out before my reappearance registered. Regardless, the back of my neck crawled with invisible eyes and my shoulders tightened again.

Peter noticed, and the joking manner evaporated. "We've got the building covered tonight. No worries. Have a good time."

I shook the creepy feeling; he was right. "Will do. Thank you. Nice to see you again."

He nodded, and I headed up to the room. Inside, I set my luggage down. The room was high enough to give a nice view between the other glass-clad skyscrapers and see the harbor and mountains looming beyond. I made myself some coffee, flopped in a chair by the window, and tried to relax.

Camille arrived an hour later, bags and dress dragging behind her.

"I'm starving," she said, and hung up her dress bag. "Lunch? Nothing too heavy; I won't fit into my dress otherwise."

I laughed. I gave her a brief hug and grabbed my purse. "Lunch. Nice to see you, by the way."

She pulled the zipper down on my dress bag and snuck a peek, nodding in approval, so I must have chosen wisely. "Do you have accessories to go with it?"

The jewelry, the necklace and earrings from David, and my clutch passed inspection. When I pointed at my black heels, she winced. "Lunch and shopping. Let's go."

*   *   *

We spent an enjoyable afternoon in Vancouver. I ate a bucket of mussels and half a baguette; Camille picked at her salad. We drank a little too much wine sitting outside on the sunny patio along the waterfront on Granville Island, and then wandered around Stanley Park in the afternoon. I bought shoes up to the fashion journalist's standard. This was another reason I was looking forward to moving back to Ottawa; seeing my best friend was a lot different than just talking on the phone.

When we returned, cameras were hanging around the entrance to the hotel. We scooted through quickly. It'd ruin the surprise if I bumped into any campaign folks now.

"Still haven't told him you're here?" she asked on the way up.

I shook my head no. "Not yet. It's a good idea, right? A surprise?"

She gave me a look somewhere between amused and exasperated. "You know him better than I do."

Two hours later, we were ready to roll. Camille's dress was a slinky orange silk sheath with carefully placed cut-outs along the side; she looked much more artsy than me.

"This dress isn't too boring, is it?" I asked as we left. I didn't want to look old.

"Not at all. You look like the prime minister's girlfriend. I look like a fashion editor. We're suitably attired. You won't embarrass me too much." She patted my hand as I glared at her.

I'd found a sapphire ball gown with thin straps and a deep V-neckline—not inappropriate, but not too modest, either. I thought the criss-crossing straps on the open back made it artsy. Camille had wrestled my hair into a loose braid off to the side so I looked like I'd wandered off a red carpet instead of emerging from a hole like I would have if I'd been left to my own devices. The earrings and necklace from David completed the look. I thought I looked presentable.

David arrived at these things early; there were special meet and greets and photos with the big donors beforehand. He would already be in there, probably wondering why I hadn't called or texted him yet to say to have a good time tonight. I squeezed Camille's hand.

"Thank you." I grinned.

"Yeah, you owe me big. We're here."

We entered through the press entrance because this was a working event for Camille. I didn't mind being snuck in the back. The venue was interesting—a brand-new building made to look like it'd been plucked out of Paris with rounded corners, tall windows, and wrought iron balconies. I would enjoy wandering around looking at the exhibits.

Tonight, we were confined to the great hall, lined with pop art and elaborate costume dresses, the kind worn at the Met Gala in New York. It was a popular place to be, with cameras everywhere and a wide range of well-to-do old folks and people who looked more like Camille. Tables were set up for the dinner, priced at some ungodly amount per head, and a stage up front where David could go on about how important the arts are to our culture and in cultivating a sense of community. In the back, there was a champagne and oyster bar. We went there first.

"I think I chose the wrong line of work." This was by far the most extravagant fundraiser event planned so far. Everything for the evening was gorgeous, from the exhibits in jewel tones to the tinkling of crystal glasses mingling with the orchestra playing in the front. It was perfect.

Camille looked smug and sipped the bubbles. "Champagne at some events is a perk. Some are disgusting, though. There was one—"

A loud spread of clapping interrupted her as the emcee announced David Reid. I caught a glimpse of him as he came in, all smiles and waving. Jessica followed in an unfortunate billowy yellow dress. But then, I was back looking at David and found it difficult to stay where we were, strategically positioned by the champagne. I wanted to see him now, but had to wait.

"He does look good in a tux, I'll give you that," said Camille. "He should have some schmoozing time before dinner… I'm guessing you want to surprise him before then?"

I nodded. "He might spit something out across the table if I surprise him over dinner. It'd be bad optics."

She was right about the tux; David wasn't a muscle man by any stretch. He might have gained a couple pounds of campaign weight, but he was still lean and handsome and rocked the black tie look, cut-to-fit and confident.

"I don't look too silly, right?" I asked.

Camille linked her arm in mine and moved us closer. "I wouldn't have let you out of the room if you looked silly. Do you see anyone else here you know?"

People watched us. We were both tall and thin, contrasts to each other—dark blue to burnt orange gowns, ebony to pale skin. Her question was an effective distraction technique. I looked around, my eyes bouncing across faces uselessly. "Jessica you already know," I said, and pointed towards her along the opposite side of the room. Her dress, the big yellow gown, made it look like she had tried to be a southern belle.

Camille winced. "I wouldn't have let her out of the room."

I giggled and continued scanning; David's back was to us. "Her, you'll like Kaitlyn. And that's Ben over on the side." He looked tired and out of his comfort zone in an art and fashion museum.

Camille started pointing out people she'd worked with in the past, a friend who wrote for Vogue, and on and on.

I was antsy. I willed David to look my way, but he worked the room slowly. This was what he was so good at, talking with people and winning them over, making people like him as soon as he turned to them. I wished he didn't care so much and would hurry up with it tonight. What if he didn't get to us before I had to sit down for dinner?

"Have you heard anything I just said?" Camille asked, trying not to laugh.

I nodded. "You said your boss worked for five years in Milan with the guy—"

And there it was. David finished talking to a couple, shaking hands with the man, air kissing the lady and glanced up at me.

There was a complete lack of recognition at first and he looked away. But then, almost instantly and somewhat comically, he did a double-take and locked his eyes on me.

I smiled, trying not to do anything too obvious that'd give us away.

He failed at not being obvious. His mouth opened in surprise, a wide grin taking over his face, and then the next couple was in front of him, shaking hands.

"If he was a cartoon character, he'd be the one with the tongue hanging out on the floor and little hearts for eyes," Camille whispered.

I laughed. "He's not that bad." And really, he wasn't. I caught him more than once finding me, smiling, before he refocused on the people in front of him.

Camille rolled her eyes and pushed us forward. "Let's introduce me and then I can go work. You can hang out with your campaign buds until dinner."

We made our way nearer; the crowd compacted the closer we got to him. Camille took my champagne glass from me and handed it off to a waiter.

"So you don't dump it down the back of his jacket when you fling yourself on him," she said.

"No flinging will be involved." We were too close to other people to talk like this. Although, the only reason there'd be no flinging was because there couldn't be. I wanted to fling. "How's Tom's residency going?"

I had to wait for two more groups of people before David was finally in front of us. I was impressed with our levels of self-restraint.

"It's a surprise to see you here, Charlotte," he said.

I don't know which one of us moved first, but I ended up in his arms and everything familiar flooded my senses—his cologne, his hands on my back, the tux jacket under my cheek—it was home. He pulled away sooner than I wanted.

"Hopefully not a bad one," I said, trying to sound offhand about it. "My friend Camille," I introduced and motioned to her, "had an extra pass and invited me along. Figured I might as well."

He looked dumbfounded, but happily so. "Of course, it's a good surprise. I…it's…" It was funny seeing him at a loss for words. He was normally so eloquent and unflappable. "Thank you, Camille," he finally said, giving up on getting anything coherent out. "You're a fashion journalist, correct?"

It was easier for them to chat. It made me a little uncomfortable that a lot of the people they mutually knew were through David's ex-wife, but at least they were talking, and he and I weren't just staring and grinning at each other like idiots.

"Charlotte. I wasn't expecting to see you here."

I turned and saw Jessica. She was in near-flats and I looked down on her head, which made talking to her awkward. She looked run ragged, a sag in her shoulders, the make-up failing to conceal the dark circles under her eyes. The campaign pace must have caught up to her. This was something she wanted badly, nearly as much as David, but it was ruining her.

"I know. Camille surprised me with a ticket. Couldn't say no," I bubbled, and gave her a hug hello.

She was flustered to see me but patted me back. "I guess not. David, you need to—"

"I know," he said irritably. "Camille, it was nice to meet you. Charlotte…" He caught my eye again and smiled. "We can catch up later tonight, after I make the rounds?"

I nodded and smiled back. "Sure, I know the drill. It was good seeing both of you again."

I shooed Camille to move and we let them go off to the next group.

"Am I allowed to let you roam by yourself now?" Camille asked. "Chaperoning over? I can trust you two to behave? You won't find a darkened corner and start—"

I interrupted her before she got much further in that scenario. "Go work. I'll meet you at the table for dinner."

She winked at me and made for the museum director, who had finished with some photographers. I turned and went towards Kaitlyn.

Ben had joined Kaitlyn, and I was happy to hang out with them until dinner. Kaitlyn bought my explanation for being here but Ben rolled his eyes. He was happy to see me, though.

"And you wanted to see us again," Kaitlyn said, looking delighted. "I miss having you as my roommate on the road." She glanced around quick and continued. "Danielle isn't quite the same."

Ben snorted. "That's an understatement."

"Is she here?" It was stupid the thought hadn't occurred to me before now. Of course she would be.

Much to my relief, Kaitlyn shook her head. "No. Had some sort of cold and couldn't come."

"So, what's she doing?" I asked, trying to hide my residual panic and get them talking. David was right. We let our guard down too much.

Between the two of them, I found out David hadn't told me about the hiccups since I'd left. Little glitches popped up, models weren't running as quickly or as accurately as they should have been. I wanted to get my hands back on it and make it run smoothly again. That was probably why David hadn't said anything. He knew I'd try to get involved.

"I'm exhausted." Kaitlyn yawned. "The last month we've picked up steam and are on the go morning to night. David's the only one not bothered by it."

"Only a month left, though. How about you, Charlotte, new job good?" Ben asked.

We continued chatting until dinner was announced. They went off to their table and I found Camille already sitting, typing away frantically on her phone.

"Get anything good?" I asked.

She set it down with a satisfied sigh. "Enough for an article. We can introduce each other to people afterwards."

Conversation was put on hold when the speeches started. Since it was an opening, the director talked for a while, the curator talked, the president of the board of directors talked… There was a lot of talking. David got a standing ovation when he finished his speech. He was on good form tonight.

Dinner finished and the tables were cleared; later this evening, the room would turn into a club party. I wondered how late David planned on staying. I guessed not for the dancing, although I wouldn't have minded staying for that. I probably couldn't have danced with him, anyway.

A DJ was getting set up and the lights dropped to after-dinner level, throwing shifting shadows across the gallery. The orchestra music disappeared, and the deeper thump of bass echoed through the room.

I'd been right that Camille and Kaitlyn would hit it off. While they talked about favorite places in Toronto, I spent the time watching David. He kept glancing over at me, keeping tabs on where I was.

"Did he know you were coming tonight?" Ben asked.

He'd made me jump. "No, it was a surprise. Camille really did get me the ticket last week."

He stifled a smile. "Just tonight, or are you making it to the other stops out here this weekend?"

I wanted to. I really, really wanted to. But I was terrified of the emails or texts or worse starting again, so I shook my head. "Just this one. I have to work this weekend."

"Actually, that's what I wanted to talk to you about," he said, and turned to business mode. "Any chance you'd be able to look at some things if I sent them to you? Danielle is…" The grimace said it all. "It wouldn't be a lot."

I hesitated, but only for a second. "Of course," I agreed. "Email it over and I'd be happy to. Just don't tell Danielle." I wanted to help, and Ben…I could trust Ben. Out of everyone, he was least likely to talk.

He looked relieved and sagged a bit. "Of course I won't tell her. I was going to reach out to you soon, so this worked out well." He checked his watch. "I'm heading out for the night. It was good to see you again."

"You, too." I gave him a brief hug and watched him hurry out of the hall. I was excited to help again and tried to shake my tingle of unease; no one needed to know it was me. My involvement would be minimal, a check here or there. I turned back and rejoined Camille and Kaitlyn, who had moved on to favorite Ottawa spots. I got sucked into the conversation.

"I think we're in trouble," Kaitlyn said, and made a mock horror face over my shoulder. I turned to see David finally coming over.

He smiled. "Not any trouble that I'm aware of. Charlotte, I was wondering if I could borrow you for a moment? There's someone I think you should meet."

I was somewhat startled but shrugged. "Lead the way."

"And steal her back for the last few weeks," Kaitlyn said. "Woo her back to us!"

He laughed. "No promises." He walked slowly on purpose, giving us more time together.

"You're pretty good at wooing," I said in an undertone.

The music was louder now, so it muffled our voices. We kept our heads together to be heard and to keep prying ears in the dark.

"Where are you staying tonight?" he asked, bypassing anything else.

I failed at keeping a smile from spreading across my face.

"Same hotel as you. What a coincidence," I said in mock shock.

"Hmm, I'm sure that's it." He laughed. "Room 1092?"

I nodded. "When are you leaving?"

He slowed down to a stop and paused at a tray of glow in the dark cocktails. I declined the one he offered. The dance club was almost ready.

"Soon. No one wants to see an old politician dance."

I glanced over at him and caught his eye. "You're most definitely not old. I'd dance with you."

He took a breath and let it out in a puff. "I wouldn't keep my hands off you, and that'd cause problems," he said quietly.

The thought made me happy. Minus the hug at the start, we'd been very careful not to touch each other again.

"Well, later it is. Who am I meeting?"

He led us over to a man and tapped him on the shoulder. He was slight with thick glasses.

"This is Sumit. Sumit, this is Charlotte, the colleague I was telling you about earlier."

Sumit's eyes widened and twinkled in a smile behind his glasses. "And now she's here?" he asked.

My eyebrows shot up, and I looked at David.

"Sumit runs a non-profit here in Vancouver for disadvantaged kids, helping them with coding, computer skills, that sort of thing," he said. "He's looking to expand."

"I was hoping to open a chapter back east," Sumit gushed. His enthusiasm was catchy, but I wasn't sure what my role was. "Mr. Reid says you are good with modeling and predictions?"

"And might be moving back to Ottawa at some point," David said. "So, I thought you'd be a good fit."

And it all clicked together.

"Yes," I said brightly. "I am. Tell me more."

We talked for quite a while, and I was glad David introduced us. I would move back to Ottawa later next month. This work was right up my line of interest. A little lower-key than the campaign, but that was okay. I'd get to run with it and work for something I felt good about. Thinking long-term, it was also the sort of thing the prime minister's partner could be involved in.

Sumit and I exchanged details and agreed to talk later in a more business-like setting. He decided to call it quits for the night and headed off.

The DJ started, the music ratcheted up to a vibrating thump, and a few professional dancers moved onto the cleared-off floor. The museum's costumes and lights sent shadows racing everywhere.

I paused a moment and watched the dancers while David talked with another group who'd come over; in a different time and place, I thought I'd make David stay for a dance or two or three with me. In the dark, it was easier for me to watch him and not be at risk of getting spotted.

He said his good-byes and came back towards me. "I think this is my cue to leave as well." He leaned forward and gave me two air kisses. "Don't stay too long," he whispered, squeezing my shoulders before slipping away.

He got a twenty-minute head start on me, enough so it wouldn't be obvious I followed him. The crowd split into two clear groups, those who were staying and those getting ready to go. Ben was gone. Jessica had predictably followed David out. I waited for four songs and then it was my turn.

I found Camille dancing away with Kaitlyn. "I'm heading back," I told them.

"Already?" Kaitlyn said, the pout audible.

I felt bad for a second. "Already. Call me and keep me more up-to-date. Send me anything you need help with."

She hugged me and waved me off.

"You out tonight?" Camille asked in an undertone.

"Until tomorrow morning."

"Have fun." She wiggled her eyebrows at me and turned.

I was free.

*   *   *

I changed out of the ball gown and into something more practical. If someone saw me heading up to David's floor in this dress, it'd be pretty obvious what was going on. Now, I could easily be a staffer, heading in for a late-night meeting.

The elevators were empty, thankfully. There was a decided lack of sneaking or avoiding any unwanted witnesses to me arriving at his room. The security by the elevators expected me, which was a little weird. The hallway was deserted, minus a guard by the door who let me knock.

David must have been hovering, because the door swung open in a matter of seconds.

"Come in," he said, any pretense of formality gone. He'd half-changed, the jacket and tie gone, his shirt partially undone.

I stepped in and dropped my bag as the door shut.

We stared at each other for a moment, not really believing we were here, before he pulled me over and wrapped me up in his arms. The last couple of times I'd been here, in my happy place with his arms around me and his head against mine, we had been in public. Now I could kiss his neck and hold him as tight as I wanted. He could kiss me beyond the polite air kisses.

We hadn't handled long distance well at all; more than one phone call had been strained, more than once one of us had frayed and snapped. Here, though, it didn't matter at all.

"How long have you been planning this?" he asked. He cupped my face and kissed me again.

"Not long…last Wednesday?" I stepped back to get some air; I wasn't thinking clearly. "I wanted to surprise you. Guessing it worked?"

He laughed, the lines around his eyes creasing; he looked exhausted, but happy. "Yes. I—you… I nearly knocked people over to get to you tonight. I nearly blew it."

I tried not to look too smug, but I was pleased. "Camille was worried I was going to drag you off to a darkened corner as soon as you came out. She didn't restrain me, but it was close."

He looked around the room and shrugged. "No reason I can't do that now, although we can probably do better than a dark corner." I was promptly scooped up and carried to the bedroom suite, grinning into his shoulder.

He set me on the bed and started to undress. I leaned back on my elbows, not able or willing to break eye contact; he had such dark eyes, coal black almost when he relaxed.

I sat up and grabbed his hands. "Come here." It came out as a whisper. The giggles from earlier had dried up, and I wanted him. There wasn't a lot about this that was simple, but that was.

He leaned over and kissed my neck while I shifted back on the bed.

"You actually took my breath away tonight when I saw you. I always thought it was an exaggeration when people said that, but…" He gave me a half-smile and kissed my nose. "You did."

My insides turned to mush and I blushed. "You're horrifically sappy," I said. "Keep going."

So he did.

*   *   *

The terrible thing about planning this, and what I'd known would happen when Camille first offered me the ticket, was tomorrow morning, bright and early, I'd have to leave again. As I lay pressed up against David, there wasn't a single part of me that wanted to leave. I certainly didn't want to think about it.

"Does your family know about me?" I asked. "Or anyone besides Ben?"

I felt his head shake against mine. "No. My mother would gossip, which we're not ready for, and my sister…no, not yet. A buddy in Montreal, he knows I'm seeing someone, but only because he tried to set me up on a date."

"When was that?" I leaned up to see his face.

He scrunched it up and looked sheepish. "Start of March?"

I mentally counted back. "We weren't… Was there someone before me?" Who'd he been seeing six months ago?

His fingers touched my cheek, turning my head towards him and he kissed me soundly. "No. I… It was after our first debate… That's when my friend mentioned he knew someone. I had a feeling I wasn't available anymore—after you wiped the floor with me in practice."

I grinned. "Good answer."

"Do you think your parents will be okay with me?" he asked.

I started to laugh before I realized he was being serious.

"Of course, they will," I said firmly. It seemed like a silly question. "You're…you're you. Why?"

"If we had a daughter," he started and picked up my hand resting on his stomach, "and she brought home a guy who was sixteen, seventeen years older than her, I'd be damn suspicious. It's not hard for me to imagine they'll think I'm too old for you."

I squeezed his hand back. "I love you, and you should stop being hung-up about our ages," I said. "Your family's going to think I'm a power-hungry gold digger."

That got him to laugh, but I wondered how I'd tell my parents about us, that I'd been seeing someone pretty damn seriously for six months. Oh, and by the way, he was the prime minister. There weren't any guidelines for that sort of thing.

It was late, close to midnight. David had to be up and functioning at a much higher level than me tomorrow, but he insisted he hadn't been getting to bed earlier than one lately. It sounded awful, but I didn't argue. Neither one of us was interested in falling asleep or lying in bed being sappy sots. We ended up pulling on the fluffy white hotel robes and popping open the mini-bar's half-bottle of champagne.

"Would you dance with me?"

The question slipped out. I'd wanted to ask earlier tonight, but now was okay, too.

He took a sip out of the champagne bottle, then smiled. "Yes." He handed me the bottle and turned on the audio. "Preference?"

It felt incredibly decadent to be lounging around in hotel bathrobes and drinking champagne from the bottle. I shrugged and leaned against the back of the couch. "Slow?"

It took him a minute before the music started, an older Ed Sheeran song. The room filled with soft music, singing about loving someone when crowds don't remember names.

"You said you liked this one?" he asked, glancing back.

"You have a good memory."

"Dance?"

I took his hand, warm and firm around mine, and let him lead.

We spent songs alternating between dancing around the sitting room space, snagging sips of champagne, and acting like lovesick fools. It was another teaser to what could be, which made it hard to move away from him. He didn't let go, either.

"Did you need to be working on something?" I asked after a bit. "I probably interrupted your evening."

"Hmm," he agreed, and leaned forward to kiss my temple again. "Not quite what I expected this morning. But I'm not going to waste tonight working. It can wait until tomorrow."

I had hoped that'd be the answer. "Do you want to sit—?"

A knock at the door interrupted any question I had.

Both of us stared at the door; we weren't in the mood for anyone else to be around. I didn't want to share him.

"Do you have to get it?" I asked.

He made a face; that was a yes. "At least see who it is. It could be an emergency."

He moved his hand from my waist and let go of my hand with the other one.

I shut off the music while David looked through the peek hole; he sighed and ran a hand through his hair, which wasn't a good sign. He came back over and kissed me. The person knocked again.

"David?"

I twitched as I recognized Jessica's voice. Guess it was business.

He winced. "I hate to ask you this, but—"

I nodded. "I'll go hang out in the bedroom. Come in when you're done." I smiled cheekily at him, scooped up my bag I'd left by the door, and hid. I hoped it wasn't anything too bad.

Having to hide in the bedroom made this feel more than a little illicit. At the same time, there was no way Jessica was going to come in and find me lounging on the couch in a robe, hair undone and rumpled, drinking champagne.

I heard the door open and Jessica's heels click-clacked in.

"This better be an emergency, Jess. If you bullied your way past Peter after I explicitly asked to be left alone tonight..." He left the threat hanging in the air.

I wished I could see through the door as easily as I could hear through it. Keeping that in mind, I sat down quietly on the bed.

"It's not an emergency," she said, sounding amused. "I wanted to review the speech for tomorrow. You usually work late." She seemed oblivious to his mood, prattling on about how the event had gone well.

"Jessica." He was pissed off. I didn't need to see his face; I'd shut up if I were her. "Is that all you're here for? I'm not working tonight."

"Is someone else here?" she asked. Her voice sounded strange and embarrassed.

"Yes. So, unless there's been a disaster or there's something that I need to do immediately, it's waiting until morning." His voice trembled in a barely-hanging-in-there, about-to-yell tremor.

She gave a disbelieving laugh. I winced.

"Really? A month before the election? You need to be focused on beating Yates, not having your head between someone's legs."

"Over the line," he spat out, and I heard the door open again. "Tomorrow."

"Get it together." Jessica sounded normal again, matching David's annoyance, all shreds of embarrassment gone. The door slammed shut.

I didn't have to wait long before David came back in; I'd been right about the angry face. The relaxed man I'd been with all night had disappeared.

"Sorry," I said. "What gave me away?"

He shook his head, then rubbed his face. "I think the robe and bottle of champagne."

"We were drinking out of the bottle. No glasses."

He cracked a smile and sat down next to me. "No, but the lipstick on the bottle might have given it away," he said, and traced my lips tenderly.

Fair point. "Well, still. I hope I didn't get you in too much trouble. At least, I didn't leave lipstick smeared on you." Not much anyway.

He half nodded. "You can try again."

I was fresh out of lipstick but smiled anyway. "I'll do my best."

*   *   *

All too soon, David's alarm started beeping. I cracked an eye open. It was only four. Neither one of us had wanted to fall asleep. What good was a surprise trip if we were comatose next to each other? But with only two and a half hours of sleep… No wonder I felt like a sandbag.

"You wake up too early," I mumbled into my pillow.

He stretched behind me, tugging the sheets. "You don't need to get up yet," he said. His voice was rough and lower than normal. "Do you mind if I work in here? I'll be quiet."

I rolled over and nodded. "Yes, please."

He smiled sleepily and kissed my head. "Okay."

I dozed for another hour or so. He was true to his word. Minus the initial getting up to grab a laptop and pulling on some form of clothing, he sat quietly next to me. My back rested against his legs, and for an hour, there were just the sounds of a keyboard tapping and David setting down his coffee cup on the glass side table now and then.

Eventually, I felt him move and shut the laptop lid. I wasn't surprised when he gave my shoulder a small squeeze. "You probably should head out soon."

Pouting or making a fuss when I knew damn well I couldn't stay was pointless; it'd just make both of us feel like crap. I took a breath and opened my eyes. "Okay."

I was ready and repacked before he was out of the shower. I sat down and flipped through emails on my phone. One of Camille's photographer friends had gotten a picture of David and me, and Camille had forwarded it to me. It must have been while we were walking over to meet Sumit, because we were by ourselves, eyes glued on each other. The picture was good, but we looked completely besotted with each other, the smiles and eyes screaming out more than a thousand words. Or maybe it was just my perspective coloring it.

"What do you think?" I asked David when he came out with damp hair and only pants and an undershirt on. I handed him my phone.

He took it and squinted; guess the contacts hadn't made it in for the day yet. A smile spread across his face. "We weren't quite as neutral as we thought, hm? Can you send that to me?" he asked, giving it back.

"Done." I tossed it in my bag and sighed. "I'll leave now." No point in delaying it.

He glanced at his watch and nodded. "You shouldn't have a problem getting back down this early. I…" He paused and leaned against the wall. "I don't want you to leave."

I opened my mouth and shut it; I didn't know what to say. It hurt. "You told me last time it was only for a couple of months. Less than that now. Six weeks."

He rolled his eyes and pulled me over. "Last time," he started, resting his head against mine, "I lied through my teeth. At the risk of sounding completely juvenile, I was worried you'd find someone else in Edmonton who was more exciting, younger, all that, and I'd never hear from you again."

I didn't mean to, but I started to laugh.

He stepped back, looking annoyed with me and probably rightly so.

"Sorry," I said. "I did the same thing. You'd forget me, find a lovely lady to move in with you, have beautiful kids with your eyes." I stopped and shrugged. "And yet, we seem to have done okay."

"Still stuck together." He smiled. "And next time, you won't have to leave." He kept looking at me in a way that made this more difficult.

I stuck my tongue out at him. "Stop being sappy," I said, although I didn't mind it too much. "You need to get ready to do your rock star candidate thing."

He laughed. "Then, get out of here." He walked me towards the door, keeping an arm firmly around my waist. It was easier to talk tough than actually be tough. "I'll see you in just over a month."

"As prime minister," I said.

"Don't jinx it," he said and grimaced. "I love you, sweetheart."

I kissed him before he saw me cry. "I love you, too. Not long at all."

"I'll call tonight." He rapped on the door and opened it.

The guard gave him the all-clear and ushered me out. It was easier to make my break without looking back at David. Only six weeks to go.

*　　*　　*

Before we had satellites or radios or TVs, I wonder how people dealt with the weather. Nowadays, if there's a thunderstorm coming or we're going to be dumped on by a blizzard, we get a heads up; it might be sunny out today, but come tomorrow, all hell breaks loose.

I'm sure you could learn to read it, the prickle of a breeze, a sixth sense, a chill. But I think a lot of the time, you don't recognize you're in the calm before the storm until it's too late.

Chapter Thirteen

"You should have told me you were going," Xavier muttered mulishly, calling a week or so after the Vancouver trip.

"It wasn't a planned thing," I said. I wished he could have been there; he would have enjoyed making fun of the weird dresses. "Besides, I hear you haven't been keeping me fully up-to-date on all that's going on in the office. What say you?"

He snorted. "'What say you?' Is that a pirate thing?"

I flipped on the TV to get my daily David visual fix. The last week we'd barely spoken; the last-minute stops and talks, the work-the-crowd speeches, they took so much time and energy. At least I could watch him on TV.

"I don't think it's pirate…more knight-like, isn't it? Doesn't matter. Tell me. I heard that people are frazzling. I want details."

For someone who claimed to be above office gossip, Xavier was a fount of knowledge. Common consensus had Danielle as the most likely to fizzle out next; I counted as the first. Apparently, when Ben had made a suggestion, something I'd done to run things, Danielle had cracked and gone on a tirade about how she was perfectly competent.

"And Mike?" I asked, figuring I'd better keep an ear on my main targets. Better safe than sorry.

"Hmph. It's too bad he's good at his job, self-righteous prick. Expects things to be done instantly, snippy comments of how things should be done… I'm surprised no one's punched him."

Some things didn't change. "You could. I'd pay to see that." The thought made me smile more broadly than it should have. The news finally shifted to the campaign trail and showed David, shirtsleeves rolled up and meeting with apple-pickers on Ile d'Orleans. He looked good with his forearms showing, all sun-kissed and healthy. I knew they did a tour of a cider press on the island as well. It was a perfect fall campaign stop.

"Oh!" Xavier shouted, making me jump. "That's something. Someone's stealing from the campaign."

I blinked and hit pause on the TV. "What?"

"Exactly." He was a gossip master. "Only in the last week, but..." he lowered his voice conspiratorially, "it's C$150,000."

"What?" How had David not mentioned this? Or Kaitlyn? Or Ben? Bah, I was out of the loop. I stared at cargo shipments and arrivals all day.

"C$150,000," he repeated.

"Just gone? Do the police or anyone know? Why hasn't it been on the news?"

Xavier laughed. "Do you really think Jessica would let that slip out this close to the election?"

He had a point. That'd be bad.

"One of the underlings in finance found it and reported directly to Jessica," he continued. "That set Mike off, as you can imagine. Jessica panicked and shut discussion around it down, so I don't think anyone else knows, but I overheard; no one notices me."

"You're good at lurking," I said. "Was the money found?"

"Jessica's looking into it. I wouldn't want to be Mike right now. It's out of the tour budget. Hey, I've got to go. The girlfriend's calling."

"Say hi from me. And keep me updated!"

He hung up.

That was a huge amount of money to go missing. I started the TV again, half-watching, half-thinking. I wondered who did it? And why? Maybe as a safety net if the election went badly? That amount missing would raise all sorts of red flags with campaign transparency watchdogs. The Centre Party led in all the polls by a comfortable margin. Anyone on the campaign, especially those higher up, would probably have a position going forward. Why risk that? The timing felt odd.

I texted David and told him he should run around more with his sleeves rolled up to attract female voters.

It wasn't until later, nearly midnight for him, that I got a message back apologizing for the late response. We texted a minute or two before I could tell he was bone-dead tired.

Get to sleep. I'll be there in a month.

One month.

*   *   *

At first, I ignored the feeling. I told myself it was my imagination; I was just paranoid. The weather changed, and like an old person, my head prickled because of where I'd gotten thumped a few months ago.

I moved a chair back in front of my door. My kettle bell relocated to beside my bed again. Something didn't feel right, but I couldn't put a finger on what.

The not knowing was most alarming. If there'd been another text or email or anything, I'd know why I was uneasy. As it was, I felt like I was missing something.

Just over a week until the election.

*   *   *

"Ben sent me the numbers," I said on my way home from work. David had scored a free few minutes before an event at a veteran's home near Halifax.

"You're pulling double-duty?" he asked. His voice was soft, raspy, almost a whisper. I couldn't tell if it was from just being tired or if he was in a somewhat public spot. "How long have you been doing that?"

"Just a few weeks, I think." With Xavier swamped running models for everyone else, and the new hires not firing on all cylinders, they were struggling. What we'd agreed on in Vancouver had been blown out the window and I'd been working most nights, with both Ben and Kaitlyn sending me things on the side; it wasn't anything much, just verification of data Danielle ran.

I knew I should stop. My common sense screamed it every time I opened an email, but I wanted to help David. Ben and Kaitlyn were the only two who knew about it. They both were smart enough to keep it under wraps.

I stepped into my apartment and tossed my bag on the chair by the door. As the door closed, I froze. The little bit of air movement from the door closing had wafted the smell of cigarette smoke and cheap cologne.

I glanced at the counter, where the workmen normally left a ticket if they'd been in, but it was empty.

"Can you stay on the phone?" I asked, interrupting him. I picked up my kettle bell and felt idiotic, but I didn't have anything else. What did I do if someone was here?

"I'm on the phone now," he said. "Why?"

I poked my head in my bedroom: empty. Bathroom: empty. Closets: empty. But my closet door was open. I had shut that in the morning. Someone had been here.

"Charlotte." David didn't quite shout but it was loud and firm.

It brought me back. "What?" I licked my lips a few times and tried not to have a meltdown. "I think someone was in my apartment."

I hadn't been imagining things. My worst-case scenario of me being here by myself and having it all start again was suddenly staring me in the face. I should never have gone to Vancouver, never showed my face around the campaign or started to run numbers again. I was an idiot.

"What? Like maintenance?" David asked.

I shook my head and sat down on the floor against my couch. "They'd leave a note. Mr. B.'s pretty good about that. He doesn't smoke."

"What..." David stopped and started. "What does smoking have to do with it?"

"It smells like smoke. And bad cologne." As I said it, I knew I was right. "It's okay now."

But what about tonight? What about the weeks I had left here? That *wasn't* okay. How did I sleep when I knew someone had been in here?

There was a long pause.

"Call the police," David said finally. "And book a hotel. There haven't been any texts or emails?"

"No." I picked at the frayed edge of my couch. "Something felt…off the last couple of weeks, but there's been nothing. I can call the police."

"Yes. And fly out early. Now," he said. "Stay with me—"

"No." I wish he wouldn't have asked. I stopped him before he got too persuasive and I said yes. "No. Not now, not this close to next Monday." Zero chance I'd bring this anywhere near him. Zero chance any of this would disrupt what he needed to do.

"Some things are more important than next Monday."

I rested my head on my knees and took a couple of deep breaths. "It'll be fine. I'll call the police. I won't be stupid."

I squeezed my eyes shut and wished to be three weeks into the future. This would be done. "I moved," I said, sounding pathetic. If I'd moved and it still hadn't stopped, when would it? "It's not just a coincidence, is it?"

"I doubt it. I've got to go. Call me or text me any time. I don't care when it is."

"I will," I promised. "I'll text you after I'm done calling the police."

"Please." He sounded stressed. "I love you."

"I love you, too," I said, hanging up in a rush before he heard me have a panic attack.

*   *   *

It didn't matter if I was in Ottawa or Edmonton; I couldn't make the police take me seriously. With nothing taken and no proof someone had been in my apartment, I knew there wasn't much they could do. Still, I'd been hoping there'd be something.

"We can't investigate nothing, ma'am," the officer said as he left. "We need more than just a hunch. Stay alert and let us know if you notice anything or anyone, and we'll come right back out." He handed me a card and drove off.

Staying alert was not something I needed to be told. I was tired of being ma'am-ed and told nothing could be done.

I was exhausted. I had never realized how many little pops, bumps, or squeaks my apartment made. Every time I rolled at night when the sheets resettled against me, feeling like someone was touching me, I jolted awake. Everything woke me up.

I sat awake for hours at night, waiting for someone to barge in, to attack, panic making me light-headed. The people walking up the stairs next to me, the car parking outside my apartment, the shutting of a door—it all made me jump. When I needed my brain to be top-notch, it felt like I was wading through mud; I was foggy from lack of sleep and everything took extra seconds to process.

Whether or not it had anything to do with my re-emerged stalker, I pulled back from Rita's campaign. I felt bad doing it, but at this stage, there was only so much I could do. Work was too busy at the moment, I explained, never mind I had finished my contract project two and a half weeks early. Backing out now was too little, too late, but I didn't know what else to do.

I wanted to leave because that seemed like the logical thing to do. But what if I put my parents in danger? Or Camille? Or David? I couldn't do that, either.

Part of me wanted to run back to Ottawa as soon as the election was done, but David needed time to either re-evaluate his party if they lost, or to form a government if they won. A move hadn't worked last time, so my confidence in it working again was low.

I was *trapped.*

* * *

Two days until the election.

I was a shadow of myself. My nerves were frayed between the election, getting maybe three hours of sleep a night over the last week, plus the stalker. I was grateful my bus home stopped right outside my apartment. I only walked half a block with many other people.

The day was crisp and cool; the smell of a neighbor burning leaves wafted through the neighborhood. When I got closer to my door, I saw a package sitting on my front step. I hadn't ordered anything, but surprise packages made me happy.

I did my normal double-check around me—nobody behind me, no people in cars just sitting on the road, no rape vans. I checked the doorknob to make sure it hadn't been tampered with; it was locked.

I let myself in, keys always clenched in my hand, and bent down to shove the box in.

It was open. There was something leaking through the box and staining the cement step. I frowned, cracked the lid open, and instantly wished I hadn't. A strangled scream slipped out and I jumped back, tripping on the stairs and tumbling onto the ground.

It was Herring, the gray cat. Someone had put Herring in a box and he was very dead. Someone had purposefully killed him.

The police took me seriously this time. They sealed poor Herring into a plastic bag as evidence. Two officers searched my apartment but found nothing.

"Are you here by yourself?"

I jerked out of my runaway thoughts and nodded to the officer who had spoken. I'd been sitting on the back of a squad car with a blanket for the last hour. I was cold. I was hungry. I was scared.

"Yes, but I think I'll stay in a hotel tonight," I thought out loud. I wasn't calling a taxi and wasn't staying here by myself. "Could you give me a ride, please?"

He looked like he was going to say no at first, but saw something on my face that said, *don't even try it.*

I had to call David. How far was it between mutilating someone's friendly neighborhood cat and mutilating a person? Not far. Serial killers often started off doing horrible things to pets; I remembered that wonderful tidbit from psychology class. How far would a hired…?

The money. Xavier had said C\$150,000 was missing. I couldn't say that to the police. I wasn't mentioning it two days before we voted, before David had his shot. But that was it. Someone had stolen money from the campaign to hire a hit man. It had to have been someone very close to the money.

"Where will you be staying?" the officer asked.

I numbly said the name of a long-term stay hotel downtown. They had little kitchens in the rooms. "Can you make sure no one follows us?"

The annoyed expression on his face softened. "Absolutely, ma'am."

They waited for me to grab a suitcase full of clothes and we were off.

The officer was true to his word. There was a lot of traffic tonight, and no way we were followed.

On the way there, I booked myself a room for the remainder of my time in Edmonton; the cost at this point was irrelevant and would eat into my savings.

Two weeks to go. What happened then?

The traffic inched forward around us, and I hugged myself.

After I checked in, the police and I exchanged contact information one more time. They told me to call with anything else I thought of.

My room was on the eleventh floor. No ground-level entry. I yanked the curtains shut, blocking out the October twilight and hid myself from the world.

I fumbled with my phone and called David. Herring's tufty face kept resurfacing in my head; I'd scratched his ears this morning. He'd wrapped his fuzzy self around my ankles. Who does that to a cat?

I deadbolted the door, jammed the office chair under the handle. The kettle bell was still in my apartment; absurdly, it worried me.

"You're early tonight," David said when he picked up. They had a dinner tonight, a country-style buffet at a fishery on the coast. We hadn't planned to talk until it was done.

"They killed Herring," I blurted out. I started shaking and couldn't stop. "They…put him in a box—"

"Hold on." I heard him excusing himself and a door shutting. "Slow down. Herring the cat?"

I poured myself a glass of water and sat on the floor, retelling him the whole story.

He took a breath, several, before speaking again. "You're okay? Not hurt?"

I gulped my water, shaking hard enough it splashed on my chest and chin. "Yes. I'm in a hotel and under a fake name. I'm staying here for the rest of the time."

"Police?"

"Yes. They're working on it."

"Please come back here," he pleaded. "Please. We'll figure out who is doing this and—"

"No, not yet," I said. "I'm not bringing this anywhere near you."

"It's going to be near me when you move back here in two weeks. You are still moving back." It was a statement. He'd asked me to move back every day for the last couple of weeks, the idea I wouldn't come back wasn't entertained.

"I'm planning on it. We think it's someone on the campaign, so after it's done it should be okay, right?"

"Charlotte… Please, think about coming back early. Please come home."

I started to cry because that was all I wanted to do. "If anything else happens, I will. No one knows I'm here. I just wanted you to know."

"Please stay safe. You're kind of it for me."

"I think you're kind of it for me, too," I said. "Tell me what you have planned the next few days."

"I… Not much at this point. Final talks, a few rallies, criss-crossing the county tomorrow." He talked disjointedly for a few more minutes. "I will call or text you whenever I can over the next few days. You," he said loudly, stopping me from protesting, "need to respond back within five minutes or I will call the police to check on you. Not negotiable."

"Fine." I took a breath and knew I had to tell him. "Do you have a few more minutes? There's something else you should know."

"I have time," he hedged. "What?"

"Did you know someone took C$150,000 from the campaign?" There wasn't any way to sugarcoat it.

Silence filled my ears and I started to second-guess telling him.

"No," he said curtly. "Who…how did you hear that?"

"Finance noticed, went around Mike and told Jessica… I don't think it's gone beyond her." I should have told him earlier; I screwed up my eyes and plunged on. "It disappeared a couple weeks ago."

"Right before someone was in your apartment," he finished, catching it faster than I had. He swore, and I heard him hit something.

I winced.

"I'll deal with Jess. Why the fuck didn't she say something?"

"Because you have enough on your mind." I agreed with Jessica on this.

"And why didn't you?" he asked. "You knew, and didn't say anything to me?"

My head dropped to my knees and I felt sick. "Because I thought Jessica was handling it. I…"

I was lost and tired. Nothing in the last couple of weeks had gone to plan, and nothing in my sleep-deprived state had been well thought out. "I'm… sorry. I thought you should know now."

He sighed loudly. "Someone has taken over a hundred thousand dollars from my campaign to hire someone to kill you. You're damn right I should know."

"Could you wait a couple of weeks to yell at me and just do it in person?" I asked. I couldn't handle him mad at me now. "I wanted you to know, but I can't do this right now."

"Charlotte—" His voice was rough with stress, and he muttered something under his breath, livid. "You and me, we're in this together. We will figure it out, but if you're holding back on me, I can't help. It's not just you; you're in the rest of my life."

"I know. Get back to work, okay? I'm good. I need to order food, though." I'd kept him long enough tonight.

"Take care of yourself. Get a steak, order a martini, and call me if you need anything at all."

What I wanted was to hear him talk all night because that calmed me down best. I couldn't ask that.

"I will. Can you call after you're done tonight?"

"Of course." And he hung up.

The abrupt end took me by surprise and didn't make me feel better. I'd made everything a mess. I looked around my little room, the tiny kitchenette, a bed, a couch, a desk. The view I'd blocked out earlier looked over the North Saskatchewan River and promised to be rather scenic in the daytime. A very generic picture of a boat on a lake hung above the bed. This wasn't a home. I really wanted to go home.

But I couldn't. I followed his advice, ordered dinner, and planned.

*   *   *

Over the next two days, I slept very little and scraped my brain for anything I might have missed. The business center attached to the hotel had poster-sized paper, so I bought some, along with multi-colored Sharpies and did what I should have done months ago.

I pulled up the emails I'd saved and started a timeline. I added the bumps and shoves and Herring's death. At the time, I'd never noted when Mike or Danielle did something or said something to indicate annoyance at me, but I tried to add in what I remembered.

My gut said Mike. Jealousy and spurred romantic interest made people do crazy things. The few times I'd told him to back off in public and embarrassed him might have burned more than I'd realized. Add in that he was in finance, the missing money, and the general unease I got around him, he was the closest fit.

I noted when I had done something good at work, showing Danielle up in a meeting or project. I added in when I'd turned Mike down. The missing C$150,000 slid in a couple of weeks ago.

On second thought, I drew in everyone else, projects I worked on, or if Ben, Kaitlyn, Xavier, or Jessica had gotten annoyed with me for not knowing something right away. I didn't know who to look at or who to exclude anymore.

All of it added up to a frustratingly unclear web of colored lines. On TV shows, the detective always solved it this way. There was a piece I still didn't have.

*   *   *

Election Day dawned dark and rainy, my city view obscured by rain splatters. I'd voted early a few weeks ago since there was no question which party was getting my vote. I was stuck in my hotel room with my timeline and evidence map.

During the day, there wasn't much to do except wait and get increasingly antsy. I wished I could be with the rest of the team, watching the results come in.

David had voted this morning in his own riding, showing up with his mother and sister, all three of them smiling and waving at voters. He, his family, and the core team would watch the results come in tonight; they had a hotel suite booked in Ottawa.

Whatever talk he'd give later tonight, either victory or concession, would be in the ballroom downstairs. Speeches would be tweaked as things changed. I wanted to be there. I wanted to be in the room with him when he got the results.

Instead, I spent the day with my timeline, adding in any details that popped into my mind.

*   *   *

Results trickled in early evening. Watching something with such an impact on my future, something I couldn't control, was nerve-wracking to the point of nausea. When the first ridings that weren't a given showed as Centre, Centre, Centre I smiled. He had this. Those were the ones I'd said to focus on, and we had. We were going to win.

I giggled, and then started laughing. Despite the fact I was hiding in a hotel room because someone was trying to kill me, I was ridiculously happy for David. He'd be prime minister.

I think you did it

I didn't expect to get a text back. He'd be surrounded by everyone else. But he did it. He won.

The news networks called the election before the last vote was counted on the west coast; we won. Centre had a solid majority moving into tomorrow and the next four years. Rita's campaign had made the election here much closer than we'd initially thought, but she'd still fallen a couple hundred votes short.

It was surreal to me. Maybe if I had been there, where I knew David and everyone else were waiting, or in the conference room full of supporters, maybe it'd seem more real to me. Or maybe if it had just been my job and I wasn't emotionally involved. I was a jumble of happiness, disbelief, and nerves. Everything we'd talked about, from normal couple things we'd do together to his work as Prime Minster, would become reality. He had won— any worry about the future was wiped out by the grin I couldn't erase.

His victory speech followed the typical pattern: the victory lap for the campaign; the thank yous to family, to staff, to volunteers. I got a jolt of surprise when he thanked Jessica, Ben, Kaitlyn, other staff, and Charlotte for all their work planning and prepping; he'd never mentioned I'd get a call out. He thanked Alan Yates for his concession call, far more politely than I'd ever heard him talk about Yates. He outlined the goals for tomorrow, the hard work ahead, rosy visions of the future, thanking supporters and all the people we'd met and talked to along the way. He promised to take all he'd heard to heart.

His voice was hoarse and sounded like a husk, but the jubilation shone through. The room cheered and screamed. Confetti and balloons floated from the ceiling. When he finished the speech and waved, shaking hands with those next to the stage and hugging his mom and sister and Jessica and everyone else, I wanted to be there to celebrate with him. I *should've* been there.

I finished the single-serve bottle of champagne I'd bought for myself; it was pretty bad but made a satisfying pop and fizzed a decent amount. Instead of wearing the pretty purple slim-fitting slip of a dress I'd bought during the summer just in case tonight happened, I wore my yoga pants and one of David's T-shirts I'd smuggled out with me. It was as close to him as I could get tonight. Instead of being around friends and celebrating into the wee hours of the morning, I was alone. I'd been angry and sad about being tossed into exile the last three months, but tonight topped it.

Tonight, I felt incredibly isolated.

*   *   *

It was another two hours, nearly two in the morning in Ottawa, before my phone rang. I'd dozed off.

"Hi you," I answered, smiling. I hadn't expected him to call on FaceTime, clearly still in full party mode. I switched the light on and tried to sit up. "Still celebrating?"

His face lit up. "Still celebrating." He maneuvered outside the party to what looked like an isolated back room. The noise level dropped so I could hear him above the music and chatter.

For a second or two, I didn't know what else to say and just smiled. Words failed me.

"I assume you watched the speech earlier?" he asked. His smile creased every corner of his face, from mouth to cheeks to eyes.

"Of course I did. They all love you," I said.

"I had another version," he continued, ignoring me. "In case you came back early and were here tonight. I wasn't going to wait the few weeks you wanted before making us public." He looked a little sheepish admitting it.

I wasn't sure if I should be annoyed or amused.

"I wanted to say thank you to you specifically, for everything you did work-wise but mainly for everything else you've been to me over the course of the campaign, and everything going forward. It didn't seem right to do it when you weren't here."

Part of me wished he would have. Maybe it would have been easier to stop all the hiding.

"I—" Saying I was happy for him, or proud, sounded silly. "You don't need to thank me for anything. You would have ended up winning without me around. And congrats," I added a bit lamely at the end.

"Possibly, yes. But the thank you is for everything you are personally to me." He smiled and shook his head in a happy daze. "I need to head back but wanted to call now."

The call was shorter than I expected. "Okay. Don't party too hard, Prime Minister Reid."

His smile stretched to his eyes; he looked exhausted and slightly disbelieving yet. "I won't."

Some of the glow faded from his face for a second. "I wish you were here. I want to celebrate with you."

Rather than admitting that was what I wanted, too, which he already knew, I tried to brush it off. "This is no time for sappy. Go have fun tonight. But save some celebrating for me when I get back."

"I'll send you pictures. We'll talk more tomorrow."

The smile never left his face as he hung up, the stunned happy a person gets when a dream comes true.

I smiled and tossed my phone on the side of the bed as I clicked the light off.

Two weeks really wasn't long at all.

*   *   *

In the days immediately following election night, I was a bit lost. For the last ten months, it was all I'd thought of or done. And now, there was nothing. Obviously, David didn't get a break as he switched to running the country, but there was nothing for me to do. Campaign work I was good at. Actual governing, picking ministers, I wanted to stay well clear of. Sitting in the hotel room for the last couple of days hadn't worn on me much because I'd worked on my timeline and had the election to worry about. Now, there was a gaping hole in my time, and the hotel room felt stifling.

I spent one day printing photos I'd taken on the campaign and ones I'd asked nicely for from the official photographer. There was a stationery and paper supply store, far more crafty than I normally would use, across the road. I felt like an idiot when I tucked my hair up under a hat, the white-blonde too conspicuous for my liking, and dashed across the road to get scrapbook materials. People in the store ignored me. There was no one vaguely threatening.

I gathered my supplies and went back, picking up something for dinner from the deli next door. I was a suspicious, paranoid lady who'd holed up in a hotel room, trying to scrapbook.

When I told David, he laughed. He commented I should get a cat to complete the crazy, eccentric cat lady look. As soon as he said it, he looked horrified and apologized. Herring still haunted my dreams.

The reaction to my scrapbook was remarkably consistent; my mom, Camille, and David all suggested perhaps being crafty wasn't my strong suit. As much as I wanted to be indignant at the response to my day's work, I had to agree. It resembled a grade-school art project.

It took me three days to remember Sumit, who I'd met just a month ago in Vancouver.

He was excited to hear from me and really wanted the help. What I'd expected to be just a quick email turned into a returned call that lasted a couple hours. A little piece of my future Ottawa life settled, and I had work to do again.

David also gave me the task of picking somewhere for us to go between Christmas and New Year's. Both tasks kept me from going too stir crazy.

Neither eliminated the fact I was holed up in a hotel room for a reason. The end of exile was in sight. I would have loved to think of it as the end of things, but I wasn't convinced and neither was David moving back would be a tidy wrap-up. It was easy to feel vaguely safe in my eleventh-story perch, adventuring out only for dashes across the street or up to the twentieth-floor patio for fresh air and an endless view across the river to the prairies; going up in the morning to watch the sunrises turned into a highlight of my day. David was the only person who knew I was here. That'd all change as soon as I moved home and plunged back into an incredibly bright spotlight.

Only five more days…

Chapter Fourteen

"Happy birthday, Mr. Eric! Are you old and achy yet?"

Eric's laugh rumbled through the phone. "Not too much, but I'm pretty sure my knee's telling me the weather's a-changing soon. How've you been?"

I caught a glance of myself in the mirror—dark circles, messy hair, and dull skin, and decided the truth was not best to share. "Oh, you know, keeping myself occupied."

The timeline was spread out on the table next to my laptop and notes from my call earlier with Sumit; I was either a crazy lady or Sherlock. I preferred to think of myself as Sherlock. "You?"

We spent a few minutes talking birthday plans, how little Henry was doing, life back there. It sounded like he was having a good day.

"Is Jessica showing up for your birthday dinner?" I asked. Now that the election was done and David was prime minister designate, maybe she'd have the time. I thought Eric would appreciate that.

"Ah, you haven't heard yet, have you?" he said.

I sat down in my stiff little hotel chair and stared outside; maybe I could get out for a walk this evening. The sun was setting, warming the buildings around me, making it look like a beautiful autumn night. Then again, the last few times I had let my guard down, I'd nearly been killed. So maybe not.

"What exciting news am I missing? You get to spill the beans."

"I thought you'd already know since you worked with her for so long. Sounds like she and Reid are more than just friends. Can you believe it—Jessica and David Reid? Ha!" He laughed.

I was completely lost. "Why do you say that?" I asked, feeling off-balance.

"She told me when she called yesterday," he said, clueless to my reaction. He sounded thoroughly amused. "They're going somewhere, just the two of them, so it must have been going on for a while. I guess when they showed up at dinner together, that should have been a hint. Really, you didn't know? Seems like it'd be hard to keep that much of a thing quiet without anyone noticing, especially when you worked with them so much."

I opened my mouth and shut it. "Maybe…"

Eric kept talking, but I'd checked out. Things slid into place with ease, no more clawing details from my brain or over-thinking. A smooth click and it opened up.

"Just a second," I interrupted. "Don't hang up."

I placed him on speakerphone and scrambled over to my timeline. David was the piece I'd missed. I grabbed a new Sharpie color and started adding our relationship. The first debate practice. Showing up to meetings early together. Maybe more than one look when we'd been in public. Jessica had noticed I'd smelled like his cologne. The look she'd given me when I showed up in Vancouver. She'd known I was in his room that night. It lined up, every single piece lined up. It was Jessica.

"You still there?" Eric asked.

"Yes. Just hold on."

Everything she had done was to get him elected; that was all that mattered to her. The last few months played out in my mind and I could see it all from her point of view. Eliminating distractions so he could focus, hiring me at Christmas because I was good at what I did and she knew I'd help the campaign. But then I'd become a distraction, a benefit cost analysis showed I was too expensive to keep. I had gone away but reappeared in Vancouver. The distraction came back, and *boom*, Herring was murdered. Of course she'd had access to the missing C$150,000.

David had won, though. So why would she say that now to Eric, that they were a couple? There was still one piece missing.

I stopped pacing and drew in the last week. David and I had talked once a day. It'd been mundane stuff, just what would happen next, what we'd do, what I'd do, David liking my plan for Banff over the holidays, getting my security cleared so I could move in next week…

Oh, shit. That had been two days ago. He'd stepped out from a meeting with Jessica when I'd called. She'd heard. She must have known then it wasn't just a campaign fling. He hadn't turned to her after she moved heaven and earth for him to win, so…

"Eric, what did she say?" I asked, feeling like I already knew the answer. I hadn't slept in two weeks. My brain was frazzled. *Please let me be wrong.*

"What did Jessica say?" he repeated.

"Yes," I snapped harshly. "When she called and said she and David were going somewhere?"

He picked up on my tone and answered straight. "That they'd been an item and pretty serious for a while. She wanted to say happy birthday because they'd be gone tomorrow—"

"When did she call you?"

"Yesterday. Charlotte, are you okay?"

David hadn't called or texted me since early morning when he'd woken up. He usually checked in on me a couple of times throughout the day. I thought the lack of communication today was due to being busy, but maybe not. "I've got to go. Thank you."

I had seen a show, maybe more than one, with a murder-suicide. It happened because if X couldn't be with Y, then nobody else could. At least they'd be together at the end.

Jessica's devotion wasn't to the party, but to David.

I had no hard proof, but as I tried to call David, nausea bubbled. I had zero doubt I was right. What if I was too late? You expected for your grandparents to pass away, or an older relative; I wasn't ready for this. We were going to have the next fifty years together. We weren't supposed to end before we had the chance to start.

"Damn it!" The call went to voicemail.

Verging on hysteria, I hung up and dialed his work phone instead. He couldn't be gone already. There would have been something on the news, or Twitter, or someone would have called me… A scream built in my chest. This whole time we had been protecting me, but now—

"What's up?"

I let out a cry; he was alive. "Are you alone? Don't say my name." She couldn't know it was me on the phone. What did I do now?

"I stepped out from a meeting with Jess," he said, sounding confused and worried. "You're not okay. What—?"

"It's her," I blurted. How did we get him out? I had to convince him. "Is your security in there with you?"

"What? No, they're outside. What do you mean—?"

"Everything," I said. "The emails, the threats, the missing money. She's in love with you, David. Jessica…she wanted you to win and hired me because I'm good, but then you, we…we fell in love, and I was a distraction. She's jealous, so I had to go. But then you won, and you still don't… She's going to—I think she's going to try and kill you. Everything lines up… I drew it in my timeline and it all matches. She's going to do something to you." I was rambling. I wanted to storm into whatever room they were in and run him out. I wiped at my eyes and tried to unclench my fist; my nails cut deep red half-moons into my palm.

"That doesn't make sense," he said, sounding unsure. "Why do you think that? Jess has probably been my best friend for the last twenty years. I can't go back in there and accuse her."

I took a breath; I couldn't sound like a crazy person. "I talked to my cousin, Eric, today. Jessica told him you two are in love and have been for months. She said she wanted to say happy birthday and good-bye because you'd both be gone today."

David couldn't be gone yet. We needed more time.

"How confident are you?" he asked.

I closed my eyes. I was good at seeing patterns; it was why I was so good at my job. "I'm sure."

"I'm going to try leaving," he said, much softer than before. "If it's nothing, there shouldn't be a problem. Do you still have Peter's number?"

My stomach churned. "Yes."

"Call him."

I nodded. "Leave your phone on," I whispered. "Don't hang up; I need to know what's happening. I'll call Peter on my hotel phone."

"He won't answer that number," David said gently. "Hang up, call him from your phone, and then call me on the hotel phone. I'll wait."

"David, I—"

"I know. And you can say it later tonight, after I call you back and we laugh about this and we plan where I'm taking you out on a date when you get back here." He was doing his politician voice, where he knew he wasn't telling the whole truth. He knew we may not get that. "We're not doing good-byes now."

My face was wet with tears and I nearly choked on my breath. *Pull it together.* "Okay. I'm going to hang up and call you back, and then call Peter."

"Okay."

I pried my phone from my ear and hung up before I could delay. Delaying was bad. I pulled up Peter's number from my phone and scribbled it down. I called David back from the hotel phone.

"I'll mute myself," I said when he picked up.

"Call Peter. It'll be fine."

I pressed mute and switched phones. Peter answered on the third ring.

"Hello, Ms. Finnan, everything all right?" He was confused. He knew I was in Edmonton and something was very wrong if I'd called him.

"Get in David's room. Now," I said in a rush.

David's line distracted me. I heard him tell Jessica their meeting was over, something had come up.

"Slow down a second…what's going on?" Peter said, jerking me back to our conversation. "Unless there's an emergency—"

"There is. Please. Jessica… I think she's going to kill him." It sounded absurd when I said it out loud.

David's phone was muffled, but I made out Jessica asking if I was on the phone. David's voice went wary, and then jumped from wary to alarmed.

"Jess, put it down." His voice sounded steady. "You don't want to do this."

For a second, I forgot Peter.

Jessica's voice came through the phone shrilly. "Everything I did was to help you get your dream," she said, the plead easily audible. "We could have everything, you and me, now…we have it, but you don't see it." She didn't sound herself, nothing like the firm and in-command Jessica I was used to.

"Jess, of course I do," David said. "You've been my best friend since college. We talk about everything—always have. Set the gun down and we can talk through this, too. I know we can."

The word gun *screamed* in my head.

"Peter, get in there! Now. She's got a weapon—a gun. Please go in. Please."

"You say she has a weapon?" He sounded more alert now. He believed me.

My attention pulled back to David's voice on the other phone. "Put down the gun."

Jessica's voice wavered and trembled out of control. "She's a nobody. You were supposed to be different. You were supposed to love me. We were supposed to be together."

"We are." David was still talking, but it sounded overly in control, like he was trying too hard. "We are together. You and I, right now. And we still will be tomorrow and in the future. Don't do this."

I relayed what I'd heard to Peter. "Peter, please…please go in."

"I'm calling for back up and going in now."

I hated he was right. Of course he'd need back up and couldn't barge in solo. "Go."

His line dropped off and I grabbed the other phone.

The two of them had stopped talking. I heard a door open and slam shut; Peter was in. There was a pause that sounded louder than any shout could. I couldn't do a damned thing, useless and stuck.

Peter started yelling to drop the gun, blowing up any calm David had created.

I nearly choked. I should have let David talk her down, not send in another threat. I heard Jessica, a loud heartbreaking sob that tore through the phone, and then David yelling at Peter to step back. A picture of a cornered animal popped to mind, always more dangerous when cornered. A lull settled on the line, dark and heavy.

"Do you love her?" Jessica asked.

Every inch and particle of me urged him to say no. I started shaking my head, mouthing *please say no*, save himself. I knew what he'd say before he said it.

"Yes, I do."

There was more shouting, indecipherable and from everyone. One, two gunshots, loud static scratches, and the line went dead.

Chapter Fifteen

I wanted to claw the evening out of my head. I wanted to scoop it out and throw it away. I wanted to wake up again this morning and have things be okay. I wanted to go back three months ago and say, "Not a chance I'm leaving you," and not waste time running away. I wanted one more smile that crinkled David's eyes. I wanted another shared looked where I knew exactly what he was thinking. I wanted to wake up and find him lying next to me. I wanted one more everything…

Instead, I curled up on the floor, very much aware of what just happened, shaking and unable to make my fingers function enough to dial back. The gunshots echoed around my head. One. Two. I'd heard David yell. I couldn't get it out of my head, the sound seared in permanently.

Jessica might have missed. It might have been Peter, as terrible as that sounded. But I had heard David. When I closed my eyes, I could see him lifeless and white in the middle of pooling ruby blood, an empty shell on a hotel floor somewhere.

The bullets *might have* missed.

I finally stopped shaking enough to hit the call button. His personal number went directly to voicemail. I tried his business phone—voicemail. And again. Voicemail. I wiped at my eyes, trying to clear them to see what I was doing. I tried Peter's line, but it just rang and rang and rang.

I paused after ten minutes. I needed to get back to Ottawa. All thoughts for my own safety were completely out the window.

I grabbed my suitcase and shoved clothes in. What if I needed black? I didn't have any black here. If there was a funeral, why would they let me near it? It was my cousin who had shot him. I wouldn't be able to get near him. I wouldn't get to say good-bye. I'd become a widow before I could be a wife.

I folded up my timeline, just in case, and jammed it in my purse. That was everything. My momentary burst of activity died. There were still no messages on my phone. I did something I shouldn't and looked at the news; there were alerts about shots fired near where the newly-elected prime minister was visiting.

I should have said I love you; I should have made him say it.

My bag slipped from my hand and I sank onto the bed. For a moment, I couldn't breathe. It didn't matter how many breaths I gasped in, I was drowning. I squeezed my eyes tight, pressed the heels of my hands hard against them until I saw stars, and screamed at myself to wake up. Except when I opened my eyes, I was still sitting in a hotel room in Edmonton. My phone still showed call after call after unanswered call. My eyes were swollen and my nose stuffed. I could still hear the gunshots.

I tried one more time before I left, giving the personal phone a ring first.

"This is David. Leave a message."

I could listen to his speeches, and events, and rallies when I wanted to hear his voice again. I had one voicemail he'd left me saved on my phone. How could I not have been fast enough? I'd sat here for weeks; how had I not put it together?

I pushed David's business phone number in again. There wasn't a voicemail on this one.

"I'm okay."

At first, it didn't register.

"Charlotte. Are you there?"

"David?"

"I'm okay," he said. "Hurt, but alive, and will be okay."

I broke down. And pinched myself hard to make sure I was fully awake, that I hadn't passed out hallucinating.

"I'm coming," I managed to say. "What happened?"

A sharp intake of breath interrupted his response at first; he was hurt. "She missed," he said. "She hit my arm, but it's nothing major. I need to let the paramedics patch me up. I'll call you later."

I nodded. "Yes. Please. Soon. I'll be there soon. I love you." No chance I wasn't saying it now.

"I love you, too."

The phone went dead.

I stared at it, my dread receding a bit. I needed to go. This time I grabbed my bag, checked out, and jumped in the first taxi I saw.

*   *   *

My mind was curiously blank on the way to the airport and while I fought to get my ticket bumped up by a few days. It cost more than the original ticket to move it, but I was scheduled now to be on the 6 AM back to Ottawa via Toronto. I'd be there by two this afternoon. I had twelve hours until I boarded and zero intention of getting another hotel. Instead, I hustled through security, set my alarm for 4 AM and set up camp in the terminal.

Every TV at every gate showed "Breaking News" banners running across the screen, announcing an assassination attempt on future Prime Minister David Reid. I couldn't handle those. I wandered around until I found a quiet corner, out of the way and free from news. I replied to two texts, one from Camille and one from Ben; they had both called earlier as well. And then I waited.

David finally called back several hours later. I was sitting against a wall, too wound up to sleep, too tired to do anything except stare and people-watch. I needed to eat.

"Do you know how hard it is to find a spot in an airport that isn't showing the news?" I asked, breaking the silence.

He gave a little puff of a laugh. "Popular guy, am I?"

Four hours ago, I'd thought he was dead. For about the gazillionth time, I said a thank you to whoever or whatever was listening.

"What happened?" I asked.

He sighed, and any sort of lightheartedness evaporated.

I'd been right, obviously. When he'd told her their meeting was over unexpectedly, she'd pulled out a gun. He sounded in shock. He and Jessica had been friends for nearly twenty years. I wasn't sure how I'd respond if Camille snapped.

"When Peter came in, she lost it," he said, tired and sad. "It seemed to click together for her that you'd figured it out and now she couldn't do this, either. I almost felt sorry for her until she shot me."

He'd meant to be glib about it; it didn't work.

"How bad?" I asked. "And Peter!" I felt horrible and guilty. I'd been so wrapped up in our own little world, I had forgotten him. "Peter's okay?"

"Peter is fine," he reassured me. "He came out the best of all of us."

"How bad are you?" I asked again. "Are you in the hospital?"

"No," he said quickly. "I'm on the plane heading towards Ottawa. The first shot just grazed my arm; the second pulled high. I got patched up and sent on my way with some painkillers. That's all."

I knew little to nothing about guns. I was pretty sure, though, they made a mess if you got hit. "Just a little graze?" I asked.

"With some stitches tossed in for good measure."

He was being cagey about it. "How many stitches are we talking? One or two, or a cross-stitch piece?"

"I'll have an impressive scar."

The nauseating thought of *what if* surfaced again and made me glad I hadn't eaten anything. "You're very casual about it all."

"Is it working?"

I rested my chin on my knees and sighed. "Not really."

"What time do you get in tomorrow? Early?" The question betrayed the bravado he'd been trying to carry.

"Two." I yawned. Only eight more hours until my flight. "That's the earliest stupid flight they could put me on."

"You're coming directly home?"

I bit back a smile; he assumed my home was with him, and of course he was right. I threw out another silent thank you. "Yes, as soon as I land. What happened to Jessica?" I asked.

"She's in custody," he said, his voice flat and hard. "The police started going through her house tonight. They found the name of the person she hired to get you, the account the money was in, a journal she kept, a suicide note for tonight…everything. The police in Edmonton arrested the hired person earlier tonight. It's over, Charlotte."

Get was a nice word for *kill*. I had forgotten there might have still been someone out for me.

"Are you okay? Not just physically?" I asked.

I heard him sigh heavily. There was a long, telling pause. "I don't know. Probably? I'm glad you'll be home tomorrow."

"Like there was a doubt," I said.

We talked for quite a while longer. When we ran out of things to say, we stayed on the line and were just quiet together. I didn't ask any more about what had happened, even though I started to brim over with questions, and he didn't mention it. We called it for the night when he was about to land.

*   *   *

My travel day went without a hitch. I didn't sleep. The flight only crossed two time zones, but I felt jetlagged beyond belief. I was shaky, stiff, and I struggled to come up with the words for a thank you as I exited the plane.

Once in Toronto, I finally called my parents. They had left messages last night, but quite frankly, I couldn't handle them. They were going to be talking about Jessica, if I'd seen this coming, and how terrible it was for my aunt and uncle.

So, I waited until morning, after I found a Tim Hortons and bought sugar and caffeine.

"Charlotte! It's about time," Mom said, a slight scold coming through. "I'm glad you called. Your dad and I were starting to get worried. You haven't talked to Eric yet, have you? I talked to your Aunt Judy—"

"Mom," I interrupted. If I didn't jump in early, I'd lose my chance to get a word in. "Stop for a second and listen to me. Well, actually, what have you heard?" My policy of no news might have backfired. I had no idea what was being said or reported at this point. David had texted me this morning and that was really all I'd cared about. In the daylight now, I was more apprehensive.

Mom started rambling on about everything she'd heard; it gave me time to eat the sprinkles off my donut, shockingly bright pink strawberry and so sugary I could smell it. News outlets had reported former Centre Party campaign manager Jessica Hage attempted to kill David Reid last night. Ms. Hage had been taken into custody immediately. Rumors were swirling it was a love triangle gone wrong; I winced. The rest wouldn't take long to come out at this point.

"Did you know they were together?" Mom asked, fishing for gossip in a hushed tone. "I never thought to ask her if she was involved with someone. I thought she'd just bring a boyfriend along to a family gathering at some point. I know Aunt Judy and Uncle Matt were worried she was so committed to work, but I just can't see her doing this. And if there's a love triangle, then there's a third—"

"Mom, you're doing it again." I swigged down a sip of purposefully strong, straight black coffee. "I'm the third piece," I blurted before I lost my opening. "I didn't want you to find out in the news. Jessica invented the triangle thing, but I'm flying back to Ottawa now because, well, David and I are very much a couple."

I stunned her into silence for a breath or two, which was more alarming than anything.

"But he's the prime minister," she finally said.

The coffee kicked in enough for me to swallow the sarcastic response that nearly slipped out. "Yes, and he's also my someone."

The silence this time lasted for a very long time before she erupted into questions. I spent the better part of a half an hour fielding as best I could. There was a lot I couldn't answer, like what we were doing now and how I fit in with him being prime minister, but also a lot I could, namely that it was serious, and yes, I was absolutely certain about it.

"Are you okay now, honey?" she asked.

I tucked my knees up to rest my head on them so people couldn't see me crying. I wanted to be back in Ottawa.

"Maybe?" I said, sniffling a little. I couldn't stop. "I was on the phone with him when Jessica—" I choked on the memory and the words tumbled out. "When Eric said she'd told him they were going to be gone, I figured it out and called David to tell him to get out, but I wasn't fast enough…"

I started to hyperventilate again, short, shallow, useless breaths in between tears. "I told him to keep me on the phone, and I heard the gunshots." Two loud and clear shots. "She shot him."

"Oh, Charlotte…" Mom sounded lost. "Where are you now? Do you need help getting back?"

"I'm in Toronto already. I flew out this morning and I board for Ottawa in about ten minutes."

"And David?" she asked, hesitating. "He's okay?"

"Yes." I sounded more confident than I felt. "I'll see him tonight when I get home. Do you think you and Dad could maybe come up sometime next week?" I asked, feeling suddenly very small again.

We set a tentative date, and eventually hung up after my gate was announced on the screen. I was jittery and ready to get on the last flight. I called Mr. Abas, and he agreed to pick me up from the airport. I was set.

Chapter Sixteen

I was grateful for the lack of cameras and press at the airport; nobody had pegged me yet. Mr. Abas had greeted me with a smile and another cup of coffee before driving us away. It was smooth as could be. And now I was here, standing in the doorway to a giant, gray stone house. I made it.

An older lady with an elegant chignon and sharp-looking business suit smiled benignly as I came through the entryway. On a normal day, if I'd arrived fresh from the airport, I'd be able to appreciate the house; it was brand-new and we'd be the first occupants. Even now, I noted it was beautiful, although calling the prime minister's official residence just a house seemed a little off-kilter. I couldn't fully appreciate the double-storied entryway, the slate floors, the elegant dark wood staircase winding up to the upper stories, or really anything else.

I gave the lady the best smile I could muster and shuffled my bag around to shake her hand.

"Hello, Ms. Finnan," she said crisply. "My name is Mrs. Martin and I'm the housekeeper. Do you have any bags that need taking care of?"

"Just these," I said indicating my suitcase and little carry-on. How would I get everything back from Edmonton? The thought barely landed before puffing away…I was so tired.

She gave a little finger motion and someone stepped forward to grab them. It was probably completely normal for the house, but after the few weeks where I'd jumped at every noise and movement, the quick movement coming from behind me made me scuttle forward. After thinking earlier I could barely walk, the adrenaline showed I could jump and jerk and stifle a scream just fine.

When I realized the movement was a porter, I knew I'd made a fool of myself. I tried to smile back as I handed my bag over. I was making a lousy first impression.

He looked at me like I was crazy and left with my bags.

Mrs. Martin touched my arm, and for a moment, the business front dropped and her eyes were soft and concerned. "You're all right here, Ms. Finnan. Safe as can be." She gave me a smile and nodded towards the stairs. "I'll give you a brief tour."

Thankfully, she turned and headed up the stairs before seeing my eyes start to water. I had no reason to be teary except she was someone who cared.

She understood I had no desire to see the full house right now. She led me through to the private residence part, away from where any of the official meetings and events would be staged, and into a house that didn't look quite like David's condo, but even after just a week, had his influence. She pointed out the living room area, the private study overlooking the park and river, and the bedroom. This was the first time David and I could actually be seen together, for it to be normal for us to share a bedroom. And to think yesterday at this time—

"Is there anything else you need, Ms. Finnan?" The polite professional returned and I pulled myself back from anything to do with yesterday.

"No," I said firmly and was happy I sounded relatively convincing. "I think that's fine."

"Very good. If you do think of something, just give us a ring on the intercom." She smiled and made her departure, leaving me alone in the bedroom.

If I stayed in this room and saw all David's things and looked too closely at the picture on the side table that I was pretty sure was of us, I'd start to cry. Instead, I changed out of my travel clothes, took my phone, and wandered down the hall to the study area. It wasn't quite the stately library I expected, but it wasn't bad. And the view was hard to beat, even in late October when the wind whipped away any trace of autumn leaves and tore the river into waves.

I sat down on an oversized leather chair next to the window and pulled down a waffled blanket laid across the back. I sent David a quick text, as requested, letting him know I was here.

I was here.

For the first time in multiple weeks—and really, if I went back to the first blasted email that Jessica had sent, first time in months—I started to unwind. The months of emails and texts, the threats, the attacks, it all uncoiled, the knot in my shoulders relaxing. Jessica was well behind bars at the moment, the hired hit man arrested and in jail across the country, and I was in the most secure house in Canada. Until it was taken away from me, I never truly appreciated the luxury of being safe. I was safe now, with no specter of a threat hanging over us, and we could just be Charlotte and David.

I slipped my glasses off and set them on the window ledge. The world went blurry and reduced to fuzzy blocks of color; it made it easier for my mind to relax. I tried to tell myself the blurriness was my lousy vision, but I felt my eyes going hot and watery. It was annoying.

I'd cry when David got home, just because twenty-four hours ago I thought I'd never see him again. But now, I was so tired and used to carrying around the stress, my emotions seemed to be running rampant without any care for what my brain said.

With the lack of tension and adrenaline, the woolly blanket around me, the warm book smell of a library, and the spittle of rain starting to ping against the window, it wasn't a surprise I surrendered and slipped into sleep.

*   *   *

When I opened my eyes, I wasn't entirely sure what woke me up. I heard voices somewhere in the house, a murmur of other people. It was dark out now. Someone at some point had been in and drawn the heavy curtains next to me; that went to show how much I'd uncoiled. I hadn't slept through the heater kicking in the last couple of weeks, let alone someone walking in next to me.

I groped for my glasses and stood up. Before I managed to shuffle across the floor, wondering if there was anything for me to crash into, the door cracked open. Lights flicked on and David walked in.

He looked beat and weary to the bone and beautifully alive. He didn't bother waiting for me to move and crossed the room in a few strides. His arms wrapped around me. I wasn't letting go again. To be fair, he didn't seem inclined to, either.

"I owe you everything," he said after a while, and pulled back to look at me. He relaxed his left arm, wincing. The bulky outline of a bandage was nearly visible through his suit jacket.

I just smiled. "You're alive." I grabbed his silly face and kissed him. It was a lousy kiss because we were both smiling too much.

"Thanks to you. And you're alive and here, too."

More relief and emotion was in that sentence than I expected and it caught me off guard. When I tilted my head back to look more squarely at him, worry creased across his face.

"Nothing to worry about anymore, right?" I asked.

He pulled me back, taking a breath against my head before answering. "What you went through last night, the not knowing, being across country and not a thing you could do about it? That's been my last three months."

So we were both a mess. I pressed my face against his neck, where I could lose myself in him and inhaled; he was right.

"We're both home," he said.

"It will take a while for that to sink in." I got one more kiss, this time not as much smile but more kiss, before we headed out of the study.

"You're quite the national hero, or will be. More famous than me." He wrapped the non-hurt arm tight around my waist, leading us towards the bedroom.

I latched on to him and found it difficult to unclench my fist from his jacket. A horrible part of me was terrified I'd wake up and find out I had dreamed everything ended okay, when in reality, the shot hadn't missed and David was dead. I tightened my grip and got a tighter hold in return.

"I doubt it," I said. "My role will pass pretty quick."

He stopped and stared at me. "'Prime Minister's Secret Girlfriend Thwarts Assassination Attempt.' I don't need PR to tell me that's going to sell."

I wrinkled my nose and winced. He was right. That would be the headline and a large part of the story. Along with interviews, TV show requests, statements, and public outings… All of it made my head spin.

But as we went into the bedroom, it hit me again. We were both here and I didn't care how much publicity came with it.

"Do you need help changing?" I asked. Now that we were in better light and I saw him fully, it was obvious he was in pain, his face gray and drawn. That she'd actually shot him made my blood boil.

He nodded. "Yes."

Maybe in other scenarios or with other couples, this turned into some sexy reunion where despite a gaping arm wound, the couple launched into bedroom aerobics. Maybe we were both boring and tired, or simply grateful we'd found ourselves together again, but it didn't go like that. It took careful maneuvering to get his shirt pulled off without snagging the wrap around his bicep. Three inches to the right, and…

"I thought you said it was just a little graze?" The wrap was big, more than normal for a couple of stitches.

He looked guilty and shrugged. "Compared to some gunshot wounds, it is just a nick. We made a stop at the hospital last night after I called the first time. I'd lost a lot of blood."

I sat on the bed before my shaking knocked me down. Part of me was angry he hadn't told me everything; I got played by a politician telling a partial truth. Telling me everything wouldn't have helped, though, and would have made me more of a wreck at the airport. Being angry now did nothing. I grabbed his hand instead and held on.

"Are we…or do we need to talk about what happened last night?" The white bandage stared at me and started the unwanted what-if questions again.

"No." He dropped it fast and firm. "Not now. I just want to be thankful you are here and I'm here, have dinner, and go to bed. I don't want you to leave my side or be out of reach. Nothing else matters tonight."

It was hard for me to argue with that. "Okay."

I'd worried dinner in the prime minister's house would be formal. I had visions of black tie, multicourse affairs. The dining room was official, but bright and airy, with huge windows and long curtains and a chandelier glowing with warmth. David let go of my hand long enough to pull out a chair for me.

"Are you okay with something quick tonight?" he asked as he sat down. He looked nearly as bad as I did, the same dark circles, worry lines relaxing but still etched in deeper than they should be.

"Quick is good." I caught a whiff of something and realized how hungry I was. My donut and plane pretzels aside, I hadn't eaten since lunch yesterday.

He leaned back in the chair with his eyes closed and sighed.

I looked around, still having a hard time taking anything in. Rather than trying to talk, I latched onto his hand and sat quietly. Sometimes silence was okay.

The staff served us soup, tasty clam chowder with crusty bread; we split a beer. The idea of someone cooking for me was weird and somewhat uncomfortable, but tonight, it was welcomed.

We touched on mundane things—my flight and his day's worth of work. He'd be sworn in as prime minister next week, and gunshot or not, needed to have his government in place. When those topics were exhausted, we fell silent and finished dinner. Part of me was still in shock.

By the end of dinner, I was nearly sleepwalking. David showed me where the towels and my PJs were, and how to use the multiple knobs and handles on the fancy shower. I cranked it to near-scalding so the smell and feel of the last day washed away. Holding shampoo bottles—my rose-scented ones already here and in place—and not leaning against the side or falling asleep in the shower took a huge amount of effort.

I stumbled out and rushed through getting ready for bed. Just a few more steps and I could fall into bed in a house with cameras and security guards and David.

When I came out of the bathroom, David was sitting on the edge of the bed, resting his forehead on his hand. I wasn't the only one who was beat.

"Okay?" I went and sat down on the bed. Just a few feet back was my pillow. Instead, I rested my head on his shoulder.

I felt his shoulder lift in a shrug. "Better. You?"

I shrugged back. "Tired."

His kiss landed on my head and lingered. "You can get into bed. I'll be there in a minute."

He stood abruptly and went into the bathroom.

I wasn't sure if he was okay, or maybe he was just stressed. Either way, I slid back and wasted no time in diving under the duvet. Now that I was closer, I could see the picture by the bed better; it was the one of us taken in Vancouver. It was only last month, but it seemed so long ago.

There was another one next to it as well. It took me a moment to place it, but I recognized it eventually from the very first debate practice I'd stood in for. It was a still from right at the end, when I'd looked up at him and smiled. He'd mentioned before that moment was when he'd known I was the one. Having a picture of the moment was lucky.

It took me approximately a minute to start drifting off. The duvet was warm, the pillow soft, and I could sleep without worrying. I hoped I didn't have to get up early.

I woke briefly when the bathroom door opened, but I didn't hear him move or slide into bed.

"Am I on the wrong side?" I asked, more into the pillow than to David.

"I didn't think I was going to see you again," he said quietly, still standing in the doorway of the bathroom, staring at me. "She pulled the gun out..."

I sat up, alarmed. "Come here." I pulled back the covers on the other side. "Please."

If he was going to do this now, he needed to be closer to me, not standing on the opposite side of the room. He shut the lights off and came over, sliding in next to me, tugging me over; I got the hint and rested my head on his shoulder.

"I've wanted this job for as long as I can remember. Everything I've done over the past twenty years has been to get here. And I did. And then, you came along and didn't seem to mind me too much," he said, giving me a squeeze. "You were everything I was waiting for and everything I never knew I was missing. When she pulled it out…" He tensed, and I got a flash of rage again towards Jessica. "…I thought that was it, and you were listening to everything. I think that made it worse. You were going to hear me get shot and I couldn't stop it because my damn phone was in my pocket. I didn't want to startle her by reaching for it. You were going to hear, and that made me sick."

Those two gunshots were still loud in my head; I wasn't sure they'd ever fully disappear. I pressed my face against his chest, close enough to feel his pulse, the steady thud of his heart against my lips. He was alive.

"It didn't end," I whispered, for myself and for him.

"No. And now I get to take you out for dinner, and we can…we can start. I've wanted to do that since you smiled at me that first debate practice."

I grinned and nodded. "Yes, please."

The idea of a first date, doing something normal like dinner seemed so simple; it was something I hadn't been sure we'd ever get. "I'm okay with being out and about with you; I want to be very public." Cameras and publicity and talking heads dissecting what we did felt so incredibly insignificant, and also seemed like not such a bad thing.

"When I heard the gun shots and then couldn't get ahold of you, I thought that was it. No one knew that we were… No one would let me know or let me do anything more at your funeral than be a public visitor." The kind of public visitor where you walked by a casket, put a flower on it, and moved on.

His arm tightened around my shoulders. "I was afraid something was going to happen to you, like your cat, and I wouldn't know. Your parents would know, maybe Camille would say something, but I had this horrible thought that…*she*," he said, spitting the word out, clearly meaning Jessica, "would just mention her cousin's funeral and that would be it."

I kissed his neck. "Dinner tomorrow?"

"Yes. Dinner, and I have to give a statement on…" He waved his hand a bit, indicating everything. "Would you mind being there? Not to talk, just on the side?"

"Of course I will. What time do you get up?"

"Six."

I closed my eyes and snuggled down. "Getting lazy now, are we?"

He nodded. "Big slacker."

We both fell silent. His chest was warm through his T-shirt. Without realizing it, our breath slowed down and fell into sync.

"I love you, Charlotte."

"I love you, too."

Even if a little part of me was still terrified this was a dream, at least I got that.

*   *   *

David left after breakfast the next morning. The press conference wasn't until later in the afternoon. I had meetings of my own all morning, with a lawyer and the police for statements, give them evidence, etc. Everything I'd packed was far too wrinkly to wear, so I raided David's closet and pulled out a light blue dress shirt to pair with jeans. With the sleeves rolled up and my hair looking decent now, it worked for this morning.

The combination of hired hit man, dead cat, and near assassination of the prime minister made the police pay a lot more attention to me. The lawyer stopped me a couple of times when I got heated, annoyed with the police officer's questions. They were acting like I should have done more. It pissed me off.

We wrapped up after one. I had just over an hour before I was supposed to be presentable.

Back in the bedroom, a large box was waiting for me from Camille. I'd called earlier in the morning to fill her in and ask to have some of my clothes sent over. In my rush to get here, packing for a press conference had not been on my radar. The note made me smile.

I pulled strings with some friends. You won't embarrass yourself or David. ⊠

She'd sent two outfits. There was a dark blue dress that fit snugly, with a neat belt across the waist. She'd included a note for what I should do with my hair. Earrings were in an envelope. Little black heels at the bottom. This was more than I had expected. I'd look perfectly presentable.

The second was a much more youthful outfit, clearly for dinner tonight. Making sure I looked good not just for the date, but for the press, was not something I was used to thinking about. I owed Camille big. I didn't know where these came from, but I was grateful.

I showered and changed quickly. I followed the instructions she'd sent, along with the makeup samples tossed in, rightly assuming I hadn't grabbed any. I slid the heels on, gave myself a once-over, and decided I'd make a pretty good first impression.

David had arranged for a car to drive me over to Parliament. Once there and through the substantial security, nodding a silent hello to those I recognized, and dodging my way through the press, I had no problem finding my standing spot. It felt vaguely like I'd stepped through the looking glass; I was no longer on the campaign staff side, but on David's side of things.

I made my way over to Kaitlyn, trying to ignore the sudden whispering and pointing that got louder and was very much directed at me; of course the core press corps from the campaign recognized me. Kaitlyn was typing on her phone and didn't notice me until I coughed.

"You!" she yelped a little louder than necessary. Any worry I wouldn't be on friend-level anymore disappeared in a tight hug. "Why didn't you say anything?" she asked, getting her voice under control.

I saw Ben standing a few people down, making his way over. He looked flat-out exhausted. I guessed the last twenty-four hours had been frantic from this side as well.

I shrugged. "Because we didn't want people talking about us—"

She rolled her eyes and waved me off. "Not that, although I want details later. The emails, the threats, all of it. You should have said something. We could have helped." She added the "we" as Ben arrived.

He smiled and gave me a tight hug as well. "All right, Charlotte?"

"All right," I agreed. "And I didn't say anything because I didn't know who it was. I was paranoid to the point of not functioning."

She grudgingly accepted the explanation. "You're okay though now, right? Nothing else?"

I shook my head. More cameras were looking towards me; it was surreal. "Nothing else."

"And how long had the rest been going on?" she asked, sounding like she was on less firm footing. "You kept it very quiet."

"Really? You didn't notice?" Ben asked.

Kaitlyn stared at him in surprise. "You knew? And you knew he knew?" She glared at me when I didn't react.

Ben shrugged it off. "I've known David since we were kids. It was obvious, knowing him that long that he was…involved with someone."

Kaitlyn huffed. "Well, to those of us not privy to being old friends it wasn't clear at all. And you didn't answer the when," she said, turning back to me.

Sharing it all was a relief. I was so tired of hiding. "Sort of since the first debate practice."

Her eyes narrowed. "You nerds. That practice turned you both on, didn't it, arguing and being smart together?"

I didn't get a chance to respond before the side doors opened and a PR guy came out. This would be harder for me than I thought.

When David had asked me to be here I knew it was partly so the press could see me and put a face with the events, but mainly to be support for him while he answered questions about his best friend shooting him. My thoughts had been focused on him, but the blind panic that hit when I thought about doing this, listening to him replay it all, made me realize I wasn't okay, either.

Right now, it didn't matter. I could do whatever I wanted afterwards—curl up and hyperventilate to my heart's content, be a weirdo and sit in our bedroom, go hang out with the nearest security officer I could find, or whatever I wanted. I didn't get that luxury for the next few minutes. I clasped my hands tight in front of me, took a breath, and held on to the fact that David was very much alive and would be talking.

PR guy laid the ground rules and shifted out of the way as David came out. The clicks on the cameras were deafening, the flashing bright. I wasn't sure what to do with my face; was I supposed to be smiling lovingly at him, acting completely aloof, somewhere in between?

David shot one glance towards us and smiled briefly when he caught my eye. I smiled in return.

He stepped to the podium and gave his prepared statement. It was very scrubbed; Kaitlyn nodded along, clearly having a heavy hand in it. It outlined that yes, his former campaign manager had tried to assassinate him. No, he was not seriously injured in any way. Yes, he was well in control. The topic flowed smoothly away from the shooting and into future policy and the selection of ministers. I squeezed my hands together; the lump of bandage you couldn't see through the shirt and coat suggested otherwise about not being injured.

When David opened it up to questions, it was overwhelming. Nobody cared about the government he was forming. Of course I'd seen this style of press conference on TV and when we were campaigning, but it was a different beast today. The questions were solely personal.

David started picking questions one at a time, answering what he could, staying mum on others. I liked watching him like this, when he was in full control and owning the venue. The questions, though, didn't make me smile.

"Why did she do it?"

"Were you alone when she pulled the gun?"

"What are your next steps?"

Almost all of it received no comment, under police investigation. He walked through the bare minimum, giving a great deal of credit to Peter; my role was left quiet at this point. I started to get the panic in my chest again and clenched my jaw to keep from chattering.

One reporter asked, "Sources say you're in a relationship with former party staff member Charlotte Finnan, and the shooting stemmed from a dispute over it. Can you confirm, or tell us how that developed?"

I froze.

A rushing noise filled my head, and I wished I could stop my face from flooding red like I knew it was doing. Several of the reporters who'd recognized me from the campaign looked at me, and cameras started to click. I tried to keep my face neutral. We wanted people to know we were together, but this wasn't exactly how we'd wanted it revealed.

David's eyes tightened and gone was the neutral politician. "It is inappropriate for me to comment on an ongoing police investigation, nor will I comment on personal questions. Thank you." His tone was icy, and just like that, the conference was done.

Kaitlyn grabbed my arm and pushed me firmly towards another side door. There were people hollering at me now. That was way beyond my depth or ability to handle.

"That's going to piss off David," she said, directing us out through a side door. "I will get a time scheduled with you and get you talking points." She switched from friend mode to communications director, which I appreciated.

We turned into a hallway and I could hear David talking heatedly with someone—I guessed the PR guy who'd come out first—and heading our way. PR guy was taking a beating.

"…not in that setting. This is not a tabloid—" David stopped short when he saw us, his eyes flickering between Kaitlyn, Ben, and me. The annoyance lessened a bit and his face lightened.

"What are you three up to?" he asked.

Kaitlyn smiled. "Getting Charlotte set up with me for Press 101. Sooner rather than later. A heads-up next time would be good." For all her joking, she sounded legitimately annoyed with us. It was hard to tailor a story or message if you didn't know everything.

He grimaced a bit and nodded. "Done. How long until the next meeting?" he asked Ben.

Ben handed over a folder. "Ten minutes. Notes and agenda are in there."

David tapped the folder absentmindedly. "How did this morning go?" he asked me.

I shrugged. "All right. I got a little snippy with the police, but the lawyer kept me in check. They said they'd call if there were any follow-up questions."

He laughed, and for the first time since I'd arrived, his eyes smiled and he looked more relaxed. "What did you do?"

He motioned for me to follow him, along with the others.

I startled when he grabbed my hand, shooting me a glance to make sure I was okay with it. There were a lot of people around giving us stares.

I smiled and squeezed back. "I told them they were idiots and should have listened to me five months ago when I first came to them. Said it was their fault before the lawyer shut me up." Thinking about it again made me want to hit something. "But they got a full statement."

We reached the end of the hall and stopped. I didn't know why David looked so amused; he was the one who'd gotten shot.

"I'll be back around 6:30. Dinner at seven. You okay getting back?"

Before I responded, Kaitlyn jumped in. "Actually, if you're free, Charlotte, we can meet now. I'd rather do this sooner than later."

I nodded. "Sure, I'm good. I'll see you later, David."

He gave my hand one more squeeze and took off with Ben.

"Ready?" Kaitlyn asked, motioning off in the opposite direction.

I took a deep breath and smiled. "I am."

Epilogue

The restaurant, Torino, looked exactly how David had described it all those months ago when he first mentioned it to me. Granted, I only caught a glimpse of it as we drove by the front—our entrance and exit would be through the back to avoid a scene. At some point, I knew we'd cause a scene with arrivals and exits, but tonight wasn't the night to start.

I could see why he chose here. The restaurant front was tucked away on a side street corner, residential and surrounded by an eclectic mix of houses. I couldn't get a good look inside through the front windows. Condensation blurred the figures sitting at tables, making everyone look fuzzy.

We pulled around the back into an alleyway that in normal circumstances would look sketchy, but there was something exciting about needing to be snuck in through the kitchen entrance and it was deserted. David squeezed my hand as the driver came around to get his door.

"I wanted to take you here as our first date."

His door opened and he slid out, being careful not to jar his arm. I took the hand he offered to me and followed him inside the open kitchen door. Instantly, the quiet of the alleyway disappeared and I blinked into the bright light. Clattering pots and pans, cooks and the chef shouting orders and times overlaid the smell of garlic, roasting meats, and other things I couldn't quite identify but made my mouth water nonetheless.

"Charlotte." David touched my elbow and pulled my attention away from watching a sous chef plate a chocolate cake, squiggling chocolate sauce on the plate with a flourish. "Charlotte, these are the owners and my friends, Julia and Luca."

The couple standing there beamed at me, giving me a hug and kiss and taking my coat in a swift movement.

"It's lovely to meet you both," I said, smiling and trying to remember the tips Kaitlyn went over with me in the afternoon. It had been such a crash course that most of the information went straight in and evaporated. "David's told me how much he enjoys eating here and I'm looking forward to it."

Julia batted David's—good—arm and laughed. "Happy to have you two here. C'mon, I'll show you the table and get you out of this noise."

We followed her, weaving between prep tables and into the dining room, which was thankfully much quieter. It was small, like he said. A long, narrow front dining area with a divider running the length. It was Italian, but the checkered floors, wicker backed chairs, and the brass and wood divider reminded me of a Paris bistro. A bar was set up in the back corner, mirrored back with shelves of bottles. Tall candles stood on each table, dripping wax down the chianti bottles that held them. The lighting was soft and acoustic music floated in the background.

A few other tables looked up at us and stared. Their whispers and points followed us to the table Julia led us to, tucked into a corner. Our security had a table nearby, my new shadow that'd go out with me whenever I had an outing or went to visit a friend.

"Enjoy you two," Luca said and set a bottle of wine on the table with a flourish. "On the house, for celebration."

They left us with two menus, although David seemed to already know what he wanted and pushed it away, relaxing in the booth with his leg resting against mine. For a second, I thought he was going to tip his head against the back and fall asleep, but he just smiled.

"So not a first date, but this looks promising as a first celebration dinner," I said, skimming the menu and quickly finding at least half a dozen things I'd order. My appetite from the prior few days had recovered with aplomb.

He nodded and looked around before rubbing his face. "I can't believe we're here," he said and almost laughed. "Seemed improbable there for a while."

I leaned against him, trying to keep what Kaitlyn said about cameras being everywhere at all times, about what our level of public affection should be, but I couldn't make myself care. Maybe that would come back to haunt me, but at the moment it felt like a long ways away.

"Like you said, we're here. I've heard this place has good food so I'm going to focus on that and my date tonight."

A camera flickered somewhere across the room. We were getting the publicity we both thought we wanted. Tucked away in the booth, any consequence of it felt a million miles away.

"Completely agree," he said, and pulled his wine glass over, swirling it so the ruby red cast jewel-like shadows on the tablecloth. "And then, we'll tackle the rest tomorrow."

"Tomorrow and together," I added and thought it sounded like a marvelous plan.

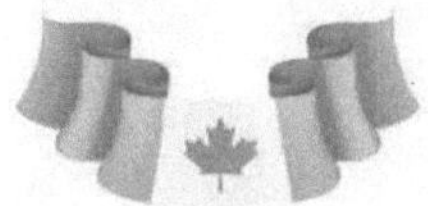

Acknowledgements

I owe a lot of people thanks for putting up with me as I daydreamed this book into reality...so thank you to everyone who I made repeat questions or who had to put up with spaced out looks from me over the last couple of years.

I'm grateful to everyone at Written Dreams Publishing. To Brittiany Koren, for taking a chance on me and seeing something in the messy first draft I submitted, to Ed Vincent for a beautiful cover design, and to Amit Dey and Maria Connor for making the inside of the book look great.

And a thank you to the first agent I pitched the book to who eventually said no, but was interested enough to give it a full read. That ask gave me confidence I was on to something and I kept going.

Thank you to my readers—Mom, Dad, Jess, Amber, and Cherry. When my eyes blurred past words and timelines, you caught my mistakes.

And a special thank you to Jon for making sure I still made it to work in the morning and remembered to feed myself. I couldn't have finished this novel without your support.

About the Author

Tatiana McArthur has been writing stories since she was ten years old. *The Girl Behind the Numbers* is her first novel. She has a degree in International Relations from the University of St. Andrews, Scotland, where she lived for four years. When not writing, she's baking or plotting her next travel adventure. She lives with her husband and daughter in Wisconsin. Follow her on social media at @TatianaMcArthur, IG @Tatianamcarthur, or learn more about her at her website: tatianamcarthur.com.